Suzanne Wright lives in England with her husband and two children. When she's not spending time with her family, she's writing, reading or doing her version of housework – sweeping the house with a look.

She's worked in a pharmaceutical company, at a Disney Store, at a primary school as a voluntary teaching assistant, at the RSPCA and has a First Class Honours degree in Psychology and Identity Studies.

As to her interests, she enjoys reading, writing, reading, writing (sort of eat, sleep, write, repeat), spending time with her family, movie nights with her sisters and playing with her two Bengal kittens.

To connect with Suzanne online:

Website: http://www.suzannewright.co.uk
Facebook: https://www.facebook.com/
suzannewrightfanpage

SUZANNE WRIGHT
VIPER
A Dark in You novel

PIATKUS

PIATKUS

First published in Great Britain in 2024 by Piatkus

1 3 5 7 9 10 8 6 4 2

A CIP catalogue record for this book
is available from the British Library.

ISBN: 978-0-349-44037-8

Typeset in Goudy by M Rules

Printed and bound in Great Britain by
Clays Ltd, Elcograf S.p.A.

Papers used by Piatkus are from well-managed forests
and other responsible sources.

Piatkus
An imprint of
Little, Brown Book Group
Carmelite House
50 Victoria Embankment
London EC4Y 0DZ

An Hachette UK Company
www.hachette.co.uk

www.littlebrown.co.uk

For somebody close to me who is currently going through a terrible time—you are a warrior for getting through this, don't ever see yourself as anything else.

PROLOGUE

New Zealand, 1994

Breathing hard, Everleigh struggled against the sheer power pinning her hands to the wall behind her. She twisted. Pulled. Arched.

Nothing happened.

Similarly, her inner demon writhed and squirmed and fought to surface. It was trapped inside her, unable to be of any aid.

Feeling a flush of anger heat her face, Everleigh glared at the strangers fanned out in front of her. "What the fuck is this shit?"

One male took a step toward her—tall, lean, imposing, his hair so blond it was almost white. "There's no need to panic. You need not fear us."

Was he serious? "You *kidnapped* me." She'd been in the middle of a wickedly hot kiss when ... it was as if her senses had shut down. She'd been conscious, but she hadn't been able to see, hear, smell, or feel a thing.

She'd been distantly aware that she was being moved. *Taken.* When her senses had rushed back to her, it could have been minutes or hours later. And she'd found herself here, in what appeared to be some kind of abandoned warehouse.

The only other people present were the six males who were evenly staring back at her, their eyes twin blue gems—striking eyes she'd only ever seen in one other person.

Everleigh swallowed. "Where is he?" She had the distinct feeling that they'd taken him, too.

"That isn't important," Blondie told her.

She felt her nostrils flare. "It is to me."

"He is nowhere near here. We have plenty of privacy for what we're about to do."

Everleigh's heart stuttered. "What does that mean? What have you done to him?" And why couldn't she telepath anyone? Whenever she tried, she hit some kind of psychic wall.

"He is safe. Unconscious for the moment, but safe."

Her instincts stirred. "You're members of the Seven archangels." Powerful beings who could, in fact, collectively do something as difficult as knock the seventh of their unit out cold. Few would manage such a feat.

A dark-haired, clean-shaven celestial inclined his head in confirmation. "Be assured that our intention isn't to make you suffer. We will simply put you to sleep. That is all."

Everleigh tensed, her heart banging against her ribcage. The word 'sleep' sounded so very final. "Why do I get the feeling that you don't intend for me to wake up?"

"Your body will not wake up, but your soul will," Mr. Clean-shaven told her. "Your life will start anew in another body, just as it has many times before."

Her gut twisted. He'd said it like it was nothing. Like she'd merely be changing outfits. "In other words, you're going to kill me. Let's just call it what it is." They could dress it up all they wanted, but it was murder.

"You could view it that way. We all see it as saving you both."

She felt her face scrunch up. "From what?"

He observed her like she was clueless. "From what will become of him if he falls."

"He has not told you?" Blondie pursed his lips. "He probably fears you would otherwise reject him. I doubt those fears are senseless, to be fair."

"No one would care if you were just a toy to him," cut in a dark-skinned, brawny male. "But you've become an obsession. He is prepared to fall from our realm to stay with you."

Everleigh knew that much. She'd been shocked when he offered to fall—it wasn't a small thing, and it meant leaving his life behind. She'd even objected at first, not wanting him to give up so much for her; not wanting him to suffer the consequences. But then he'd told her a little about his life, about how the darkness of it weighed heavily on him, and she could see how it was eating at his soul. So she'd ceased protesting—and no, it wasn't at all a selfless decision. The fact was that she loved him and didn't want to be without him.

He had wished to first say his goodbyes to these archangels he'd considered family. Falling meant leaving them behind. Going by their reaction, that had been a mistake.

"An archangel should never fall," Brawny added. "One of the Seven? That cannot happen. If you knew what it would do to him, you would agree with us."

She licked her lips. "I know about the curse. I know what he'd have to do to survive."

"For one of the Seven, that is only the tip of the iceberg," said

Brawny sadly. "He would change. We cannot bear the thought of him becoming *that*. We care for him too much."

"*Care* for him? You really see killing someone he loves as 'caring'?" Everleigh ran her gaze along the line of archangels. "He spoke of you. Each of you. You're all important to him. How shitty for him that it doesn't go both ways."

Mr. Clean-shaven's brow pinched. "This is not a betrayal on our part. We look out for him as he does us. This is for his own good."

"And yours," Blondie chipped in. "A being with the volume of power he possesses . . . It is not good for such a person to love. It only makes them more unstable, more dangerous."

Her pulse skittered as Blondie moved closer, the set of his jaw telling her there'd be no changing his mind. Helplessness battered at her, amping up her demon's anger. "You may not see this as a betrayal, but *he* will," she said. "That doesn't bother you?"

Blondie waved that away. "He will not believe we were responsible. He will suspect our superiors. He would be right to do so—they would have come for you if we hadn't. They wouldn't have settled for hiding you, they would have obliterated your soul to rein him in."

Her head swimming, she shook it. "Hiding me? What does that mean?"

"When he claimed you as his own, he placed an imprint of himself on your soul. It allowed him to know where you were. But we will take away that imprint. He will not feel you, and so he will not know that you have been reborn. When time goes on and your soul appears to have not been reborn, he will assume it is either in hell . . . or that it has been destroyed."

Oh, fuck.

Right then, all six of the archangels began to close in on her.

Panic wrapped around her throat and squeezed. Everleigh shook her head. "Don't do this."

Blondie stared at her, his expression implacable. "As we have explained, it is for your own good as well as his," he stated with such unbelievable arrogance and condescension . . . like she was a child who knew no better.

Her panic gave way to a fury that heated her skin. "He won't be fooled, he'll find me," she swore with a snarl. "Maybe not straight away. Maybe not for a while. But eventually, he'll find me."

Brawny shook his head. "No, no, he won't. He's exceedingly powerful—one of the most powerful of our kind. But without the imprint, there is no way for him to track you." It was said with such assurance that her belly flipped. "He will never find you. No one will, not even us."

"There will be no need for him to search for you anyway because, as I said, he'll presume your soul now dwells in hell or no longer exists," Blondie reminded her.

Fuck, fuck, fuck.

"Now be still," Blondie told her, all business. "We shall put you to sleep—there is no need for you to suffer as you die."

A cold force *delved* into her mind, and she cried out with the shock of it. The force spread, turned even colder, seemed to numb her thoughts. She felt herself fading; felt a thick, gray cloud move through her mind.

"I am not so sure there is truly a point in this," said one of the archangels, his voice seeming so far away.

"This is the only way to save him from himself," Blondie insisted.

"But it will only work if he believes she hasn't been reborn. We will then have time to talk him out of falling. But if he does not believe it—"

"He will be blind to her location without the imprint, so it matters not."

"Perhaps. But we know our kind can be very obsessive when they want something—she has brought that out in him. Do you honestly think he will cease looking? That he will accept she has gone?"

Other words were spoken, but she couldn't make them out. The archangels were too far away. Or she was. And she just kept fading and fading and fading until, finally, it all went dark.

CHAPTER ONE

Las Vegas, present day

Ella Wilde parked at the curb and pulled out her phone. *Running late, have to make a quick house call,* she texted to her sister.

Mia quickly responded: *No problem, I'll order drinks.*

Usually, Ella would turn down any jobs that cropped up on a Friday evening—it was routine for she and Mia to meet at their local pool hall to eat dinner, knock back beer, and shoot some pool. But there were some matters that required a swift intervention, and this was one of them.

Having plopped her cell back into her jacket pocket, Ella slid out of the car and took in the cute two-story home. It was pretty with its window boxes, porch rocking chairs, and ropes of ivy trailing up the walls.

It made her think of the house that she and Mia had recently considered renting, but then their apartment complex had come under new management. The place had since been spruced up—new security system, fresh paint, working elevator, better lighting for the parking lot, major cleaning job.

Ella strode up the path and rang the doorbell. When the door swung open, she smiled gently at the human male staring at her through tortured grayish-blue eyes. "Hi, I'd like to speak to Mr. or Mrs. Mills."

He cleared his throat. "I'm Mr. Mills."

She'd suspected as much, given how haggard the poor guy looked. Any father in his position would be so haggard. "I'm Ella Wilde," she said, holding out her hand. "I believe you're expecting me."

He gave a slow nod as he briefly shook her hand in an absent manner. "Thank you for coming." Stepping aside, he waved her into the house.

She accepted his silent invitation, and he then closed the door. Her inner entity eyeballed their surroundings, hypervigilant as ever.

He scrubbed a hand down his pale, drawn face that hadn't seen a razor in several days. "I, we, it . . . Neve, a friend of my wife, told me you could fix this. Fix my daughter."

"I can," Ella assured him.

A local practitioner, Neve knew much about all things that went bump in the night. She was talented at her craft, but she couldn't work the sort of magick that would aid this family. Not like Ella, who was an incantor—a breed of demon that could wield magick.

So, whenever Neve came across a situation that she felt required demonic intervention, she contacted Ella, who consulted for many people. Neve had told her all about Annmarie and Edgar Mills, as well as their daughter.

He looked at the ceiling. "Malia's . . . I don't know what's wrong with her. I don't know—" He cut himself off and pinched a nose that had clearly once been broken. "I wanted to call a doctor here, but my wife begged me to try something else first." He let his arm fall back to his side. "She's afraid our daughter would be hospitalized."

That wasn't a senseless concern. Such a thing had happened to humans in Malia's present condition. "I can help your daughter, if you'll let me. But if you would rather seek medical help, I completely understand. It's your choice."

He carved his fingers through his tousled chestnut hair, his hesitation clear. Finally, he sighed and said, "Malia's in her bedroom."

Ella followed him as he trudged up the stairs, exhaustion in his every step. She ran her gaze along the framed pictures mounted on the wall. Some featured he and a woman, who was presumably his wife. Others featured a girl who could only be Malia at varying ages. Many were of the entire family—posing, smiling, laughing.

It made her think of the wall of her mother's staircase—there was an overabundance of pictures of Ella, her older sister Mia, and their parents. Well . . . their idiot-for-a-father's *body* could be seen. Their mother had covered his face with those of various male celebrities that she'd cut out of magazines. Something that still made Ella smile.

"Neve said you're a kind of psychic," said Edgar as they reached the top of the stairs.

Uh, not even close. But the truth wasn't something that Ella could share. "In a manner of speaking," she lied.

The *snick* of a lock sounded at the other end of the hallway. She looked to see the dark-haired, middle-aged woman from the framed pictures stepping out of a room.

"I don't believe in psychics," said Edgar, drawing Ella's

attention back to him. "I don't believe in God or the devil or heaven or hell." A heavy sigh slipped out of him and pulled down his shoulders. "Or I didn't, until now," he added in defeat, his voice breaking.

Her heart squeezed in sympathy. She didn't get the chance to respond, because he immediately began making his way to his wife. Ella trailed after him and gave the woman a soft smile. "You must be Annmarie. I'm Ella."

Her arms filled with soiled blankets, Annmarie swallowed hard. "I appreciate you coming." Looking as drained and weary as her husband, she cast the bedroom door a quick glance. "She's in bed. But awake. We had to cuff her to the bedframe so she couldn't hurt herself anymore." A shaky breath left her. "What is it you're going to do?"

Ella pinned her with a sober look. "No harm will come to your daughter at my hands."

Annmarie's hazel eyes went wet and glassy. "She's only thirteen. I know it was stupid of her and her friends to fool around with a spirit board, but—" She stopped as tears trailed down her cheeks. "Neve said you had experience at this. Can you really help Malia?"

"Yes, I can. And I will," Ella swore. "You should both wait out here."

Her brow dented. "Won't it be dangerous for you to go in there alone? Neve said you wouldn't need the aid of a priest, but I thought you'd have *someone* with you. Perhaps a nun or spiritual practitioner of a sort."

Ella felt her nose wrinkle. "Exorcisms don't always happen the way they do in movies." Technically, what she was about to do wouldn't be an exorcism; it would involve a little magick. She couldn't explain that to humans, however. "It'll work better if I'm alone."

"But why can't we be there?" Edgar gruffly challenged.

Two reasons. One, they would learn things they shouldn't. Two ... "The presence inside Malia will feed off your misery and panic. That will make it stronger; give it fuel to fight me."

He looked as though he'd argue, but then his shoulders drooped once more. "All right. Just ... just get it out of her."

Annmarie moved away from the door. "Be careful. It claims to be Beelzebub."

Ella's demon let out an impatient sigh. "I won't be long." She walked into the bedroom and closed the door behind her.

A sense of oppression lay heavy in the room. A room that was nothing short of girly. Posters were tacked on the pink walls. Makeup littered the surface of the chic vanity. A neon *Malia* sign hung above the bed. Shelves were lined with books, artificial plants, framed photos, and little knickknacks.

What held Ella's attention, however, was the teenage girl who'd been cuffed to the bedframe by her wrists and ankles— her face pale, her lips chapped, her matted, sweat-slick chestnut hair plastered to her head. Slices, burns, and bruises decorated her body. Dark smudges circled her eyes—eyes that weren't hazel like on her photos. No, her irises were now as black as her pupils.

Awake, it locked that cold gaze on her. A wicked grin curved its mouth as it chuckled, but there was unease rumbling through the sound. The damn thing *should* be uneasy—it would recognize an incantor on sight, and it would know what an incantor could do to it.

"You told them you're Beelzebub?" Ella rolled her eyes at the wraith. "How cliché."

"It's not my fault humans are so naïve," it said, its voice deep, grating, and eerie.

Hell was filled with all kinds of creatures. Some had ways of psychically attaching themselves to people who lived in other realms. Spirit boards were their main gateway, though such breeds of demon couldn't actually walk the Earth. Sometimes, it was because they were incorporeal. Other times, it was because—as was the case with wraiths—their forms wouldn't survive in this realm, so they could only leech onto the mind of someone who could.

When it came to possessions, it was very rarely the devil or any of his minions responsible—they generally considered that sort of thing beneath them. No, it was most commonly low-level demons like wraiths, who often tossed out names of biblical demons to scare the families of those they'd possessed.

"Ella Wilde," it drawled.

That was another thing about wraiths. They could 'scan' a person; could tell many things about them on sight.

"You have two choices," she told it, moving to stand at the foot of the bed. "You can release your grip on Malia's soul and toddle off home, or I can destroy you."

"I vote that we instead come to an agreement."

Wraiths always made such proposals, and she always refused. "I'm not taking votes. Your choices are simple. Pick one. I have somewhere to be."

"But you haven't even heard my proposition yet."

"I don't need to. Choose."

It cocked its head. "Wouldn't you like to know the future? There's much I could share."

No doubt, considering that wraiths had foresight. "Not interested. I prefer surprises. Besides, I don't make deals with anything that dwells in hell." That kind of shit tended to backfire on a person.

"You have no interest in learning about the future, hmm?" It narrowed its eyes. "What about your past?"

She frowned. "I can remember it pretty well, thanks."

"I mean your *soul's* past." One corner of its mouth tipped up into a sly smirk. "Surely your past lives would interest you. I could tell you things. So many, many things."

Maybe, but none of it was worth trading the soul of a teenage girl. She lifted her chin and called to her magick—threads of green, red, and yellow shimmered like flames as they hissed and snapped against her palms. "Release Malia's soul, or die."

The wraith tensed, its gaze briefly dipping to her hands. Anger rippled across its face. "The human should be the least of your concerns. Forget her. It is *your* soul that you should worry about. He will come for you."

A frown tugged at her brow.

"You will be chained to him forever, and you cannot imagine what that will mean for you." It started to laugh.

Knowing it was just screwing with her, she hummed. "So you've decided to meet your end? Okay."

It froze. "Wait."

"No." Chanting beneath her breath, she unleashed her magick. Two flickering, fiery ribbons rushed from her palms, streamed through the air, and slammed into its chest like cardiac arrest paddles. Malia's eyes rolled back, hers head jerked hard, her body bucked and spasmed. With one last chant, Ella snapped her hands closed.

Black particles all but burst out of Malia's body as it sagged to the bed. Those particles disintegrated fast, and the oppressive feel left the room.

Malia coughed, her eyelids lifting to reveal a beautiful, hazel gaze that was bruised with pain and terror. Those lids quickly fell shut again, but her breathing swiftly steadied.

Satisfied, Ella let Malia's parents into the room. They thanked Ella even as they faffed around their daughter. Having assured them that the demon would not return, she left the house and headed for her car.

She usually made such 'house calls' four or five times a year, and it was usually wraiths responsible for the possessions. Considering they weren't difficult for incantors to kill, you would think they would give up their human victim voluntarily. Weirdly, though, they rarely did.

He will come for you.

Ella felt her brow crease as the words drifted through her mind. They meant nothing. The wraith had simply been messing with her—she knew that. Knew it well. As did her demon. So why did something about that phrase make her skin chill?

She was late.

Viper clenched his hand around his beer bottle, the pads of his fingertips tingling with both unease and a restless anticipation.

The redhead at a corner table—one who resembled *his* redhead—checked her phone, but she didn't seem concerned. Maybe Mia had received a heads-up that there was some kind of delay.

The sisters were close. Best friends, really. They had little rituals; things they routinely did together. Like come to this particular pool hall every Friday.

'Ella' was his woman's name in this life. It had taken him quite some time to find her. *Too* long.

Many things had delayed his locating her. He'd only had two clues that would aid him. One, she'd again be a demon. Two, her date of birth would be roughly nine months after the very day that her life as Everleigh had ended.

It didn't help his search that, due to demons being exclusive and secretive, lairs didn't have accessible birth records. Also, demons weren't rare creatures, they existed all over the globe— that was a whole lot of ground to check out.

The timelines of the various realms were out of sync. Just returning home to the upper realm for a brief rest from searching for her had sometimes meant that months had passed when he returned to Earth to continue that search. At other times, it was only mere minutes.

Making it even harder, the six traitorous bastards he'd once considered 'family' had laid a false trail that—in his anger and desperation to find her—he'd been naïve enough to follow. They'd sure gone *all* out to keep him away from her so that he wouldn't choose to 'doom himself'. Their words.

On first seeing Ella here in Vegas, he'd known it was her. She had the same mannerisms and personal style. Even the same graceful, confident walk.

A *slip* into her mind as she'd slept had been enough for him to confirm it. Her brain might be physically different, but the psychic *feel* of her was the same.

It had taken him twenty-eight fucking years, but he'd found her. He'd fallen, along with thirteen angels who'd been part of his branch in the upper realm's army; men he called brothers now that they'd formed a motorcycle club. And Viper was finally so very close to what he wanted most.

Not that he'd done anything about it yet. He'd had to hold off.

Viper had known that those in the upper realm wouldn't easily accept that he'd fallen. He'd known that they'd try to persuade him to return and, more, that they'd try having him executed when he refused.

He'd also known they'd assume that he'd fallen because he'd managed to track down his woman. They would have taken her; would have outright destroyed her soul to get him in line. So, to keep their attention away from her, Viper had kept his distance from Ella over the past several months. He'd made it look to celestials as though his decision to fall had had nothing to do with her; that Vegas was a random choice of location on his part.

He'd butchered every slayer that the upper realm had sent, all the while focusing on getting his club settled, establishing their presence in Vegas, and forming necessary alliances with demons to get one foot in Ella's world.

Viper had also spent a lot of that time observing his quarry from afar. At first, it had been strange to see his woman in a whole other body answering to a whole other name. But at this point, after several months of watching her, he'd gotten used to it; had even ceased refering to her as Everleigh in his mind.

In fact, he considered the situation similar to how he'd dropped his old identity after falling. They *both* now had new names, new circumstances, new families.

Before, she'd been a reaper. Now she was an incantor.

Before, he'd been an archangel. Now he was something ... other.

Neither of them were *exactly* as they were before. But it meant they could start fresh as Ella and Viper. Meant they could get it right this time.

They weren't so different than before that it would affect how well they 'fit'. Small elements of a person's character would vary with each life, but never their core nature.

He'd watched her closely so he could learn her patterns, familial situation, power-level, personal details, etc.

Basically, he'd discovered and filed away every aspect of her life to identify the easiest way to infiltrate it.

He'd already moved some pawns around, placing himself on the periphery of her world. Example: he'd recently bought this very pool hall that she frequented, and now he came here every Friday. Each time, he chose a table that was just a little closer to where she and Mia routinely sat.

Essentially, he'd set himself up to step fully into her life—something he'd soon do.

The coast was now mostly clear. The attempts to execute him had ceased. Celestials sometimes came to pass on messages from the Uppers, but there were no shows of violence. However, a new issue had cropped up. Once he'd resolved it, he could focus on Ella.

He planned to take things slow with her. To move with care, give her his full attention, and drag her so far under his spell she would accept all that he'd eventually have to reveal to her.

Some might say it made him a selfish bastard. There was no denying that since falling he'd become a literal stain upon this world. She deserved a life that wasn't touched by him. But Viper hadn't been 'good' in a long time, so here he was.

There was nothing sweet and flowery about what he felt for her. It wasn't romantic or anyone's idea of progressive. It was obsession and greed and a dark sense of ownership all tangled up with a blindingly intense emotion that, until her, had always eluded him.

She'd been easy to fall for—no pun intended with the whole 'fall' thing.

She was a person who would rise to any challenge. If she couldn't move through something, she'd find some way to flow around it or leap over it—nothing was a true obstacle to her. Something he respected and admired.

She loved fiercely. Had a capacity for compassion that he found staggering. Anyone who'd heard about the life he'd led—a life that had weighed him down, darkened his soul, and stole so many choices from him—might have judged and shied away from him. She hadn't. Nor had she shied away from being with him after hearing of the subsequent curse.

And she was *happy* for others. Too many people were jealous of those around him or resented them for having what they didn't. Not her. Not as Everleigh or Ella, because they were one and the same.

In her previous life, she'd *remembered* him after their first meeting—nobody after did that unless he allowed it. Until her.

Sometimes, when Ella looked at him a certain way, he could even think she remembered him now. But that was likely wishful thinking on his part.

He tossed back a mouthful of beer and took an idle scan of his surroundings. The hall was dim—a deliberate effect of the tinted windows and low lighting. The neon 'Beer' signs hanging above the long mahogany bar did nothing to brighten the place.

Waitresses took orders from the patrons who'd either claimed tables or were playing pool. Other patrons sat at bar stools chatting, scrolling through their cell, or watching the darts game playing live on the wall-mounted TV. A few people hung at the back where gaming machines, an ATM, and a jukebox lined one wall.

An image shot to the forefront of his mind. An image of every single one of those patrons dead, their throats slit, their bodies gutted, their blood everywhere.

The image came from the once-holy being with which Viper shared his soul. Bored, it was 'suggesting' they instigate a bloodbath. Not unusual for the sadistic entity.

Viper focused on his five club brothers who were gathered around a pool table engaging in regular shit talk.

On falling, they'd all chosen the biker lifestyle. It fit the dynamic they already had after their years in service to heaven's higher-ups. And they didn't feel that they could connect with this realm's normative society. They collectively had different values, different beliefs, different priorities.

Having secrets to protect, they hadn't invited others into

their club. Ella *would* join eventually, obviously. She just didn't know that yet.

After doing a few 'jobs' with some local imps, they'd ended up with a surplus of cash that enabled them to buy land, businesses, and vacant buildings. They had no involvement in any sort of trafficking, and their businesses were legitimate—earning them no human attention.

But did they keep their hands perfectly clean? No. They hunted any hell-born demons who'd escaped from that place.

Old habits and all that.

Where the fuck was Ella?

She always arrived at six-thirty, give or take ten minutes. It was now seven pm, but there was no sign of her. He didn't like it.

Viper rolled back his shoulders, struggling to tamp down his unease. The world of demons was brutal, and Ella . . . he'd swear she'd been hexed or some shit. Danger seemed to constantly dog her heels like a puppy chasing after its master.

She just *stumbled* into situations, always in the wrong place at the worst time. Like a month ago, when she'd come across a woman being mugged. Ella had intervened, only to subsequently get hit by a psychic punch that knocked her unconscious.

Viper had stepped in fast, killing the bastard who'd dared harm her and wiping the memory of it from the mind of the woman who'd been mugged; replacing said memory with a false one of the mugger sprinting away.

He could have instead played the white knight who'd killed Ella's attacker, yes. But he hadn't been ready to plant himself in her life at that point. Plus, it would have meant lying to her about why he'd been close by.

Viper was no stranger to lies or trickery. He'd mastered deception long ago. He was good at it. Typically, it didn't bother him to rattle off untruths. But Ella wasn't just anyone.

A round of crowing rang out from one of the far tables, pulling him from his thoughts.

"Do you really have to bitch at me?" complained Ghost, rubbing a blue chalk square over the tip of his cue, his gray eyes locked on the club's Road Captain.

"I'm not bitching, I'm saying." Razor bent over the pool table and took his shot, sending a ball tumbling into one of the pockets.

"You can't *tell* me what to wear," Ghost insisted.

Razor shot him a glare from pale-blue eyes that stood out against his dark skin. "I can when you're talking about buying a fucking Deadpool suit."

"I like the style."

Viper exchanged an amused look with Dice. What Ghost *liked* was to fuck with his opponents to better his chance of winning. They all knew it. But Razor, being an ornery son of a bitch, was easy to rile.

"We're supposed to be *blending*," Razor reminded Ghost. "Blending means acting like regular people." He stretched his bulky frame across the table as he smoothly positioned the cue between his thumb and forefinger. "Regular adults don't go round wearing superhero costumes as everyday clothes." The ball he hit smacked into another and sent it shuttling into a corner pocket.

"I'd make a hot superhero," said Ghost, wiping chalk dust from his fingers on his faded black jeans.

"I'd make a good cult leader," Darko piped up from his stool.

Beside him, Dice snorted. "You sure have the Messiah look going on," he noted, gesturing at their brother's shoulder-length chestnut hair, mustache, and light beard.

"It's why I make such a good Chaplain for the club," said Darko, snatching a nacho from a small tray he'd set on his thigh.

Viper frowned. "You're not the Chaplain. We don't *need* a Chaplain." It was something they'd already covered.

"We also don't need *you* riding around in a Deadpool suit," Razor told Ghost.

Dice sighed at the Road Captain. "He's just yanking your chain to throw you off your game. Stop letting him."

Ghost idly rasped a hand over his dusting of stubble that was the same dark brown as his short hair. "Out of curiosity, are you gonna bitch at me if I get cowboy boots as well?"

It was Dice who pinned him with a hard stare this time. "You get cowboy boots and I'll shred them."

"Why?" asked Ghost, his brow creasing. "Some bikers wear cowboy boots."

"But we both know you'd get them in fucking bright orange or something," said Dice.

Ghost raised his shoulders, all innocence. "And what would be wrong with that?"

Razor snickered at Dice. "*Now* who's letting him yank their chain?" He potted another ball.

Viper exhaled heavily. "Ghost, give the boys a break, yeah?"

The shit-stirrer grinned but quieted.

Right then, Jester's mind touched his. *We got him, V*, he telepathed, no doubt referring to the mystery male who'd been earlier hovering around their compound and had then followed them here. Viper had instructed two of his brothers to nab the guy.

Want us to bring him inside? Jester asked.

Yeah, take him to my office. Setting his beer on the table, Viper spoke to the others. "Jester and Omen have our watcher."

"Want me to question him?" asked Razor, who had a knack for making people talk.

Viper gave his head a slight shake. "I got it covered." It would give him the distraction he needed.

Dice rose from his stool. "I'll come with you."

Together, Viper and his VP headed through a door labeled 'STAFF' and strode down a hallway. A tall, bronze-skinned male was casually leaning against the wall near the office door, wearing his usual stony mug. Jester was asocial, tactless, and lacked a sense of humor. Yeah, the club was being sarcastic when they branded him Jester.

Viper flicked a look at the door. "I take it Omen is inside there with him?"

The Sergeant at Arms nodded, his deep-brown eyes as sober as always. "Caught our friend walking the perimeter of the building, peeking through windows. Not sure what he expected to find."

Dice lifted a brow. "Did you ask?"

Pulling a face, Jester skimmed a hand over his dark buzzcut. "Nah, I didn't see any point. He'll just lie. I don't have time to listen to bullshit," he added, as if he had a thousand things eating up his time and attention. Which couldn't be further from the truth.

Viper frowned. "And what is it that you're scheduled to do?"

Jester only twisted his mouth.

Inwardly sighing, Viper reached for the doorknob.

"By the way, I figure you'll be interested in knowing he ain't a demon like we assumed. The guy's an Earth-bound angel."

"That so?" Viper narrowed his eyes. "Interesting." His entity stretched out inside him, hoping their evening was about to perk up.

Personally, Viper thought it messed up that some angels were placed on Earth and then forced to earn their halo, especially when they hadn't done anything to warrant that. The struggle was forced upon those whose parents had angered the powers-that-be in the upper realm. Basically, these angels paid for the sins of their parents.

There were plenty of Earth-bound angels in this realm. They tended to keep their distance from his club—they wouldn't want to risk upsetting heaven's higher-ups by consorting with the Fallen. That was no way to earn a halo.

Viper opened the door and stalked into the office. He exchanged a brief nod with the lean, olive-skinned male who stood near the window. Only then did he switch his attention to the stranger sitting in a chair with his back to Viper—a back that was currently ruler straight. The guy didn't turn to check who'd entered the room, just remained perfectly still.

Viper prowled further into the office and moved to stand in front of his guest. It was easy to sense that the slim, balding, narrow-faced male was an angel—he gave off the same low-hum frequency that all celestial beings did; a frequency only other angels would pick up.

But . . . there was something not quite right here. The male's face was as blank as that of any doll. But his light-green eyes? Alive with emotion.

Someone had taken the guy's mental wheel; had made him their—perhaps willing, perhaps unwilling—puppet.

Viper tipped his head to the side. "And just who might you be?"

A smile lit the angel's gaze. "I suppose it's not easy to recognize me in this get-up."

Only one celestial he knew would describe a person whose mind they'd hijacked as a 'get-up', as if he wore their skin. A celestial who Viper had considered a friend until, over the course of their 'careers', they'd lost touch. "Ophaniel."

The archangel gave a graceful incline of his head.

Omen shifted, swearing low.

Viper felt his jaw harden. Ophaniel was a seasoned slayer who'd been forced to retire when he'd . . . changed. Centuries of killing could do that to a celestial—mostly because their innately pure inner entity, not built to destroy, would eventually fracture from the strain. Those fractures would affect the other half of their soul, and so the celestial would turn.

Ophaniel's kills had become unnecessarily gruesome. At times, he'd killed not only his target, but their families. There were even occasions when he'd butchered archangels within his own unit because they'd annoyed him. Not out of cruelty, but because he'd come to feel numb.

That same numbness had once crept up on Viper until he'd found Ella.

No longer useful to the Uppers, being that Ophaniel was difficult to control, they'd dropped him from his unit. But, as they considered him an extremely expendable asset, they would offer him jobs that had proven difficult for others to complete. Better to lose a retired and 'damaged' slayer than one of their active and proficient slayers.

Viper narrowed his eyes. "If you've come to execute me, this wasn't the best way to go about it." When using a puppet, Ophaniel couldn't access his own offensive abilities; only those whose mind he'd taken over. His current celestial 'get-up' would stand no chance against Viper.

"I had thought the Uppers would offer me a substantial fee to end you," said Ophaniel. "But they feel that killing you would require more caution and control than I possess."

They weren't wrong.

"They came to me because you and I were once friends, so they feel you'd be more likely to hear me out. I would have just appeared at your compound and requested an audience with you, but you wouldn't have come to the gate."

Viper turned away any celestial who came for a 'chat', because they were only ever acting as messengers for the Uppers; pressuring him to return to heaven.

Viper leaned back onto his office desk. "My answer is still no."

"Doesn't matter. Our superiors don't care what you want, they care that you do as ordered. You know that."

Yeah, see, the Upper Realm wasn't all love, peace, and divine light. Nor were the beings who ruled over it. In fact, they enjoyed tempting the innate darkness that brewed inside humans, and they'd once used Viper to do it.

He had spent most of his life executing their will at any cost. His life hadn't really been his own. That was the rub when it came to being so high-ranked. Your life was about serving, not *having* or owning. No one had ever belonged to him until Ella

He'd seen the worst that man had to offer. Too many times he'd easily tempted someone off a righteous path. It had left him jaded and cynical and in need of something *good*.

His woman was good.

Well . . . to an extent. She was a demon, after all.

"You had to have anticipated that they wouldn't let you be," Ophaniel added. "The Seven are considered sacred and heroic. You have tainted that image."

Snorting, Viper crossed his legs at the ankles. "*The Uppers* will have tainted that image by spreading a bullshit story about how I fell to escape punishment for some kind of betrayal." When Ophaniel didn't deny the charge, Viper added, "They could have just told people the truth, that I fell willingly."

"You know why they didn't. It would have emboldened any celestials who might be considering falling—they all regard the Seven through awe-filled eyes. If *you* deem it acceptable to fall, then surely such a thing isn't quite so bad. That would be the line of thinking some would have. The Uppers can't allow that. And they can't allow you to stay on Earth. They insist on you returning."

"I don't answer to them anymore. They really should have noticed that."

"They'll undo the curse if you return," Ophaniel threw out. "They'll even restore you to who, what, you once were."

Like hell they would. The Uppers weren't that merciful. And they liked to 'make examples' of those who demonstrated any form of rebellion.

The process of falling wasn't as dramatic as humans would assume. It wasn't a physical fall. It was a simple decision to leave the upper realm.

There was no dropping from the sky, no crashing to the Earth, no having stumps where their wings used to be. Not all angels actually had wings. But ... leaving the realm *did* have consequences.

Angels and demons were similar in that they had a dualism to the soul. The entities within demons were cruel and psychopathic, totally at contrast to the pure and innocent beings within angels. But that purity and innocence became warped and twisted from the fall—they were then dark and unfeeling, lost any grace they had, and only one thing made them feel alive. A thing they were cursed to forever need. Crave. Feed on.

Blood.

It was their punishment for 'abandoning' their people and home. And if you were one of the Seven archangels, your punishment would be so much worse.

Even if the higher-ups were to undo the curse, they'd still make an example of him so that no other archangels thought to repeat Viper's actions. "There's nothing they could offer me that would make me return. I would've thought they'd have clued in to that by now."

"You cannot say that you're enjoying life on Earth. Not when one or all of you have become so bored that you're recklessly snatching humans, despite knowing that their disappearances will eventually attract attention."

Viper felt his brows almost lift in surprise. For Ophaniel to know about the disappearances of the local humans, the Uppers must still be having Viper and his brothers watched. A disconcerting notion, considering they hadn't sensed that they were being closely monitored. They usually did. "That has nothing to do with us."

Ophaniel cast him a doubtful look. "Two of the missing women frequent your nightclub. One of the missing men is a regular here at the pool hall."

"I'm aware of that." He and his club were investigating the disappearances, since these humans were practically being plucked from the Black Saints' metaphorical doorstep. "We don't yet know who's responsible, but we'll find out."

"You expect me to believe that it is a coincidence? That none of your brothers, caught up in bloodlust, have—"

"You can believe whatever you want. I don't give a fuck. Fact is we have nothing to do with the disappearances."

Ophaniel's brow pinched. "You are saying that someone is counting on you taking the blame?"

Viper was more of the opinion that they were taunting him and his club, but he wasn't yet sure. He didn't really care *why* they were doing it, he just wanted it stopped. No one got to use his territory as their personal hunting ground.

"As I said, we're looking into it. We'll have our answers soon enough." Viper pushed away from his desk. "Now ... to be blunt ... it's time for you to fuck off."

Ophaniel sighed. "You are far too stubborn."

"It's not a matter of being stubborn. It's a matter of my being content where I am."

"I will never believe you could be content being a walking leech. What are you holding out for? Why delay your return? If you're expecting them to beg—"

"All I expect is for them to leave me and my brothers be. Nothing the Uppers ever say, do, or offer will tempt me to return. You be sure to communicate that," he said, a silken menace woven around the words.

Exhaling heavily, Ophaniel stood. "Fine. But I will be surprised if this makes a difference. As I've already pointed out, they don't care what you want. This is about so much more than just you. You're a fool if you think otherwise." With that, he teleported away.

Viper's entity slumped its shoulders in disappointment. It had hoped to 'play' with the archangel a little. Mostly by slicing into his skin over and over. Yeah, the entity with whom Viper shared his soul was no one's idea of pleasant.

"He's right, you know," said Omen, taking a slow step forward. "No amount of clear statements from you will make the Uppers back off. Your refusal will continue to fall on deaf ears."

To say that heaven's higher-ups loathed when angels fell would be an understatement. They detested it more if angels bred with humans. Though what really got under their skin was when angels reproduced with demons, particularly since no one from heaven could afford to go round slaughtering the hybrid children—it would spark a war between the light and the dark. Their disinclination to start such a war was one of the reasons Viper had been intent on securing alliances with very powerful demons.

Viper shrugged. "There ain't much I can do about that." He crossed to the open door, where Jester waited.

"What did the angel want?" asked the Sgt at Arms, though he didn't sound all that interested.

"The angel was just a puppet. It was Ophaniel who wanted to speak with me." Viper gave Jester a quick recap of the conversation as they walked along the hallway side by side, their other two brothers trailing close behind.

"It has to piss some of the celestials off that they're sent to talk to you over and over," mused Jester. "Most will have accepted that you won't go back on your choice. The Uppers, though? They seem determined to ignore that."

"That's pretty much what I said," Omen chipped in.

"Part of it is they're so used to being able to order us around, they find it hard to believe they've lost all hold on us," said Dice. "The other part is that they simply can't just let one of the Seven fall."

"They'll eventually have to face that you won't willingly return," said Jester. "At that point, they'll either send more slayers . . . or they'll just tell their people you're dead and proceed to act as though you are."

While Viper would prefer the latter, his entity rather hoped it would have the chance to butcher more slayers.

Just then, Darko's mind touched Viper's as he telepathically spoke . . . *She's here.*

CHAPTER TWO

Viper's pulse did a little jump as both relief and anticipation seeped into him. Reaching the door that separated the private area from the public section, he shoved it open. His gaze roamed over the space. And there she was. His woman. A beautiful, sensual, willowy sight.

She walked to her usual table on those long legs, moving with the grace and lightness of a dancer. She'd pulled her striking hair back into an intricate knot and wound little white flowers into it—they stood out against the rich ruby red mass. A mass he wanted to stroke. Fist. Toy with. Bury his fingers in.

As Everleigh, she'd been brunette. Small and curvy. A default-smiler. But no less beautiful than she was now.

Or any less fierce.

In terms of her soul's core character, she made him think of a swan. She was smart. Elegant. Calm. But she could be vicious if the situation called for it.

Even as he made his way back to his other brothers, Viper

continued to watch her. Recognizing her, his entity sat up straight, its mood instantly improving. Even before falling, it had never seen those in this realm as equals. Merely toys. Ella was no exception, just as she hadn't been in her past life. But the entity didn't view her as an interchangeable toy the way it did others.

Even now, despite being twisted from the fall, it didn't consider her disposable. It didn't want to hurt or break Ella. She was its favorite.

It wanted to keep her. Hog her. Squirrel her away. Ensure that no one else played with her.

There was no denying that the woman had marked both him and his entity. Not physically, but *inside*. She'd left some part of herself there, buried so deep they'd never get her out.

"Aren't you tired of only fucking her with your eyes?" asked Jester, sidling up to him. "Other parts of your anatomy must be feeling left out."

Viper shot him a hard look.

"Well, as the proud owner of her favorite hangout *and* the dive bar next to her store, what're you gonna buy next? Because you've already bought her apartment building, so that's out. I'm thinking you—"

"Don't," said Viper, retrieving the beer he'd left on the table.

Jester arched a brow. "Don't, what?"

"Start rambling about how I need to make a direct move already."

"I never said that."

Viper tipped his bottle at the Sgt at Arms. "But you're thinking it."

"Of course I am. We're *all* thinking it."

"Don't speak for me," Razor cut in, his brows drawing together.

Jester lifted his shoulders. "So I'm wrong?"

"No. But I don't need you to be my voice." Razor potted the

black ball, ignoring Ghost's curse. "Instead of getting on Viper's case, convince that asshole over there not to buy a goddamn superhero suit."

His eyes dancing, Ghost twirled his pool cue between his fingers. "You're just jealous that, unlike you, I'd look good in spandex."

Razor gifted him a flat look. "Yeah, that's exactly it," he deadpanned.

"Can we focus, please?" Jester demanded.

Ghost's brow pinched. "On what?"

"Me," Jester replied.

"Uh, okay, narcissist." Ghost turned to Darko. "He'd make a good cult leader, too."

"You know, I was thinking the exact same thing," said Darko.

Jester ground his teeth. "I hate you all."

Ghost smiled. "That's nice."

Shaking his head, Jester refocused on Viper. "I get that you'd rather see to our current problem first so she doesn't get caught in any crossfire. But I don't see a need for it; she's unlikely to get touched by it. It's humans who are being snatched, not demons."

Viper guzzled down some beer. "I don't want to take any chances. Not with her."

"But you can't keep chasing off every guy who shows interest in her."

Yeah? Watch me.

"She hasn't noticed it's happening yet, but she will."

"Probably." Viper found his attention zipping back to Ella. Their gazes clashed, making his insides seize. Her inky blue eyes narrowed slightly as a line creased her brow. Probably because he was blatantly staring at her. But fuck if he could avert his gaze.

She didn't look tired today, which was good. Too often lately she'd seemed fatigued. He didn't like that she might not be getting the sleep she needed, but it wasn't his place to do anything about it yet. At least not in her view.

The waitress materialized at her table, blocking his view of Ella; breaking their connection.

"You sure you're not just stalling because you've got it in your head that you don't deserve her?" asked Omen. "Because that'd be dumb."

Viper frowned at him. "I'm no martyr. And I'm not stalling. I'm simply intent on not risking her. I've waited this long—I can hold out a little longer." Maybe.

His entity snorted, confident it could tempt him into acting much sooner. Honestly, it probably could. Viper supposed they'd soon see.

Placing her food order, Ella beat back the heat that tried rising to her cheeks. It wasn't so easy to ignore the way her skin tingled in awareness, however. Having that compelling blue gaze drilling into her—something that had happened on a number of recent occasions—seriously messed with her composure.

Once the waitress melted away, Ella lifted the bottle of beer that her sister had earlier ordered for her. "He reminds me of someone."

Leaning back in the chair across from her, Mia slanted her head. "Who does?"

"Viper, the president of the Black Saints." Ella had seen him from a distance many times. Each occasion they made eye contact, she had that nagging sense of familiarity. "I can't think who he reminds me of," she groused, planting her elbow on the table as she put the tip of her bottle near her mouth. "It's probably a celebrity."

Mia hummed. "Dark and dangerous generally doesn't get my engines running, but it must be said that he's hot as a motherfucker."

"Actually, you *do* like 'dark and dangerous'."

"Correction, then: I tend to avoid guys like that because I've had bad experiences with them in the past."

Ella's eyes unconsciously tried straying back to him. Ugh, it was *his* fault. The big, indecently attractive bastard loped around dropping a sexual candy trail of pheromones, testosterone, and unbridled alpha energy. Ella was not immune to it. Or him. Which she very much blamed on her obsession with biker romance novels.

Dominant alpha males, a badass brotherhood, tattoos upon tattoos, typical club chaos ... Yeah, she was *all there* for those novel ingredients. Viper was a real-life dark, gritty, I-am-who-I-am-and-don't-give-a-fuck biker.

He was almost frighteningly beautiful in a savage sort of way, his face harshly masculine. Every part of him sang with a power that pulsed around him. Power that showed in his solid build, roped muscles, compact shoulders, and flat abs she'd seen peeks of through his tees. That same power even somehow came across in his penetrating eyes that shimmered like blue diamonds.

"I'm kind of partial to one of his brothers," Mia went on, idly fussing with her tight braid. She and Ella were similar in many ways. Same eye color. Same hair. Same tall build. But Mia had enviable curves, longer lashes, and her eyes were slanted rather than wide like Ella's.

Knowing her sister's type, Ella guessed, "The blond who happens to be the club's VP?"

Mia smiled. "It's his eyes, mostly—they grab hold."

Unlike his president's, Dice's eyes were a very pale blue that were no less striking.

Ella tipped back her bottle and gulped down some beer. "All the Black Saints are pretty to look at."

They sure got around, because she often spied a couple of

them hovering here or there—including in the Underground. Which was surprising, since the subterranean location was generally exclusive to demons. It seemed that Viper had managed to form an alliance with Knox Thorne, the demon who founded and owned it—the billionaire was exceptionally powerful, but no one seemed to know just what breed of demon he was.

Another thing that surprised her was Viper purchasing the pool hall. This place wasn't exactly a money maker, though it had become more popular since the club took it over. Hence why it was currently on the rowdy side. The sounds of the tournament playing on the TV blended with the chatter, laughter, cursing, cheering, balls smacking balls, beer bottles clinking, and gaming machines bleeping and blooping.

Leaning forward, Mia planted her lower arms on the table. "I'd give you shit for sneaking looks at Viper—don't think I haven't noticed you do it—but I figure it would be criminal to not admire someone that hot, even if they are an angel." She paused. "Do you think he could really be an archangel like the rumors say?" she asked, lowering her voice. "Maybe even one of the Seven?"

Pulling a face, Ella set down her bottle. "I do think he may be an archangel, what with how much power he oozes. But one of the Seven? Surely none who'd risen so high in the ranks would want to fall."

"Maybe he was kicked out of the Seven and, ultimately, out of heaven itself. His brothers could have followed him in a show of support, or maybe they were kicked out, too."

"It's possible, I guess."

"Considering how often he glances your way, I think we can safely conclude that he seriously wants to nail you."

"So aptly put." Ella probably shouldn't like that she might have caught his attention. Since almost the beginning of time, angels and demons had been foes. There was a lot of ugly history there. More, there had been instances where angels who'd regretted falling had subsequently killed random demons in a bid to please those in the upper realm and, thus, earn their way back up there.

A few of her ancestors had been victims of such crimes, so incantors generally weren't among the demons who flapped a dismissive hand about it all. But Ella personally saw no sense in holding crimes against people who didn't commit them. She certainly wouldn't let it stop her from admiring Viper from afar. He was such a visual wonder . . .

"But even if you'd be willing to look past the fact that he's one of the Fallen, Luka would never let such a person near you," Mia went on. "He's hyper protective of you."

That was because he and Ella were anchors. Demons came in pairs, meaning they all had a psychic mate who would anchor them and their inner entity, ensuring said entity never turned rogue. A demon gone rogue was no joke, and they were always hunted down to be executed.

"Is Luka any closer to identifying the mugger who flattened you with a psychic punch?" asked Mia.

"Nope, and it's making him crazy." Ella couldn't be of any real help, because she hadn't seen her attacker's face—he'd worn a mask.

"What did Luka make of the note you received?"

Ah, yes, the little note that someone had stuck under her windscreen wiper: *Let sleeping dogs lie*.

Such a silly, innocuous phrase. But there'd been power embedded in the ink. She hadn't noticed it at first. When she'd absently gone to read the note aloud, her magick had leaped up to spark the air like an alarm.

On taking a closer look at the note, Ella had spotted the glimmer of power in the black ink. A snare. Saying the words aloud would have activated it—she knew that much. But she had no clue what would have happened.

Its purpose could have been *anything*. To make her sleep. Make her hungry. Make her sad. Make her smell bad.

The possibilities were endless, so she had no idea whether the author of the note meant her real harm or was just playing some weird prank on her.

If the snare had been a work of magick, she could have read its intent. But it was infused with power—one she didn't recognize and couldn't seem to unravel.

Luka, too, had tried. So had Mia. Neither had had any luck.

The note had been typed, not written by hand. The paper it was printed on was standard paper you could buy anywhere. As such, there was no way to trace it back to a particular person.

"Luka agrees with you that it's likely from the mugger, which only made him more furious." Ella grimaced. "I'm still not convinced you're both right. The note wasn't addressed to me, it could have been an idiotic joke that was meant for anyone."

"Why would a prankster choose your car at random when it wasn't parked in a spot that would be easy for some passer-by to reach? They had to go through the trouble of smashing CCTV cameras just to get near it. Why go that extra mile?"

"Why would the mugger write that note?" Ella shot back.

"All the digging that Luka's doing has to worry him. I mean, who *wouldn't* be worried that a demonic crime boss was on their ass? Especially since they have to know that he won't let it go easily. They might be thinking *you* can convince him to back off, so they put a snare in their note that was designed to compel you to do it—I don't know. But you have to admit it's possible."

"Yes, it's possible."

Mia nodded, placated. "I have faith in Luka. He'll flush out the shithead eventually."

"Speaking of psi-mates, what's happening with you and Joe?"

Mia grimaced. "He's still being a tool. I should never have slept with him. In my defense, it was only supposed to happen once. I didn't think we'd topple into a full-on fling."

Possessiveness easily came into play with anchors, so it wasn't uncommon for them to do the dirty. In fact, Ella had years ago spent the night with Luka. It hadn't in any way tainted their friendship, but not all demons were so lucky.

"I texted Joe earlier asking how much longer he planned to be all weird and distant," Mia told her. "He hasn't replied yet, so I'm thinking it's gonna be a while."

Hating the hurt lacing her sister's voice, Ella gave Mia's wrist a supportive squeeze. "He cares for you."

"But not in a way that would sustain a relationship. It's the same for me. I love him, but not in a *I need him to be mine, I can't live without him* way. That's why I wasn't upset when he chose to end the fling. I would have eventually done it if he hadn't."

"Maybe he doesn't know that. Maybe he's avoiding you because he worries he's hurt you but doesn't know what to say."

Mia let out a haughty *hmph*. "I'm sure he'll enlighten me when he finally deigns to contact me. I'm not going to reach out to him again. He'll have to make that move."

Just then, the waitress reappeared with their food.

Ella and Mia talked as they ate, laughing at this or that. Despite herself, Ella repeatedly found her gaze flitting to the Black Saints. Or, more specifically, to Viper—she couldn't help it.

She almost choked on her hot dog when his eyes abruptly locked with hers, an intensity glimmering there that made the hairs on her nape stand up.

A loud shout made her look to her far right just as two males dived at each other, arms swinging, meaty fists smacking flesh hard. *Not pretty.*

Two of the Black Saints hurried over and dragged the brawlers apart, not hesitating to get up in their face. A few harsh words were exchanged, and then both fighters were ordered to leave. There were complaints and curses, but both fast-bruising demons stormed out.

"That's the third fight to have broken out since I got here," said Mia, before taking a bite of her burger.

It did happen a lot in the pool hall these days. In fact, it also occurred often at the dive bar that the club purchased. "It's almost as if the demons are sending a snarky, *We were here first and we'll do what we want whether you now own the place or not* message to the Black Saints. Or something like that." Ella shrugged. "Whatever the case, it's pretty reckless of them."

Mia nodded. "The Fallen are as dangerous as any demon."

They talked about lighter stuff as they finished their food. Fresh drinks in hand, they then claimed a pool table. Ella deliberately chose one that wasn't close to where Viper stood. He unnerved her enough from a distance.

Twenty minutes into their game, Mia frowned and asked, "Are we losing our touch?"

Ella bent over the table, careful not to knock her head on a low-hanging light. "What?"

"Once upon a time, we'd have guys come over, offering to buy us drinks, asking to play with or against us, and watching our asses each time we bent over to take a shot. They leave us alone nowadays. Those two goofballs standing at the ATM would *always* flirt with us. Now they won't even glance our way."

Ella felt her brow furrow as she studied the two men. "Yeah, they do seem to be making a point of not looking in our direction. Come to think of it, even the regulars we've known and indulged in playful shit talk with for years don't approach us anymore."

Mia bit into her lower lip. "Maybe we really are losing our touch. A dreary thought." She frowned when Ella potted two balls in quick succession. "And now I'm also gonna lose at pool. This day sucks."

Ella snorted. "Game's not over yet. You could still win."

But Mia didn't. Which she griped about even as they later left the building and walked into the dimly lit parking lot.

Her mouth curving, Ella said, "I'll see you in the morning."

"Whatever," Mia mumbled, making a beeline for her car.

Shaking her head with a smile, Ella began heading to her own vehicle. She was almost at it when she heard something. A rustle. And it was coming from the shadowy alley adjacent to where she stood.

Coming to a halt, she narrowed her eyes, able to make out two figures. One lay still on the ground, the other hovered over them in a way that seemed . . . threatening. He was lanky. Pale as death.

Her demon stilled as his head whipped to face her. Air got trapped in her lungs as blood-red eyes met hers, cruel and animalistic. Yeah, *red eyes.*

Ella's brows snapped together. "The fuck?"

He hissed at her. Like a freaking alley cat. His body tensed as his legs bent, as if he was poised to lunge.

Oh, the hell no. Ella called to her magick, letting it crackle against her palms, and then chanted under her breath as she sent ribbons of magick gushing through the air toward him. Before it could touch him—holy mother of God—he seemed to *explode* into a billion pieces . . . only to become a bat. A *bat.* One that promptly flew away.

Gaping, Ella could only stare after it. That was . . . She was . . . He couldn't have . . .

Fuck, she needed to sit down.

Instead, she cautiously walked into the alley and approached the figure lying on the ground. A human male, she quickly realized. It took no detective work to conclude that he was dead. He *smelled* it. The stench made her demon sniff in disdain.

Hinges creaked as the side door of the pool hall opened. Several people piled into the alley—all of whom were members of the Black Saints. They stilled as their gazes bounced from her to the human at her feet.

Ella lifted her hands. "Uh, yeah, it wasn't me. I just found him this way."

CHAPTER THREE

Taking in the scene, Viper wanted to groan. The universe couldn't have just let her get in her car and drive home, could it? No, it had to make sure she stumbled into yet another 'situation'.

"Something was just here," Ella went on in that low and scratchy voice, dropping her arms to her sides. "I don't know if they killed him in this spot or dumped him here, but . . ."

"I believe you." Viper crossed to the corpse with his brothers at his back. He instantly recognized the body as belonging to one of the missing humans. The guy looked surprisingly peaceful, his eyes closed, his face free of lines.

There were no signs of torture. No tears in, or stains on, his clothes. The only visible injuries were on his neck—four pairs of puncture wounds.

"He's been dead a day or so," noted Darko, crouching beside the body.

If Viper remembered rightly, this particular human had vanished a week ago. So where had he been all that time?

Viper met Ella's gaze again—and sexual connection slammed into him, making his body go tight and his blood go hot. Her eyelids flickered, telling him she wasn't unaffected by the close-up eye contact either. His entity grinned, liking that.

"You said *something* was just here," Viper prompted.

She nodded. "He had red eyes. Seriously pale skin. Long nails. And he hissed at me like an honest to God's cat. Then he morphed into a bat and flew away. As you do." She twisted her lips. "I'm thinking vampire."

Some vampires could shapeshift, and one of the three vampiric breeds did in fact boast red irises. But they typically didn't go around senselessly killing humans.

There was another creature, however, who fit the physical description she'd reeled off. A creature who could shift into bats, would kill without thought, and needed no motivation to do so.

"He didn't touch you?" Viper checked.

"He went to pounce, but when I struck out with magick he shifted into a bat to evade it. I'm an incantor," she added, as if to explain why she could call on magick.

"I know."

Her eyelids lowered slightly. "How do you know?"

Viper let his lips curl. "I pay attention when something or someone intrigues me." He saw no harm in making his interest in her clear now. It would give her some time to get accustomed to it.

"Huh," was all she said, clearly thrown by his blunt response—just as she'd always been in her past life.

He wanted to smile, finding her cute as fuck when she was off-balance. But right now, what he wanted most was to get her away from this scene—there was no need for her to be further touched by this matter.

Viper tipped his chin toward the parking lot. "Go. We'll handle this."

A line dented her brow. "But—"

"This happened on our turf. It's for us to deal with."

Her delicious mouth tightened. "If there's a human-killing vamp on the loose—"

"They won't live long," he stated firmly.

Visibly reluctant, she glanced down at the human. "You swear you'll find out who did this?"

Viper felt his brows inch up. "You think we'd overlook it?"

"What I think is that a lot of the preternatural population wouldn't much care about the death of a human."

She wasn't wrong. "I'd be lying if I said I'm aching to avenge him, but what I won't tolerate is anyone dumping corpses on my doorstep. So yes, I will find out who did this. It won't be overlooked."

She exhaled heavily. "All right." She moved as if to leave, but then instead held her hand out to him. "I'm Ella."

I know, baby. I know a whole lot about you. "Viper," he said, letting his hand swallow hers, both comforted and enlivened by the zap of static that bounced from their palms. It startled a silent gasp from her, but she didn't pull back. Neither did he.

Decades. He hadn't been this close to her in fucking decades. It had felt more like centuries. Her soul might wear a different body this time, but it didn't matter. She was still *her*. Still belonged to him. And it was all he could do not to yank her to him and devour her mouth.

"You'll definitely take care of this?" she double-checked.

Viper forced himself to allow her palm to slip out of his grasp. "It'll be handled."

"Okay." She spared his brothers a quick look and then left.

Viper watched her stride out of the alley, knots forming in his stomach with each bit of distance she placed between them. His entity bared its teeth, annoyed that he'd let her walk away.

Much like Jester, it saw no reason why they couldn't claim her now.

Only once she was out of sight did Viper return his attention to his brothers. "Anyone think they know the cause of death?"

It was Darko who responded. "My guess? Exsanguination. The body's almost empty of blood."

"A vamp wouldn't drink a human near to death unless they were converting them," said Razor.

"But a strix would," Viper pointed out.

Darko rose to his feet. "That fits."

Human mythology often confused the two species. Unlike vampires, strix were never human. Nor were they immortal. These creatures were born in hell and all typically looked alike—tall figures, dark hair, red eyes, long fingernails, canine fangs, skin so pale it was almost translucent. They had various abilities, including the power to shift into bats, owls, or even mist.

"I hate to be the voice of doom and gloom," began Darko, "but there's never a lone strix, so I doubt only one escaped from hell. There'll be a colony. One it's safe to say is responsible for the recent human disappearances."

"And they know we're here." Dice waved a hand at the corpse. "This is a taunt. A gauntlet. Their queen is basically pitting the colony against us."

"I accept her challenge," Viper muttered darkly.

Colonies were usually made up of around seventy strix. Though there were generally more males, their societies were largely matriarchal. Females held higher positions and were often warriors, though they rarely fought except in situations of war. Males served mostly as hunters and protectors.

"The strix probably felt drawn here by you," mused Omen, looking at Viper. "Or, more to the point, drawn by what you are."

"Probably." Staring down at the puncture wounds on the dead human, Viper didn't doubt there were more wounds. Victims were often covered in bites, because many of the colony would descend on them all at once.

Strix rarely drained their prey of blood in one sitting, though. They were known to keep several humans around at a time, drawing out each one's inevitable death.

Ghost folded his arms. "If the other missing humans aren't already dead, they soon will be. And the strix will no doubt dump them near or on our properties."

"We need to track and kill them," said Jester. "Fucking hate strix."

"Are we much different from them?" Viper asked. "We prey on people like parasites. We can't survive without the life-force of others. We're addicts for whom there is peace only in death."

The Fallen were pariahs even among monsters. Unnatural due to their curse, they belonged on no realm. Had no 'place'. They were not angel, demon, or vampire, but they possessed the dark qualities of all three.

Drinking from animals did nothing for them, so they didn't have the option of sticking to what would emotionally be an easier diet to handle. Their prey had to be people—whether human or preternatural.

Dice gave him a grave look. "We don't kill those we feed from. We don't make our bites painful. We don't enjoy the hunt. And we *never* touch children."

All true. The strix, by contrast, had no self-control or humanity. Their primal appetite overwhelmed them. But when the Fallen were in bloodlust, the same could be said about them.

Bloodlust could strike them any time, whether they fed regularly or not. Mindless as they were when bloodlust struck, they had to be confined during such times. There was no avoiding it, no 'fixing' it, no snapping a person out of it. They just had to let it run its course.

Darko gestured at the dead human. "What do we do with him?"

"We let him be found *far* from here, but not in this state," Viper replied. "Put him in either a vacant house or a car and set it alight. We don't want anything but dental records IDing him." More to the point, they didn't want any preternatural evidence on his person.

"Done," said Dice with a nod.

Ghost looked to the end of the alley and then back at Viper. "I guess we were wrong in thinking she wouldn't get caught up in our newest issue. It's probably best that you've held back. If the strix are watching us, they would see you with her."

"You know, V, with the way she looks at you ... You're *sure* it's not possible that she remembers you?"

"Yes." Though people retained memories from their past lives, they didn't consciously have access to them—such memories were carved into their soul, not lodged in their brain. Still, they could meet a person from a past life and feel an instant familiarity with them; could feel they'd met them before, or simply be at total ease in their company.

But this couldn't apply to Ella, because ... "When those fuckers upstairs scrubbed the imprint of me from her soul, they scrubbed away the memories there as well."

Ghost bit into the inside of his cheek. "There's a chance they didn't scrub hard enough."

"They would have been thorough. They wanted no trace of me to linger on her soul."

"Doesn't mean they effectively erased all of those traces," Ghost insisted. "Fragments could remain."

Razor nodded. "You kept your distance from her, but you've

been in her periphery. It might have shaken the memories loose. It would only have been on a subconscious level, but still."

"She loved you, V," said Dice. "Loved you enough that she didn't care you'd need blood to survive—she was *all* in. I personally don't think it'd be so easy to rid a soul of every memory of someone they loved *that* hard, powerful archangels on the case or not."

A warm mouth pressed hot, damp kisses to the back of her shoulder, lulling her out of sleep. Her eyes closed, she frowned and shifted slightly.

"Morning, baby," a deep voice breathed.

Everleigh writhed, restless, as he trailed kisses all over her back. He took his time, exploring and marking everywhere he could reach, causing her anticipation to rise and rise.

Fingertips danced down the side of her breast as his hand slid down, down, down . . . and dived into the back of her shorts. She bucked as one finger swiped between her folds.

"Slick for me already." His warm breath fanned her ear as he lowered his broad body onto her. "That's because you know you're mine."

Two fingers sank inside her, and she inhaled sharply. Then those fingers were moving. Swirling. Plunging. Scissoring.

A soft but guttural growl sounded in her ear as she lifted her hips to meet each thrust. "Yeah, take it," he urged.

Moaning, she scratched at the bedsheet, loving the feel of those clever fingers slicing into her again and again. As his mouth latched onto her pulse, she tilted her head to give him better access to her neck. His tongue licked. Teeth nipped. Words of praise were whispered against her skin. The friction inside her built and built and built.

Then she came. Hard.

He hummed. "That's my baby." Gentling kisses were pressed to the back of her shoulder. "Now it's my turn."

Waking to the beeping of her alarm, Ella blindly reached out and switched off the offensive noise. Fuzzy snippets in her mind's eye plucked at her attention. *Erotic* snippets. She tried grabbing on to the threads of her dream, but they slipped away too fast.

Damn, if she was dreaming about getting laid, she definitely needed to give her libido some action soon.

She wasn't someone who typically had those kinds of dreams. Though . . . there had been one several months ago. She couldn't remember it well. There'd been a mouth trailing kisses up her back until it reached her ear. Then a voice had rumbled, "Found you." She'd woken with a start.

Weird, to say the least.

Rubbing at her tired eyes, Ella edged out of bed and then began her morning routine—paid a visit to her small but bright en suite bathroom, got dressed in her cozy bedroom that was all cool blues and greens, and then headed down to her dark-wooded, plant-dominated kitchen. Once she'd tossed back a cup of tea and chowed down a bowl of oatmeal, she left the apartment.

As usual, she found Mia waiting for her in the lobby. They often rode to work together, and they'd alternate on who would drive. This morning, it was Ella's turn.

Mia pushed off the cream leather sofa, her brow pinching. "You look tired again."

"I had another restless night's sleep." Lately, she'd been plagued by dreams she couldn't remember on waking. "Ready to go?"

"Yup."

As they drove, Mia nattered about a TV series she was

binge-watching. Ella nodded and smiled, but her mind drifted back to the previous night. It should be the poor deceased human who snatched her thoughts, but no. It was Viper.

His hyper-intense gaze had pinned hers with a hormone-melting focus. Always did. The very first time they'd locked gazes many months ago, for a single moment, she'd had the thought that she *knew* those eyes. They'd somehow seemed familiar.

Last night, her pulse had jumped when his hand engulfed hers. Ella wasn't the type to get all flustered and nervous around guys, but Viper did things to her head. And ovaries. Oh, her poor ovaries.

Her demon was intrigued by him but also wary. He was one of the Fallen, after all. And her entity didn't quite trust how very *aware* Ella's body was of this perfect stranger.

He'd been a little too slow in releasing her hand, but she'd chosen not to call him on it. Mostly because she hadn't been in any rush to walk away.

One thing had been kind of weird ... When she'd shaken hands with Viper, the VP had worn a weird 'fucking finally' expression. Like he'd been eager for them to meet.

"You've zoned out, haven't you?" accused Mia.

Her mind flicking back to the present, Ella cast her sister a quick look. "Sorry. It's just that something odd happened last night."

Mia tilted her head. "What?"

"I saw a vampire."

"A vampire?"

"And he wasn't a very nice one. Looked kind of, I don't know, feral." Ella hadn't come across many vamps in her time, but the ones she'd met had behaved like regular people to a large extent. They'd blended well while walking among humans, hiding fangs with closed-mouthed smiles and concealing oddly-colored irises with sunglasses. The guy she'd come upon last night had been very different.

"Feral?" Mia echoed, twisting to better face Ella. "In what way?"

"He hissed at me. He had weirdly long nails. And get this: he shifted into a bat. An actual bat."

Mia's lips parted. "When did this happen?"

"In the alley outside the pool hall. I caught him dumping a dead human there. He wasn't pleased that I'd spotted him. He might have pounced on me if I hadn't given him a little magickal demonstration."

"He might have killed you, and you didn't think to lead with that?" Mia asked, the bite of disbelief in her voice.

Ella shrugged. "I said he might have, not that he tried. Anyway, the Black Saints appeared. Viper assured me he'd deal with it."

A slow smile curved Mia's lips. "Oh, you talked a little with Viper, huh?"

"Briefly." Ella shifted gears as she sped up, contemplating whether to add his little implication that she'd piqued his interest . . .

"It's such a shame that he's one of the Fallen. I mean, I don't hold their nature against them—or what others of their kind have done. But there'd be no wisdom in a demon getting involved with one."

Ella pressed her lips shut, deciding to keep Viper's intriguing little comment to herself. "Agreed," she eventually said. Begrudgingly. Very, very begrudgingly.

A short time later, she parked in the lot outside a club that happened to be built on top of the Underground's entrance. After a quick venture down to the basement, she and Mia were descending an elevator that took them to a subterranean version of the Las Vegas strip that catered to the dark and addictive natures of demons.

Walking side by side, they passed an endless number of businesses—bars, eateries, casinos, stores, a mall. There were various forms of entertainment down here, including racing stadiums for hellhounds and hellhorses.

Finally, they arrived at their herbalist store. A pretty *From the Wilde* sign hung above the door. It sold a whole lot of stuff such as seeds and herbs, many of which were either enchanted or could be used when practicing magick.

They also sold all-natural products like soap bars, aftershave balm, beard oil, facial cleanser, and shampoo. All were made using pure essential oils, other natural ingredients, and a little magick.

Stepping inside the store, Ella smiled. The bright and earthy color scheme went well with the witchy feel of the place. Some aisles featured bath and skincare products. Others had shelves lined with glass jars, elixirs, pastes, oils, clay pots, various plants, and even medicinal tea blends.

Strong scents danced in the air. Mint. Herbs. Honey. Fragrant plants. Soaps made from oils such as mango and coconut.

Their mother Elodie and aunt Jocelyn made the soaps etc., and they operated from a small workshop at the back of the store. Which was exactly where Ella found them.

Opposite to the store, the workshop was on the messy side. Bunches of dried herbs and flowers dangled from the ceiling. Pots of cream, powders, grease, and other ingredients were propped on shelves in no particular order. Garlic braids hung from precarious-looking hooks on the wall. Despite the clutter, the workshop was pristine clean. The sisters were big on cleanliness, but they thrived on chaos.

Jocelyn stood at one of the four counters, carefully pouring black powder from a bowl into a jar. Melodie was busy putting the finishing touches to what looked exactly like a three-tiered cake, only it wasn't really a cake. It was slabs of pastel pink soap covered in colorful decorative flowers that were mini bath bombs.

Unlike Ella and Mia, the two sisters didn't bear a very close resemblance. Melodie was tall and curvy with blood-red hair. Jocelyn was medium height with a slim frame and curly auburn locks. But they both had the same blue eyes and sharp cheekbones.

"Morning," Ella called out, making the women's heads snap up.

Melodie smiled. "Morning, my babies."

"The cake looks good," said Mia.

"Of course it does." Melodie gave Ella the side-eye. "Heard you came upon another wraith problem yesterday."

"Oh, yesterday got even weirder later on." Ella lifted an open jar filled with honeycomb from the counter and took a sniff. "I actually came upon a vampire dumping a body in an alley."

Jocelyn sighed, her expression droll. "And of course *you* were the one to find it. Where exactly was this alley?"

"Outside the pool hall," Ella replied.

"The one the Black Saints bought? They also got their hands on the dive bar next-door, you know. Angels in the Underground." Jocelyn shook her head, her mouth tight in displeasure. "Your uncle would be rolling in his grave."

"He's not dead yet," Mia told her.

Jocelyn's brow furrowed. "He's not? But I thought he died, I'm enjoying being a widow."

Ella stifled a smile. Most of their lair lived in Idaho, but the four of them had relocated to Las Vegas years ago after Jocelyn's mate left her for her best friend. Predictably, Jocelyn hadn't reacted well. Some curses had been cast, and everyone—including the Prime of their lair—had deemed it a good idea for Jocelyn to put some miles between her and her ex-mate.

"I heard through the demonic grapevine that he met his end at the hands of a Prime he'd wronged," Jocelyn went on.

Mia's shoulders lifted and fell as she leaned against the butcher's block table. "Last I heard, he was living in Ohio and had angry imps on his ass."

"Then he won't be alive for much longer," said Melodie, giving her sister's back a soothing pat. "The imps will see to it. On that happy note, let's officially open the store, shall we?"

"Before we do," began Jocelyn, looking from Ella to Mia, "you should know that Dionne called to say she can't come to work today—apparently, she's having another severe migraine."

Ella felt her lips thin. She'd had the occasional migraine herself, so she knew they were beasts. And if she truly believed that Dionne was regularly afflicted by them, she'd greatly sympathize and totally understand why the woman begged off work so often. But that was the thing, she *didn't* believe it. Because one too many times she'd bumped into the woman here in the Underground on days Dionne was supposedly unable to get out of bed.

"A migraine," Mia echoed, clearly doubtful. "Right."

"Honestly, it sometimes seems like she's pushing us to fire her. But why not just quit?" Ella didn't get it.

"No idea," said Mia. "Whatever the case, we've warned her she needs to step up. She hasn't. She always says she will, but it's clear that she has no real intention to do so. We have to let her go."

Ella nodded. "We'll do it Monday."

Their mother gave a satisfied nod. "Let's get moving, then."

CHAPTER FOUR

Arriving at Luka's illegal gambling den later that day, Ella left her car with the valet and then crossed to the entrance. An overly broad, dark-skinned male wearing an earpiece manned the door. She smiled at him. "Hey."

"Ella," the security guard greeted simply, pushing open the door. "Luka's is expecting you. He said you'll know where to find him."

She did know, having been to Infernal plenty of times since forming the anchor bond with Luka six years ago.

Stepping inside, she was assaulted by the scents of alcohol, perfume, cologne, hot machinery, and a floral air freshener. Her demon wrinkled its nose, not a fan of the abundance of smells.

There was nothing dingy about the illegal gambling den. It was modern, classy, and fashionable with purple and blue LED uplighting, soft leather sofas, an uber-long chrome bar, and strobe lights that slashed through the air. Domed security cameras were mounted on the high ceilings, catching every little thing.

The den also had fighting cages in the basement, but no one talked much about that.

The soft patterned carpet muffled her footsteps as she wandered through the place. People were perched on stools at the backlit slot machines. Others were gathered around card tables, roulette wheels, or the trendy bar. Servers walked back and forth, taking orders and passing out drinks. Suited-up security guards prowled around the space, their eyes sharp.

Sounds were plentiful. Gamblers chattered, dealers called out for bids, alarms dinged to announce winners, dice tumbled over felt. Despite the noise, the place wasn't rowdy. The atmosphere was fairly calm until someone won. Then a round of cheers would go up.

The den was exclusive to members, most of whom were demons. Some were from Luka's lair, which had relocated here from Russia long ago. Others were outsiders.

A girl didn't exactly dream that her anchor would be firmly entrenched in the dark underbelly of the preternatural criminal underworld. But crime boss Luka Belinsky had a code of honor. It was skewed and fluid and sometimes ignored, but it was there.

Typically, though demons could be found in just about any walk of life, they tended to aim for positions of authority. It answered their inborn hunger for power, respect, and control. Therefore, it was easy to see why being the boss of an underground crime syndicate might appeal to some.

It was a fitting position for Luka's breed of demon. A breed that was relatively rare and often avoided. He was what was known as a legion, a demon who shared his soul with not one malevolent entity but three. As such, his yearning for power and authority far exceeded that of an average demon.

Ella couldn't imagine what it would be like to have *three* inner entities. She found having only one to contend with quite a trial.

She'd once told him as much, asking how he was able to handle it. He had shrugged and said that he had nothing to compare it to; that it was all he'd ever known.

She personally didn't see how it being his norm would ever have made his struggle to remain dominant over multiple entities any easier. Managing to maintain supremacy over just one could be tricky enough. It was why legions were always so determined to find and bond with their anchor—it relieved them of the pressure of having to always be on their guard to avoid one of their entities attempting to take over.

Since legions were quite literally a one-man army, people smartly avoided getting on their bad side—or bad sides (*plural*), to be more precise. As such, you never saw patrons at Infernal causing scenes, verbally abusing staff, or counting cards. People wouldn't dare.

Well . . . unless they were imps. They were both immoral and reckless, which had led to quite a few being executed by Luka. Something he never made quick or painless.

Of course, the Primes of those imps hadn't at all liked the situation. They also hadn't wanted to take him on, though. So they'd formed an agreement with Luka—they would keep their lair members away from his businesses, and he would stop sending their severed heads to their families. It worked out for everyone.

Reaching a roped-off set of stairs, Ella exchanged a nod with the familiar burly guy there. He unclipped said rope, allowing her to pass. She clambered up the steps and into the massive VIP area. It certainly screamed 'luxury' with the chandeliers, backlit tables, and the lilac and blue velvet sofas on which many people lounged.

Luka stood near the bar with his shoulders back and his feet planted, clothed in a dark-gray tailored suit. No amount of smart clothing would hide the apex predator in him. There was just something too uncivilized about him. Too precarious. Like he could burst into violence at any given moment.

He was a sight for sore hormones. Long. Lean. Dark. His eyes were velvety black, just like the light layer of scruff on his strong jaw.

Ella did a double-take as she noticed two of the Black Saints hanging near a slot machine not far from the VIP area. Huh. She hadn't known that Luka had granted the fallen angels memberships to Infernal. The Black Saints sure had a talent for squirming their way into the good books of powerful demons.

Continuing toward the bar, she refocused on Luka. His two bodyguards, Nikandr and Mikhail, stood relatively close. The identical twin brothers were never far from Luka. It seemed ridiculous that he'd have such protection, given how powerful he was. But someone with his position in life would always attract danger and cultivate enemies. Bodyguards came with the package.

It wasn't only the twins who were with him. He was deep in conversation with a tall, dark, so very fine male who was none other than Knox Thorne. At Knox's back was his broad and equally tall personal guard and sentinel, Levi—a reaper who was also a good friend of Ella's.

For a crime boss, Luka had a surprising amount of allies who you might expect to avoid someone with so little respect for law and order. But she supposed it wasn't too shocking that he'd be friendly with Knox—they had the whole 'merciless' thing in common.

Her attention went to her left, where Thorne's mate and anchor stood alongside another of their lair's sentinels. Rather than interrupt whatever conversation was taking place between Knox and Luka, she headed over to Harper and her guard.

Harper smiled. "Hey, Ella." No one would question how the petite sphinx had snared the attention of her supremely hot mate. She was beautiful, though not in a classical way. Harper made an impact with all that dark hair tipped with a gold that matched the color of her eyes—eyes that were reflective and glassy, like those of a cat. At any time the color of her irises could swirl like liquid and become a completely different color.

Honestly, Ella's demon was a little jealous of the latter.

Ella felt her lips curve as she looked from the sphinx to Tanner. "Hi, guys, good to see you. How're things?"

"Fine, thanks," replied Harper brightly.

Tanner merely grunted, though it wasn't an expression of rudeness. He was just busy keeping an eye out, protective of his female co-Prime. The hellhound's wolf-gold gaze repeatedly scanned their surroundings, slow and thorough.

Harper tilted her head. "Don't take this the wrong way, but you look kind of tired."

Ella shrugged. "Story of my life lately. How's little Asher?"

A glowing smile split Harper's mouth at the mention of her son. "Still the embodiment of trouble."

Ella could believe it, given that his personality was very imp-like. An unsurprising fact, since most of his maternal relatives were imps.

It was claimed that, like his mother, Asher was a sphinx. But Ella had been near him a few times, and he didn't *feel* like a sphinx. He was something else. Something powerful. She just didn't know what. Her inner demon very much agreed with Ella's suspicion.

"I'm hoping you're not here to ask Luka to have mercy on some of your imp-relatives or something," said Ella. "He didn't hurt any, did he?"

"No, nothing like that," Harper assured her with a flick of a hand.

Well, that was good. Because the majority of those imp rela-tives belonged to a lair that was run by Harper's grandmother,

Jolene Wallis—a shrewd, batshit, unpredictable she-demon who made a *bad* enemy.

"He and Knox are having a quick meeting," Harper explained. "I don't actually know what it's about, only that it's nothing bad. I came with him because I've heard so much about Infernal and wanted to check it out."

"Your mate sure has a lot of contacts." Ella angled her body ever so slightly as she subtly slid a look at the Black Saints. "Case in point."

"Yeah, I wasn't expecting Knox to consent to them having access to the Underground. But he seems to like Viper. So does Maddox, and he generally isn't a fan of people outside his lair."

Maddox Quentin's breed of demon generally kept to themselves. He was a descendant, part of a race who came into being after some of the first fallen angels mated with demons. Those offspring then mated with demons as well, and so on and so on until descendants became a species in their own right. Still, they were often thought of as mutts.

Maddox *did* mingle a little outside his lair now that he was mated to Harper's friend and business partner, Raini. He was also, if the rumors were true, allied with Viper.

"Ah, it appears the meeting is finished," said Harper, pulling Ella from her thoughts.

She glanced over her shoulder to see both Knox and Levi approaching.

"Ella," Knox politely greeted with an incline of his head.

His aura of power unnerved her demon slightly, so it watched him warily. "Your mate was just kindly keeping me company while I waited for you and Luka to round up your conversation." She looked at her friend. "Hi, Levi, how are you?"

Gunmetal gray eyes landed on her, and his lips tipped up. "Good, what about you?" His brows dipped. "You look tired."

She was getting a little fed up of hearing that. "I'm fine. How's Piper?"

His smile widened and took on a proud tilt, just as it always did when he spoke of his mate. He was *so* gone for her it was cute. "She's fine, she—"

"Why are you all hogging my anchor?" complained Luka as he came up behind them.

Mirth lighting his gaze, Knox said, "I wouldn't call it hogging, but be assured we're leaving now so you can have her all to yourself." He gave her a quick nod, amusement still dancing in his eyes, and then ushered his mate away.

Ella said her goodbyes to the group and then turned to face Luka, who crossed to her with a small but genuine smile. "Hey." She kissed his cheek. "Kill anyone today?" she joked . . . though, yes, he might have done.

"He's not yet dead, but he'll have bled out before the night is over."

What a cheerful prospect.

"Drink?" he offered with an arch of his brow.

"Just water, thanks. I'm driving."

He gave her order to a passing waiter as she said quick hellos to Nikandr and Mikhail, both of whom responded with respectful nods.

Luka shepherded her to the L-shaped sofa he typically claimed. "Sit," he invited. "You look tired again. I don't like it."

She slumped onto the sofa. "Me neither. It would be understandable if I was sleep-deprived, but I'm not. I just don't wake up feeling refreshed these days."

"As if your sleep is restless," he mused, angling his body on the seat to better face her.

"Yes. That. I guess the effects of it are catching up to me now, since I tend to look drained a lot."

"I would have thought the psychic punch was responsible, but you were having this problem before the mugging." A hardness slid into his eyes. "I've spoken to many people about the incident. If anyone knows who he is, they're not talking. And it's rare that people don't talk to me."

Probably because he tortured them until they did.

"It definitely won't be anyone from the other criminal. We consider mates, children, and anchors off-limits."

"All I know is that he's a burly guy with enough power to pummel me with a severe psychic punch." It still galled her that he'd been able to disable her that way.

Something very dark seemed to move behind Luka's eyes. "I've made no secret of who you are to me. The criminal element of the demonic population would recognize you in an instant. Yet, this person dared harm you."

The protective anger in his voice brushed over her skin like a cold breeze. All demons were incredibly protective of their psi-mate. Luka took it to a whole other level. It was just in his nature to keep those in his inner circle safe.

"He didn't set out to target me. He was in the process of mugging another woman. I just happened upon them. It all happened pretty fast, so he probably didn't recognize me until it was too late."

Luka shook his head. "Such predators always have to be sure they're not going to anger another and more dangerous predator. Their survival depends on their ability to make snap decisions that aren't going to bite them on the ass. Even if he didn't know who you are to me, it would not matter. He will still pay for what he did to you."

"Yes, he will indeed." She'd make sure of it.

His eyes went slitted. "He's mine to kill."

Ella felt her lips curve. "Only if you find him first."

"Oh, I will," he swore, his expression hard. There was no missing the thread of menace in his voice.

Right then, a waiter materialized and handed her a glass of iced water.

"Thank you." She took a sip of her drink, letting her gaze idly roam the den. When it again landed on two familiar fallen angels, she said, "I didn't know the Black Saints were members here."

"It's a recent development."

"They seem to be everywhere lately."

"And they're buying a lot of property," he noted. "I have a strong feeling that their club's president is most definitely an archangel."

She cocked her head. "You've met him?"

"Once. I intervened when the local MC club chapter talked of going to war with them."

"War?" she echoed, more than a little shocked. Demons were brutal but generally avoided full-on wars.

"They're humans and completely oblivious to what they're dealing with."

Ah.

"Uninterested in sharing their territory, they'd suggested that the Black Saints join them. They hadn't taken too kindly to Viper neither accepting their offer nor heeding their subsequent warning to relocate. They also hadn't liked that he refused to traffic drugs for them. He wants to keep his club clean."

"I see." It was a little surprising, really. Viper hadn't struck her as the moral type. It was strange for a celestial being maybe, but there was just something very dark and ruthless in his manner.

"I advised the national president of the club—who, unbeknownst to the human chapter, happens to be a demon—that they should leave the Black Saints be. He took my advice, not wanting to tangle with a fallen angel who was not only rumored to be a fallen archangel but who'd secured alliances with powerful demons like Knox Thorne and Maddox Quentin."

It had been smart of Viper to do so. "It's good that you stepped in. Archangels are dangerous. Fallen archangels? His danger factor will be off the charts."

Luka caught her gaze with his. "Which is why I want you to stay away from Viper."

She blinked. "You say that as if I follow him home."

"You have nothing to do with him, I know. But in purchasing certain properties, he's on the edge of your life. That's too close for my liking. I have nothing against their kind, but I don't want them near you."

Ella rolled her eyes. "You think all guys are too close to me for your liking. You can't tell me who I can and can't talk to."

"I just did."

"And you think I'll heed and obey?"

He exhaled heavily, put-out. "No. You don't fear me like other people do."

Because she had nothing to fear from him. He'd never hurt her.

"Just give Viper a wide berth, Ella. That's all I ask. Now, tell me all I've missed since I last saw you."

"Well . . ."

CHAPTER FIVE

Driving through the chain-link fence of his compound Sunday evening, Viper noticed a number of his brothers gathered in a circle. He parked his bike among the others outside the clubhouse and then switched off the engine. Tugging off his safety helmet, he frowned. Voices were yelling—voices that came from *within* the circle of people.

Having set both his gloves and helmet on the bike, he dismounted it. He didn't actually need protective gear. None of them did. It would take more than a traffic accident to severely injure them. But blending with humans often meant following their rules so as not to attract the attention of their law enforcement.

As he strode toward the gathering of people, he noticed that Jester stood off to the side. "What's going on?" Viper asked him.

"So—and don't ask me how, because I don't get it—Hustle managed to convince Rivet to stake his bike during a game of poker," Jester explained. "A game he then lost. Rivet, naturally, doesn't wanna part with his pride and joy. Hustle doesn't see how that's his problem."

Viper sighed. Honestly, his brothers had been easier to manage when part of the holy host. Since they'd fallen, they'd become more mercurial—a result of not only their inner entities twisting but the lessening of action, combat, and adrenaline since retiring from their old positions. Half the time, he'd swear they started shit with each other out of boredom.

Viper waded in, shrugging his way through the crowd. "All right, enough."

The yelling stopped, and the two glowering angels took a step back from each other.

His club was made up of two breeds of angel. Both kinds were powerful, though one was slightly more dangerous than the other. Unlike angels who sported wings or halos, the two breeds here didn't boast typical physical traits that made them identifiable. A fortunate thing, since not one of their kind would be welcome by the demon population.

Rivet pointed at Hustle. "*He* needs an ass-kicking."

"Because he won at poker?" asked Viper.

"No, because he *cheated.*"

"I resent that," Hustle piped up.

He shouldn't, since he probably *had* cheated.

"Resent it all the fuck you like," Rivet sniped. "I'm not handing over my bike to you or anyone else. I would have won if you'd played fair."

In the crowd, Prophet sighed. "When does he ever play fair?"

"He said he would this time," Rivet claimed.

Jester frowned. "You didn't suspect he was lying, considering he's a person you can always rely on to bullshit and swindle people? Seriously?"

Rivet ground his teeth. "I believe in giving people the benefit of the doubt."

"Then you're stupid," Jester bluntly told him.

A psyche right then bumped Viper's, a sense of urgency coming from it. Then Dice's voice flitted through his mind ... *I found some strix.*

Viper stilled. *Where?* He wasn't surprised that Dice had located them within a day—he was an expert tracker.

A bunch of them are hovering and sniffing around a camping spot. Seems like they're trying to track the humans who recently used it. He paused. *One human left behind a sock. A real small one, V.*

Viper silently swore. Strix always preferred the blood of children. *I need your coordinates.*

Dice rattled them off. *Be fast.*

Viper refocused on his brothers. "All right, listen up. Dice has tracked the strix. We need to act quickly, because they seem to be hunting a party of campers that includes at least one kid." He gave out Dice's coordinates and then teleported straight there, finding himself stood within a tight cluster of trees. His brothers appeared behind him in a mere millisecond.

They could all teleport—or shimmer, as they sometimes called it—with complete ease. All celestials could, fallen or not.

Dice nodded their way. "They're still sniffing around the camp."

Celestial-vision not hampered by low lighting, Viper locked his gaze on the pale, long-limbed figures that were prowling around a patch of uneven ground that was ringed by trees and shrubs. One of them held the sock that Dice had mentioned. Yeah, it definitely belonged to a child.

They appeared to be debating something, two pointing long-nailed fingers in separate directions; possibly arguing over which way they believed the campers had headed.

"There's only a dozen of them, and none are females. This can't possibly be the entire colony." Which was a shame, because eradicating them all in one go would have been easiest.

He drew in a breath through his nose, taking in the scents of grass, dew, and pine needles. There were no sounds of nature— no owls hooting, no coyotes howling, no mosquitos buzzing. As if every living thing had fled on sensing the strix. All that could be heard was the rustle of leaves and the crunch of gravel beneath the strix's feet.

Viper shed his jacket, and the others followed suit. The fight would get ugly, and none wanted their jackets being ruined.

"We move now," said Viper. "Circle them. None can leave here alive."

"Do we have to kill them fast, or can we play?" asked Darko.

Viper felt his lips tip up, his entity *all* for the latter. "We can play."

Darko grinned, as did several others.

They teleported straight to the camp, forming a circle around it . . . placing the strix in the center.

Startled, the demons tensed, their blood-red eyes skimming over the Black Saints. Hissing, they shifted nervously, though a hunger for violence seeped into their gazes.

Inside Viper, his entity smiled in sadistic delight. "I've been looking forward to this." He let out an archangelic blast of warped holy fire. The ultraviolet wave shimmered through the air, lethal as the sharpest of blades. It rammed into three strix, severing their bodies in half—halves that then crumbled to ashes.

The other strix hissed again; baring canine fangs. Then, like a switch had been flicked, chaos ensued.

A strix leaped in the air as if it had bounced off a damn trampoline. It came right at Viper, striking out with a black whip of fire that smelled of sulphur and brimstone.

He lurched to the side, but the whip lashed his arm and shoulder. The scorching-hot lash hurt like a motherfucker. It corroded his skin, ate through his tee, and infuriated his entity.

Adrenaline pumping through his system fast, Viper lobbed an ultraviolet orb at the demon's chest, sending it careening into the picnic bench behind it. The wooden table gave beneath the strix's weight, collapsing into a pile. An agonized cry burst out of the strix as he stared down at his wound.

Just as the fall from heaven had twisted Viper's inner entity, it had also twisted his ability to conjure holy fire. The latter left clean burns that hurt like nothing else. But the flaming orbs Viper and his brothers now wielded? They blackened flesh, burned like hell, and carried the astringent scent of acid.

The strix in Viper's sight didn't look up in time to see the second ball he aimed its way—it caught the demon right in the head, killing it instantly.

He jerked back as a hellfire orb whizzed past him and crashed into Sting's chest.

Sting regarded his attacker like he was no more than a child throwing pebbles. "That all you got? How disappointing."

He probably *was* disappointed, because he actually liked pain.

Confident that Sting could take out the strix easily, Viper zeroed in on another demon—one who was attacking Darko from behind and clawing at his back. He pelted the strix with a shower of unholy orbs that reduced it to ashes. He couldn't lie, the feeling of release that came when he allowed violence to take him was thrillingly addictive.

Viper and his brothers fought how they always fought: Viciously and without pity. Which wasn't to say that they were all *kill, kill, kill*. As pre-agreed, they had some fun with the strix. They bit them, burned them, broke their bones, drank their blood, blistered their skin. And they enjoyed every fucking minute.

The strix retaliated hard with claws, fangs, hellfire orbs, and whips of black fire. Again and again the demons evaded strikes by shifting into mist or exploding into molecules. They sometimes attacked as oversized bats or owls, and they were gruesome in every form. But they were also outmatched—the power of the Black Saints too raw, their savageness too primal.

"Jesus, he's heavier than he looks," grumbled Merchant.

Viper tracked his brother's voice, his brows lifting at the sight of Merchant and Rivet holding a demon by its wrists and ankles while swinging it from side to side. They sang something about shaking a bed and turning the blanket over before promptly dropping the strix face first onto the fire pit they'd lit with unholy fire.

Leaving them to it, Viper turned. And found a demon almost on him. He growled as it swiped out and dragged its razor-sharp nails across his face, scoring deep.

Fucker. He fisted its sweater, hauled it close, and sank his teeth into its throat. Blood hit his tongue, carrying a charred tang. He wasn't crazy about the taste, but he drank the liquid down, letting it help him heal. His blood clotted, his wounds closed over, his energy—

A large impact blindsided him, breaking his hold on the strix and sending him stumbling to the side so hard he almost lost his footing.

Viper whirled on the new threat and lobbed an orb its way. The demon burst into molecules, evading the orb. Those molecules quickly reformed into an overly large bat that swooped down toward him.

He wacked it with a telekinetic hit. The winged little shit rammed into a tree with such force that wood cracked and bark—

His peripheral vision screamed a warning. The strix he'd fed from was advancing on him fast.

Viper didn't move. He let it crash into him, let it bury its fangs into his neck, gritting his teeth against the sharp pain.

The demon jerked back with a loud screech, and Viper's entity smirked. His once-blessed blood, now so acidic it poisoned any who drank it, immediately went to work on the strix. The demon dropped to its knees as his blood killed it from the inside out.

Viper glanced around, braced for more threats. There were none, to his entity's supreme disappointment. Few strix were left alive, and his brothers were focused on them as a group.

He took that moment to take stock of his brothers. None were fatally injured, but many sported puncture wounds, burns, and rake marks. No fatigue could be seen on their expressions. No, they were as amped up as always when battle came their way.

"Let's end this," he called out . . . just as an owl dropped down on his fucking head.

Viper grabbed it, slammed it on the ground, and stomped his foot down hard on its body. A screech erupted from the owl. It squirmed, twisted, *shifted*. And then a strix lay beneath Viper's foot in its standard form.

It coughed up blood, its body sporting burns, bruises, slices, and broken bones. The demon was dying and knew it.

Viper cocked his head as he stared down at it. "If that was supposed to be one last ditch effort to kill me before you die, it was a totally shit one. Did you really think it was wise to come after us? Did you think you could take us out?"

It bared bloodstained teeth. "My brethren will keep trying. They will eventually succeed."

Viper pursed his lips. "Nah, they'll just be slaughtered."

He didn't bother asking for the location of the colony. Strix never gave up their own, not even under heavy interrogation. But there was another way to extract information from it. Few mental shields could keep Viper out.

"Don't do it," Dice said to him, clearly sensing what Viper was considering. "We'll find the colony another way."

Jester nodded. "It ain't worth the pain you'd go through, or the psychic burnout. And you can't afford to be weak when you have celestials *and* hell-born demons to contend with."

Excruciating pain hit any angel that tried delving into the mind of a demon, and vice versa. It also rendered them weak on a psychic level. Hence why Viper hadn't stayed in Ella's mind long the one time he'd invaded it to confirm his suspicion of who she was to him.

"We'll find the others," Jester went on. "We'll keep chipping at their numbers until what's left of the colony finally launches an attack. Then we'll wipe out the rest."

"No," the strix objected, its red eyes like lasers of hatred. "*They* will wipe out all of *you*. My colony—"

"Stands no chance against what we are and what we can do," finished Razor. "You should have just stayed away."

The demon slid Viper a look. "He calls to us."

That wasn't something Viper could control. Neither could they, but they weren't compelled to act on it. "You could have ignored that call. You didn't." He shrugged. "Now you die."

CHAPTER SIX

"I didn't do it," Dionne insisted, stood in front of the office desk with her head held high. "I would *never* do something like that."

"Huh." Sinking further into the leather chair, Ella licked her front teeth. "Can't say I believe you."

She'd arrived at work that morning resolved that she'd fire Dionne first thing, just as she'd told her family she would. But the hellcat hadn't arrived until after noon, while Ella was busy with a customer. It was afterward, when she and Mia had peeked over at where Dionne stood at the register, that the sisters had discovered a *whole* new reason why the woman needed to be fired.

Dionne's lips thinned. "I'm not the only person who works here. Any number of people could have stolen money from the till. Just because the others are related to you doesn't mean it wasn't them."

"True. But I know for a fact that it was you, so . . ."

Dionne folded her arms. "Oh, I see. Because you don't like me, you're going to claim I stole the money."

"I'm claiming you stole it because I *saw* you do it." Ella leaned forward in her seat. "Now, here's what's going to happen. You're going to give me back the cash you stole. And then you're going to grab your shit and go."

Dionne gaped. "You're firing me?"

"This truly surprises you?" Unreal. "You're never on-time. You call in sick at least once a week. You keep claiming you need a bathroom break when, really, you're going to your locker to check your cell phone. I already warned you that all that shit needed to stop. Mia warned you. My mom and Jocelyn warned you. But you didn't listen to us, and *now* you're stealing from the till. What did you think would happen?"

The hellcat's nostrils flared. "Like I really wanted to work here anyway." She fished the wad of cash from her pocket, slapped it on the desk, and then stormed out.

God, the woman was a pain in the ass.

Ella snatched the money from the desk and left the office. Since she needed to leave work early to check out a situation for Neve, she retrieved her purse from her locker and kept a close eye on Dionne as the hellcat grabbed her stuff from her own locker.

Once they were both done, Ella followed her to the shop floor and then slipped behind the counter. Dionne stormed out of the place, almost crashing into someone who'd been trying to enter.

Joe.

Ella sensed her sister tense beside her.

Looking sheepish as he crossed to the counter, he tipped his chin at Mia, an awkwardness in his manner. "Hi."

His blue eyes met Ella's for the briefest moment as he nodded in greeting. They were civil toward each other, but they'd never been anything close to friends. Whereas Luka was protective of Ella's family purely because of who they were to her, Joe didn't extend his protectiveness beyond Mia. Which had been fine with Ella right up until he *stopped* being considerate of her sister's feelings.

Mia stared at him, her expression wary. "What brings you here?" she bluntly asked him.

He drifted his fingers through his scruffy ash-blond hair. "I figure we should talk."

Mia inhaled deeply. "Okay." She walked out from behind the counter and headed to the nearest corner, gesturing for him to follow.

Ella stuffed the cash in the till, *totally* intending to eavesdrop.

He cleared his throat. "Thanks for speaking with me," he said to Mia. "I wouldn't have blamed you if you'd flipped me off." He stuffed his hands in his pockets. "Listen, I . . . Can we just forget all that happened between us recently?"

"Forget?" Mia's eyes went squinty. "Forget you've been an ass to me, or forget stuff from before that?"

He grimaced. "We should have kept things platonic, but we didn't. I don't want it to ruin our friendship. Can we just pretend it never happened?"

Ella couldn't help but wince. If Luka had told her he'd regretted that they slept together and wanted them to act as though it had never occurred, it would have stung big time. Your anchor was supposed to be a person you'd always feel safe with, emotionally and physically. They weren't supposed to hurt you.

Mia folded her arms, her posture defensive. "So you've been acting weird and distant because you regret that we slept together but didn't wanna say so?"

He averted his gaze. "Yes."

Ella tensed, telepathically reaching out to her sister. *That was a lie.*

Mia's mind stroked hers as she telepathically replied, *It was. There's more to this.* She gave him a brittle smile. "Sure. Why not?"

He swallowed. "Great."

He doesn't sound as though he thinks it's great, Ella mused.

No, he doesn't, Mia agreed.

He let out what seemed to be a relieved breath, but it was a little too exaggerated to be genuine. "Glad that's all sorted."

"As am I," Mia told him, studying him closely.

Again, he cleared his throat. "Well, I . . . I guess I'd better go."

Mia watched him scurry out of the shop before turning to Ella. "That was weird. *He* was weird."

Ella bit her lip. "I hate to say it, I really do, but I think he said that stuff to you. Why else do it? He could have omitted that he allegedly regrets that you two had a fling. Could have just apologized and asked that you focus on your friendship from here on out."

"I don't get why he'd want to hurt me, though." Mia flapped her arms. "I'm stumped. And pissed. I was already angry, thanks to what Dionne did. Speaking of that, did she deny it?"

Sensing that Mia wanted to change the subject, Ella went with it. "Until she realized we have cameras, yes. She was actually surprised that we fired her. I can't think why."

"Seems like people are set on acting strange today." Mia sighed at the shop door.

"Are you gonna be okay?"

"Fine. You go handle whatever situation Neve has tossed your way. I'm good here."

"You're sure? I can cancel—"

"I'm completely sure." Mia tilted her head. "Did Neve give you specifics?"

"Just that human friends of the Mills were asking to speak

with me, wanting my help with a 'personal matter'." Ella shrugged. "Hopefully it won't be a weird one."

"Our house is haunted."

Ella blinked at the middle-aged blonde sitting across from her. "Haunted?" She glanced to the woman's husband, who stared back at her steadily.

Though pleased that she'd arrived as promised, the couple hadn't invited Ella into their grand Victorian home. They'd urged her to follow them through the side gate that led to their backyard. It was beautifully maintained, bordered by trees similar to those in the massive wooded area behind this particular street of houses.

Very 'Zen' with the pretty pond, Japanese-style bridge, and stone lanterns, the garden possessed a relaxing feel. But there was nothing relaxed about the humans sitting opposite Ella at the patio table. They were nervous. Twitchy. Looked a little worn-down.

The woman, Nestor, licked her lips. "The Mills said you helped them with a similar situation. That you got rid of whatever was in their home."

Ella couldn't say that the situations were similar, since they so far didn't appear to be. "Why don't you tell me a little about what's been happening?" she invited.

"There was nothing until four months ago," replied Nestor's husband, Martin. "We've lived here a decade, never had any issues. Then *bam*, the place turned into a hub of supernatural activity."

Nestor rubbed her arm. "Things move around by themselves. Or they go missing and then turn up in odd places."

"And by move around, she doesn't mean something as simple as a glass sliding along a kitchen counter," added Martin. "We've had objects thrown at us. The TV was knocked off the wall. Light bulbs randomly implode. Food gets taken out of the fridge and dumped over the floor. Our bedcovers were once yanked away from us in the middle of the night, and something *laughed*. It was a horrible sound."

"We hear footsteps in the attic, but nothing is up there—we've checked," said Nestor, a manic light in her eyes that conveyed she'd reached her limit. "Or, at least, it's nothing we can see."

Okay, well, they definitely had a preternatural problem of some sort.

Martin thrust a hand through his russet-brown hair, making it stick up in parts. The poor guy was the picture of frazzled. "We had the local priest bless the house, but it didn't help. We're hoping that *you* can."

Ella had helped with hauntings in the past. For her, it wasn't a matter of banishing spirits or guiding them to 'the light'. She simply used magick to provide enough of a tear in the veil between this realm and that of the dead for the ghosts to *slip* through. Though, yes, sometimes she had to give them a violent magickal shove to get them moving. Not all wanted to pass on; some clung tight to their old lives.

She leaned forward slightly. "How about you two stay out here while I go take a walk around the house?" she proposed. "Would that be okay?"

Relief rippled over Nestor's face. "That would be fine. *Anything* you can do would be fine."

Martin gave Ella a jerky nod. "Thank you for not laughing at us or telling us we're going crazy." He flicked a look at the patio doors. "They're unlocked."

She flashed the couple a gentle smile, pushed out of her chair, and crossed to the doors. Slipping into the house, she glanced around. All dark woods with the typical Victorian color scheme of red, brown, and blue, the place was stylish and neat as a pin. Though modern, it had retained its original features such as the terracotta tiled floor.

Her fingertips prickling with her at-the-ready magick, she advanced through the house; explored the kitchen, dining room, large den, and half-bath before making her way upstairs.

She'd walked through haunted locations before. They had a certain *feel* to them. An atmosphere that was coldly electric. There was no such vibe here, but she didn't believe that the humans were lying. Their fear and exhaustion were very real.

Wood creaked.

Ella halted in the master bedroom, her head jerking up. The sound had come from above. Narrowing her eyes, she made her way to the hallway and moved to stand beneath the attic's rectangular hatch door. She released a thread of magick and used it to tug down both the hatch and the attached fold-down metal ladder.

She snapped her hands around the cool metal as she began to ascend the ladder. Reaching the attic, she felt her nose wrinkle. The stale air stank of dust, mold, and old fabric.

The space was predictably dim, the only shaft of light coming through the sole circular window, which was positioned at the front of the house. Cobwebs dangled from the exposed wooden beams. A fine layer of dust seemed to coat every surface. Shadowy spots were everywhere.

She called on her magick, shaping it into four balls of light. She tossed one into each corner of the attic, giving her a better view. Sheets were draped over pieces of furniture. Boxes—some sealed, some open—were stacked here and there. Filled garbage bags were scattered around. Random items could be seen, such as an old trunk and a broken sewing machine.

Winding her way through the cramped space, she paused at

the slight *give* of the floorboard beneath her. Something caught her eye. A rumpled blanket. Beside it were candy wrappers, a flashlight, and some comic books.

Muffled footsteps coming from the other side of the attic.

Ella didn't whirl around. She planted her feet and chanted beneath her breath as she sent out a wave of magick. It slammed the attic hatch closed, flicked the lock on the window, and further illuminated the space. Only then did she turn. A young teenager stood several feet away, poised as if to run for the hatch.

"You won't get it open," she warned, studying him. He was thin and pale with dull-blond, unkempt hair. He was also a demon. *Imp*, she sensed. "Just what would you be doing here?"

He jutted out his chin. "I'm not here to steal."

"No?" She cast the candy wrappers a quick glance. "I doubt *you* bought that food."

His cheeks reddened. "I was hungry."

He was also in need of a wash and fresh clothes. "Which lair do you belong to?"

"I don't belong to any. I'm a stray."

She gifted him an impatient look. "Don't lie to me. I'd rather not have to hurt you to get answers, but I will."

He glared at her, but his shoulders slumped in defeat. "Jolene Wallis' lair."

"Want to tell me why you're hiding out here terrorizing a human couple?"

His brows snapped together. "I'm not terrorizing them."

"You used telekinesis to make them think their house is haunted. You made them feel unsafe in their own home. You were trying to scare them into leaving."

He averted his gaze, his shoulders hunching.

She slanted her head. "You didn't answer my question. Why are you here?"

He shot her a belligerent look. "My family wants to move away. I don't."

"So this is a protest. You ran off to make a point." She heaved a sigh, and her demon rolled its eyes. "They're probably worried sick about you. Something you know well, since they're likely telepathing you."

"If they are, I wouldn't know. I'm not close to home, and I can't receive telepathic messages over long distances."

Neither could Ella, actually. "What's your name?"

He hesitated. "Jacques. Look, I don't know why . . . Wait, what are you doing?"

Having pulled out her cell phone, she scrolled through her list of contacts. "I'm going to call a friend of mine. I feel for you, kid, I do. But you can't stay here, and I think you know that."

It took a few rings before Levi answered simply, "Hey." The reaper wasn't what you'd call chatty.

"Listen, I have an imp situation. But I don't have a way to personally contact Jolene Wallis. I was hoping you might, what with Harper being her granddaughter."

"What kind of situation?" Levi asked.

She elaborated, watching Jacques' flush deepen in what seemed to be embarrassment.

"Imps," said the reaper with a disgruntled sigh. "I'll get word to Jolene. She'll probably send someone to pick the kid up."

"Thanks." Not wanting to bring more imps here—mostly because she didn't trust that they wouldn't nab some antiques to take with them—Ella gave him the location of the coffee shop on the corner of the street. "We'll wait for them there." She rounded up the conversation and tucked away her phone.

Sulkily, Jacques folded his arms. "My family's gonna lose their mind."

"Maybe, but they'll also be relieved to have you back. Now, I'm going to go tell the humans who own this house that it's no longer plagued by ghosts, since I can't exactly tell them the truth. You are going to sneak out of here. I'll meet you at the coffee shop. Ignore any temptation you have to make a run for it. Such a move won't end well for you."

He mumbled something under his breath but nodded in acquiescence.

In the backyard, she had a quick chat with the humans, informing them that 'the spirits' were at peace and had moved on. They were beyond relieved.

As she was walking to her car, her step faltered and her stomach dropped. Because something was tucked under her windscreen wiper.

Scanning her surroundings, Ella registered nothing suspicious as she crossed to her car. She snatched what turned out to be a folded slip of crinkled paper from under the wiper. Opening up the slip, she frowned. It read: *You know what happened to the curious cat.*

Like with the previous note, the ink shimmered with power. Another snare.

Ella bit back a curse, angry sparks yo-yoing around her belly. Her demon prowled to the forefront of her consciousness, tense and braced for battle.

Whether this was the work of whoever psychically assaulted her, Ella didn't know. But it definitely wasn't someone playing a simple prank—you didn't follow a person around just to play jokes on them.

Fucker.

What bothered her *way* more than the note itself was that he'd touched her vehicle again. He'd been physically far too close to Ella twice. And she hadn't known.

Gnashing her teeth together, she tore the note in two, de-activating the snare. She so didn't have time for this right now.

Putting a pin in the matter, she drove to the coffee shop, half-expecting to find no sign of Jacques. But he was sulkily slumped on a chair at one of the outdoor tables. Once she'd parked her car, Ella joined him at the table.

It was no more than thirty seconds later that two familiar imps from Jolene's lair came striding out of the nearby alley. Ella was guessing one of them could teleport, because no cars had driven down there, and it was a dead-end.

The siblings—who were also Jolene's grandchildren—greeted her with chin-tips and then moved to stand in front of Jacques, their faces molding into masks of disappointment. He all but shrank under the weight of their disapproval.

Khloë shook her head. "Dude, I'm all for rebelling. But imps don't run. We stir shit, we break bones, we set fires, we bathe in the blood of our enemies. But running? Never."

Jacques grimaced. "I know. Sorry."

"Great pep talk," Ella deadpanned.

Khloë smiled, smug. "I thought so. Thanks for bringing this little matter to my lair's attention."

"No problem."

"Jacques, over here," Ciaran ordered.

The teenager didn't hesitate to obey, his metaphorical tail tucked between his legs.

"We'll see you around," Khloë said, saluting her.

"Take care," Ella told the three imps.

Ciaran responded with a chin-tip while Jacques just glowered petulantly.

Ella might have smiled at the latter if she wasn't feeling ready to murder the crap out of someone. She returned to her car, pulled out her phone, and called her sister.

"Greetings, bitch," Mia answered so lovingly.

"I got another note," said Ella, the earlier sparks of anger rekindling in her belly.

"*What?*"

"It was left under my windscreen wiper, just like the last one. It has a similar tone, too—threatening, yet in a non-scary way." As she'd deactivated the snare, Ella was able to say aloud: "*You know what happened to the curious cat.*"

Mia let out a dark hum. "The first note mentioned sleeping dogs. Now curious cats. Maybe our boy is an animal lover."

Rubbing at her temple, Ella let her head tilt back to hit the headrest. "It feels like this is some sort of game to him."

Mia made a speculative noise in the back of her throat. "Was there power embedded in the ink?"

"Yes."

"Then I don't think it's a mere game. He has a purpose here."

Ella righted her head. "But the compulsion could be something minor, like to make me shave off a chunk of my hair for his own amusement."

"He could be having fun, but I don't think the compulsion is something as innocuous as that. Neither do you."

As it happened, no, Ella didn't think so either. She'd just prefer for that to be the case. "My demon is raging right now."

"*I'm* raging. He must be following you. That takes the threat level up a notch, because it's stalkerish behavior. Not that I think he's what you would call a typical obsessed stalker, but he's certainly employing dark tactics."

Yes, but *why?*

"We should lay some kind of magickal trap for him. Bespell your window wipers, maybe."

Ella's demon perked up at the idea. "Ooh, I'm liking the

endless possibilities sifting through my brain right now. We'll definitely get on that."

"In the meantime, be careful, Ella," Mia half-pled, half-warned. "Seriously careful."

"I will. I'm not dismissing this as a silly prank, I promise."

"Good. Now I'm wishing I went with you. I don't like that you're alone right now."

"I'm fine. Not hurt, not scared, just pissed." Ella wasn't about to allow this idiocy to ruin her day, though it would for sure play on her mind if she didn't distract herself. On that note . . . "You up to anything later?"

"Actually," began Mia, a mischievous note lacing her voice, "I'm thinking of venturing to the Red Rooms."

Ella blinked. "Seriously?"

"Why do you sound so surprised?"

"It's owned by the Black Saints. You know that, right?"

"It's not as if the Fallen are the only people who go there. Demons are regular patrons. So are oblivious humans. I've heard it's the kind of club where a person can go get laid right there on the dance floor and then head on home. I prefer that over the idea of taking someone home *with* me. I just want to get fucked— no conversations, no aftermath, no exchanging numbers."

"And they say romance is dead."

Mia barked a light laugh. "I'm done with romance for a while. But that doesn't mean I should have to forgo sex, does it?"

"There are similar clubs in the Underground. Why not head to one of those?"

"Because I want to go somewhere different. And I'm curious to see if this place really lives up to its hype."

"You're not going there alone, are you?"

"No. You're coming with me."

Ella snorted. "I am?"

"Yup. You're my wing-woman, remember? And you need a release valve, too. Come on, wouldn't you like someone to fuck the annoyance you're feeling right out of you?"

"Having sex with a stranger in public isn't my jam." Ella was no shy flower, but she wasn't an exhibitionist either. And intimacy felt awkward for her when it was someone she didn't know or trust.

"Make an exception," Mia urged.

"Look, I'll come with you so that you're not going alone, but I'll just hang at the bar."

"*Boring,*" her sister droned.

"Yeah, that's me. Totally boring. What time do you want to leave?"

"Say . . . eight-thirty?"

"I'll be ready."

"See you then. Remember to stay vigilant," Mia pushed. "And make sure you tell Luka about the note."

"I'm going to call him after I get off the phone with you."

Luka didn't take the news any better than Mia did. He spat out a gust of Russian words that were a mix of curses and threats. "As if it isn't bad enough that he psychically assaulted you," he began, a gruff edge to his voice, "he now dares follow you and hand-delivered yet another note."

"He's not scaring me, if that's his plan," said Ella.

"Doesn't matter. Fucking with you this way, leaving written snares for you that have God knows what intent, isn't acceptable."

Ella tapped her fingers on the steering wheel. "I think he's getting ballsier, even if his notes are still petulant."

"*I* think I'm going to subject him to several kinds of twisted, torturous, mind-warping pain and may not stop for a very long time."

And what could she really say to that except . . . "Oh. Okay."

CHAPTER SEVEN

Sitting in his office at the Red Rooms, Viper looked up as one of his brothers materialized in front of his desk. Taking in Omen's dark expression, he sighed. "What you're about to say is gonna piss me off, isn't it?"

"Yeah. I just found another body."

Viper felt his jaw clench. "Where?"

"Behind our clubhouse. It was another of the missing humans. A young woman," Omen added, his voice dropping with anger.

"Did you check the security footage?"

"Yes. The person who dumped her there was definitely a strix. And they *knew* they were on camera. Even smiled."

Viper swore and pushed out of his seat. The entity inside him bared its teeth, its ego smarting from the taunt. Some demons who'd escaped hell did their best to lay low. Others, being natural thrill-seekers, tried challenging those who could end them.

It wasn't something humans would understand. They sought safety and security, for the most part. They typically didn't put their lives at risk for the thrill. Demons were different. Hell-born demons even more so.

Viper planted his feet. "They obviously guessed we're responsible for the deaths of their brethren, just as we'd anticipated." They would have traced their brethren back to the camp; would have noticed the scattering of ashes and the telling scorch marks on the ground and trees. "This was their way of striking back at us."

"Dice will track them. He always finds his target."

He did, but there was no saying how long it would take. Strix knew how to hide, and they wouldn't taunt the club the way they were doing unless they were confident that their colony was well-hidden.

"Her body was in a bad state," Omen went on. "It was covered in bruises. The strix beat her, but most of the damage seems to have been done postmortem. It's as if they took out their fury on her in lieu of us." He scratched his jaw. "I take it you want the body to be burned like the last one."

Viper nodded. "It's the only real way to get rid of the evidence."

Jester materialized a few feet away from Omen. His brow furrowed as he absorbed the dark tension in the office. "Everything all right?"

"One of the missing humans was left behind the clubhouse." Viper further elaborated, bringing him up to speed.

Jester's jaw hardened. "Figured it'd happen. Fucking strix need wiping out. Like wasps. I hate them as well."

"Is there any creature you don't hate?" Omen asked, genuinely curious.

Jester thought about it for a second. "No." He cut his gaze back to Viper. "I don't know if my news is going to improve your mood or not, but ... Ella walked through the door a minute ago."

Viper felt his entire body go still. Ella was here, on what was essentially his territory?

His inner entity grinned, its anger rapidly replaced by anticipation. It wanted to see her. Smell her. Touch her.

Bite her.

Viper ground his teeth so hard it was surprising that no molars cracked. Her coming here ... That wasn't supposed to happen. Not yet. Not until the danger had passed and she'd be here at his invitation.

Turning to the security monitors hanging on the wall behind his desk, he studied each one in search of her.

"Did she ask for Viper?" Omen asked.

"No," replied Jester. "She's just meandering around with her sister."

Omen hummed. "They're probably here to hook up."

Yeah, that wasn't gonna happen. Not a chance would he allow another man to touch his woman.

It was right then that Viper spotted her on camera. She was shouldering her way through the throngs of people on the lower level with her sister at her back, glancing around curiously. And she looked fucking edible in a little black dress that was more of a shirt.

Viper looked at Jester. "Tell the boys on the ground floor to put the word out that she's not to be touched."

Jester nodded, his gaze then going inward as he telepathically reached out.

Satisfied, Viper turned back to the security monitor.

"Wonder why she'd come here of all places to hook up with someone," Omen pondered, sidling up to Viper. "It's not her usual scene."

No, it wasn't, from what Viper had observed of her habits. She didn't go clubbing often. She seemed to prefer low-key bars and dives. Yet, there she was.

He stared at her image on the screen. *You shouldn't have come here, baby.* She couldn't waltz into his metaphorical den like this. Couldn't put herself in his path. He only had so much restraint.

"You gonna go talk to her?" asked Omen.

Viper turned away from the monitors. "You already know the answer to that question." While he was determined that she wouldn't get pulled into his world just yet, he wasn't going to hang back in his office and act like she wasn't here.

Plus, he wouldn't have to worry that any strix would see him near her here. None would dare come inside the club.

"Then you're going to feed, right?" pushed Jester, giving him a solemn look. "We can't have you going without. Bloodlust will hit—"

"I told you earlier that I'll feed tonight, and I will."

Pursing his lips, Omen lifted his shoulders. "You could drink from Ella."

The idea was far too tempting. Viper could easily remove the memory of it from her mind afterwards, so he wouldn't be revealing his secrets too soon. But ... "I want her to give me her blood willingly, not because she's under a thrall." That wasn't possible just yet.

"Fine," Jester grunted. "But I don't see why it matters, just as I don't see why you're delaying—"

"I'm well aware of what you think. I don't need to hear it again."

Jester shrugged. "I like repeating myself."

"I've noticed. But saying the same stuff again and again doesn't make you right, it just makes you repetitive."

"Also annoying," Omen tacked on.

Jester shot him an even look, unbothered. "I don't live to please others. I don't even make an effort to please myself, so why the fuck would I care if you're annoyed?"

Omen's head flicked to the side. "You know, I overheard a female demon telling her friend that you're *the* most unpleasant person she's ever met."

"Again, why would I care?"

"It's not about whether or not you should care," Omen stressed, "it's about whether or not you want to alienate yourself from the world at large. Is that your grand plan?"

"Yes. Though I don't consider it a plan, more of a calling. And it isn't grand, it's relatively simple—I shouldn't really have to point that out."

Rubbing at the center of his forehead, Viper sighed. "Right, I'm heading off to find Ella. If you're gonna tag along, be sure to keep your distance so I get some private time with her."

"Okay, but let me just say that *he*"—Omen jabbed a finger in Jester's direction—"needs an attitude adjustment or he's gonna walk through life alone. He might think he wants that now, but there'll come a day when he'll regret it."

"Unlikely," said Jester. "Very, very unlikely."

Yeah, Viper would have to agree with that.

Ella had been to a fair amount of clubs in her day. None had been quite like this one. It spanned five floors, each featuring a dance floor that streamed through several ultra-spacious rooms, like a wide road.

The club's color scheme was simple enough, sticking to varying shades of red and black. There was lots of chrome, leather, and dark woods. The consistency in style tied the rooms together, making each one feel like a continuation of the last rather than a separate space.

Every room boasted a bar, seating areas, and shadowy alcoves. A film of fog ran throughout, providing some cover for those who might wish to tuck themselves into a corner and enjoy a little privacy.

There was one thing the venue had in common with other clubs. It was hectic. People were *everywhere*. Not just at the bar or on the dance floor or sitting at the tables. The place was packed with clubbers.

Her demon, no more a fan of crowds than Ella, wanted out of here. *Soon*, she promised it. Which didn't improve its mood, since it wasn't a patient being.

The bass of the loud music thumping beneath her feet, she made her way through the crowds to the long, busy bar. Passing an alcove, she caught movement in her peripheral vision; noticed a guy kissing a woman's neck while she moaned in delight. He was one of the Black Saints, going by the patch on his jacket.

Ella would bet other alcoves were similarly used by couples wanting to indulge in raunchy stuff out here in the open.

As she and Mia reached the bar, the nearest bartender turned to them. "What can I get . . . " He trailed off as he got a good look at Ella, which was weird to say the least. Clearing his throat, he wiped his face clean of emotion. "What can I get you?"

"A gin and tonic, please," Ella said absently, her brow creasing at his reaction.

"I'm good," Mia told him.

He began busying himself with Ella's order. He was average height with compact shoulders and ruffled dull-gold hair. She didn't recall having seen him before, but the patch on his jacket proclaimed him a member of the Black Saints.

She turned to her sister. "How come you're not having a drink?"

"I will, just not yet. I want to eat first." Mia scanned the dancers as if it was a buffet.

"By eat, you mean fuck."

"Exactly. You sure I can't persuade you to join me out there?"

"I'm sure. Now, go get laid already."

"With pleasure. Hopefully mine." With that, Mia sauntered away.

Right then, the bartender set Ella's glass on the bar. She paid with her card and then took a long sip of her drink. His gaze zipped to something over his shoulder—like that, the tension in his features eased.

"This is a surprise."

She stiffened. The voice came from directly behind her. A voice rich, deep, and loaded with gravel. It was also familiar. *Viper.*

Her demon stirring in interest, Ella slowly turned. Dark-ringed striking blue eyes snared hers; seized her full attention. And her pulse promptly did a hop, skip, and a jump. With major enthusiasm.

"Hi," she said, resisting the urge to lick her lips. But she totally failed resisting the temptation to drink him in. Damn, he was quite a spectacular sight. All rough and badass in a casual dark tee, black leather jacket, and faded jeans—none of it hid his muscular build.

He stood close, loitering on the edge of her personal space. So there was no missing the sexual need that briefly flickered in his gaze. Nor was there any way to avoid having his intoxicating scent twine around her—her demon liked the dark zest of it.

There was also no stopping the atmosphere from snapping taut. The chemistry between them was electric. Flustering. Unbridled.

"Ella," he greeted. It was more like he *tasted* her name. Like he rolled it around on his tongue. "I haven't seen you at my club before." He slanted his head. "First time?"

She took a steadying sip of her drink. "Yes."

"You here alone?"

"No, I'm with my sister. She's ... somewhere." Ella gestured at the dance floor. "I just came to keep an eye on her." Which would have been a lot easier if the place wasn't so dark and foggy.

Viper's hum was low, thoughtful, and held the merest rumble. The sound skittered down her spine and almost made her break out in a shiver.

She glanced around. "I don't think I'd have guessed that a bunch of angels would open a place that's all decadence and debauchery."

A corner of his mouth hitched up. "I suppose it may seem strange that we would plunge ourselves into the sexual underbelly of demonic society.. But we're no longer angels in the real sense of the word. When we fall, we lose any grace, purity, or piety we had. Our proclivities and inclinations change."

"You don't sound at all cut up about it."

"I'm not. I have no regrets."

Catching movement not far behind him, she noticed a woman watching them closely—her glare bouncing from him to Ella. "Someone seems to be waiting for you. Blonde. Tight curls. Big boobs. Large hoop earrings."

Annoyance flickered in his eyes. "Some people don't like the word no, and even refuse to hear it." He stepped a little closer, as if to make clear—maybe to her, maybe to the blonde, maybe to both—that the only woman who currently had his attention was Ella.

She had to admit, she liked that. Ella took another sip from her glass. "Why did you choose to settle in Vegas of all places? It fairly crawls with demons, and we're not always friendly toward the Fallen."

He hesitated. "There's something here that holds value to me—let's leave it at that."

"No, let's not. It sounds intriguing."

His mouth curled. "Maybe I'll tell you another time."

"And maybe you're full of shit."

He inclined his head. "Maybe."

"Is it that you have a child here? I've heard how angels sometimes tumble into the beds of humans and demons." She could understand why he might fall to protect the child—such hybrids weren't accepted by those in the upper realm.

Then again, if he *was* an archangel, he'd likely never stepped foot in this realm before. They usually didn't. But how else could there be something here that he'd in any way value?

"No offspring," he said, the ring of truth in his voice. "I'd ask if you have children of your own, but I already know the answer to that. As I said outside the pool hall, I pay attention when someone intrigues me."

Downing more of her drink, she narrowed her eyes. "Pay attention, or look into them?"

"Both."

That should annoy her. Right? She wasn't sure—it was hard to think straight when he kept his stare locked on hers. A stare so steady and unrelenting that the hairs on the back of her neck rose.

Ella had never had anyone watch her with *such focus.* It should have been off-putting. Should have made her bristle. Instead, it made her blood heat.

She also probably should have been uncomfortable with how close he stood or, at the very least, unnerved by him quite possibly being a fallen archangel. But instead, she felt at ease. Safe. Unfazed.

Maybe he had that effect on others, too—a left-over product

of him once having been a holy being. One thing was clear. "You like to stare, don't you?"

"At you, yes." Viper gave her a slow eye-bang, and need swallowed his pupils. "There's much to look at. I don't think I've ever seen hair your shade of red." His brow lifted. "Dye?"

Having knocked back the last of her gin and tonic, she set the glass on the bar. "No, it's my natural color." But she got that question a lot. "I don't think I've ever seen eyes as blue as yours." They were too blue. "Contacts?"

His lips twitched. "No."

A loud laugh sounded as a rowdy group pushed through the crowd.

Viper smoothly herded her aside, the move almost protective ... and suddenly they were in the alcove where she'd minutes ago seen two patrons having a 'moment'. Said patrons were now gone. The only people stood in the shadows were her and Viper, which seemed to make her body more painfully aware of him.

Her demon should have been wary at being alone with him, all things considered. But the entity was more curious than anything else. Then again, it had no actual aversion to danger. Quite the opposite.

A warm, calloused fingertip whispered down the side of her throat, leaving a trail of fire in its wake. "Tell me something."

She swallowed, butterflies going nuts in her stomach. "What?"

"Did you really only come here to watch over your sister?"

"Why would you ask that?"

"You could have worn something subtle and concealing to help send the message that you're not here to partake in any ... activities. But you chose this little black number that's all satin and lace and bares lots of skin."

If she was honest with herself, she could admit there was

some part of her that wanted to follow Mia's lead, despite the fact that . . . "A quick fuck in the dark with a stranger isn't really my thing."

"Doesn't mean you can't try it at least once." He glided even closer and palmed the sides of her face, his gaze drifting over every feature. "You're fucking breathtaking." He lightly brushed his thumb over the corner of her mouth, tracing the curve. "The first time I saw you, you were wearing the same lipstick you're wearing now."

She tried recalling what color it was. Nude, maybe. It was a little hard to think when explicit images were raining down on her, threatening to stain her cheeks with a blush.

A gleam of uncurbed need in his eyes, he dipped his head. "All I wanted to do was smear it all over your lips while I fucked them." The words were low and smooth but with a guttural edge.

Her stomach clenched so hard it hurt. "Is that a fact?" Her voice cracked, and his eyes lit like those of a jungle cat scenting prey.

He ghosted the tip of his nose along the side of hers. "Oh, it's a fact."

She gasped as his hands skated upward and dived into her hair. Her demon hummed, seduced by his power and strength and . . . some darker element. It was as if beneath his skin buzzed a sense of depraved restlessness. She couldn't quite explain it.

Having his hands on her felt like she was being touched by sin. Which was a really weird way to put it, but there was just something *dark* in his touch. Not evil, not defiling, but . . . corrupt, maybe?

It wasn't off-putting, it was seductive. Drugging. Enticing.

His pupils completely blown, he stared down at her as he gave a slight, reprimanding shake of the head. "You shouldn't have come here."

She felt her brows draw together. "What? Why n—?"

His lips dropped down on hers. He ravaged her mouth with a kiss that was hot, wet, and woven with brutal need. It lit up her body, hardened her nipples, fogged her brain . . . and everything around her faded away.

CHAPTER EIGHT

Viper tightened his grip on her hair. The feel of her body flush against his, her hands grabbing at his shoulders, her tongue tangling with his own ... It was everything he needed.

The moment he'd brought his mouth down on hers, there'd been a soul-deep *click* inside him. A feeling of absolute rightness. Of finally reconnecting with what he'd lost.

He herded her backwards and pinned her against the wall, growling when her body arched into his. A possessive greed stretched out inside him, making him kiss her harder.

Their teeth gnashed, and his incisor accidentally nicked her lip. The rich taste of her blood settled on his tongue, dragging a groan from him.

Roughly peeling up her dress, he kissed her *brutally*. Lapped up every bead of blood as the chemicals in his saliva kept it flowing.

He yanked aside her panties. Heard cloth tear. Did not give a shit.

Viper slid a finger between her folds. *Slick*. He drove two fingers inside her, grunting as her inner walls clutched them tight.

A whimper slipped from her, and the sound squeezed his balls. *Fuck.* He pumped his fingers, wanting her wetter, needier. All the while, he explored every crevice of her mouth; made her moan, arch into him, dig in her nails, chase his lips for more.

She scratched at his nape as she tore her lips free. "Viper—"

"If we were alone right now, I would strip you bare. Make your body my personal playground. Do whatever the fuck I want to you."

Those rough, need-edged words whispered their way up Ella's spine like teasing fingertips. He abruptly withdrew his fingers, and then he was unzipping his fly.

Exquisite excitement humming through her system, she didn't question if this was a good idea. She shoved down her underwear with trembling hands, watching as—holy shit, he was thick—he rolled on a condom.

No sooner had she stepped one foot out of her panties than he caught the underside of her thighs and hiked her up. He caged her against the wall, and she gasped at the insistent press of his hard shaft against her clit.

Ella dove one hand into his hair and clutched at his nape with the other. "In me."

"This is gonna be rough."

"Good."

Viper jammed every inch of his cock deep, groaning at the slick, scorching hot clasp of her pussy. He let his dick settle there, wishing he could lock it inside her.

She looped her legs around him. "Move, move, move."

He jacked his hips upward over and over. He didn't hold back. Couldn't.

Years he'd waited for this. For *her.* Fucking years.

He could live out his entire existence right there. Her taste in his mouth, her scent in his lungs, her skin under his hands, his cock in her body ... It was home. *She* was home.

His hunger for her was bottomless. Wild. Primitive. And it all poured out of him, speeding up his already frenzied pace.

"Harder," Ella demanded, knowing she'd come soon. He gave her what she asked for, burying his face in her throat. The rasp of his stubble on her neck made her gasp. She dug her fingers into the solid muscles of his shoulders, feeling the contained power there.

Honey-slick flames began to spread through her veins—slow, roasting, maddening. Her release was almost on her, and she knew it.

A strange tension gathered in his shoulders as he scraped his teeth over her pulse. His warm breath washed over her ear. "Come for me, Ella." He angled his hips, sawing his long shaft over her clit.

Like that, the flames inside her turned into a full-on roaring fire as the tightness in her belly snapped. An avalanche of pleasure tumbled through her, sweeping her away.

He growled against her skin as he pounded into her even harder, his pace all but feral. Then he came, every blast of his release hot and harsh as he thrusted, grinded, and groaned.

They both stayed there for long moments, neither moving; both struggling to catch their breath.

Once his orgasm had finally subsided, Viper lifted his head to find himself staring into fuck-drunk eyes. Damn, that look tightened his gut.

His entity pushed against his skin, wanting to surface—feed from her, talk to her, touch her, play with her.

Not this time, Viper told it. *You'll scare her off.*

It growled its annoyance but subsided, knowing he was right.

They needed to ease her into certain things or they'd risk losing her—neither of them were prepared to allow that.

Viper dipped his gaze to her lip. The spot where he'd nicked it was already healing just fine. An accelerated healing rate generally came with the demon package.

She nervously chewed on the inside of her cheek. "Uh, thanks?"

Humor plucked at one corner of his mouth. "No thanks necessary." Easing his cock out of her pussy, he lowered Ella to her feet and released her—all of which proved to be seriously fucking hard when all he wanted to do was keep her close. "I'll want more of that. Of you."

Pulling her panties back on, she cast him a look he couldn't quite read. "This was just a one-off."

Yeah, he'd figured that was all she'd intended. He peeled off the condom and tied it. "Oh, so you mean to use and discard me? I'm hurt."

"You're ridiculous," she said with an eye roll, righting her dress.

"Seriously," he said, zipping up his fly as he pinned her with a sober look. "I want more of you."

"I hate to point out the obvious, but you're an angel; I'm a demon. Common sense says it's better for us to stay on our own sides of the fence."

He shrugged. "I don't see why there has to be a fence. Forget about what others would say you should do, Ella. Let yourself have what you want."

She nervously swiped her tongue over her bottom lip. "I have to go. My sister's probably looking for me."

It was a good sign that she'd prefer to escape the conversation than tell him outright that there'd be no repeat. It meant she was at least a little conflicted. They'd done this dance before in her previous life, and he'd managed to sway her back then. He'd do it again.

Viper caught her chin between his thumb and finger. "Come back to me sometime soon. You don't, I'll come for you. One way or another, Ella, I'll have you again." He let his hand fall away and stepped back.

She gave him an uncertain look and then walked away, her knees looking a little rubbery. He watched as she disappeared into the crowd and, fuck, it was hard not to follow her. But he knew from prior experience that moving too fast would make her dig in her heels.

Straightening his jacket, he exited the alcove to find Omen and Jester waiting nearby.

Jester flicked a look in the direction that Ella had walked off. "All good?"

Viper adjusted the collar of his jacket. "You could say that." He shrugged his way through the crowds as he made his way back to his office, conscious of his brothers trailing after him.

Inside, Omen closed the door behind them. "You fucked her, didn't you?" he guessed, his tone non-accusatory.

"Of course I did." Viper walked to stand behind his desk. "There wasn't a chance she was going to leave this club without me putting my cock in her." He didn't have the kind of restraint needed to hold back.

This was his woman. One he'd claimed long ago. One who'd marked him just as deeply. Plus . . . "She hadn't admitted it to herself, but she came here looking to hook up. I wasn't going to let anyone else oblige her."

Omen stalked further into the room. "Made any plans for it to happen again?"

"No." Viper sank onto his chair. "But I made it clear that it would."

"And what did she think about that?" asked Jester.

"She's hesitant."

"That won't last," Omen upheld. "You two have major ... what do humans call it? Zing."

Jester folded his arms. "What now? Because it looks to me like your plan to take things slow just shot out of the window. We both know you ain't gonna hang back until the strix are gone. Not now that you've touched her."

Viper rubbed at his temple. "You're right, I can't hang back anymore." Nor did he want to. He was fucking tired of battling the incessant daily urge to see her, talk to her, touch her. It was agonizing to be so very near to what he most wanted; to what he'd spent years attempting to find.

His entity grinned, stretching; both relaxed and eager to start officially hunting their woman.

"Not only because it would be impossible," Viper added, "but because she'd either mistake if for a withdrawal of interest, or think I was playing games."

"And then she might find herself a different bed-buddy," said Omen. "Let's face it, you wouldn't let him live."

"Did you feed from her?" asked Jester.

"No," replied Viper. Droplets of her blood didn't count. "I won't drink from her without her consent."

Omen's brow furrowed. "You do it to others."

"But she's not some random human. She's mine. That makes it different." Viper let his head fall back to hit his chair's head-rest. "I don't look forward to explaining I can't survive without feeding on the life-force of others."

Jester frowned. "She was prepared to accept it when you knew her as Everleigh and warned her about the curse."

"Back then, it wasn't the same. She accepted that I was an archangel, yes, and she showed no fear of what would happen to

me if I fell—only compassion. But now I have fallen, and we're
not dealing with things that would happen; we're dealing with
shit that's already occurred.

"Asking her to accept my new reality is a hell of a lot different from my sharing what could become of me. Plus, I hadn't
gotten round to telling her what happens to members of the
Seven who fall. I don't know how she would have reacted to
that."

"She'll accept you," Omen maintained. "She loved you in her
previous lifetime. I don't see why it would be different in this one.
And with love comes acceptance."

Viper sure as fuck hoped so. If she didn't accept him, he deeply
suspected that his entity would take the situation into its own
hands and tie her to them anyway. There wasn't anything it
wouldn't do to ensure it got to keep her this time. Much as it
made Viper a huge fucking bastard, he couldn't even judge the
entity for that.

"When are you planning on telling her that this ain't the first
lifetime you've known her in?" asked Omen.

"When I'm sure she cares for me. She'll more easily digest it
that way." Viper sat up straighter in his chair. "Besides, if she
hears it from a relative stranger, she might struggle to believe
it. Once she knows me, once she knows I'd never mess with her
that way, she'll be more open to the idea."

Considering that, Omen gave a slow nod.

"Much as I'm done keeping my distance from Ella, I'll still
have to be careful not to be seen with her in public until the
strix are dead and we can be certain there are no celestial spies
keeping watch."

"I haven't found signs of any spies," said Jester.

His other brothers had given Viper that same assurance,
but ... "The Uppers told Ophaniel about the local human

disappearances. They could only have known about it if someone reported it to them."

"Maybe they're no longer watching us. Whatever the case, we won't let our guard down. And if any spies do turn up and somehow notice you're spending time with Ella, they won't live long enough to share any suspicions they might have with the Uppers."

No, no, they wouldn't.

"Just so you're aware, your private time with Ella was almost interrupted."

Viper felt his brow furrow. "By who?"

"The blonde. Neta. She tried marching into the alcove, but Omen blocked her path. I convinced her to leave."

Viper felt his mouth tighten. The woman in question was a member of Maddox Quentin's lair. A descendant just like her Prime, Neta was a regular at the club . . . and at the dive bar . . . and even turned up at the pool hall on occasion.

A few of his brothers had fucked her, but the others had turned her down. Why? They'd come to learn that her goal was to bed every one of them—and then eventually be claimed by Viper.

Even if there'd been no Ella, he wouldn't have been interested. "That she'd dare charge into the alcove was fucking ballsy. What could she possibly have thought would come from it?" All he would have done was send her away.

Omen shrugged. "Maybe she wanted to break the moment. Or scare Ella away. Or just plain piss you off. I don't really know what's going on with Neta. I don't quite get why, when her plan was to seduce you last, she suddenly switched shit around."

"She might have seen how you look at Ella, V," Jester mused. "Maybe when at the pool hall or dive bar."

It was possible. "I don't much care so long as she stays away from my woman. It's not gonna be easy to coax Ella into pushing past all her reservations about demons getting involved with angels. The last thing I need is someone making it harder."

"Yeah, you don't want Ella realizing until it's too late that you're more trouble than you're worth," said Omen.

Viper shot him a hard look. "Thanks," he said, his voice dry. "Do you know if Neta's still here?"

"She stormed out of the club after we blocked her path to the alcove and told her to leave," replied Omen. "What are you gonna do if she reappears and again makes a move on you?"

Viper rubbed at his jaw. "I'll talk to her one last time. I'll get it firmly across that she's chasing after something she's never gonna have."

He would rather not piss off Maddox by threatening his lair members, since it would be a fast way to lose an alliance. Making an enemy of demons wouldn't endear him to Ella. But . . . "If she persists after that, I'll contact Maddox and communicate that either *he* deals with her or I will." Because Viper also couldn't allow any woman to make attempts to chase off Ella. No one would get in the way of him making her his this time. Absolutely fucking no one.

CHAPTER NINE

I'll come for you.

Cursing beneath her breath, Ella paused in topping up the box of small on-sale products near the till. Viper's words from last night wouldn't leave her alone.

She'd done her best not to think about him. Had tried hard to mentally shove aside their little encounter in the shadows. It was just sex. There was no reason to think about it.

And yet, snippets of it kept replaying in her mind. His mouth moving insistently on hers, his hands possessively fisting her hair, his cock driving into her over and over, and making her explode more fiercely than she ever had before.

Okay, so it hadn't been 'just sex'. There'd been nothing regular or simple about it. It had been incredible. An unparalleled experience. Blindingly hot.

But that wasn't to say they should repeat it. Their kinds weren't supposed to mix. A one-time fuck, well, that could be overlooked. It had just been a spur of the moment thing brought on by the mere fact that she'd been thinking with her pink parts.

Parts he'd pleasured exceptionally well.

Ella gave her head a little shake and went back to adding products to the counter.

There was another—and admittedly silly—reason why his words kept swimming back to the forefront of her mind. They felt slightly reminiscent of those spoken by the wraith: *He will come for you.*

This was sheer coincidence, of course. The wraith had merely blurted out crap to mess with her—there'd been no truth in it, let alone any reference to Viper.

The only person who might 'come' for her was her little note-deliverer, but that concept didn't gel with the rest of the wraith's weird warning ... "*You will be chained to him forever, and you cannot imagine what that will mean for you.*"

Plus, the demon had also said something about how it was *her* soul that she needed to worry about. There was no reason why her pen pal would pose a risk to her soul. No one would. So yes, the wraith had been rambling nonsense.

Viper, though? She didn't get the sense that he'd thrown out his little warning lightly. If she didn't seek him out, he might very well come find her. Which shouldn't make a little tingle of excitement ride her spine, but their chemistry was, like, *whoa*. The kind of chemistry that made a person make unwise decisions.

Case in point.

If he sought her out, well, she'd just remind him that casual fucks weren't her thing. It would be for the best, wouldn't it?

Her demon didn't think so, no longer bothered by, or uneasy about, him being one of the Fallen. It liked the darkness that seemed to cloak him. *Weirdo.*

Mia appeared beside her, one hand on her hip. "You keep zoning out, and I'm wondering if your thoughts might be flying to the mystery guy who ravished you last night."

Ella had confessed to her sister that she'd slept with someone at the Red Rooms, but she'd kept his identity to herself. Mia might toss out comments about how hot Viper was, but she wouldn't approve of this. She would instead lecture her on the evils of tangling with the Fallen in such a way. Ella was in no mood to hear one.

"I'm just tired." It wasn't a lie.

"Hmm, you do look like you could fall over and nap any second."

"Ever the flatterer," Ella sardonically muttered.

Mia snickered and braced her elbow on the counter. "Why won't you tell me who the mystery dude was? It's *killing* me that I don't know."

Ella frowned. "You haven't been all that open with me either. I'm still waiting to hear about whoever fucked a smile onto your face at the club."

Mia's brow dented. "I already told you all about him."

"Oh, yeah. '*He was uber hot and had some serious skills. You woulda liked him.*' Very detailed."

"There wasn't really anything more to tell."

The *ding* of the bell above the door made them both look over.

"Oh, here we go," Mia muttered as Dionne's mother strode into the store looking like she was sucking on a lemon. *Knew this would happen*, she added telepathically.

We're not rehiring Dionne no matter what this woman says, Ella stated.

Maxine appeared at the counter, her chin up high. She wasn't a hellcat like her daughter and mate, she was a harpy. And since people generally swerved from getting on the bad side of a harpy, the woman was used to getting her way and not dealing with resistance. So used to it, in fact, that she'd come to feel entitled to it. Which meant she could be a pain in the ass at times, *especially* when things didn't pan out like she wanted.

"Ella, Mia." Her voice was as sharp and cutting as broken glass. "I heard you fired my daughter yesterday."

Ella folded her arms. "I did."

The harpy's lips flattened. "And just what makes you believe it's fair or acceptable to fire someone for having frequent migraines?"

Whoa, was *that* what Dionne had told her? "That isn't why she lost her job. She's lazy. Frequently late. Wanders off to check her phone notifications. And, just yesterday, she also helped herself to cash from the register."

Maxine's shoulders tensed. "The latter is a very serious accusation."

"Not an accusation, a fact. And before you try to pressure us into giving her back her job, know that it won't be worth it. You run a business, Maxine." A very successful clothing store, in fact. "Would you keep such a worker on your team?"

Maxine's eyes flickered. "She is young and has much to learn."

Which did not answer Ella's question. In fact, it was a clear evasion.

"She could learn working for *you*," Mia pointed out.

"I would be thrilled to have Dionne as one of my staff," the harpy claimed, "but she has no interest in fashion."

"She has no interest in working here either." Another good point by Mia.

The bell above the door went again. Another woman walked inside—this one equally familiar, but more welcome. Ella cast her a quick smile before refocusing on the harpy.

Maxine's eyes narrowed. "Does your aunt know that you let Dionne go?"

"Of course," said Ella. "The decision to fire her was a unanimous one."

The harpy's gaze hardened. "Knox will not like this."

"Not like what?" asked the woman behind Maxine.

The harpy whirled to face the dark-haired, long-legged nightmare. "Oh. Piper."

Ella bit back a smile at the nervous tremor in Maxine's voice. She had probably planned to embellish what happened here on reporting it to Knox, whose name she often wielded like a sword. But now she couldn't lie. Because Piper would be able to tell him it was pure bull. And, as Levi's mate and a close friend of Harper, Knox would take Piper's word over Maxine's *any* day.

The harpy flicked a hand. "Nothing terribly important. Do say hello to Levi for me." With a dignified haughtiness, the woman left the store.

"What was that about?" asked Piper.

Mia puffed out a heavy breath. "We had to fire her daughter."

Piper's nose wrinkled. "It's a pretty frequent thing. She always tries intimidating Dionne's ex-employers into giving her 'one last chance.' You know, personally, I think Dionne purposely gets herself sacked just to get at her mom."

Ella cocked her head. "Like an attention seeking thing?"

"Maxine is a workaholic who doesn't have much time for her daughter," Piper reminded her. "I think Dionne sabotages every job both because she's determined to be the opposite of her mom but also because it's the only time Maxine really notices anything that's happening in Dionne's life."

Mia sighed. "It's kind of sad. I feel sorry for Dionne, but we can't keep her on."

"And you shouldn't," Piper stated firmly. "Maxine might whine about it to Knox, but he won't step in on her behalf." Her pale-green eyes glinted with concern as they cut to Ella. "You look tired."

Ella really wished people would stop pointing that out. "I'm not sleeping well."

She'd had more dreams last night. Each had woken her at various times, but she'd never managed to cling to the threads of them. They'd slipped from her mental grasp, leaving her clueless as to what she'd dreamt about.

"Can't you whip up some kind of potion that would help you sleep right through?"

"I could, but they always leave me feeling *bleh* the next day. I have zero enthusiasm, and my vigilance level suffers." Rendering herself drowsy and unalert wouldn't be smart when she clearly hadn't shaken off her stalker.

"Don't worry, I'll be making her a talisman that fends off dreams," Mia told Piper. "All she'll need to do is stick it under her pillow. That should work."

"Fingers crossed it does." Piper looked from her to Ella. "Hey, why don't you both come have a drink with me and my girls at the Xpress bar later?"

Ella pulled a face. "Last time I went there, I nearly got into a fight."

Piper waved that way. "Pretty much *everyone* almost gets into a fight with Khloë. It's like the law."

A snort popped out of Ella. The almost-fight hadn't whatso-ever tainted the growing friendship between her and the imp. On the contrary, it seemed to have strengthened it, since Khloë had found the whole thing wildly entertaining. "I'll think about it. Now, what can we do for you?"

Music blasted, drowning out Ella's voice as she yelled at Khloë, who got right up in her face. Ella couldn't hear her words, could barely hear anything over the music. Only her pulse pounding in her ears and . . . and Khloë suddenly wasn't Khloë anymore. It was a tall brunette. And the club wasn't a club anymore. It was a dingy bar.

Everything here was . . . different. Accents. Music. Smells. People.

The brunette pointed in her face, accusing her of trying to flirt with the bitch's boyfriend—a guy Everleigh had just rejected at the bar, for Christ's sake.

Everleigh would have lunged at the little bitch for then calling her a whore, but her friend held her back. Pushed her toward the restroom. Encouraged her to calm down.

Everleigh stumbled through the crowd, a strange fog at the edges of her vision that distorted her view of everything else. That fog thickened and churned, only to part as a stranger appeared. No, not a stranger. She'd seen him here and there. There was no way to miss someone who looked like that. A guy who was hot as hell and had 'danger' written all over him in capital letters.

"My opinion?" he rumbled, his voice as delicious as him. "She would have had it coming if you'd punched her."

Everleigh blinked. "Sorry?"

"She called you a whore, right?"

"Right."

"Then she would have had it coming." He stalked toward her with the animal grace of a predator on the hunt. "Everleigh, isn't it?"

Her demon narrowed its eyes, sensing he was no demon himself. If she wasn't mistaken, he was a celestial. "Yes. Who are you?"

He grinned. "Let me buy you a drink and I'll tell you."

The fog swished around them, blocked her sight, muffled her hearing, and misted her thoughts.

Her surroundings seemed to melt as every color spread and changed shape, looking more like a pastel painting. Then it cleared, every detail coming into view. Her house. She was walking toward her house.

A figure prowled out of the shadows—tall, dark, sinfully gorgeous. And a man who had some serious game in the bedroom.

Everleigh slowed, taken aback that he'd showed up here. Had she told him where she lived? She didn't think so, but she'd been pretty tipsy that night.

She'd tried not to think about him since. Really, really tried. And failed. Oh, failed so very dramatically. "I have to admit, I didn't expect to see you again."

He blinked. "You remember me?"

She frowned. "Of course I do. I wasn't that smashed last weekend." But he still appeared strangely thrown. "What brings you here?"

"You," he replied bluntly, the heat in his eyes making it clear what he wanted from her.

Temptation fluttered in her belly just as a sense of excitement rushed through her veins. Her demon's mouth curved, liking his blunt response.

She didn't believe in playing dumb, so she reminded him, "That night we had was supposed to be a one-time thing." She'd made that clear, and he'd agreed.

"Supposed to be," he allowed.

"It's not a good idea to do it again."

His shoulders lifted and fell. "Don't much care."

To her dismay, she found that neither did she. Her inner entity didn't see why she should consider it a big deal. Sex was sex, in the demon's opinion.

Much as Everleigh wished it was that simple, she knew it wasn't. Not merely because he was a freaking angel, but because nothing about the night they spent together had felt casual. They'd connected on a level she couldn't explain. "Don't you think once was enough?"

His gaze darkened. "No. And neither do you."

The fog swallowed everything in front of her. Every image, every noise, every emotion. All gone.

Her mind seemed to drift, blissfully empty. Clear. At peace.

Sensations penetrated, making her surroundings come into view once more. The fog hovered on the edges again, smudging all but what was in her line of sight. Him.

He was above her, in her, thrusting hard, stuffing her full, eating her up with his gaze.

"I could live right here in this pussy, never leave it," he gritted out, forcing his cock deep. "No one fits me better than you."

An alarm blared, dragging Ella out of her dream. Her eyelids fluttered open as the haze of sleep began to disperse. Images, words, and sensations lingered. Lingered but faded. Faded and faded and faded.

And still, she remembered. Remembered one thing: Familiar piercing blue-eyes staring into hers while a long, thick cock was buried *so deep* inside her.

Huh. Apparently, she was having sex-dreams about Viper now. Ugh.

Scrubbing a hand down her face, she sluggishly sat upright, her shoulders slumping with fatigue. As if it wasn't bad enough that the dude flowed into her waking thoughts far too often, it now seemed he also featured in her dreams. Wonderful. And unfair.

Ella threw back the covers and shuffled to the edge of the bed, letting her legs dangle over it. What was with the X-rated dream content lately? It obviously wasn't caused by sex deprivation, given she'd let Viper ravish her a couple of nights ago.

And why hadn't the talisman worked? It should have. Mia's magick had never failed her before.

Not having the time to ponder this just now, Ella forced herself out of bed. Forced herself to get ready. Forced down food and coffee. And when she met her sister in the foyer, Mia winced.

"I look that bad?"

Mia twisted her mouth. "I'd like to say no. I really would. But I can't. Didn't you get any sleep?"

"Oh, I did. I also dreamt, though. I swear, it's like dreaming takes a toll on my brain these days or something."

Mia's brow creased. "Dammit, I really thought the talisman would work. I can't understand why it didn't." She walked in a circle around Ella. "You haven't been jinxed or anything—I'd sense a spell if one clung to you." She sighed. "What's happening with you isn't normal. Dreaming doesn't tire the brain. It just doesn't."

No, it didn't. And Ella couldn't work out why that would suddenly change for her.

CHAPTER TEN

Standing in the center of the main clubhouse area, Viper crossed his arms over his chest as he glared at his brother.

"It's not what you think," Darko defended, raising his hands slightly.

Viper shot him an incredulous look. "It's not?"

"No."

Digging deep for patience, Viper took a long breath. "You're stood here covered in blood, and Omen found you looming over the dead body of a male demon outside the Red Rooms. Seems to me that you killed that demon."

"Then, yes, it is what you think," Darko admitted with a brief tilt of his head. "But I had valid reasons."

Oh, this should be good. "Which are?"

"He threw a hellfire orb at me."

Viper waited, but his brother said nothing more. "First of all, that's one reason. Second of all, I doubt this was an unprovoked attack." Darko had a way of making even the most tolerant person blow a fuse. "What did you do?"

He grimaced. "I might have called him a pussy. Things kind of escalated from there."

Viper heaved a sigh.

"I caught him slapping his girl around, and it was obvious he did it regularly," Darko continued. "I don't like that shit."

"Most people don't, and they'd have intervened if they could have. But did you genuinely feel that the only way to deal with the situation was to erase the demon's existence?"

Darko's brow furrowed. As if no other course of action had even occurred to him.

Viper clenched his jaw. "We already have local humans disappearing—that's going to lead to people knocking on our door eventually if we don't get rid of the damn strix fast. You really want to draw the attention of a demon lair as well?"

Darko's expression was the facial equivalent of a dismissive hand flick. "I made his corpse vanish. No one will trace his death back to me. And, if they do, I'll handle it."

"How?" challenged Viper. "By killing them, too?"

He shrugged. "It's the quickest way to get rid of a problem."

Viper sighed again. He did it a lot around this particular angel. In fact, the majority of their club did.

"Why are you riding *my* ass but not *his*?" groused Darko, indicating at Ghost. "He was told not to buy a Deadpool suit. Look at him."

Lounging on the sofa, Ghost pointed at Darko. "Two things. One, I'm wearing a mask, not a suit, so it doesn't really count. Two, this is a Spiderman mask, not a Deadpool one. You need to get your facts right."

"You need to get that mask off your face," Darko countered.

"I second that," Jester piped up from the other side of the

room, swiping darts out of the wall-mounted board. "And it don't look like a spider. Just saying."

Viper caught Darko's eye. "Stop trying to divert my attention. We're talking about you, not Ghost—he'll get bored of wearing the mask when you all stop reacting to it. Your problem is a lot bigger. And I'm not talking the issue of a dead demon. I'm talking of how you seem to be using any excuse you can find to kill someone.".

Darko inched up his chin. "I was trained to kill. I was made to do it regularly. The Uppers can't then put me out in the world and expect me to be normal."

"They didn't actually put you out into the world," Jester pointed out. "You fell by choice."

"Don't you get tired of being technical?" sniped Darko.

Jester's response was instant. "No."

Right then, Dice teleported into the room. He did a double-take at the sight of the blood on Darko. "You have a run-in with someone? Tell me you didn't do that thing again where you pounce on any reason to kill someone."

"I don't pounce on reasons, my actions are always justifiable. You're not more curious about why he's wearing a Batman mask?" Darko asked, flicking a hand at Ghost.

"Spiderman," Ghost corrected.

Dice angled his head. "I'm thinking it might actually be a Batman mask. I mean, spiders don't have upward-pointing black ears. That does."

A dart hit the board with a *thunk* just before Jester slid a look at Ghost, who'd yanked off his mask to study it. "I did say it didn't look like a spider."

Viper slowly blinked, thinking that none of the people who watched his brothers warily would ever for a moment guess that these conversations took place between them.

Dice did a double-take as he looked out of the window. "The fuck?"

"What?" Viper tracked his gaze to see—*motherfucker*—a strix stood outside the chain-link fence at the rear of the compound, looming over a corpse.

"Son of a bitch," spat Jester. "That'll be another of the missing humans."

The strix noticed them looking but didn't scamper. It remained in place and grinned cockily. Viper didn't worry that the little shit would bypass the fence. The entire compound was protected by wards that were powered by his blood—no demon would get through them.

Abruptly, the strix did a one-eighty and dashed across the stretch of unused, barren land that led to a wooded area.

"It could have dumped the body and then snuck off," mused Ghost. "It waited for us to see it. It's trying to lure us to the woods."

Dice nodded. "It won't be alone."

"No, it won't." Viper reached out to their other brothers on the club's 'channel': *Everyone get to the main area of the clubhouse. Now.*

They appeared in fast succession, and Viper quickly brought them up to speed before adding, "The strix won't all be waiting in the woods. It's too predictable."

"Where will they be?" asked Rivet.

Hustle rubbed at his jaw. "They'd want to blindside us."

Viper swept his gaze over the land outside. Realization hit him fast. "Mist."

Razor's brows dipped. "What?"

"They're hiding in mist-form on either side of the land beyond the fence," Viper elaborated. "Look. *Closely.* You can see faint clumps of mist."

"Do we pretend we've fallen for their trick?" asked Jester.

"Don't really have much choice." They could attack from the safety of the compound, but the strix would retreat if they were unable to land any blows. Viper and his club couldn't eat at the colony's numbers if they didn't battle them.

Viper felt his lips thin. He wasn't in the mood for this. Normally, he'd perk up at the prospect of battle. But he planned to head to the pool hall soon, just as he did every Friday. He wanted to see Ella, corner her, coax her into giving in to him.

He hadn't seen or heard from her since he fucked her at his club on Monday night. She hadn't come to him—disappointing, but unsurprising. He *needed* her to take a step toward him, but he was prepared to make a move of his own; had warned her that he would. Viper didn't want to rush her, though.

Viper slipped off his jacket and placed it on the nearby pool table. At least they wouldn't have to worry about witnesses. The compound was out in the middle of nowhere. It wasn't vulnerable, though—not when it housed a collection of fallen celestials as dangerous as that of Viper and his brothers.

"We teleport outside the fence, forming two lines that stand back to back and fully face the mists," said Viper.

"In our usual formation?" asked Sting.

They'd used such a move in the past during battles. "It'll work best."

Once the others had all removed their own jackets, Darko arched a brow. "We get to play again, right?"

Since Viper had somewhere to be ... "Not for too long, so make the most of it."

As one, they shimmered outside—seven forming a line facing the left of their land, the others forming a line facing the right.

Viper didn't hesitate to make a move. He struck with a telekinetic wave that slammed down on the mists from above, forcing them to crash to the ground. The mists flickered, thickened, and rippled before reforming into a row of fifteen strix. Red eyes gleaming with pain, rage, and bloodthirst slammed on the Black Saints.

"I feel bad for them," mocked Darko beside Viper. "I mean, how honestly devastated would you be if your eyes were red? I'd wear contacts for life."

Two strix leaped to their feet and rushed him. Viper hit out with an archangelic blast. The rippling wave of unholy fire rushed out and sliced through their bodies like a knife through butter. Bodies that fragmented into ashes.

The fight turned ugly fast. Hisses, screeches, laughs, the crackling of flames and orbs—all of it echoed across the vast spread of land. Orbs of hellfire and unholy fire bounced back and forth; slamming into bodies, blistering flesh, eating at cloth. The scents of blood, acid, pain, sulphur, and brimstone clogged the air and fed his entity's hunger for violence and death.

A strix propelled itself into the air and landed on Viper, knocking him flat on his back. His breath gusted out of him but, the thrill of battle on him, he didn't hesitate in telekinetically 'throwing' the strix backward, sending it flailing through the air before it hit the ground hard. He jumped to his feet and slammed it with orb after orb until, finally, it exploded into ashes.

A whip of black fire cracked out and wrapped around his wrist, yanking him to the side. Gritting his teeth as his skin sizzled beneath the boiling heat of the whip, Viper tossed a blazing orb of unholy fire at his attacker, hurtling it right at the strix's face.

The demon's head snapped back from the force of it. Viper took instant advantage of its disorientation—smacking it with a lethal archangelic blast.

Beside him, Ghost tossed a fast-dying strix on the ground and spat. "Why does their blood have to taste like it's been burned?"

On Ghost's other side, Razor shrugged. "We've tasted worse."

A strix leaped at Viper. No, *over* him. A pale arm then wrapped around him from behind as fangs knifed into his skin. The strix took only one gulp of blood before rearing back with a shriek of pain.

Leaving his acidic blood to kill the demon from the inside out—it made for an excruciating death—Viper switched his focus to yet another strix. He hurled an unholy orb at its head. The demon shifted into a tight ball of mist, avoiding the hit, and just as swiftly shifted back.

Awkward little bastard couldn't just die easily, could it?

Viper tossed out a series of orbs. The strix evaded all . . . bar one. The final ball of flames wacked its head hard, killing it instantly.

Breathing hard, he took a quick moment to quickly scan the metaphorical battlefield. All his brothers were still standing, still fighting. Several were covered in ultraviolent flames, blasting streams of it out of their palms. The surviving strix were in bad shape—patches of their flesh were black, burned, and corroding. There weren't very many left.

He heard a *wrench* as Darko plucked off a strix's head. The bodily remains crumbled to ashes. "Bastard tried ripping a chunk out of my throat," he told Viper, indignant. "It seemed excessive."

Viper could only shrug.

More and more strix came his way. Nails raked at him. Fangs punctured him. Whips lashed him. Orbs punched him.

To the music of his brothers' perverse laughter, Viper kept on fighting; pelting the strix with blasts, orbs, and telekinesis.

A hellfire orb crashed into his skull so hard his head snapped to the side. The move sent pain streaking up his neck and made his ears ring.

Another flaming ball came his way. He dodged it, struck out with an archangelic blast, and grunted in satisfaction when his attacker—

Blazing trails of fire raked down his back. *Fucking razor-like nails.* He pivoted to face his new foe, dived right at the little fucker, and roughly buried his teeth into its neck. The strix burst into molecules, escaping his hold, and darted backwards out of reach.

Realizing that the sounds of battle had greatly dimmed, Viper looked around ... and frowned at a cursing Jester, who was wrestling with a bat that was biting at his face, its leather wings flapping at his hand.

Jester snapped its neck, coughing as it then burst into ashes that showered his face. "Fucking. Hate. Strix."

"So you often say," intoned Ghost before puffing out a breath. "Looks like the battle's over."

It did. Jester had killed the last of the strix. Ashes littered the ground and peppered his brothers' clothes and skin.

No one was badly hurt—or they had drunk enough blood to heal any severe injuries.

"That was a decent-sized bunch of strix we just killed," remarked Omen as he approached.

"There'll be many more," commented Razor.

Omen granted that with a stiff incline of his head. "But the colony has taken a good hit, if you count the amount of strix we've killed in total since they shoved themselves onto our radar."

"They sent more this time, but not a *lot* more," Viper noted. "Like they believed we'd won the last battle by some stroke of luck."

"I reckon the next batch that come after us will be bigger again," Ghost predicted. "But not too big—the queen won't want to have to send any who she doesn't consider expendable."

Omen nodded. "Yeah, we have to remember that these won't be her strongest fighters. She'll be keeping those close for her own protection."

Done with strix bullshit for the day, Viper blew out a long breath as he took stock of himself. "Let's head back. We need to move the human corpse that was left outside the compound. Then I need a fucking shower and change of clothes. Fast." He had a pool hall to get to.

CHAPTER ELEVEN

Ella was folding clean laundry in her bedroom when her phone rang. Dropping a hoodie back into the basket, she retrieved her cell from the nightstand. *Mia.* Feeling her lips curl, she answered, "Hello?"

A sheepish sigh drifted down the line. "Hi. I'm sorry to do this to you, but I need to cancel our pool-hall plans for tonight."

"How come?" Ella asked, surprised. It wasn't like her sister to bail. "Is everything okay?"

Mia made a noncommittal sound. "Joe telepathed me. He asked if I'd meet him at his place tonight. Apparently, he wants to have a—and I quote—real talk."

"Oh, well, that's good. It's about time he decided to be honest with you."

Mia hummed in agreement. "Not sure why he didn't sooner, but I'm sure he'll explain. I'm sorry that—"

"Hey, there's no need to be sorry. He's your anchor. Things

are strained between the two of you; of course you want to give him the chance to fix it."

"I thought about putting it off until later, but delaying the conversation will bug me. I'll spend the time wondering what he has to say, so I won't make good company for you."

"Mia, really, it's *fine*," Ella stressed. "Go see him; get the matter settled. And call me later to let me know how it went."

"Will do. Love ya."

"Love ya, too." Ella rang off and placed her cell on the nightstand.

While she was glad that Mia and Joe might just finally get things back on track, she was a little disappointed that the pool-hall plans had been canceled. If she was honest with herself, Ella could admit that she'd been looking forward to going there tonight. All day—stupidly, annoyingly, unreasonably—she'd felt a little frisson of excitement at the thought of seeing Viper.

They wouldn't have talked or anything, but it didn't matter. The idea of being around him had made her feel kind of energized.

Shoving *that* irritating tidbit out of her mind, Ella silently wished her sister good luck with Joe and then went back to her laundry. After folding and putting away her clothes, she ate dinner while watching TV. And the longer she went without hearing from Mia, the more antsy she got.

Either her sister and Joe were having one hell of a long talk . . . or they were sexing each other up.

Hoping it wasn't the latter, Ella headed into the kitchen and made herself a mug of tea. She didn't dislike Joe *per se*, she just didn't like how greedy he was with Mia's time and attention. Not that that was atypical for psi-mates. But Joe could be pretty selfish about it.

Take this situation, for example.

He was well aware that Mia and Ella routinely met up at the pool hall on Fridays. He could have asked her to meet him later tonight, or some time tomorrow. Instead, he'd asked Mia to push aside her plans for him—which wasn't a first. There'd been many occasions when he'd pressured her to cancel on Ella, insensitively not caring he'd be cutting into the sisters' girl time. He seemed to feel threatened by how close they were.

Usually, his efforts to make Mia cancel didn't work. She rarely begged off unless it was necessary. That she'd done it tonight was understandable. Getting things straight with Joe definitely counted as necessary.

Leaning back against the counter, Ella took a cautious sip of her drink. Which was right when her phone beeped. *Finally*. Though why Mia would text rather than call she didn't know.

Ella swiped the cell from the counter. Her brow furrowed, because whoever had sent her a message wasn't her sister. It had come from an unfamiliar number.

You wouldn't be avoiding me, would you? it read.

Feeling her brows draw together, Ella set her mug on the counter. *Who's this?* she asked, typing fast.

Three dots danced on the screen. *Viper.*

Her pulse jumped just as her insides seized. She blinked at the screen, shaking her head. What the hell? Her demon's brows arched in both surprise and curiosity.

There was no way he should have her contact details. How did *that* come about? And would the little bubble of excitement skipping around her belly fuck right off, please?

She texted: *How did you get this number?*

I have my sources.

Oh, how very mysterious. She was about to request some elaboration, but then more words appeared on the screen.

You usually come to my pool hall on Fridays. Tonight, you were a no-show.

And he apparently thought that she was going out of her way to avoid seeing him. Not the case, but she didn't need to explain that to him. Didn't need to say *anything* to him. In fact, she should end this conversation, block his number, and go on about her evening.

It would be smart. It would also drive home the point that she had no interest in conversing with him. To continue the conversation would be … well, not quite *flirting*. But it would encourage him, wouldn't it?

Yeah, she should definitely block his number.

What Ella instead did was settle at the dining table, her phone in hand, and type a response: *I'm not avoiding you. My sister has a situation that needs her immediate attention.*

Setting her phone down on the table, she sighed at herself for having such poor self-control. Ella couldn't say what it was about this guy that made her go against her own good sense, but there seemed to be no changing it.

At least her demon wasn't passing judgement. As it happened, the entity quite liked that he'd gone through the trouble of getting her number. It liked the idea of being pursued by someone as dark and powerful as him.

If Ella was honest, she could admit to herself that she did, too.

When she'd seen nothing of him following that night at the Red Rooms, she'd concluded that the whole "I'll come for you if you don't come to me" claim wasn't something that she'd needed to take seriously.

She'd spent days telling herself that she didn't care; that it was for the best. But in truth, she'd found it slightly disappointing. Not shocking, though. After all, why would he need to pursue Ella when women no doubt regularly flung themselves at him?

Her gut went tight at the thought of that.

Another message popped up on the screen: *Anything I can help with?*

Ella double-blinked, surprised by the offer. The Black Saints were an exclusive bunch. They made alliances, but they generally didn't get involved in other people's business. Or so she'd been told.

She picked up her cell and texted: *Thanks, but Mia has it covered.* Pausing, Ella nibbled on her lower lip. *I'm not sure if I should be annoyed that you went ahead and got my number without my permission.*

More dots bopped on her screen. *I couldn't ask your permission without talking to you, and you haven't come to me yet.*

Ella swallowed, her stomach dropping. *Why would I?*

You want to.

"Arrogant bastard," she muttered. "A *correct* arrogant bastard."

Why fight it?

Sighing, she typed: *I told you, I'm not into meaningless sex. I get that my behavior the other night might have given a different impression, but that was an aberration for me.*

Sex doesn't have to be meaningless, Ella.

Well, that was true. She'd had flings that, though they hadn't been serious or stepping stones to relationships, hadn't been meaningless. They'd been fun, light, and even made her smile when she thought back on them.

But he wasn't asking for a fling. Or, at least, it didn't seem that way. He just wanted them to roll in the sack again.

Right then, another message appeared: *Come to me.*

"Why do I have to be the one who goes anywhere?" she grumbled even as she texted: *Do you do this a lot? Text women demanding they go tend to your needs?*

The phone in her hand began to ring, his number showing on the screen.

She stilled. "Oh, shit." Her demon chuckled, amused that he had Ella all befuddled.

Clearing her throat, she thumbed the screen and answered, "Hello?"

"Baby." The word was low. Soft. An amused reprimand. "I'm not demanding anything of you. I want you to come to me of your own free will."

It was wrong that she was developing a crush on his voice.

"Sure, I could instead kiss your consent right out of you. But then you'd tell yourself you got swept along for the ride again; that you had another moment of weakness."

Ella felt her lips flatten. Yes, fine, that was pretty much exactly what she'd do. "Does it really matter when all you want is a fuck anyway?"

"Who says that's all I want from you?"

A frown pulled at her brow.

"There are many things I'd like to do to you, Ella—it'll take more than one night to get through them." A pause. "There's no other man in your life right now, is there?"

"No," she replied, even though she had the feeling that he already knew the answer.

"Then what's the problem, other than my being one of the Fallen, which doesn't need to have any real bearing on anything unless you want it to?"

Well ... she supposed that was true. She was *letting* it be a factor, but she didn't have to. Not really. Particularly in her demon's opinion.

"Give in to me, Ella," he murmured.

She squeezed her eyes shut. "Stop talking. Really, just ... stop."

"Why? Because you're tempted to do what I ask?"

"No."

A rumbly, deliciously sexy chuckle drifted down the line. "Liar." A soft, teasing statement.

Yup. She was a total liar.

A double-beep sounded, signaling that another call was trying to come through. Ella peeked at the phone screen and then told him, "My sister's trying to call me. I need to answer."

"All right, I'll get off the phone. I'll give you a few more days to come to me. If that doesn't happen, I *will* come to you. There's only so long I'm prepared to wait." He hung up.

Deciding she'd process *that* little tidbit later, she answered Mia's call. "Hey, how did it go?" The long sigh that came down the line raised Ella's hackles.

"Not great," Mia mumbled. "I don't know what I expected the subject of the 'real talk' to be, but I definitely wasn't expecting to hear that he's met someone."

Ella felt her mouth fall open. "*What?*"

"It's his boss' new assistant, apparently. He ended our fling so he could start something with her."

Ella did a slow blink, utterly shocked. "I'm . . . I have no words."

"I was a little speechless myself," Mia muttered, her tone flat.

"Why didn't he tell you this before now?"

"He claims he thought it'd hurt me, so he kept it to himself. But now he feels bad about lying to me, so he decided to cough up the truth."

As a thought occurred to Ella, she narrowed her eyes. "Did he touch her while he was with you?"

"He swears he didn't. At one time, I would have taken him at his word. But now? Now I feel let down by him, and that's new for me."

"What did you say to him?"

"Not a lot. I was too stunned. Just before I left, I said I hoped it all worked out for him."

"And, is that true?" Ella carefully asked.

"Yes. I totally get why he'd stop wasting time on a fling and instead go after the woman he wanted. I'm not upset about that. But I don't like the way he handled this whole thing. He could have been honest with me right from the start, or at least not acted all distant. I'm his anchor, for Christ's sake. You'd think he'd be too protective of me to mess me around like that."

"Yeah, you'd think so."

"I've said this before, I know, but you lucked out with Luka. I know he's no one's idea of a teddy bear, but you can rely on him. That's worth its weight in gold."

"It is, and I don't take it for granted." Ella leaned back in her chair. "How come you waited so long to call me? Was it a long conversation, or did you need time to calm down?"

"I was a little pissed with Joe for being a dingus, so I hit a club on the way home and hooked up with a guy who swore he'd fuck my anger out of me."

Well. "That's quite a job you set him," said Ella, feeling her mouth kick up. Mia's nerves weren't easy to settle, even with great sex. "Tell me more about this dude."

"I will when you tell me who *you* hooked up with at the Red Rooms a few nights ago."

Not happening. "A lady never tells."

"Lady. Ha. That's funny."

Ella frowned. "Hey, I'm all grace and manners and serenity."

"Sure you are," Mia mocked.

"Now, seriously, are you sure you're okay about this Joe thing?"

"I wouldn't say I'm *okay*. Especially because he seemed to think I'd be heartbroken. Yet, had he turned up at my apartment—my safe space, where I'm most comfortable—to reveal something that he thought would hit me right in the heart? No. He'd requested that *I* go to *him*. Like he couldn't be bothered making the journey even to make it easier on me. And it's just an extra kick to the gut."

Ella shook her head hard, as furious as she was stunned. "I don't get why he's being such a jackass." In the past, he'd been intensely protective toward Mia. Loyal and reliable. A good friend and confidant. "Apparently, he's forgotten that you're anchors or something."

"I could honestly think I've done something to upset him. But we haven't argued or anything. We didn't end the fling on a bad note. *He'd* been the one to cut it short, not me. And with good reason, since he had his sights set on someone else. Where's my crime, please?"

Nowhere to be seen.

"I had to leave fast or my demon would have surfaced and . . . well, it wouldn't have been pretty. It's a little calmer now."

"Thanks to the guy you're not going to tell me about?"

"Yes. Thanks to him."

"You're seriously not going to tell me who it was?"

"Not until you give me more deets on who fucked you in the Red Rooms."

Yeah, that wouldn't be happening. "Fine. I didn't really want to know anyway."

A cackle. "Liar."

The one word echoed Viper's earlier accusation, bringing the memory of his voice—oh, she was pretty sure she could come just listening to him talk—to the forefront of her mind.

I'll give you a few more days to come to me. If that doesn't happen, I will come to you.

Going by the way that simple promise riled up her hormones, Ella couldn't honestly say she'd resist him if he did.

CHAPTER TWELVE

"She's going to steal my soul."

Ella stared at the human male opposite her, words failing her. Neve had texted his address earlier, adding, *This one is weird even for me. I leave it in your capable hands.*

Ella had to admit she'd been curious. And so here she was, sitting at his kitchen island while he stood on the other side of it. Brock was his name. Only twenty years old, he still lived with his parents and was home for his college break.

He was also presently a nervous wreck—biting at his lips, rubbing his nape, tugging at his tousled brown hair, restlessly rocking back and forth on his heels.

"She comes every night," he said, a tremor to his voice. "It doesn't matter what I do, it doesn't matter that I removed all the mirrors and that I've covered all reflective surfaces." Desperation glinted in his slanted, green eyes. "She always finds a way in."

"Who?"

He hesitated before blurting out, "Bloody Mary."

Oh, Lord. Her demon shot him a look of contempt. It urged Ella to leave; felt they had better shit to do and bigger things to deal with. Like tracking their annoying pen pal, or even heading off to see Viper, who she hadn't heard from since he'd called two days ago.

"You don't believe me," the human mumbled, a self-depreciating smile curving his mouth.

"I don't think you're lying." She believed *something* was going on. But the real Bloody Mary had merely been a witch who died a long, long time ago. The legend that had built around her wasn't something to be taken seriously. "All sorts of things happen in this world that we don't understand," she added vaguely.

Mollified, he shoved a hand into his hair. "Neve said you can break curses. She said anyone could do it, really, if they had training in herbs and rituals and stuff. I don't. And I'm going to die unless you help me."

She tilted her head. "How is it that you came to be cursed?" She almost stumbled over the latter word, quite sure no such issue was at play here.

A flush crept up his neck and face. "It was my own fault. You don't mess with this kind of stuff, I know that. But I didn't believe it would really work. I said her name in front of a mirror six times while holding a candle."

"And she appeared?"

"Not in the mirror right then. She came that night. She comes every night. Each time, she moves that *little* bit closer." He swallowed, absently fisting his tee, fear a flickering flame in his gaze. "Soon, she'll be close enough to touch me. Then it's game over."

Her demon gave an exaggerated eyeroll as it let out a sigh weighted with boredom. "When was it that you invoked her?"

"Five days ago. It was a dare. I was at a party, and someone dared me to do it."

Ella squinted. "This someone. Who was it?"

"Oh, my ex-girlfriend, PJ." He waved off her interest, as if the mention of his ex didn't matter. He gave Ella a pleading look. "Can you help me?"

"What time does Mary usually come here?"

"Always midnight."

Ella planted her lower arms on the surface of the island. "Okay, here's what we'll do. You'll pack some things and go to a hotel for the night. I'll perform a blessing here that will undo the curse."

Relief crossed his face first, but then his brow wrinkled. "I can't be here for that?"

Nope, but such a response would make him suspicious, so she replied, "You can if you want. I'm just thinking you might wish to skip having to smell all the herbs and listen to lots of chanting. It's not a quick or quiet process. The scents can give people headaches, and you're unlikely to get any sleep."

An O shaped his mouth. "Well, I'm happy to sleep elsewhere. But . . . are you sure she won't come to wherever I am?"

"I'll have broken the curse before midnight, but I'll stay here until then. Text me after midnight, let me know if she has come to you. If she has, I'll drive straight to your hotel." Ella rattled off her number, which he saved to his cell, and then slipped off her stool. "I'm going to get my ritual bag out of the trunk. You go pack whatever you need for your stay at the hotel."

Once both held their respective bag, Brock said, "I'll leave you to it." He cleared his throat. "Thanks for this. It will definitely work?"

"It will work," she assured him.

He didn't seem entirely convinced, but he did appear hopeful. After he'd driven away, Ella tossed what was really just an overnight bag on the sofa. She always kept it in her car, just in case a job required her to stick around awhile. It did contain herbs and stuff, but they were really just for show.

Following the directions he'd earlier given her, she went upstairs to Brock's bedroom to check it out. It would have been easy enough to identify without his help, what with all the sports posters, the dirty male laundry, and the collage of pictures featuring him and many other people his age.

Ella eyed his closet doors. They were slatted, so she'd be able to spy through them if there was enough space in there. A quick look showed that, yes, she could fit. When the time approached that Mary would show, Ella could hide in there to wait.

She'd just shut the closet doors when her phone beeped. Pulling it out of her pocket, she glanced at the screen. Her pulse leaped. She had a text from Viper.

Ignoring the butterflies fluttering excitedly in her stomach—someone really needed to shoot the little fuckers—she pressed the pad of her thumb on the screen to unlock it and then opened the message.

A redhead walked into my club just now. For a moment, I thought it was you. Almost went over there, thinking you'd finally come to me.

The idea of him approaching another woman shouldn't have embedded a shard of jealousy in her chest. Frustrated at herself, she typed: *Maybe you should still go over there. I'm sure she'd see to your needs.*

A reply came fast: *I want you.*

Her demon's mouth curled. Ella didn't smile—she was too busy cursing her belly for doing a happy little flip. *I never would have guessed, you hid it well.*

I'm subtle, I know.

Her lips quirked, the traitors.

What are you doing now?

Ella left the bedroom as she responded: *Nothing very interesting. I'm on a job.*

So late at night?

It happens sometimes.

Stop by the club on your way home.

Narrowing her eyes, she jogged down the stairs. *You're a tenacious bastard, aren't you?* And, honestly, all that tenaciousness was annoyingly attractive while directed at her this way.

When I want something bad enough, yes.

In the living room, she sank onto the sofa. *You've already had me.*

Three dots danced. *I want you again. Stop by the club.*

She groaned, far too tempted despite her better judgement. *I won't finish up here until a little after twelve anyway.*

I'll still be here.

Squeezing her eyes shut, she pinched the bridge of her nose. She was so close to caving. So very, very close. And she would bet he knew it.

Dropping her hand back to her lap, she opened her eyes to find a new message: *Come to me, Ella.*

Oh, fuck him sideways. Because every time he said that, every time he coaxed her that way and she imagined him saying it in that gravelly voice, parts of her went tingly and warm.

She needed to end this conversation. *I have to go. I have work to do. Go do club stuff, whatever that is.*

When no reply came, Ella plonked her cell on the coffee table. The man was a sexual nuisance, in her opinion.

Her demon didn't agree. As a matter of fact, it felt she was stupid for not just succumbing to temptation already. But then, by nature, it had no problem doing such a thing.

At this point, honestly, Ella was struggling to hold out. Mostly because it seemed senseless when she was pretty sure she'd give in eventually.

It wasn't really him being an angel that made her hesitate. Not anymore. Nor was it that he was a practical stranger. It was how unnerving it was that he could so easily sway her.

It was like he knew what mental buttons to press, what words to use, what physical hot spots to target.

She had been braced to resist him at the club . . . but then he'd crowded her, touched her, whispered to her. All kinds of sexual levers had gotten flicked, and then she'd found herself thinking a fuck in the dark with a relative stranger wouldn't be so bad.

She could have a firm opinion in mind . . . but he could blow holes in it. Could have her looking at things from a different angle; could make her second guess her stance. And then she'd be thinking that maybe it wasn't a big deal for angels and demons to mix.

She had been set on ignoring any further advances on his part . . . but then he'd begun texting and calling her, flattering her demon with his attention, luring her with little phrases that went straight to her core. And now she was thinking it wouldn't really be so bad to go get herself some.

Ugh.

Inwardly shaking her head at herself, Ella inhaled deeply. She wouldn't think about it anymore tonight. She needed to focus on the present situation.

She flicked a look at the wall clock. It would be a few hours before Mary arrived and Ella would need to 'lift the curse'. She figured she could watch some TV while she waited.

Ella switched it on and pulled up a movie on the streaming service. She had no intention of falling asleep. But her eyelids became heavy and she eventually nodded off . . .

Everleigh paced up and down in the kitchen of her home, refusing to look at the man who claimed to love her yet seemed set on keeping her at arm's length. "Why don't you trust me?" She heard the hurt lacing her voice.

"I do trust you," he promised her. "I don't trust many people, but I do trust you. I wouldn't have told you who I am if I didn't."

Yeah, learning that had been a shock. Especially when she'd assumed he was just an average angel. Halting, Everleigh turned to him. "Then why not tell me about the curse as well?"

"I already have."

"No, you told me a curse would befall you when you left heaven. You have not explained what that means." She'd asked and asked, but he'd evaded the question each time. "It can't be worse than what my imagination has conjured up."

He gave her a sober look. "Don't be so sure."

"There's only one way either of us can be sure." She crossed to him. "Tell me about it."

A resigned sigh slid out of him, and his shoulders lowered. "Something happens to angels who fall, Everleigh. It changes them. Twists them. Turns them into a kind of monster."

A loud beep pierced her sleep, making a dozen cracks spiderweb through the scene in her mind. She groaned, feeling her dream slip away image by image, word by word, thought by thought.

Ella opened her eyes, her brows meeting. She rubbed at her throat. It felt thick with emotion, as if she'd been sad during the dream. She frowned, striving to dredge up snippets of it. None came to her, annoyingly.

Realizing it had been the arrival of another text message that had woken her, Ella sat up and reached for her phone. The message was from Neve: *Is Brock's situation as weird as it seemed?*

Checking the time, she swore. It was 11:45pm. She had fifteen minutes before Mary would appear. *I'll soon find out,* she texted.

Ella tossed her cell back on the table, pushed off the sofa, and then went upstairs. Inside Brock's bedroom, she confined herself in his closet. There she waited, still and quiet, alert for any noise.

It was when 12am hit that she heard it. The *slightest* buzzing sound. It was coming from the en suite bathroom, and she recognized it as being the sign of a portal opening. Not one that enabled people to travel from realm to realm, only from spot to spot within *this* realm.

Ella would need to act quickly to subdue her visitor or they'd escape her clutches by opening another portal. She called to her magick, not yet bringing it to the surface of her palms but letting it dance beneath her skin. The magick would otherwise be seen and heard; would glow through the door slats and slice through the silence with all its crackling and zapping.

The light patter of bare feet on tile came next. Each step was slow, deliberate, taunting. The bathroom door lazily creaked open, and mist spilled out of the room.

Mary then came into view. Petite. Dark-haired. Clothed in only a ratty nightgown that, like her hair and every visible inch of her skin, was streaked with blood.

Ella acted fast. She burst out of the closet and unleased her magick, chanting quietly as the shimmering ribbons of red, green, and yellow rushed at Mary and snapped around her like a full-body straightjacket.

"The fuck?" the newcomer burst out.

Ella gave her a polite smile. "Hello." She walked over to Mary, easily noticing the spell that clung to her. Ella didn't need to take any time to 'read', it, she'd seen many such spells before.

She focused on unraveling the magickal threads, picking at them; unwinding them; tearing them. Finally, they fell away . . . and the vision before her altered in an instant. The petite woman's face morphed into another, her lank black hair turned a shiny golden-blonde, her old-style gown became pajamas dotted with tiny sheep, and every streak and dot of blood vanished from her body.

"Nice glamor spell," Ella praised. "You're PJ, Brock's ex, I'm guessing. And a demon to boot." A fellow incantor, as it happened. "But I imagine he doesn't know that last part."

PJ bared her teeth, struggling to free herself from Ella's magickal hold. A hold so secure that it prevented PJ's own magick from rushing to her rescue. "Let me go."

"Just why did you want him to believe that he'd invoked a vengeful spirit?" asked Ella.

PJ jutted out her chin. "He deserved it. He fooled around with my best friend, and then he *lied* to me about it."

Ah. "That makes him an asshole for sure. But all this? A little melodramatic, don't you think?"

PJ's ears turned red.

"Look, I don't judge those who seek revenge. I do the same myself. But he hired my services, and I don't let down my clients."

"You can't make me stop."

Ella gave her a hard smile. "Of course I can. I wouldn't have taken the job if I wasn't sure I could deliver on my promise to ensure the 'curse' is undone. For instance, I can make it so that no glamor spells—whether cast by you or anyone else—ever work on you again."

PJ's lips parted, a reluctant admiration flaring in her eyes. "No way."

"Yep way. Is he worth that?"

Her shoulders slumped. "No," she mumbled.

"Don't you think you've scared him enough? Do you really see a need to drag it out any longer?"

"He really pissed me off," she groused.

"I can tell. But I'd say you've had your revenge. And surely you have better things to do with your evenings than come here every night. You're giving him way too much of your time."

PJ grunted, a *that's true* look on her face. "Fine, I'll stop."

Ella flicked a hand, freeing the other woman from her magickal hold, and then held out the aforementioned hand. "I'm going to need you to shake on it."

PJ blinked, realization dawning on her. "You're going to bind me to my word, aren't you?"

"Correct."

"Devious. Brilliantly so." She placed her hand in Ella's. "I really don't want to like you, but it's happening anyway."

Ella's magick sparked from her to PJ, who solemnly swore she'd leave Brock alone from now on. The magick then sank into PJ's skin, stamping the promise to her body; ensuring it could never be broken.

As always when it came to spells, Ella tangled it with a few others so that it would take a *lot* of time, sweat, magick, and incantors to ever unravel it. She liked giving such layers of protection to her spells.

Once PJ left through another portal, Ella closed the closet doors, nabbed her things from downstairs, and noticed she'd received a text from Brock to say that Mary hadn't showed at his hotel room. Ella informed him that she hadn't turned up at his home either—technically not a lie, since it had been PJ, not Mary—and so 'the curse had been lifted'. She also sent a message to Neve, informing her of all that had happened.

Driving away from Brock's house, Ella debated on what to do next. She wasn't feeling all that tired. Maybe she could take a hot bath, drag on some comfy sweats, and read a book in bed.

Or you could go get laid. You know you want to.

Ella gritted her teeth. Okay, yes, she did. While she *liked* that Viper wanted her official consent rather than to seduce her into caving, the idea of toddling off to the Red Rooms to see him . . . it felt a little too much like answering a summons.

As an alternative occurred to her, she lifted her brows. She could instead go to the dive bar he owned. He wouldn't be there, but he could join her there. Then he'd basically be meeting her halfway in this 'come to me or I'll come to you' thing.

Her demon smiled, totally in support of that option.

Reaching a turn that would take her to the club that doubled as the entrance to the Underground, Ella tightened her grip on the steering wheel, warring with herself.

She took the turn. Her demon's smile widened.

Ella parked the car, headed down to the Underground, and went straight to the dive bar. Stepping inside, she was greeted by the scents of yeasty beer, wood polish, spicy foods, and liquors.

Like the pool hall she frequented with Mia, the bar was dimly lit and featured some slot machines. One might be tempted to term this place dreary or in need of a makeover. But the choice of dated and eclectic décor was deliberate. It had an old-style, well-worn charm that she preferred over glamor and glitz.

Music played on the old-fashioned jukebox, mingling with the sounds of chatter and laughter. Unlike most other bars in the Underground, the dive was small and rarely cluttered with people. The drinks were cheap, the food menu was simple, and the clientele were mostly regulars.

She weaved her way around the heavy wooden tables as she began making her way to the bar. More than its usual skeleton crew was manning it this evening. Necessary, since not a single stool there was empty.

Feeling eyes on her, Ella looked to see the blonde from the Red Rooms staring at her. No, *glaring* at her. Huh. It appeared she still wasn't happy that Viper had paid Ella any attention.

Unbothered, Ella shrugged it off and finished crossing to the bar.

Foam spat out of a beer tap, making the dark-skinned bartender swear beneath his breath. "Omen, need you to change this keg over here," he grumpily called out. His blue gaze slid to Ella and . . . changed. Sharpened.

She pointed at the fridge full of beer bottles, preferring that brand. "I'll have one of those and some sweet potato fries," she told him.

He acknowledged the order with a tip of his chin. Moments later, he plonked her drink on the bar. "Fries will be ready in fifteen minutes."

She curled her hand around the bottle. "Thanks."

Ella claimed a corner booth and pulled out her phone. She texted Viper: *Your bar's pretty busy tonight.*

There. That was pretty much a hint that he had the option of meeting her here.

If, however, Viper hadn't responded by the time she'd finished her fries, she'd head on home. If he *did* respond and then subsequently drag his ass here . . . well, then, she'd hopefully get fucked good and proper.

Time would tell.

Viper stared at the steel door as growls rumbled from the angel trapped behind it. An angel who was pounding his fists on it with preternatural strength. If it weren't for the wards securing the door closed, Merchant would have knocked it down for certain.

It was this very room, down in the basement of their clubhouse, where any brothers who went into bloodlust were confined. There was no other choice. Not when they would kill indiscriminately and glut themselves on the blood of anyone they came across.

"I never saw any signs that he was going into bloodlust," said Prophet, who'd been the one to contact Viper and inform him that Merchant had turned.

"It took him fast and hard, completely out of nowhere," added Sting.

"Happens like that sometimes," Viper reminded them.

A red haze would abruptly fall over your vision and flood your mind, shoving down everything but your predatory instincts; turning your thoughts, needs, and wants feral and rabid. Several days would pass before you snapped out of it, and you'd have no memory of what happened during that time.

Blackjack folded his arms. "I suppose we should be grateful that we usually get enough of a warning that we can lock ourselves away before we hurt anyone. But I ain't feeling grateful, I'm feeling pissed that this is our reality."

Viper narrowed his eyes. "Do you regret falling?"

Blackjack seemed surprised by the question. "Shit, no. I just hate that we were lumbered with this curse. We thought we could handle it, thought we understood how it would be, thought we were prepared."

"I don't think you can really prepare for this life," hedged Prophet. "Do you ever regret making the decision to fall, V?"

"No. It was chipping away at everything that made me who I am; chipping away at every bit of my entity's innocence. I was on my way to becoming like Ophaniel when I found Ella. She saved me. And if I hadn't fallen, I wouldn't be able to make her fully mine." Viper would pay any price to keep her at his side.

"I don't have any regrets," said Sting, idly swinging one fist into his open palm. "This curse just makes me resent the Uppers even more. The last thing I'm itching to do is go back up there."

Jester nodded with a grunt. "We had no life before. Not really.

Our choices weren't our own. Individuality was discouraged. We were numbers within a legion, not people."

"Any of our other brothers ever mention regrets?" Viper asked no one in particular.

"Nah," replied Prophet. "Not now that they've had a taste of freedom."

Viper studied him closely. "And you?"

"I don't wish I hadn't fallen. But I do wish it hadn't come to that; I wish life was different in the upper realm." Prophet teleported out of the basement.

"He's lying," Jester stated.

Darko sighed. "You think everyone is either lying or planning to lie to you."

Jester arched a brow. "You reckon I'm wrong?"

"No, Prophet definitely lied. I'm just saying, you expect it of everyone."

"Well, if people didn't bullshit me so often, I wouldn't."

Razor materialized, his gaze flying straight to the steel door that was still taking a serious beating. "I heard that Merchant had to be contained."

"The bloodlust hit him quickly," Sting told him. "He went from laughing at a joke to almost choking on his own breath while the red haze took over. We managed to restrain him before he could hurt anyone."

Razor twisted his mouth. "He didn't seem himself yesterday. I asked if something was wrong; he said no."

Darko frowned. "He would have said if he'd felt bloodlust creeping up on him, so it must have been something else bothering him."

"Or he lied," Jester put in, wrenching a sigh out of Darko.

Razor turned to fully face Viper. "Just wanted to let you know that Ella's at the dive bar. She's alone."

A spark of pleasure coursed through Viper. She'd come to him. Finally.

He dug out his cell, intending to tell her that he was on his way. It was only then he saw that she'd texted him—he hadn't heard the beeping of his phone over all the noise.

Your bar's pretty busy tonight.

Yeah, that was more or less an invitation right there. He replied: *I'd better come see for myself just how busy.*

Darko's brow pinched. "I thought you wanted her to meet you at the Red Rooms."

"I asked her to," said Viper, pocketing his phone. "This is her coming to me on her own terms, and wanting me to meet her in the middle."

"It has to have killed you to stay away the past week," Sting commented.

It had, but he'd needed her to make the informed decision to allow him into her life. He could have pushed his way into it by seducing her—she would have let him, because then she wouldn't have had to take any responsibility for having a fallen angel in her bed.

"Playing the waiting game clearly worked," said Darko. "Bet you're glad it's over."

"Fucking ecstatic," said Viper, a sense of purposeful determination filling him. Now he could go get his woman.

CHAPTER THIRTEEN

Ella felt him before she saw him. Something about Viper's presence made the air feel charged. A little electric.

Chewing on one of her fries, she instinctively looked to her right. He was stalking toward her table, his expression determined. The gorgeous, sensual, badass sight of him made her hormones tingle in excitement. Her body *instantly* responded to all that natural authority and raw sexuality.

He'd gotten here sooner than she'd expected. Either he had already been at the Underground when he'd texted her, or he had an ability that allowed him to travel fast.

Or ... maybe he had wings, though she doubted it. They would have been clipped from the fall.

Halting before her table, he inclined his head. "Ella," he said, his tone humming with a note of sexual invitation.

"Viper," she greeted.

"You came. Sort of," he said, a tiny upward lift to his mouth.

"I did. Sort of."

A hotly sexual gleam in his eyes, he slid onto the cushioned bench opposite her. "How'd the job go?" The question was so casual and light, totally at contrast to the intense *I am going to fuck the holy hell out of you* look he pinned her with.

Her belly fluttered. "Smoothly."

He slowly leaned forward—the simple move making an effervescent tension tauten the air—and braced his lower arms on the table. "Tell me about it," he urged, his voice low and deep and intimate as it brushed over her skin.

She wasn't sure how he did that. Maybe it was that his power bled into his voice, making it seem tangible. But sometimes, when he spoke to her a certain way, she honestly felt like his voice touched her. Stroked her. Teased her. As if it had vocal fingertips.

"A human thought that Bloody Mary was on his ass. Turns out it was his ex—a demon, though he didn't know that—using a glamor spell to fake her appearance."

His mouth quirked. "I take it you've put a stop to the problem." Not a question. A confident statement.

"I have." She tipped her chin at her box of fries in invitation.

A little warmth leaked into his gaze, mingling with the sexual promise there. He took a fry and shoved it into his mouth.

As she bit into her own, his eyes drifted down to her lips. Stared. Heated. Darted back up to meet her gaze. "You get jobs like that a lot?" he asked.

She might have told him to stop with the small talk, except . . . this wasn't mere chit-chat. His interest was genuine. He was also enjoying letting the tension simmer. She had to admit, it was ratcheting up her nerves.

"I've consulted with people who think either they, or someone around them, has been cursed in some way. But Bloody Mary? That was a new element." She cocked her head. "How did the club stuff go?"

"My night was pretty boring until I got your text." He hummed. "I should have guessed you'd show up here so I'd have to meet you halfway."

"Why should you have guessed? You don't know me."

"I'm good at reading people." He dipped his head toward hers. "You should come with me." It wasn't a suggestion. It was a lure, plain and simple.

There was something so deeply compelling about his tone. She could almost think magick was at work. But there was no spell, no manipulation. Just a combination of his natural magnetism and the weight of sexual chemistry pressing down on her.

"Where would we go?"

The corner of his mouth tipped up. "Somewhere I can fuck you blind."

She touched her lower lip with her tongue, her insides doing a happy jig; her demon smirking its approval.

"You on board with that?"

"If you'll make it worth my while."

"That I can do."

"I'm quite sure you can, since you've done it before."

At her capitulation, waves of relief, triumph, and pure male satisfaction rushed through Viper. His entity grinned, smug as a motherfucker. It wanted to take her to the bar's office and bend her over the desk there. Viper had other plans.

Raised voices rang through the air, and he quickly realized two demons were raring to start a fight. Wanting Ella away from the trouble, he slid out of the booth and took a single step toward her. "Come," he bid, holding out his hand.

Standing, she took it easily. The lack of hesitation on her part pleased Viper. It wasn't quite an indication of trust, but it illustrated that she felt comfortable with him; that she was completely sure of her decision to give herself to him.

As he tugged her a little closer, the scent of her magick wrapped around him like perfume—heady, feminine, spiced with power. The urge to dip his head into the crook of her neck and drag that scent all the way into his lungs near took him over.

Instead, he led her behind the bar and away from prying eyes, not wanting others to see as he teleported them out of there—he didn't broadcast his abilities. When they abruptly appeared in his bedroom, she jerked slightly as their surroundings changed.

"You can teleport. This explains how you got to the bar so fast." She scanned their new surroundings, her gaze brushing over the bare white walls and basic oak furnishings. "Are we at your clubhouse?"

Viper didn't move his eyes from her as he shed his jacket. "Yes." He tossed it on the armchair.

She flicked a look at the large bed. "This is your room?"

"It is."

"You're surprisingly neat."

Viper noticed her pulse beating fast in her throat. He found that little show of nerves delicious. It made his dick—already full and aching—throb in the confines of his jeans; made the predatory streak in his entity come to life.

"I'm gonna take a guess at something," he said. "You're used to taking the lead in the bedroom."

She stilled, her eyes going slitted. "Why would you think that?"

"At the club, it set you off-balance that I was so forward and touched you without invitation, but you liked it. Liked when I took over and fucked you as hard as I did."

"It was all right, I guess."

He chuckled. "You liked it."

A huff. "Fine, I did. What of it?"

"And I'm right, you're used to taking the lead?"

Ella sighed heavily, admitting, "Yes." She'd somehow always found herself in bed with guys who were careful and tentative. While there was nothing wrong with 'careful and tentative', it had frustrated her to have to speed them along, to have to give them direction. She didn't need to do any of that with Viper, and it had allowed her to sink into the moment.

"I'm not a man who likes to be led. That said, I'm not looking for you to be submissive. The fact is I will take over because that's just how I am, but you can handle that however you want."

In other words, he would dominantly assert himself—it was part of the fabric of his personality—but he wasn't expecting her to roll over and obey.

"I wouldn't ask you to trust me so soon, but you can trust yourself. And you feel sure I won't harm you, don't you?"

Strangely, yes, she did. Though she barely knew him, she had this utter surety that she was safe with him. It made no rational sense. Especially when her defenses weren't usually so lax around others. "Yes."

Satisfaction bled into his eyes. "Good. Now, quick warning: I can get rough. Intense. And I fucking know I'm gonna be greedy when it comes to you. But you're in no danger with me. You tell me to stop, I stop."

"I believe you."

Something in him seemed to settle at that. With a satisfied nod, he took three steps back. "Clothes off, Ella. I want to see every single inch of you."

Not at all shy, Ella peeled off her t-shirt and threw it on the armchair where his jacket rested. He slowly circled her as she stripped, each step he took fluid and predatory.

Behind her, he said, "No other woman has ever been in this room."

Surprise pricked her, making her pause in removing her bra. "Then why bring me here?"

"Because"—a mouth brushed her ear—"I want to fuck you in my bed."

The words fell like sexual bullets. Little bumps rising on her skin, she flung her bra on the chair. After removing her panties, she kicked them aside, leaving her naked.

He did another slow circuit around her. Somehow, she could feel the intensity building in him. Feel his sexual energy heightening and coiling and twisting.

As he came to stand before her, his eyes darkened, flaring with sheer avarice. He fisted the back of his tee and yanked it off, baring inked skin that covered smooth, taut muscle. He tossed his tee on the armchair, crooked his finger at her, and pointed to the floor in front of him. "Come."

The little order might have rankled, except she knew he didn't expect obedience. Knew she could instead stand here and make *him* close the distance between them. But she had no interest in engaging in a power struggle.

What she wanted was to get thoroughly fucked as soon as possible, which meant not delaying things merely to make a point. She didn't *need* to make that point. He'd already been clear that he didn't expect total compliance.

Ella moved to him, watching masculine contentment flare in his eyes. Those twin blue pools of devastating intensity lowered to her mouth; stared at it with such hunger it caused her belly to clench.

His gaze flicked back to hers, the storm of energy inside him dancing behind his eyes. "You'll look so pretty choking on my cock," he said, his voice a mere whisper that nonetheless held a sensual punch. "We'll save that for later."

She gasped as he tangled a hand in her hair and wrenched her head back.

"The things I could do to you ... *Will* do to you ..." He caught her lower lip between both of his and gave it a tug. "By the time this night is over, you're gonna know one thing."

"What's that?"

"You'll know what it is to feel owned." A low growl scraping his throat, Viper closed his mouth over hers. Once again, that feeling of rightness clicked into place. Possessiveness surged up inside him and swallowed him whole.

He dragged her against him, not wanting an inch of space between them. He didn't stop eating at her mouth. Couldn't. He settled in and feasted.

Fire blew through his veins, scorched his blood, and hardened his cock even more. He skated his hands over her, rough and proprietary as he stroked, squeezed, and shaped.

Finally freeing her mouth, he abruptly hefted her up and set her on the bed. She looked perfect there. His own personal feast. And very much where she belonged.

A pretty flush stained her skin, sweeping up the valley between those full breasts he intended to get his hands on. Fuck, he wanted to drink from those breasts. From her throat. Her inner thighs. Anywhere and everywhere.

He wouldn't—couldn't—do it tonight, but soon.

Glassy eyes watched him as he moved to the foot of the bed. "Fuck me. Now."

"Not yet." Planting his fists on the bed, Viper curled over her and captured her nipple with his mouth. He suckled, licked around it, dragged his teeth over it, suckled again. He drank in every moan and whimper and gasp.

He moved lower, leaving suckling kisses along her belly, not bothering to check his teeth; wanting her to feel the sting.

"Enough playing," she hoarsely ordered.

"I'm not playing. I'm indulging."

"Indulge later." Ella pressed her nails into his shoulders, feeling a little desperate. She was hot. Too hot. And more than ready to come.

He ignored that and went to his knees on the floor. Then his mouth was on her pussy and, fuck it all, did he have to be good at everything? Her eyes fell shut as he devoured her. He pulled her under with every wicked swipe or pump of his tongue, every light scrape or nip of his teeth, every soft rhythmic suckle on her clit.

Hot zings of sensation skipped over her skin and set fire to her nerve-endings. It wasn't long before her release hit her, sending white-hot bliss winding through her body.

Straightening, Viper deftly tackled his fly one-handed, tore open a small packet, and rolled on a condom. He joined her on the bed, lowered his body over hers, and lodged the broad tip of his cock inside her. "Believe me when I say I am going to fucking defile you tonight."

Ella flinched as he crammed every thick inch of his shaft into her pussy with one brutal thrust. *Jesus.* She clung to his shoulders and wrapped her legs around his hips.

"Fuck, you feel good."

"You're not moving. Why aren't you moving?"

Because Viper was battling his entity for supremacy. It wanted to surface, take over, take *her* over.

You'll scare her, he reminded it. *We go slow, or we lose her.*

It backed down, grumbling its displeasure.

Viper smoothly reared his hips back, gritting his teeth as her pussy clamped down on him. "When we fucked at my club ... that was fast. This won't be."

He slammed his cock home. That's what she was to him. Home.

He pounded into her hard, unleashing the knot of dark

emotions inside him. Every bit of want and greed and possessiveness and love.

His entity blasted him with a sensory memory: *Blood, warm and addictive and spicy with magick.*

Viper clenched his jaw, the burn of thirst tickling the back of his throat. The bastard was trying to tempt him to feed from her. He clamped his jaw shut and wrestled back his thirst—the frustration of that only made him fuck her harder.

"Viper," she rasped, her inner walls rippling and heating. Then she came.

He didn't stop. Kept ramming his dick into her. Soon enough, she came again. He still didn't stop. He drove her higher and higher, until he sensed it building in her once more. "Come."

She shook her head. "I can't," she breathed. "Not again."

"You can. You will."

She did.

Ella imploded with a hoarse scream, digging the heels of her feet into his lower back, absently aware of him jackhammering into her with a rumbly snarl. He pitched his hips forward one last time, lodging his dick impossibly deep, and then she felt his cock throb as he filled the condom.

She melted into the mattress, all hollowed out. He sagged over her, burying his face in her throat. Neither of them moved for long moments. But then, keeping her with him, he rolled onto his back.

Sprawled over him, she lifted her head, finding her gaze drawn to the ink on his neck. There was a lot of it. Curves, lines, symbols, runes, images. She skimmed a finger down the scythe there, following it down to where a bunch of other symbols were inked into the skin right above his heart. "I don't recognize these."

"They're ancient writings that are only used in the upper realm."

Cocking her head, she met his gaze again, curious as to what he'd have stamped over his heart. "What does this bit say?"

He waited a beat, pursing his lips. "Maybe I'll tell you some other time."

Yeah, she'd heard that before. She gave him the same response she had last time: "And maybe you're full of shit."

"Maybe," he said, his lips bowing up.

Feeling his softening cock slip out of her, she told him, "I have to go clean up."

"I want a hand in that." After removing and disposing of the condom, he carried her to the shower. Under the hot spray, he washed her down ... only to then eat her out right there, after which he fucked her again. So they had to clean up once more before they finally left the stall.

Slumped on her stomach on his bed, she felt a very proprietary hand sweep down her back in a smooth, covetous glide that gave her tingles.

He palmed her ass. "Stay the night," he coaxed.

"There you go using that tone on me again."

He looked genuinely confused. "What tone?"

"The one that wraps around someone's will like a spell."

His lips winged up. "So you'll stay?"

"I'm not sleepy."

His smile widened. "Who said I had plans for us to sleep?" He gave her ass an encouraging squeeze. "Stay."

She let out a mock, long-suffering sigh. "Okay." Because she found that she'd completely ceased caring that he was a celestial.

Her mother would tut at that and brand her dumb. Her aunt would concur. Mia probably would as well. But Ella found that she gave no fucks about any of that either.

"All night?"

"All night."

"And you'll come back tomorrow?"

"I'll come back."

"Often," he pushed.

Her eyes narrowed. "What is it exactly you want from me?"

Everything, baby. But Viper didn't say that, because she wasn't ready to hear it yet. For now, he'd keep it simple. "I want you in my bed. Or your bed. Or pretty much anywhere. I want you as often as I can get you. And I don't want any other man touching you." Even he heard the blatant possession in his voice.

"And there'd be no other women for you?"

"No, I don't want anyone else." He slid his hand from her ass up to her nape. "We can see where it goes. Can't we?" he prodded, aiming to sound casual when in reality he wanted to officially claim her right there, right then.

She chewed on her lower lip. "Okay."

Relief settled into his cells. "Good."

"We'd have to keep it on the downlow, though."

Yes, they did. Because he didn't want either the strix or any potential celestial informant to see them together—none of which he could explain. "You ashamed to be seen with one of the Fallen?"

"No. I keep most of my flings and relationships on the downlow. My anchor, who's something of an overprotective meddler, pokes his nose in. He likes to threaten guys to treat me well. He wouldn't like me spending any kind of time with you, so he'd be problematic."

Viper did a long stretch and rolled onto his back. "I'm not worried about Belinsky." The legion was an exceedingly dangerous demon, but he'd have a fuck of a time taking Viper out.

Suspicious eyes gazed into his. "How do you know he's my psi-mate?"

"Belinsky makes it well-known who you are to him as a

protective measure." As a thought occurred to Viper, he went still. "Did anything ever happen between you two? I know demons sometimes share a bed with their anchor."

She spluttered. "It does happen. Mia had a brief fling with hers. I'm pretty sure she regrets it now, though. She and Joe are having issues. I personally think—"

"You're rambling."

Indignant, she frowned. "I am not."

"You're rambling, and you're avoiding my question."

"Speaking of cocks, didn't you earlier say you wanted my mouth on yours?"

Viper's brows slid together. "I didn't just say the word, 'cock.'" But now that *she* had, his own was twitching back to life—no doubt intentional on her part.

"It's what I heard. Well, am I sucking you off or what?"

"This is manipulation, pure and simple."

She gave an innocent blink. "Yes or no?"

He shoved his hand into her hair with a growl and pushed her head down. "Be warned, baby, you're not just going to suck me off. You're gonna get your throat fucked."

They didn't sleep. They stayed awake all night—talking, laughing, teasing, sexing each other up. It shouldn't have been so *easy* to be with him. Shouldn't have felt so natural for Ella. But it did.

Even her demon was at ease around him. And that damn entity wasn't relaxed around anyone.

He also gave her a tour of the compound at one point. He introduced her to any of the club members they came across, all of whom seemed strangely satisfied to see her there.

When it was time for her to go home, so she wouldn't be late for work, she felt a pang of disappointment. That, too, was strange. She *liked* space. Liked alone time. Yet, here she was lamenting that her very long night with Viper was over.

When he teleported them to the front door of her apartment, she narrowed her eyes at him. "How do you know where I live?"

He shrugged. "Same way I know your phone number."

"Ah, yes, your mysterious sources." She was beginning to think there was little he didn't know about the demon world. But then, it made sense that he'd delved deeply into it. How else could he ensure that his club slotted right in with minimal issues?

Her eyes went wide as she remembered something. "Shit, my car—"

"Is parked outside your building," he finished. "I had one of my brothers collect it for you. They got it started without a key—it's one of their many talents."

"Huh. I feel like I should be irritated that you just went ahead and did that without saying a word to me about it."

"Why be irritated? It's your car. You need it. I wanted to make sure you had it, so I did. It's not as if I spray painted it green."

Huffing, she dug her keys out of her pocket. "I like that color. But no, don't spray paint it."

"Don't worry. Not my idea of a good time." He frowned as his gaze landed on the floor. "What's that?" He bent and snatched—*oh, fuck*—a folded slip of paper from the hallway carpet. Before she had the chance to take the note from his hand, he opened it . . . and his face went rock hard with anger. "What the fuck is this?"

CHAPTER FOURTEEN

"*Don't* read it out loud." Ella snatched the paper fast and looked down at it. *Back off if you want to live.*

She felt her brows draw together, because that . . . that wasn't such a typical note. The other two she'd received were more like turns of phrase. Easy to snicker at. This was a direct threat. And coming here, letting her know that he was aware of where she lived; making it clear that he could get *this close* to her—it was all part of the threat.

Like it wasn't bad enough that he'd dared *come to her home*.

Oh, she was gonna kill the motherfucker when she finally got her hands on him. Her demon wanted to rip out his intestines and wear them like a necklace.

"*Ella*"—his eyes dark as flint, Viper jabbed a finger toward the note—"what is this?"

A private matter. "Someone apparently thought it would be fun to leave a stupid note on my doorstep. Ignore it. I intend to."

Just to be safe, she tore it in two to deactivate the snare. The last thing she needed was him unknowingly setting it off.

"Baby." The word was darkly amused. "You think I can't tell you're trying to blow me off?"

Well, she had hoped she could. "It's just a stupid note," she reiterated, unlocking her front door.

"And you don't seem shocked to see it, which tells me this isn't the first threat you've received." He followed her into the apartment, bypassing her magickal wards like they weren't even there.

Ella stared at him, surprised. "My wards should have kept you out." Her demon was kind of impressed that they hadn't, though not particularly pleased that someone had circumvented their personal security so easily.

"Not a lot can keep me from somewhere I want to be. Now, what is happening?" He shot her a look of warning when she would have waved away his concern. "Ella, I spent last night making you mine—and you know it. That places you under my protection. No fucking way am I going to ignore that note. Don't ask me to."

She narrowed her eyes. "If me being yours means you have the right to know my business, it works both ways, right?"

"Right." The answer was cautious.

"Then I'll explain about the notes once you answer my question. What happened with that vampire who dumped a body outside your pool hall? Did you catch him?" Ella had wondered about it a few times.

He looked as though he might dismiss the questions, but then he sighed. "It wasn't a vampire. It was a strix. A colony of them have somehow made it to this realm. They're taunting my club by snatching local humans and then dumping their bodies near our properties."

Okay, *that* took her off-guard. "Why taunt your club? It would surely be more sensible to not bring their presence here to your attention."

"Strix aren't known for being sensible. I have some of my brothers tracking them. They're typically good at hiding, but we always find them eventually."

"You've had run-ins with them before?"

"Part of what me and my brothers did in the upper realm was deal with rogue hell-born demons. You could say we haven't quite retired, though we now take them out because we want to, not because we're under orders." He folded his arms, his expression turning expectant. "Now it's your turn. Tell me about the notes."

She rolled her shoulders. "There's only been two others."

"And they were both delivered here?"

"No. The previous two were tucked under my windscreen wiper on separate days. They had dumb little warnings typed on them. The first said, *Let sleeping dogs lie.* The other said, *You know what happened to the curious cat.*"

Viper felt his brow furrow in surprise. Not exactly the usual threats a person would make. "Did the ink in those have power stamped in it like that one?"

She looked surprised he'd sensed it. "Yes, they did. I can't tell what compulsion was buried in the ink. You?"

Viper shook his head, forcing his back teeth to unlock. "But I doubt it's anything good." Hence why his furious entity was making all sorts of sadistic plans.

"Same. Even though this note has a different vibe, it has to have been typed by the same person. I mean, how many damn people hand-deliver death threats these days?"

People who wanted to die. And the person sending notes to Ella would in fact die soon—both Viper and his entity would ensure it. "You have no idea who left them for you?"

"It has to have been whoever psychically assaulted me a

month ago—I came across them mugging someone, and they put me unconscious when I tried to help. I don't think he likes that my anchor won't stop pressing for answers as to who he is. Luka will kill him if he ever finds him."

It wasn't her assailant typing the notes—Viper knew that for certain, because that fucker was dead. But he couldn't really tell her that without admitting he'd been on the scene, which would beg two questions: why he'd been there, and why he hadn't stuck around. He wasn't ready to answer those yet.

"Nothing else has happened?" he checked.

"No, nothing."

Viper flicked a look at the torn, crumpled note in her hand. "Whoever wrote that clearly knows where you live, so he's probably been following you around." *Fucker.*

She glanced at her front door. "I normally wouldn't worry that someone would get passed my wards, but *you* did it."

"As I said, very little can keep me from somewhere I want to be. It doesn't reflect on the strength of your wards. They're powerful. I can feel it." Viper telepathically reached out to Jester and said, *Round up the brothers, I need to hold a meeting.*

Done, said Jester.

"If you receive any more of these, I want to hear about it."

"Viper, I have this situation covered—"

"Clearly not, because this shit is escalating." He inched closer and cupped her neck. "The bastard came to your home, baby. And this note isn't as petty as the others. He's getting bolder. He could do something worse next time. Might even harm you or someone you love. Take what help I'm offering so we can get to him faster."

She huffed. "You'll involve yourself no matter what I say."

He gave a small shrug. "Figured it'd serve me better to let you think it's on your terms."

She tried stifling a smile, but it didn't work too well.

"You'll reach out if you receive another, yeah?" he pushed.

Her shoulders dipping in surrender, she rubbed at her forehead. "Fine."

Relief filled him, and his entity relaxed ever so slightly.

"But if anything more happens with the strix, you have to tell me."

Shit. He'd rather none of that touched her, rather she didn't . . . He let his thoughts trail off, knowing he'd have to give in here. If he didn't, neither would she. "If and when there's anything further to share, I'll be sure to tell you."

She sniffed, seemingly mollified. "Okay, then."

"In the interests of full disclosure, you'll have guards on you from now on." Watching her bristle, Viper added, "They won't be seen. You won't even know they're there. Give me this, Ella. I have to know that you're safe. Wouldn't you rather make it harder for this fucker to get to you?"

She let out a long sigh. "Fine. But only because you're right; he's getting bolder; we need to catch him before he hurts someone."

Hiding his satisfaction, Viper gave a nod and lightly squeezed her neck. "I'll see you later." Neither he nor his entity wanted to leave her, especially when they now knew there was a threat hovering over her head. But they also wanted to get rid of said threat.

"I have work, but I'll be home around six."

"I'll come to you then. In the meantime, you need anything—absolutely anything—you call me."

She swallowed. "Okay."

He released her neck. "Take care, baby." With that, he teleported to the meeting room in his clubhouse. His brothers were seated at the long table, all looking varying degrees of curious.

Viper claimed his usual seat at the head of the table. "Many of you came across Ella at the compound last night, so you'll know she was here. The rest of you no doubt heard about it." News traveled through the club fast.

"I was hoping you were going to tell us she'd let you claim her already or something like that," said Ghost, lazily sprawled in his seat, "but you look kind of pissed."

"I am." Viper splayed his hands on the armrests. "On taking her home, I discovered she's been getting anonymous notes."

Jester's brows knitted. "What kind of notes?"

"Threats," Viper bit out.

Dice straightened in his chair. "Someone's threatening her?"

"Yes." Viper idly rapped his fingers on the table. "Two were tucked under her windscreen wiper. The third was left outside her front door, which means they teleported into her building since they wouldn't have otherwise gotten past the security measures ... or they live in it."

"What exactly do the notes say?" asked Ghost, his posture having lost its lazy edge.

"The first two were oddly phrased warnings. *Let sleeping dogs lie,* and *You know what happened to the curious cat.* The third read, *Back off if you want to live,*" Viper added, his entity baring his teeth at the memory.

"Back off from what?" asked Omen.

"That I don't know." There was a creak of leather as Viper leaned forward in his chair. "Ella thinks they're from the demon who knocked her out with a psychic punch; that he's trying to put her off digging to uncover his identity. But we all know that isn't true, because he's dead."

Darko scratched at his jaw. "What else would she need to 'back off' from?"

"Again, I don't know," replied Viper. "But I do know that there's power stamped in the ink."

"Power?" echoed Blackjack, frowning.

Viper dipped his chin. "A compulsion of some sort. It was impossible to tell more without triggering the trap, and Ella was quick to deactivate it. It was probably best that she did. If the target is her, it might not matter who speaks the words; only that they're spoken aloud."

Sting regarded him closely. "Do you think someone from the upper realm is sending the notes?"

"The compulsive power didn't feel either celestial or demonic in nature to me, so I can't be sure," Viper told him. "But, really, why would the Uppers pay Ella any attention? I've been very careful not to give them reason to. The only people who know that she means anything to me are the people in this room."

Jester froze. "V, none of us would ever dick with Ella this way. It would be no different from dicking with you."

Hustle edged forward on his chair. "Wait, you think it was one of us?" His gaze bounced from brother to brother.

"I think it could be." As did Viper's entity. Hence why it was currently eyeing them all suspiciously. "Maybe none of you have a personal hand in what's happening, but you could have clued in the Uppers as to who she is to me."

A stunned silence greeted that statement.

Staring at his club members, knowing that one of them could very well be responsible for taunting Ella ... It hit hard. He wouldn't have thought that any would betray him. But then, he hadn't thought that the last six people he'd counted as family would ever fuck him over, and look what had happened there.

Darko shook his head. "No. We wouldn't give the Uppers the steam off our shit, let alone any valuable information. Nor would we ever threaten or scare Ella. We know what she means to you. And come on, there's no real reason why any of us would target her *or* give up her identity."

"Someone might do the latter in exchange for a ticket back to the upper realm," said Viper.

Prophet's jaw went hard. "If that was the case, they'd be gone from here already. They wouldn't stick around, risking you finding out what they've done."

"Maybe not," Viper allowed. "But there's no saying for sure. Just as there's no saying for certain that someone here isn't writing the notes."

Rivet slashed a hand through the air. "No. It's gotta be one of the Uppers."

"Her anchor will have plenty of enemies," considered Razor. "One of his could be responsible."

Unlikely. "They'd know it would be beyond stupid to target Luka Belinsky's psi-mate."

Razor gave a loose shrug. "There are lots of stupid people in this world."

"There are also lots of people who do shitty things for what they believe is the right reason." Viper drummed his fingers on the table again. "Fact is, I'll have to tell Ella all our secrets eventually—everyone here knows that. Knows that having her in my life comes with many risks to us. Maybe someone here fears she'll share our secrets with outsiders and so, for the good of us all, they want her out of the picture."

Many expressions turned pensive.

"Now, everyone in this room is a ruthless motherfucker," Viper went on. "We've all done way worse things than type some compulsion-embedded threats. Can any of you honestly tell me you're positive that one of us hasn't been sending Ella notes to protect our club and all we hold secret?"

Dice sighed. "Put like that, no. We've watched each other's backs for a long time. There ain't a lot we wouldn't do to keep each other safe."

"So, then, you get why I ain't prepared to take the word of everyone here when they assure me that they didn't do it," said Viper. "I'm more of the opinion that someone outside our club is responsible, but I have to be certain that nobody here is an actual danger to my woman. I have to know there's no traitor among us."

Sting's gaze sharpened. "You're gonna search our minds, aren't you?"

"I'm hoping it won't come to that. Hoping the person behind the notes holds up their hands and admits to it, if it is someone here." Viper ran his gaze along each of his brothers. "I'll understand. Protecting each other is what we do. And Ella hasn't been harmed. But if you lie to me, if you play innocent and I later learn you lied, I can't promise I won't skin you the fuck alive. So, does anyone have anything to confess?"

Gazes darted around as everyone waited to see if anyone would admit to sending the notes. Nobody did.

Viper licked over his front teeth. "Then let's get started." He gestured at his nearest brother, which was Hustle. "You first."

An explosion of Russian curses flew out of Luka's mouth as he fisted the slips of torn paper he held. "I am fucking done with this shit."

Watching him pace up and down the store's workshop like a caged tiger, Ella leaned back against the counter. She didn't fail to notice how Mia, Melodie, and Jocelyn backed up to give him space. Not that they feared him—being the close relatives of his anchor, Luka considered them under his protection. But he could be something of a scary sight when angry.

The skin of his face, neck, and hands currently rippled . . . as though snakes were slithering beneath his flesh. It was his inner demons. His anger called to them and fed their own fury just as theirs fed his. A vicious cycle for sure.

She'd gathered everyone here in the store to tell them about the note all at once. She hadn't told them that Viper would be conducting his own investigation into the notes, though—not even Luka.

Her anchor had nothing against the Fallen in general, but every part of him would bristle at another male thinking they had any right to look out for her. He considered it his job; he wouldn't want his toes stepped on.

He also wouldn't like that Viper had edged his way into her business, and he'd demand to know why the president would even want to. That she was sharing Viper's bed was something she'd be keeping to herself for now.

Ella wasn't sure exactly how Viper planned to go about getting answers for her, but she'd welcome any aid she could get. Having all hands on deck made sense.

"The guy must get off on riding the edge of danger," said Mikhail, his steel-gray eyes focused on Luka. "That little note in your hand is, in effect, a signed death warrant."

Nikandr gave a slow nod. "He might as well have dared you to come after him."

"I will when I find out who he is." Luka's gaze bled to black as one of his entities surfaced. "He will beg for death before we are done with him, and it will be some time before we are done," it said.

Belial, Ella sensed.

A funny thing about legions? Their inner demons tended to name themselves, possibly to ensure they each stood out as separate entities. Inside Luka were Abraxas, Belial, and Dagon.

Ella had learned to tell them apart. Though they shared many of the same traits—remorselessness, impulsiveness, fearlessness—they each had distinct personalities.

Abraxas was extremely narcissistic and possessed a superficial charm. Dagon was moody, manipulative, and a compulsive liar. Belial was a pure sadist who didn't seem to derive pleasure from anything other than hurting or humiliating others—hence why it was a particular favorite of her own inner demon, who could be somewhat coldhearted.

Melodie turned to Ella. "I can't believe you didn't tell us about the notes."

"I didn't want you to worry," she defended.

"And you weren't taking them very seriously, I'll bet," Jocelyn accused, pursing her lips.

"I'll admit, I thought the first note could be a random kid completing a dare or something," said Ella. "But due to the snare, I wasn't feeling at all blasé about it."

Melodie shot her a look of reprimand. "You can't keep things like this from us. You always do it." She glanced from her to Mia. "*Both* of you do. Whenever anything happens, you keep me and your aunt in the dark."

"For the good of the world," said Mia.

Jocelyn's brows met. "What's that supposed to mean?"

"It means there's a reason our Prime asked us to relocate rather than just kick us all out of the lair," Mia elaborated. "The pair of you turn into magickal terrorists when any wrongs befall you or yours."

Melodie lifted her chin a notch. "Glitter bomb potions don't count as terrorism."

Mia looked at Ella. "Remember that time my ex lost his hearing for six months?"

"That had nothing to do with us," their mother swiftly denied.

Yeah, right. "And the time my old sleazy, touchy-feely neighbor kept snorting like a pig when he tried to speak?" That had gone on for a whole five months.

"Again, not connected to us," Melodie insisted.

"Or the time the unapologetic drunk-driver who crashed into my car realized he'd been declared dead in every country and was never able to get tipsy again no matter how much he drank?" asked Mia.

Jocelyn nudged Melodie with her elbow. "I suppose we should take it as a compliment that they consider us so powerful."

Melodie sniffed and then turned to Luka, whose eyes were back to normal now that Belial had retreated. "You're no closer to finding out who it was?"

Luka gave a resentful shake of the head. "I have left not one fucking stone unturned. *Not one.* The people I'd originally suspected of assaulting her all have solid alibis. Everyone I've questioned swore that they have no idea who he is."

Melodie let out a sound of distress. "What do we do?"

"We lay some magickal traps," said Ella. "He'll probably expect that, so I doubt he'll touch my car again or go near my apartment. But if he does, I'll know."

Luka fixed her with a hard stare. "You're going to have bodyguards from now on," he declared, his tone empty of negotiation. "Don't argue. This last note says he means business. I'm not taking any chances with your life."

Ella had figured he'd say that. "Okay."

His eyes narrowed at her easy acquiescence. "Okay?"

"I'm not going to turn down an offer of protection if it means he'll be caught." It was why she hadn't fought Viper's insistence on putting guards on her.

"I'm not offering it, I'm telling you it's happening," Luka stated. "I will not allow any further harm to come to you."

Mia sighed at him, almost longingly. "Luka, will you be my anchor, too?"

His brows dipped. "No. You're Joe's problem."

"Problem?" Mia echoed.

"Yes."

Mia folded her arms. "And you see my sister as a problem?"

"'Course not. She's mine." Luka resettled his attention on Ella. "And she should have told me about the recent note *immediately*, not waited until now."

Ella heaved a sigh. "I'm just tired of letting this, *him*, take up my time."

Luka crossed to her and rested a supportive hand on her shoulder. "Come to Infernal tonight. We'll eat. Talk. Get your mind off things."

Ella couldn't, since she had plans to see Viper. "Sorry, I have some stuff I need to do. I'll come to Infernal another night, though."

His lips flattened. "I don't like seeing you so weary. It makes me want to kill someone—I don't even particularly care who it is."

"Seriously, Luka, *be my anchor*," Mia pled.

Melodie turned to her with a frown. "What's wrong with Joe all of a sudden?"

Luka's eyes narrowed on Mia. "Did he harm you?"

"No, nothing like that," Mia assured him. "He's just being an idiot. It'll pass."

Luka grunted and looked back at Ella. "I'm leaving now." He squeezed her shoulder. "We will catch him, Ella. It's just a matter of time."

As she'd earlier temporarily closed the store so they'd have privacy while they talked, Ella led the way to the front door and unlocked it for Luka and his guards. He gave her a quick hug, warned her to be vigilant, and then swanned out of the store with the twins.

Flipping the Open/Closed sign, Ella looked out of the shop window to see two of the Black Saints loitering outside the dive bar. Her new guards, maybe? She wasn't sure.

They made eye contact and offered the most subtle of nods before looking away, saving her from having to either rudely not return the gesture *or* politely nod back . . . and have her watchful sister pounce on it.

"Much as I know you'd love to get your hands on the mugger," began Mia, "I hope it's Luka who finds him. He'll make him *pay* pay. You'll be more merciful."

Given the way her note writer was behaving . . . "You shouldn't be so sure of that," muttered Ella, crossing to the counter with her sister at her side.

"I am *beyond pissed* that the bold little prick went to your front door. He might have only left a compulsion-ridden note, but it was still a scare tactic—a kind of 'I know where you live and can get close to you' message."

Ella slowly nodded. Her demon, showing no signs of calming, was still as infuriated by it as it had been when first discovering the note early this morning. "I worry he'll target you, Mom, or Jocelyn. Please be super careful."

"I will. But *you're* the one in his sights. He's focused on you."

Hearing the bell above the door chime, Ella glanced over. Her body went still. Because Maxine and Dionne were filing inside the store. Wonderful.

CHAPTER FIFTEEN

Ella's demon sneered, in no mood to tolerate either female right now. It was clear by their tight expressions that they weren't here to browse the shelves or buy something. And while there was nothing particularly confrontational about their posture, it was very *all business*.

Moving a little stiffly, they purposefully made a beeline for the counter. Reaching it first, Maxine gave a strained smile. "Ladies," she greeted simply. "Dionne and I would like to apologize."

"You would?" asked Ella, because it didn't *seem* as though either of them truly wanted to.

"Yes. My behavior last week was uncalled for. I was simply defensive on hearing you accuse my daughter of theft. But she has since admitted to me that the accusation was not actually false."

Ella exchanged a quick look with her sister.

"All right," said Mia.

Dionne did a little head flick that made her hair bounce. "I'm sorry for taking the cash. I shouldn't have. And I should have apologized before now so, yeah, sorry."

Neither of them are being sincere, Mia telepathed.

I know, it's weird that they'd even come here. "Apologies accepted." Not entirely true, but there was no sense in dragging out the conversation, so it was best to round it up.

Maxine's mouth curled into a placid smile. "Thank you. For Jocelyn's sake, I would like for there to be no friction here."

"As would we," said Ella.

"Wonderful." The harpy turned her smile on her daughter . . . only to see that the hellcat was idly scrolling through her cell. "Dionne?"

The hellcat didn't look up from her phone screen as she absently responded, "Uh-huh?"

"*Dionne.*"

The young woman's head snapped up. "What? What now? I said what you told me to say. Can't we just go?"

Ella clamped her lips shut to hold back a smile.

"You're supposed to be . . . " Maxine trailed off.

"*Come on*, Mom, they're not going to give me back my job. *I* wouldn't give me back my job."

Which clearly pleased Dionne immensely, Ella noted, but the same could not be said for Maxine. "You're right, we won't. But we wish you the best of luck in what comes next."

The hellcat gave a whatever shrug and then headed for the door. Maxine bounced her gaze from her daughter to Ella and Mia, clearly torn on what to do. Reluctantly, she followed Dionne, muttering something too low for the words to carry.

Watching them leave the store, Ella frowned as a thought came to her. "You know, it just occurred to me . . . Dionne's had a lot of jobs."

"Yeah. And?"

"And Maxine is always the one to get her these jobs."

"Right."

"And Dionne never seems to want to work in any of these places." Or so each of her past employers had claimed when Ella spoke to them before hiring the girl.

Mia lifted her shoulders. "Yeah, so?"

"So, what if Maxine is choosing her daughter's jobs for her? And what if it's because she wants to use Dionne as a plant?"

Mia's lips parted, her eyes widening. "You could be right. People do that. Information is an important currency in the demon world."

It was, and it was sometimes used as blackmail material.

"And you know something, I always thought it was weird that Maxine befriended our aunt. I mean, they have nothing in common."

Ella dipped her chin. "So maybe she just hoped to get info on our lair . . . or maybe even on Luka, come to think of it." It was more likely the latter, since their lair wasn't in Vegas or at all influential. "Nothing's been going on in our lives over the past few months that would make Maxine inclined to send a spy our way."

"If Dionne resents being made a plant, it would explain why she ensures she gets herself fired," said Mia. "It would also explain why Maxine's now pushing for her to get her job back. Damn, I'd better warn Jocelyn to be even more careful than usual in what she says in front of Maxine."

"Do we pass on our suspicions to Knox? He's Maxine's Prime, but would he even want to know?"

Mia twisted her mouth. "You could tell Harper just in case. If she feels it's noteworthy, she'll mention it to her mate."

Ella nodded again. "I'll head over to her tattoo shop on my lunch break."

*

Arriving at Urban Ink, she pushed open the front door. The place was trendy and bright but with an edgy vibe. Customers lounged on the leather recliners at four almost identical stations. Beyond them were doors to various rooms, along with a tracing table and other equipment.

Waiting clients could hang here in the very neat reception area on the comfy-looking sofas while watching TV or flicking through the tattoo portfolios on the table in front of them. There was also a vending machine for anyone who might be feeling peckish.

Ella smiled at the imp who stood behind the reception desk. "Hi, trouble."

Khloë saluted her. "Yo, demon witch."

Snickering, Ella walked to the desk. "I was hoping to speak to Harper. I only need a minute."

Khloë briefly glanced at the sphinx over her shoulder. "She's with a client right now, but she'll be done soon."

Noting that Harper had set down her tattoo gun and seemed to be giving her client aftercare advice, Ella said, "I'll wait. No Piper today?" She couldn't see her anywhere.

"She left early—had to go somewhere with her mom."

Shame. Ella loved chatting with her. She was about to take a seat on the sofa, but Khloë held up a staying hand.

"No, don't go sit," the imp pled. "Stay here with me." She leaned forward, propped her elbows on the desk, and gave Ella a huge smile. "Tell me how life's treating you these days. I'm interested."

"No, you're not. You want something." It was easy to sense.

The imp scratched her cheek. "Well, now that you mention it, there is something you could do for me."

"I'm not going to convince Luka to let your family into Infernal."

Khloë frowned. "Oh, come on, they'd behave themselves."

Ella snorted. "Imps have no concept of what that means."

"That's not true. We learn. We evolve. We—"

"Do as you please," Ella finished. "And it mostly pleases you to disregard warnings, ethics, rules, and your own damn safety. I have no clue why."

Khloë stared off into the distance, a pensive look on her face. "No, neither do we."

"Hey there, Ella," cut in Raini as she sidled up to the imp. A succubae, the tattooist was positively stunning, but she often tried toning down her looks—which didn't work well. "Love the earrings."

Fingering one of the dragonflies, Ella smiled. "Aw, thanks."

"You here about a tattoo?"

"No, I just want to speak to Harper about something."

"Well, if you change your mind on that, I recommend you have a baby hippo tattooed on you," Khloë interjected.

Raini frowned. "Didn't we agree you'd stop trying to—"

"Do not badmouth Fritz, he hasn't done a damn thing to you," Khloë griped.

"Of course he hasn't. Because he isn't a 'he'. He's a cock with a pair of hairy balls. But you insist otherwise. As if we can't see what you draw."

"Imps don't always follow logic," Ella pointed out.

Raini grunted. "Don't I know it."

Right then, Harper's client appeared at the desk, stealing Khloë's attention.

Harper approached Ella mere seconds later. "Hey, what brings you here?"

Ella folded her arms. "Well, I got a little story." She quickly relayed her business with Dionne and Maxine to the sphinx, adding her suspicions.

Harper dug her teeth into her lower lip. "Hmm, I'll mention it to Knox. I hadn't suspected Maxine of planting little spies around, but I wouldn't be surprised if that's her game. Her old business partner used to do it."

"I'm not positive she *is* doing it," Ella clarified. "And I'm not outright accusing her of it either. I just wanted to make you aware of my suspicions."

"Knox will talk to her," said Harper. "If it turns out you're right, he'll put a stop to it."

Ella cocked her head. "You think Maxine would admit to doing such a thing?"

A cunning smile surfaced on the sphinx's face. "People are very hesitant to lie to my mate, and he's very good at making them part with information they'd otherwise keep to themselves."

A little like Luka, then.

Devon—another tattooist as well as someone who specialized in piercings—appeared out of the back room with a darling little infant in her arms. Devon also happened to be Tanner's mate, which surprised a lot of people since hellcats and hellhounds generally didn't get along at all.

"She won't settle," complained Devon, casting her hellpup a quick look. A smile took over her face as she spotted Ella. "Oh, hi, I didn't know you'd stopped by. No one tells me anything." Her cat-green gaze danced from person to person. "Am I missing interesting stuff?"

Khloë pulled a face. "No, it's super boring."

Clapping for what appeared to be no reason, Anaïs babbled at Ella, her liquid-gold eyes smiling.

Ella grinned. "Aw, Devon, she's so cute." Violent, according to Levi—whose face she'd clawed several times—but cute. Though she had Tanner's eyes, she had the same gorgeous ultraviolet ringlets as her mom.

Anaïs looked about a year old, but demonic babies were advanced that way, so she was probably nine or ten months old—Ella couldn't remember what month the kid was born.

Devon offered her to Ella. "Wanna hold her?"

Spluttering, Ella leaned back slightly. "Uh, no. No, I don't." She liked her eyes exactly where they were. "But thanks."

Devon's lips flattened, and she cast a look at the others. "They've been telling you that Anaïs tries to kill people, haven't they?"

Ella spluttered again. "That's simply not true. I'm just not great with kids." *Lie.*

Huffing, Khloë turned to the infant and gripped her small fist. "People are so mean to you, aren't they, Anaïs? So mean. You're sweet and adorable."

"Wanna hold her?" offered Devon.

The imp reared back. "Fuck, no."

The hellcat flushed. "*Oh my God, you're all such assholes.*"

Ella started to laugh.

"Hate to say it," began Darko, sitting on the grass with the neck of a beer bottle caught between his thumb and finger, "but I really did think it might be one of us. Glad I was wrong."

So was Viper. He'd raided every psyche over the past few hours, and he'd swiftly come to the realization that none of his brothers were responsible for the notes. Nor had any of them been a source of information for other celestials.

While it was a relief, it wasn't necessarily comforting. Because the likeliest theory at this point was that Ella was being targeted by a celestial. Such a thing would only occur if the Uppers had become aware of who she was to Viper. And that meant that the club was somehow being closely monitored without them sensing it.

Gritting his teeth at the idea, Viper gazed beyond the chain-link fence, eyeing the barren land and black forest suspiciously. It was no sweet view. The yard, too, was no one's idea of pretty. There were no plants, no flowers, no decorative items. Only a large patch of mowed brittle grass, some concrete paving, and several picnic benches.

Most of his brothers were currently gathered in the yard. It was easy to tell by their expressions that some were still offended that he'd suspected them. Nonetheless, they understood his need for caution, so they weren't holding it against him. Their main concern was that an outsider might have somehow acquired *inside* information.

Viper's main concern was Ella.

He currently had Ghost and Rebel watching her; neither had spotted anyone loitering near her home or car, and they'd confirmed that she wasn't being tailed. Well . . . aside from the guards that her anchor had wisely put on her.

On the bench across from him, Prophet leaned forward and rested his lower arms on the wooden table. "I don't see how any outsider could get close without our knowing."

Sting caught Viper's eye from the neighboring bench. "If it *is* a celestial writing these notes, the only thing I can think is that they've been following your financial activity. You bought her apartment building. You bought the bar next to her store. You bought the pool hall she frequents. Ella's the common denominator there."

"Yeah," allowed Dice, who was seated on Viper's right, "but he buys a lot of property—there's no reason for those three to stand out. And how could any celestial know he bought the bar anyway? It's located in the Underground."

"They could have heard about it," Sting suggested. "Demons talk. Especially when they've got something to whine about.

And a lot of them aren't happy that our club has a presence in the Underground."

"That's true." Dice looked at Viper. "If I was watching you, I'd be very interested in any properties you purchased in the Underground. I'd wonder if you'd done it to be near your woman. So I'd look at what staff worked there; I'd take note of what businesses are close by, and I'd notice Ella's store. A celestial could teleport down to the Underground and move about unseen, if they were careful enough. They just wouldn't be able to linger for long."

Razor nodded as he scooped up a dead bird and tossed it over the fence. "If a watcher cottoned on to how Ella also lives in a building you own, their bat senses would be tingling."

"Spidey," Jester corrected.

Razor waved that away. "Whatever. If the celestial also watched you at the pool hall, they'd have noticed you eye-banging Ella, V—they could have then put the pieces together and suspected who she is to you. It wouldn't take much detective work to figure out she's been going there for years. Dots would be connected. Assumptions would be made. Why notes would then be written, I don't have a damn clue."

"It'd help to know the intent of the compulsions," said Dice, absently running a fingertip along his eyebrow. "They were cleverly written, when you think about it. The phrases on the first two notes are harmless enough that someone might say them out loud in a kind of amused surprise. The third was more threatening but, coupled with how it was delivered to her door, it meant there was a chance Ella would read it aloud out of anger."

"I personally don't get why anyone would go down a note-writing route at all," said Blackjack, perched on the edge of a bench on Viper's left. "The Uppers would surely want her dead. A professional slayer would get the job down fast and bail."

Jester pursed his lips, considering that. "Maybe it ain't a slayer at all. Do you think it could be one of the now-Six archangels, V?"

"They'll have found someone to replace me by now. There'll be Seven of them again at this point." Viper rubbed at his jaw. "As for whether any of them would do this, I don't know. We didn't exactly part on a pleasant note, but I don't see what reason they'd have to target Ella."

"They killed her once," Jester reminded him.

Like Viper could ever forget. "To keep us apart. It didn't work. They failed. They'd be likely to just accept it. The Uppers, though? They'll resent her since, in their view, she 'seduced' me down 'a dark path' that resulted in an obsession I never shook off."

"What if it's not a celestial, what if it's someone close to her?" Rivet suggested. "Like her sister?"

Omen's brows met. "What?" he asked, pure incredulity ringing through his voice.

Rivet lifted his shoulders. "They live in the same building, so it'd be easy for Mia to leave the note."

Jester shot him a derisive look. "That's the stupidest idea ever. Why would Mia do any of that?"

"It could be a prank. Maybe she's bored." Rivet raised his brows at Jester in challenge. "You got a better theory?"

"*Any* theory would be better than that," Jester stated.

On the grass, Hustle stretched his legs out in front of him. "What if Ella's sending the notes to herself?"

Jester did a long blink and then looked at Rivet. "Scrap what I said. It turns out there *is* a theory that ain't better than yours."

Hustle raised his hands. "People have done weirder shit for attention."

"Hey, here's a thought," said Omen. "What if it's Neta?"

Blackjack blinked. "Who?"

"Neta," Omen repeated.

Darko tilted his head. "You mean the delivery company?"

Omen's brow furrowed. "No. And you're thinking of Letta."

"Then what's Neta?" asked Darko.

"Not a 'what'," Rivet cut in. "It's a 'who'. She sewed the patches on our jackets. How can you not remember her?"

Dice sighed. "That was Esta."

Rivet lifted his shoulders. "Then I don't get who you're talking about."

"Neta is from Maddox's lair," Omen reminded him. "She's always hanging around the club, bar, and pool hall." He paused, but Rivet still appeared confused, so Omen continued, "She's blonde. Has an impressive rack. You fucked her in the parking lot."

Rivet's eyes went wide with realization. "Oh. Neta. Right. The hot petite one with the pixie haircut."

Omen's mouth tightened. "No."

"Then I really have no clue who she is."

"It won't be Neta," Dice said to Viper. "She didn't like seeing you with Ella at the Red Rooms, but your woman was receiving notes *before* that. Neta would have had no reason to go after her back then."

Sting raised an index finger. "*Unless* the descendant had noticed how often he watches Ella. The compulsion could be to pressure her to stay away from you, V."

Personally, Viper doubted it. Neta's interest in him wasn't *that* profound. But he wouldn't dismiss the idea.

"Are you going to tell Ella that the mugger is dead?" Blackjack asked him.

Viper dipped his chin. "I'll have to. I'm not yet ready to go into specifics, but I'll make it clear that he's a goner. Right now, she has it in her head that he's her note-sender. It's blinding her to other possibilities. I don't want her in the dark." He rose to his feet. "But before I do that, there's someone else I need to see."

Fastening the tie of her towel robe, Ella exhaled a rough sigh. A hot bath never failed to calm her mind and sweep away any tension from her muscles. Tonight, it had done nothing. Her mind was too hyper over the little mystery of the note situation.

It made matters worse that her demon was all worked up. The entity's need to hunt, nab, and avenge wound her even tighter.

Hearing the chiming of her cell phone, Ella padded out of her en suite bathroom, batting at one of the curls she'd gathered into an unruly ponytail to keep dry as she bathed.

Entering her bedroom, she jerked back as Viper came striding inside. Ella put a hand to her pounding heart. "I need to put a bell on you."

He raked a searching gaze over her, his eyes darkening as pure need moved over his face.

Her muscles bunched. Damn, he could make her feel hyper-aware of herself with just a look. She liked it, even though it made her ovaries do a damn jig.

"I told you I'd be coming," he said as he erased the distance between them in purposeful strides.

"I didn't think you'd be here so soon."

He pressed a kiss to her mouth, sweeping a hand down her back. "I wanted to check on you."

"I'm fine. All is well. Nothing to report. I think my body-guards are having the desired effect."

"Yeah, I heard that Belinsky put guards on you. Good."

"Heard it from who?"

"Ghost and Rebel. I had them watching over you." Viper an-chored his palm on her hip, the heavy warm weight of it nothing short of proprietary. "I like that Belinsky's so protective of you. Yet, I don't."

Her brow knitted. "You do, and you don't?"

"The more protection you have the better. But I don't like that another man has those rights to you." Viper moved his face closer to hers, his voice lowering as he added, "Especially when I know you've been in his bed."

"I never said I'd been in his bed."

"You didn't have to. It was obvious by how you were spluttering and rambling and avoiding the question when I asked about it."

She wasn't touching that subject. "I didn't tell him you're having me guarded, by the way. He'd freak and ask the kind of questions I'm not feeling inclined to answer truthfully." She frowned at the odd look on Viper's face. "What is it?"

He drew in a breath through his nose. "There's something I need to tell you."

She tilted her head. "What?"

He hesitated, his eyes drifting intently over her face. "I was there the night that you interfered with that mugging."

She double-blinked. "What?"

"I heard you shouting. Well, cursing. I came over just in time to watch you take the psychic hit. I stepped in and killed the fucker that assaulted you."

"But ... why ... why didn't you ..." Ella shook her head, struggling to gather her thoughts. "Why would you come to my rescue and then vanish?" That made no sense. Unless ... She narrowed her eyes. "Or were you up to no good at the time? You couldn't afford to be seen in the area?"

He ran his tongue over the front of his teeth. "Something like that." The hand cinching her hip breezed a thumb over her hipbone. "I'm telling you this because I don't want you hunting the wrong person. Whoever's writing the notes isn't the fucker that assaulted you. He's long gone from this world," he added, his voice dropping, sheer menace threaded through each word.

Something told her that her attacker had died *hard*.

While it was annoying to only learn of this now, she couldn't really blame him for keeping it to himself. He hadn't known about the notes; hadn't realized how hard she was searching for the identity of her mugger. Once he did learn of it, he chose to be upfront with her . . . even though it meant revealing something he'd apparently prefer to keep quiet.

Okay, so he hadn't been upfront with her straight off the mark. He could have told her this morning but hadn't. She was guessing he'd wanted to speak with his club about it first.

Ella sighed. "How am I supposed to tell this to my family and Luka? They'll want to know how you could possibly have known about the notes. I mean, there'd be no other reason for you to admit to being at the scene."

"Belinsky already knows. I paid him a visit earlier."

Yet again, she rapidly blinked. "You did, what?"

"You said you wanted to keep us on the downlow. That meant I needed to handle this a different way. I told him I'd overheard that he was searching for information on who'd assaulted you that night. I admitted to him what I just admitted to you. He hasn't called you?"

"He might have done. I was in the bath. I left my phone over there on the nightstand."

"He'll want to let you know about our conversation, because he'll have no reason to assume that I'd be the one to tell you."

"Thank you for being honest. You could have hid it from me to conceal your whereabouts that night. You didn't. I appreciate it."

"I told you, you're mine. I protect what belongs to me."

She probably shouldn't like it when he used the M-word, but she did.

"Is there no one else who could be sending you these notes? No enemies, old or new?"

She blew out a breath that slightly rattled her lips. "Not really. I mean, I recently fired someone. But that was *after* I'd received the first two notes, and she didn't actually want to work for me, so she doesn't care."

He kissed her forehead. "We'll eventually find out who it is." His brow creasing in concern, he breezed the pad of his thumb beneath her eye. "You look a little—"

"Tired. Yeah. Normal for me recently."

"Why?"

"I rarely wake feeling like I've slept well. It'll pass."

He bumped his nose to hers gently. "I'll make sure you get a good night's sleep tonight."

"If that means you intend to fuck me to sleep, I'm all for it."

"Glad to hear it." The hand on her hip tugged her closer as he glided his free hand up her spine to settle on her nape ... smoothly pulling her into a hug.

"You're good at this."

A wolfish smile tipped up his mouth. "You said that last night. I was going down on you at the time, wasn't I?"

Her belly clenched at the memory his words conjured up.

"Now, it's fucking with my head that you're wearing nothing beneath that robe," he said, his voice dropping to a whisper; need blooming in his eyes. "I want to see it on the floor."

Smiling, Ella opened the tie. "I think I can accommodate that wish."

CHAPTER SIXTEEN

Everleigh stared up at him, biting her lower lip. "Are you sure you want to do this?"

He held her gaze, his expression grave. "I'm sure."

"I just don't want you to have any regrets. I'd understand if you later did, and I'd even understand if you came to hate me for—"

"I could never hate you." He framed her face with his hands. "I love every fucking inch of you, inside and out. And I would never regret falling to be with you."

"Even though you'll have to survive partly on blood?"

"Even though. I have been alone for a very long time. Alone and numb. I didn't live, I existed. Until you. I'm not going to let you go, and I'm not going to leave you. I fucking refuse to be without you."

She took in a shaky breath. "I should really push you away to spare you the consequences of falling—especially when I get the impression that there's some things you haven't told me about the curse—but I'm too selfish for that."

She kissed him. Hard, deep, and slow. She truly should push him *away for his own sake, but she just couldn't find it in her to do it, couldn't—*

Everything went black.

He was gone from her arms. There was no noise. No smells. Nothing to see.

But . . . she was moving. No, being moved by someone or something.

She opened her mouth to speak, to ask what the fuck was going on, but no words came out.

Finally, her back met something hard and cold. Her arms were wrenched high above her head. Her vision came back to her . . . and she found herself facing six—

A horn beeped, cutting into her sleep, sending the dreamy images dispersing and making them fade away too fast for her to remember any.

"Some people should *not* be allowed to drive," snarked Mia, flipping a finger at a fellow driver.

Ella straightened from her slouch in the front passenger seat. "I fell asleep?"

Her sister spared her a sideways glance as she turned the steering wheel. "Yes. I didn't wake you, because I figured a nap might do you some good. I *had* thought you'd take advantage of us having the morning off work to sleep in. Didn't you?"

Ella rubbed at her face. "No." She'd spent the extra time with Viper.

"Did you sleep at all last night?"

"Some." Viper had insisted on it, concerned about how tired she looked. He often did coax her to get some sleep while in his bed, and she always slept better at his clubhouse.

For just over a week, they'd officially shared a bed. Something which showed no signs of stopping anytime soon. Thankfully.

Because she didn't want it to stop. Neither did her demon, who'd grown to like the angel. Or archangel. Whichever.

She'd repeatedly asked if the rumors about him were true, but each time he'd merely given her a mysterious smile. Or he'd said something like, *'Maybe I'll tell you one day,'* to which she'd said, *'And maybe you're full of shit.'* The dude had secrets for sure. A whole bunch of them.

So often he and his brothers would resort to telepathic communication in front of her. Viper would claim they were simply discussing 'club business'. That was no doubt sometimes true, but she didn't think it was *always* the case.

She wasn't exactly in a position to push him to spill private stuff, though. It wasn't like they were a couple. Although ... much as they'd agreed to keep things mellow and simple, she couldn't say that the arrangement centered solely on sex. They didn't go on dates or make demands of each other, but they'd each spend time at the other's home sharing a meal, watching TV, and exchanging stories.

She still hadn't told anyone that they were sleeping together. Only his brothers knew. Several times she'd turned to her sister, tempted to just blurt it out. But the words always got trapped in her throat, and she'd tell herself there was no point in saying anything unless, or until, she and Viper became serious about each other.

Otherwise, where was the sense in it?

It wasn't as if she generally talked of her flings.

"What were you dreaming about?" asked Mia, pulling Ella out of her contemplations. "You seemed ... distressed."

Ella blinked. "I don't know. I don't remember. I rarely remember *any* of what I dream these days."

A long, guilt-ridden sigh eased out of her sister. "I really can't understand why my talisman isn't working. I'll make you a stronger one and see if that helps. If it doesn't, maybe you should reconsider knocking back some sleeping potions. I know you avoid them because you want to be at your sharpest, but you won't be if you're tired all the time."

Point well made.

Ordinarily, Ella would have been resolute on not using them when sleeping beside someone else. But she didn't believe Viper would ever cause her any harm. Neither did her demon.

It felt strange to be so sure of someone when they were near strangers, but he made her feel safe. Her demon didn't read him as any kind of threat to Ella.

Not long later, she and Mia were striding through the Underground, passing pedestrians and vendors and various types of premises. The guards that Luka had assigned to Ella—Kasper and Arman—followed them, though they didn't come *too* close.

Despite the cacophony of sounds—chatter, laughter, footsteps, music filtering out of windows—she easily heard Mia's phone ring.

Her sister fished her phone out of her purse, and her brows knitted. "It's Leif."

The name rang a bell. "Joe's best friend?"

"Yeah," confirmed Mia, slowing to a stop. "Just give me a sec." She walked into a side alley where there was less noise to take the call.

Ella held up two fingers to her guards, indicating that they'd be on the move again in a matter of minutes. Nodding curtly, they took positions close by and let their sharp gazes wander their surroundings.

Ella did the same, humming to herself as people walked around her, heading in various directions. A lot of them were walking to and from eateries. One person caught her attention—firstly because they were familiar, secondly because they were staring at her.

The blonde from the Red Rooms who, according to Viper, didn't like the word 'no'.

Ella's demon narrowed its eyes, disliking the woman on principle. She could have been the sweetest creature to have ever walked the Earth and the demon *still* wouldn't have liked her because she apparently had a thing for Viper.

She also apparently thought it a good idea to approach Ella, because she did exactly that. The blonde didn't speak, just stared. *Hard*. It wasn't an attempt at intimidation. No, she looked at Ella the way you would at a math equation that made no sense to you.

Both Ella and her demon stared right back at her. *Descendant*, the entity sensed. She probably belonged to Maddox's lair, then.

A male psyche touched hers. *Need us to deal with her?* asked Kasper.

Ella responded, *I doubt it'll come to that. I'll let you know if I need backup.* "Can I help you with something?" she asked the blonde.

The woman blinked twice. Poking her tongue into the inside of her cheek, she leaned forward and said, "I know."

Ella's insides seized. "Sorry?"

"I know something's going on between you and Viper," the woman elaborated, her voice not loud enough to carry to others.

Personally, Ella doubted that the woman 'knew' anything. The descendant was more than likely just guessing, throwing out the comment to test Ella's reaction.

Though she and Viper spent a lot of time together, it was only in the confines of their own homes. Ella never drove to and from his compound, just as he never drove to and from her apartment complex. They traveled together using teleportation, and no one ever saw. Other than for his brothers, of course. They'd never tell anyone about it.

"I don't need you to confirm or deny it," the blonde added.

"And I'm not looking to cause trouble for you or to spread your secret around."

Again, doubtful. The descendant would have no reason to protect Ella's privacy.

"I just wanted to warn you, one woman to another, that you are wasting your time with Viper," the blonde explained, her voice laced with a candid sympathy.

Oh, so *this* was her game. She was going to pressure Ella to steer clear of Viper, acting as though she was doing it in the name of sisterhood.

"He'll never commit to a demon. There are too many things he'd be unable to share with you. And before you ask how I could know that, given I'm not part of his club"—a gentle smile curved the descendant's mouth that carried a hint of condescension—"I just know."

"If you feel the need to chase away any women you think might be involved with him, you very obviously are looking to land him. Which begs the question: why would you bother to try when you believe he'd never commit to a demon?"

"He'd make an exception for a descendant. We have similar secrets."

So she was eluding to things that were connected to his angelic nature, then.

"I understand him in ways you never will. Ways only my kind and his own could understand."

"How marvelous for you. Thanks for sharing what is totally irrelevant information. I'll, uh, see you around, I guess. I mean, you *are* around a lot."

The blonde's eyes narrowed at the taunt.

"Okay, I'm done," announced Mia as she sidled up to Ella. She did a slight double-take at the sight of the descendant, who appeared equally surprised to see her.

Worried the blonde might blurt out something she shouldn't, Ella quickly guided her sister away.

"You know her?" Mia asked.

Ella gave a small, flippant shrug. "I don't know her name or anything, but I know her face." *Change the subject, change the subject.* "Anyway, what did Leif want?"

Mia heaved a sigh. "Apparently, Joe is having 'a bad time' and Leif feels it would be good for me to go visit him. I got the feeling from some of the stuff Leif said that he's not aware of how Joe's been acting toward me lately. He seemed to think I'd be like, 'yeah, sure, I'll track him down right now.'"

Maybe it made her a little insensitive, but Ella wasn't feeling too bad for her sister's anchor—he'd behaved like an ass recently. Still, she'd support Mia in whatever she wanted to do. "Are you going to check on him?"

"I don't think he'd want to see me. And, if I'm honest, I don't really want to see him. There's too much tension and bad vibes between us at the moment. Giving each other space makes more sense."

Ella gently bumped Mia's shoulder with her own. "It'll all sort itself out eventually. I truly believe that."

"I hope you're right. I really do."

At Ghost's telepathic news, Viper felt his hand flex around his mug. *What do you mean, Neta approached her?*

It didn't seem that she was being confrontational or rude, Ghost replied. *I couldn't hear any of what was said, I wasn't close enough. But Ella didn't look upset or rattled. More like . . . inconvenienced.*

Viper clenched his jaw, biting back a curse.

At the breakfast bar, Jester caught his eye and flicked up a questioning brow.

Viper raised his forefinger, wanting more information from Ghost before he relayed the conversation. *You're sure Ella ain't upset?*

She doesn't look it. She waltzed off with her sister, shrugging off the whole thing with Neta easily. She seems more focused on Mia.

That was something, at least.

Want me to nab Neta?

No, stay on Ella. I'll have someone else do it. Focusing on Jester, Viper informed him, "Neta spoke to Ella in the Underground just now."

Jester's brows slid together. "Spoke to her about what?"

"Ghost doesn't know." Viper set his cup down on the counter. "He says Ella doesn't seem fazed or upset. While I'm confident she can handle Neta just fine if need be, I still don't like it. And I want to know what was said."

"It could be that Neta simply asked her if you two are seeing each other. Maybe talk to Ella first. *She's* more likely to spill all."

Viper rolled his shoulders. "Not really feeling in the mood to delay—" He cut off as Darko teleported into the kitchen of the clubhouse, the light of urgency in his gaze.

"Hudson, we have a problem," Darko announced.

"You mean Houston," Jester corrected.

Darko shrugged. "Whatever. There's a problem."

"Which is?" asked Viper, pushing away from the counter.

Darko planted his feet. "I tracked down some strix, but they're in a pretty public place."

Viper felt his eyes narrow. "How public?"

"They're at a damn carnival."

Shit. "Coordinates?"

After Darko rattled them off, Viper telepathically sent them to each brother along their club's 'channel', adding, *Other than Ghost—you need to stay on Ella—I want everyone to teleport to this spot. There are some strix there.* He refocused on the angels in front of him. "Let's get gone."

As one, they teleported to a shadowed spot among the trees at the carnival's perimeter. It was like walking into a wall of noise. So much talking, laughing, circus-like music, chugging machinery, screams of riders, and the spooky theatrical sounds filtering out of the haunted house.

"They've separated into groups," said Darko, who then pointed to the clusters of strix that were hovering out of sight near amusement rides; watching the children with a predatory gaze.

In quick bursts, more of Viper's brothers materialized, gathering into a tight huddle as they spied on the demons.

"There's, what, twenty of them?" estimated Omen, a slight question in his tone.

"Looks like it," replied Razor.

"We can't really afford to have our usual fun," said Viper. "Too many people would see things they shouldn't, not to mention get hurt."

Jester cocked his head. "What are you thinking we should do?"

Viper pursed his lips. "I'm thinking we teleport behind each of them, snap their necks, and then whisk their corpses out of here."

Rebel frowned. "Do we really have to make their deaths fast? They're about to snatch *kids*. They don't deserve quick and easy."

Viper sighed. "Fine. We teleport behind them, grab them before they can act, and whisk them away from here so we can kill them in privacy."

Darko grinned. "I like that plan better. Where do you wanna take them?"

Viper chewed on the inside of his mouth, pensive. "Strix hate water, right?"

A smile curved Omen's mouth. "You're thinking the small stretch of beach where we once had that party."

"No one goes there, and it's far away from everything." The perfect spot.

"The beach it is," decided Merchant, who'd been out of isolation for a few days now. He pointed at a particular strix. "I want *that* one in the green jumper. Which one do you want?" he asked Sting.

At that, each of the brothers chose their own target. Several of the angels would return for the last cluster of strix before they could notice their brethren had been taken.

"Right, let's move," said Viper. He teleported to a particular demon, grabbed it from behind, and teleported it straight to the destination in mind.

As he and his brothers all stood in a long line on the shore, they became instantly smothered by the scents of salty air, brine, and seaweed.

Release them, Viper telepathically ordered.

As one, the club let go of their captives, who all lurched forward and then spun to face them. The strix's gazes darted around, taking in their new surroundings.

It wasn't a pretty beach. There was no white sand, no turquoise water, no seagulls crying overheard, no signs of human life.

Small and cramped, it was bordered by tall-as-hell cliffs. The tawny-brown sand was littered with grit, sharp pebbles, and seaweed. Frothy, dark-blue waves tumbled inland and turned into foam. Other waves angrily crashed against rocks. Thick gray clouds blocked the sun and cast shadows everywhere, giving the beach a gloomy look.

Unease flickered in the demons' red eyes as they stared at the sea. A strix's aversion to water wasn't about fear. They just hated being wet. And Viper had no reservations about exposing fucking child eaters to anything they hated.

All the strix are now here, including those we had to go back for, Jester reported through the telepathic channel as everyone shrugged out of their jackets.

Viper dropped his on a rock that protruded out of the sand. "You were all gonna feed on children? Really?"

"What do you care?" a demon sniped. It stepped back but then stilled as water lapped at its feet. "They are human. Cattle."

The strix beside it hissed at Viper, greed carved into its face. "Now we feed on you instead." It leaped at him.

Viper didn't try to dodge it, just braced himself for impact so he wouldn't tip over. The strix landed on him, snapped its limbs around his body, and sank its teeth into his throat. It was a hard, vicious, feral bite that hurt like a bitch.

But not as much as it hurt the strix to drink Viper's blood.

It slumped to the sandy floor at his feet with an agonized cry. Arching and writhing on the ground, it hissed and cried out as Viper's blood ate at its insides.

Letting out a shriek of grief, another strix came at him. Viper telekinetically shoved it hard, sending it zooming backwards. The demon hit the water with a plop. It emerged, staggering under the pull of undertow; its shriek getting lost beneath the sounds of battle as chaos broke out.

Viper released an archangelic blast that gleamed as it rolled toward the demon. The slice of unholy fire severed the body with no effort, sending its ashes scattering into the sea.

Battle adrenaline flooded his bloodstream as he fought alongside his brothers. Orbs were volleyed this way and that. Whips of black fire cracked out. Strix were dumped in the sea or thrown against the cliffs.

The earlier peaceful vibe to the beach disappeared, its natural music disappearing beneath the *cracks* of whips, the snapping and popping of flames, the harsh splashes of water, the grunts and hisses and laughs and shrieks.

The fresh smell of the sea air became tainted with those of sulphur, brimstone, acid, blood, and pain.

Even as sand stuck to his blistered skin, even as splatters of salty water stung his wounds, even as fucking Darko annoyingly sang "Under the Sea" in a Jamaican accent, Viper kept fighting.

A sweltering hot orb collided into his chest, punching the breath from his lungs and sending pain radiating through his torso. He tracked its sender, conjuring an orb of unholy fire. But then Dice curved his covered-in-flames body around the strix, burning it alive with a bear hug.

All right.

"Coming to the beach was a bad shout," clipped Jester as he stomped out of the water. "Fucking hate salt water."

Blackjack smirked. "You hate everything."

A series of flaming balls whooshed through the air toward Viper. He returned fire. Literally. Hurled several orbs of unholy fire at his foe until, finally, the fucker became ashes.

A heavy weight landed on his back as two hands grasped his head in a viselike grip. He grunted as sharp nails dug into his scalp like thick needles.

As those hands tried wrenching his head to the side, Viper teleported them both right into the sea, the shock of the cold water making him go still for a split second.

With a dramatic shriek, the strix strived to rise and escape. Viper surfaced at the same time, nabbed the demon by the throat, and plunged its head back into the sea. Its limbs flailed frantically, splashing water everywhere. He tightened his grip on the strix, not allowing it to resurface. Finally, its struggles ceased and the body disintegrated in his hands.

Viper teleported back onto the shore, water sluicing down

his body and weighing down his sodden clothes. He noted with relief that none of his brothers were badly injured. In fact, they were laughing and grinning and living their best lives. As for the strix? Their numbers had dropped fast.

Omen groaned, his face all scrunched up. "Think I've got sand in my eye."

Jester grunted, his back covered in sand as if he'd fallen at some point. "Think I've got it down the crack of my ass."

A stream of ultraviolet fire gushed past Viper, lighting up the strix who'd *just* been coming at him from the side. Before he could give Jester a nod of thanks, another strix advanced on him, all nails and fangs and long limbs. Viper was impressed it was still alive, considering its skin was a collage of blisters, burns, cuts, and rotting patches.

The demon vaulted its body right at him . . . but was incidentally knocked down by a wayward telekinetic strike from Dice. The strix zoomed backwards and hit the sand, sending it *puffing* everywhere. Before the strix could rise, Viper telekinetically snapped its neck.

An enraged hiss emerged out of a nearby strix, who then pinned Viper with a hateful glare.

Viper flicked up a taunting brow. "Problem?"

The demon rushed him, kicking up a cloud of sand. Viper slashed out his arm, telekinetically slamming the strix into a rock wall. The impact caused little stones to break away and patter the sea below as the body sank into it. But the strix surfaced, shifting into a bat in the process, and then bulleted through the air toward Viper.

He slammed up a telekinetic hand to stop its momentum and shoved it hard, sending the bat crashing into a rocky outcropping. Maybe the impact cracked its skull or something because, like that, the strix was dead.

A fiery whip slapped at Viper's face, splitting his lower lip and burning a line along his cheekbone. Even as his injured skin began to prickle and sizzle, he turned toward the new attacker; saw a strix charging toward him. Viper flicked a hand, telekinetically wafting up a shit load of sand toward the demon.

It coughed and rubbed at its eyes, stumbling to a halt. He took advantage, driving his teeth down hard into the prick's throat. He gulped down blood, letting it heal his injuries, and then sliced downwards with an archangelic blast that split its body in a vertical fashion.

"Nice," praised Omen.

Viper grunted, gratified to see that the battle was over. No strix were left. Ashes mingled with the sand and floated on the water.

"Well, I enjoyed that," Rebel announced, shoving at the wet strands of hair clinging to his forehead. "Though I have sand in places it has no right being."

Sting snickered, scrubbing away the bits of grit dusting his face. "Don't we all?"

Jester crossed to Viper. "When these demons don't return to the colony, the queen will know it was likely us who'll kill them. This makes three times we've chipped at their numbers. She's going to launch a mass attack eventually."

Since it would enable his club to eradicate them in one swoop . . . "I look forward to the day she finally does."

CHAPTER SEVENTEEN

As her sister parked her car in the lot outside their complex later that day, Ella pulled in a steadying breath. Throughout her shift at work, she'd thought about her little chat with the blonde descendant, wondering just how truthful she'd been when claiming she wouldn't expose Ella's arrangement with Viper.

Ella wasn't ready to talk about it with others yet. She knew her loved ones would pressure her to end it. She also knew that Luka would pressure *Viper* to end it—especially since he was currently in full-on protective mode due to the notes.

Ella didn't believe that Viper would cave to her anchor's demands. *She* certainly wouldn't. Luka would be pissed, and he could strike out at Viper. Then there'd be fighting. She didn't want that.

But she might not have the option of continuing to keep her fling with Viper on the downlow. Not if the blonde intended to blab. So maybe it was best for Ella to be the one to tell her loved ones. They'd only react worse if they heard about it secondhand.

She needed to start with someone, and her sister was the least likely person to overreact and call up Luka, banking on him ensuring the fling came to an end.

So when Mia went to exit the car, Ella blurted out, "Before we head inside, I have to tell you something."

Her sister blinked, her eyes lighting with interest. "Ooh, I'm all ears."

"You can't tell anyone, though. Not even Mom or Jocelyn. I need to do that myself."

"It's a secret? Awesome. I'm even more intrigued now. What gives?"

"*Promise* me you'll keep it to yourself."

Mia lifted a hand, palm out. "I solemnly swear to guard your secret—I will tell no one."

Ella exhaled heavily and twisted in her seat to better face her sister. "Quick warning, you probably won't like this. I don't *think* you'll judge, but you might well call me all kinds of stupid."

Mia's expression registered surprise. "I would never call you stupid."

We'll see. "You know how this past week you kept insisting I was *definitely* getting laid on the regular?" Mia hadn't bought her denials, but she hadn't pushed too hard.

"Yeah," Mia replied.

"Well, you were right."

"I know that. I just can't figure out who's been doing the laying."

"It's the same guy I hooked up with at the Red Rooms." Ella drew in a preparatory breath and straightened her shoulders. "It's Viper."

Mia's lips parted. "Viper as in the president of the Black Saints Viper?"

"One and the same," Ella confirmed, studying her sister's face;

picking up nothing. "I didn't tell anyone—well, until right now—because I know there'll be stern looks and lectures. I also know Luka will be *seriously* against it. And, yeah, those reactions would be perfectly understandable. But . . . but I like Viper, Mia. A lot."

On pins, Ella nibbled her lower lip as she waited for her sister to speak. Only . . . Mia didn't. She just stared dumbly. Ella frowned. "Say something."

"Uh . . ."

Ella leaned back slightly. "You're not gonna be all judgy, are you?"

"As your baby sister—"

"You're the oldest."

"Well, I like to pretend I'm the younger one. Getting old scares me." Mia flapped a hand. "Anyway, as your sister, I should tell you that this isn't wise and point out that it could go tits up *big style*. But if you like Viper and enjoy being with him . . . then I'm happy for you."

"Why?"

Mia's brows snapped together. "What do you mean, why?"

"I mean why would you be happy when he's one of the Fallen?"

Mia bristled. "They're not only *the Fallen*. They're people. Not bad. Not good. Just some of both, much like everyone else. And, well, I'd be a hypocrite to lecture you."

"A hypocrite? Why a . . ." Ella trailed off as the pieces fell together. She gawked at her sister. "Oh my God, that dude you slept with, who fucked your frustration out of you—it was one of the Black Saints, wasn't it?"

Squeezing one eye shut, Mia scratched her cheek. "Yeah."

"Which one?"

"Dice. And, uh, we didn't just do it that one time."

"It happened again?"

Mia gave her a sheepish look. "That was sort of an accident.

But the times after that, well, they weren't so accidental. It's basically become a regular thing for us to meet up for sex."

Ella gaped again. "Why didn't you say anything before?"

"I thought you'd lecture me and I didn't want to hear it. Sound familiar?"

Ella's mouth snapped shut. To think she'd been nervous of her sister's response when, in actuality, Mia would have taken it well.

"I was going to tell you. I kept meaning to. But after what happened with Joe, I'm enjoying what I have with Dice—it's simple, casual, no expectations or demands. I'm not ready to walk away from it yet, and if there's anyone who could talk me into doing that it's you."

Ella let out a long breath. "I don't know why Viper didn't tell me about you and Dice."

Mia's nose wrinkled. "Uh, Dice hasn't yet told him. He plans to do it today."

"Oh. And he didn't tell you about me and Viper? He *definitely* knows I'm sleeping with his president—I see the VP at the compound often."

"He said nothing about it to me," she said, shaking her head. "But in his shoes, I probably wouldn't have either. The messengers are never thanked. And I would have worried it would cause trouble between siblings if they found out secondhand."

Yeah, that made sense. "Dice probably thought it would hurt you to not hear it from me. Are you guys exclusive?"

"Oh yeah, he was pretty insistent on it. And I saw no need to object, because I didn't want to."

"Then we're in very similar situations."

"Crazy, isn't it," Mia marveled. "So, this is how you know Neta, then?"

"Who?"

"The blonde you were talking with earlier. Dice and I once

bumped into her, and she made no bones about eye-fucking him. He told me her ultimate goal is to be claimed by Viper."

Ella felt her eyelid twitch, possessiveness clutching her chest. No happier, her demon cricked its neck. "I see. That explains why she wants me off the scene."

"So she's aware you're doing the sexual rodeo with Viper?"

"I think it's more of a guess on her part. She didn't threaten to tell people. Actually, she said she *wouldn't* tell. But I'm not sure I believe her."

"She might mean it. If she revealed stuff she shouldn't, it would piss off Viper in a mega way. She won't want to do that. It won't actually endear him to her," Mia pointed out.

"She said he'll never commit to me because he has the kind of secrets only descendants and celestials would understand. I don't know what exactly she meant by that."

Mia nibbled on her lower lip. "Dice admitted to me that he is keeping secrets. The club as a whole are secretive. I've asked him to part with at least one, but he says he can't. And really, why should he? We're not serious. We're just having fun."

"I've asked Viper some personal questions. He often teasingly blows me off. Which would annoy me, but I don't get the feeling he wants to hold me at a distance; just that he's not in a position to share easily."

Mia hummed. "I can't complain, because I know all about keeping your own council and holding your secrets close."

"Yeah, you don't go round dropping secrets like they're candy. You share them with people you know will stick around. And I don't know if Viper even wants me to stick around."

"All you can do is see how things play out. Fingers crossed they play out in your favor."

"Fingers crossed."

*

Hearing a knock on his bedroom door, Viper slipped on his jacket as he called out, "Come in."

Dice stalked inside, an uncharacteristic uncertainty in his gaze. "You got a minute?"

"Sure. What's up?"

He planted his feet, flexing one hand. "You should know that this might piss you off, but ... I've been seeing Mia."

Both Viper and his inner entity went still. "Mia?"

"It ain't anything serious, but—"

"As in Ella's sister Mia?"

Dice notched up his chin. "I first slept with her shortly after you fucked Ella at the Red Rooms. I can't even tell you how it happened. It just did. I never lose control. But every bit of rationality I had went out the damn window," he grumbled.

Viper blinked. It was true that his VP was always in complete control of himself. "And it didn't stop at one night?"

"I meant for it to, but no. Like I said, I'm not all that rational around Mia. I do shit I shouldn't. Like refuse to give her my dick again unless she agreed to an exclusive arrangement." Dice shook his head in a kind of resentful wonder.

Viper ran his tongue over his front teeth, amused despite himself.

"I like what we have, but I can't say it will go the distance. I'm not built for relationships, and Mia's not looking for one anyway. If you want me to walk away from ... Why don't you look pissed?"

"Why would I be pissed?"

Dice's brow creased. "I can think of several reasons."

"I don't like that you kept this from me. I don't like that you slept with her regularly knowing her connection to Ella—if things had gone badly with you and Mia, she might have told Ella, and that might have made it harder for me to get on my woman's good side. But I'm the last person who's in a position to judge someone for going after the woman they want."

"I know, but I'm your brother. Your VP—"

"When I pursued Ella in her previous life, I did it knowing it would piss off a *lot* of people—some of whom I considered family." He just hadn't thought they'd hide her soul from him. "I knew I was breaking every rule there was; knew there'd be people who'd be upset, or angry, or disappointed. I did it anyway. Nothing could have stopped me."

"I still wouldn't blame you for being pissed."

"How can I be, when I know you wouldn't have gotten even slightly entangled with Mia if she hadn't snagged your interest in a major way? No woman has done that in a very long time."

"You're not worried that if I hurt Mia it'll lead to Ella not wanting anything to do with the Fallen?"

"You wouldn't hurt Mia or any other woman." Viper took a step toward him. "Look, I want you and the rest of our brothers to find some fucking happiness in this life where we subsist partly on the life-force of others and have to randomly suffer bouts of bloodlust. If Mia can give you that, even temporarily, I'm not going to stand in the way."

Dice cleared his throat. "Appreciate it. Not sure I'd have been so reasonable."

"Well, you're not me."

The angel's lips curled.

"Now I gotta go, I'm heading off to see Ella."

Dice tipped his chin. "Later."

"Later."

Viper teleported straight to the living area of Ella's apartment. And there she was, tucking a hoover into a closet. "Hey there, baby."

She jumped a little and then put a hand to her chest. "Yeah, we're *definitely* putting a bell on you."

Feeling his mouth curve, he crossed to her, hooked his hand around her nape, and planted a quick kiss on her lips. Or that was the plan. But the kiss fast turned deep and wet and wicked.

She hummed against his mouth. "That was a promising start to the evening."

His entity fully agreed. "I plan for it to end on an equally good note."

"You're my favorite angel. Just sayin'."

He felt his lips quirk. "I'm the only angel you know well."

"I am getting to know your brothers, though. Speaking of them . . . did you have a particular talk with Dice today?"

Surprise plucked at his brows. "I did."

"I confessed to Mia that you and I were sleeping together, and she then confessed that she and Dice were also regularly doing the dirty. She said he meant to share it with you today."

"He did. It took me aback, but I'm glad. He's been on his own too long. Even something simple and casual will be good for him. What prompted you to tell her?"

She hesitated. "I was approached by that blonde from your club. Mia said her name is Neta."

At the reminder, anger zipped through both him and his entity. He felt his face go hard. "Ghost mentioned it earlier—he was watching over you today. What did she say?"

"She wasn't hostile or anything. Just said she's of the opinion that you'd only ever commit to a fellow celestial or descendant."

Viper's entity growled. "The fuck?"

"Something about you having secrets you wouldn't be able to share with any other race."

Son of a bitch, she'd tried manipulating Ella into walking away.

"Is that true?" Such a deceptively casual question.

Viper gave her nape a light squeeze. "No. If I trusted someone all the way, there's nothing I'd keep from them." One day, he'd tell her everything. It just wouldn't be any time soon. "Which she'd know if she knew *me*, but she doesn't."

"She still seems intent on having you."

"*You* have me, so she's wasting her time. She'd be wasting it even if there was no you. I don't want her."

"Shame she's not getting that." Ella paused. "She said she wouldn't tell others that you and I are involved with each other, but I worry she might. Not that I'm ashamed to—"

"I get it, Ella. You already explained what happened to some of your ancestors at the hands of the Fallen, so I know why your family isn't a fan of my kind; I understand why you'd hesitate to tell them. And of course you'd rather they heard it from you, if they ever hear of it at all. I'll talk to Neta, I'll ensure she keeps her mouth shut."

Ella eyed him, her face soft. "I'm not sure I'd be so nice about this if I were you. I'd feel at least a little offended that you're intent on keeping me a secret from those around you."

"As I told you, I get it." And it worked to Viper's benefit that they hadn't made shit public, considering it was vital he keep her off the strix's radar. It might already be too late to keep the Uppers' attention away from her, unfortunately. "Does your whole lair have that opinion of the Fallen?"

"Most."

"Is it hard not living near the majority of its members?"

She gave an easy shake of her head. "I wasn't close to any of them."

"Not even any of your relatives there?"

"Nope. And I actually prefer living a distance away from my father. He's a complete tool."

Viper was well-aware of that, because he'd looked into her background, but he couldn't say as much. "In what way?"

"Turns out he had a 'secret family'. They're humans. We didn't find out until he one day announced he was leaving us for them. Mom wasn't heartbroken, she was furious. She would have left him years before; she'd only stayed with him thinking it'd be best for me and my sister. So for him to up and leave us on revealing he'd actually built another family elsewhere? Yeah, I'm surprised she let him live."

Viper nuzzled her neck, holding her close. "I'm sorry, baby."

"I wasn't cut up about him leaving, I didn't really know him. He never had much time for me or Mia. Was always 'at the office'. Or so we thought. But I was upset to hear about his other family. Honestly, though, we're better off without the idiot around."

For certain. "Do you have contact with him?"

"No, I have no time for him. Neither does Mia. And he never asked to stay in touch with us anyway."

Yet more proof that the guy was, in her words, a complete tool. "Want me to kill him for you?"

Her lips twitched. "Nah. For some people, the punishment is in letting them live."

"If you're sure."

"I'm sure. I think maybe . . . " She trailed off, her brows drawing together as her gaze dipped to the collar of his jacket. "You have blood on you. What the hell?"

Viper silently cursed. It had to be blood spatter. "So, keeping to my word, I gotta inform you that I had another run-in with strix."

Her eyes flared. "Tell me."

"One of my brothers tracked a bunch of them to a carnival. The bastards had their eyes on some of the children there. We teleported them to another location and killed them."

"So, they're all dead?"

"Not the entire colony. There'll be more."

"How many more?"

"Depends. Could be thirty. Could be forty. Could be more. Strix colonies aren't small."

Damn. Ella knew a fair bit about some hell-born demons, but not all. With others, like strix, she merely knew *of* them and possessed few details.

"We'll keep working to track them, and we'll eat at their numbers until they're all gone."

"They really go after little kids?"

Viper gave her a grim look. "They prefer the blood of children."

"Then they definitely need killing." She took stock of him. "You aren't hurt?"

His expression softened. "No, baby, I'm good."

"I'd rather see that for myself."

"Yeah?" His lips tipped up. "Feels more like you're just trying to get me naked so you can take advantage of me."

Busted. "You have a problem with that?"

"No."

"Good."

He lowered his head to hers. "Turn around. Bend over. Hold onto the arm of the sofa."

Gladly.

CHAPTER EIGHTEEN

Neta's glare bounced from Viper to Dice, a hint of wariness there. "Just to note, I don't appreciate being summoned like some minion at your beck and call."

Well, Viper didn't appreciate *her* going near his woman, so . . .

"What's this about?" she demanded, trying for indignant.

Twisting on his stool at the not-yet-open dive bar, he arched a brow. "You can't guess?"

Neta sighed and pulled a face. "I wasn't a bitch to the incantor or anything, I just talked to her."

His entity narrowed its eyes, annoyed that she'd attempt to downplay it. "You told her that our kinds have secrets."

"It's not like she won't have already picked up on it."

"And how would you know?" he challenged. "Do you spend a lot of time around Ella? Is she someone you've spoken to before yesterday?"

She flicked her blonde hair over her shoulder in a nervous

gesture. "I just think it's unlikely that she isn't aware you keep things from her."

Which wasn't the point *at all*. "You basically prompted her to ask me uncomfortable questions. You wanted her to think that anything with me is a dead-end." That infuriated his entity most of all, because they weren't yet in a position to make Ella the kind of promises that would prove otherwise—she wasn't ready to hear those yet.

"You can't exactly claim a mate outside of your own kind. Not when you have secrets to protect from outsiders."

"Why? Your kind does it sometimes. What's the difference?"

Neta blinked. "Wait, so you're saying you *will* claim the redhead?" It wasn't a question, it was a query that demanded justification.

Viper gave her a hard look. "Tell me how *anything* I do is your fucking business," he said, the words rough with a faint growl.

She licked her lips. "I just . . . "

"My guess is that, for whatever reason, you want to leave your lair. You thought joining our club would be as good as joining another lair. You wouldn't have to hide the curse, and you wouldn't have to keep secrets from whoever you took as your mate. But *you*, Neta, wouldn't be content with mating one of my brothers. You want to have status. And that would mean being taken as my mate. That's what this is about."

Her eyes flickered.

"I made it clear to you more than once that I'm not interested in what you're offering. That hasn't changed. It won't ever change."

"Viper," she implored, "can we—"

"I definitely wouldn't have any interest in a woman who'd try to come between me and what's mine." His entity wanted to ring her neck.

"Okay, so I went about things the wrong way. You're right, I want out of my lair—and for real good reasons. Tell me what I have to do to earn a place in your club, and I'll do it."

"That ain't gonna happen." She was fucking high if she thought differently.

Her brow pinched. "But—"

"You fucked with my woman, Neta. You think I want anyone near her who'd do that?"

Her eyes drifted shut, and her shoulders slumped. "I really messed up, didn't I?"

That was putting it lightly. "There are other descendant lairs; other groups of fallen angels. If you're really that desperate to leave your own lair, switch to one of those."

She swallowed. "Are you going to tell Maddox about this?" she asked, not quite masking the dread from her voice.

"Don't see the point—I made myself clear, you listened, and I'm gonna assume you won't fuck up like that again. But if you do, or if you tell anyone about my involvement with Ella—and I mean fucking *anyone*—I will call him. It'll only be fair I let him know that I tortured one of his demons."

Fear washed over her face, pleasing his entity.

"From now on, you're barred from every premise I own. You stay away from my businesses, you stay away from my brothers, and you stay away from my woman. You got that?"

Her eyes went wide, and she took a fast step forward. "Please don't bar me from the Red Rooms. The only other place I'll be able to feed is my lair's club. I don't like being there."

"Not my problem. I told you, I don't want anyone around my woman who'd fuck with her."

Neta pressed her lips tight together, resignation flitting over her features. "Right. Okay." She paused, looking from him to Dice. "I'd like to leave now."

Viper tipped his chin toward the door. "Go."

She didn't hesitate to spin on her heel and scamper.

He looked at his VP. "You have any idea why she'd so badly want to leave her lair?"

Pursing his lips, Dice shook his head. "Not one."

"Look into it. I wanna know just how likely she is to push back at me for not offering her a place in our club. Demons are good at holding grudges."

Dice grunted his agreement. "So are we."

Yeah, very true.

Having finished drawing symbols on her kitchen floor, Mia rose to her feet and set the chalk on the circular black, glass table. Rubbing her hands together to brush off the powdery residue, she looked at Ella. "I'm ready when you are."

"Then let's find out what we're dealing with." Ella squatted down, unzipped the small suitcase she'd earlier placed on the floor, and then flipped it open. It was empty aside for the vintage porcelain doll.

It was in perfect condition and boasted the usual features you'd expect to see on such a toy—doe eyes, small mouth, light blush, alabaster skin tone, blonde ringlets, pretty dress. But there was something . . . *off* about it.

The doll was honestly spooky as hell. Maybe because it looked so lifelike. Maybe because, no matter what angle you stood at, its eyes seemed to be staring right at you. Or maybe it was something to do with its tiny smile that looked kind of sinister.

Ella pulled it out of the case, grimacing at the not-so-nice vibe it gave off.

Mia's nose wrinkled. "Eerie little thing, isn't it?"

"For sure." Ella placed it in the center of the protective circle on the floor, which would contain any aggressive power or magick that might be attached to the doll.

Mia began to circle it, careful not to cross the lines of chalk. "And the couple is convinced it's a conduit?"

"A conduit for pure evil. Their words." Ella folded her arms. "Their son believes it's actually possessed."

"Have you met them?"

"No. They wanted rid of the doll, not to consult about it. They gave it to Neve, who dropped it off here so I could take a look at it." Ella had accepted the suitcase from her, taken one peek inside, sensed the magick it gave off, and instantly closed it. She'd had the instant feeling that she'd need her sister's input on this.

"It smells like a musty attic," Mia groused.

"Considering it's been sitting on a shelf in a kid's bedroom, it shouldn't."

"That poor kid must have hated having it in their room. *I* wouldn't want to look at it every day."

Ella would likely have dumped it in the trash when no one was looking. "At first, when Neve told me it supposedly moves around by itself, I thought maybe a telekinetic demon was acting as some kind of puppeteer. But I sense a hint of magick here. I think someone bespelled it."

Mia dipped her chin in agreement. "Where did the family get the doll?"

"A second-hand toy store. So, if there's a jinx at work, it's likely not personal to them; more to its original owners. You're the expert when it comes to jinxes and all that stuff, so I figured you'd recognize what we're dealing with here."

Mia leaned toward it without breaking the circle. "It has been jinxed. I don't think an incantor is responsible. More like a witch or dark practitioner." She stood up straight. "Have there been any fires at the house?"

"Yeah, actually. Two. One in the kitchen, the other in the dad's home office. They thought the first one was an accident; that someone left the gas on. But the second fire had no obvious cause. The doll was somehow in the office—a place it *shouldn't* have been—and it was the only thing that suffered no smoke damage, aside from the patch of carpet on which it lay."

Mia juddered. "Creepy."

"That was when the humans decided it was time to get shot of the doll. For a while, the parents thought that their kids were just pranking them; they didn't believe it was moving around by itself."

"Not many human adults would. Most instinctively shy away from anything paranormal."

Ella unfolded her arms, letting them fall to her sides. "What was the purpose of the jinx? To cause fires?"

"No, to cause destruction for the family that owned it. That takes lots of forms. For instance, by moving around, the doll caused fear in the children. The parents didn't believe their claims, which made the kids feel betrayed. And as the adults felt they were not only being pranked but lied to, they were upset and probably punished them. The destruction eventually turns physical—fires, falling furniture, malfunctioning electrics, etc, etc."

Ah. "So whoever bespelled the doll had a *lot* of beef with whatever family they ensured it reached," Ella mused.

"It was definitely personal. Always is with such jinxes."

"Can you dissolve the spell?"

"Yes, though it's going to require a delicate hand. If you give me an hour or so, I can have it done. But I'd advise you to destroy the doll afterwards, because negative energy will still cling to it. Not the kind that's harmful, but it won't be pleasant to have around."

"I get that. I'll—" Ella stilled as a dart of magick shot up in front of her and burst outward like a firework.

"What was that?" Mia asked.

"The magickal alarm I put on my front door." *Shit*. Ella tore out of the apartment, her sister close behind her. She didn't bother waiting for the elevator. Her heart pounding like crazy, her demon losing its mind, she sprinted down the stairwell— descending one floor and then another before finally arriving at her own.

Dashing down the hallway toward her apartment, she frowned. Because there was no one there. Coming to a stop near her front door, she breathed hard and fast. "They're gone."

Mia swore, panting. "It has to have been your note writer."

Ella scanned the carpeted floor around them. "There's nothing here. If they came to leave another letter, they forgot to drop it off before they left."

"Do you think they were trying to get inside?"

"Possibly." Ella briefly chanted under her breath, causing the four wards protecting her door to become visible. The size of her palm, they were all gold, glimmering circles containing glyphs and old arcane writings. Scanning each of them, she froze. "Wait."

"What?"

"Look at that." Anger scraping at her nerves and boiling in her demon's gut, she pointed to the ward on the top left of the doorframe. "See the shadow there?"

Mia studied it closely, and her nostrils flared. "Motherfucker, they took a shot at unraveling your wards."

"Only one, so maybe . . ." Ella trailed off on noticing that her sister's gaze had turned inward. "What is it?"

Mia blinked, refocusing on her. "Dice telepathically reached out to ask what time I want him to pick me up. Can I tell him what happened here? He'll only brood if he later finds out I didn't say anything at the time."

"Yeah, that's fine. Tell him to relay it to Viper—I would have texted him about this anyway." Ella turned back to the front door. "Whoever came here was cocky to think they'd unravel my personal wards. I mean, people literally pay me to build wards for them. It's no secret that I'm good at it."

"They stupidly thought they were up to the challenge, I guess."

Just then, Viper and Dice teleported a mere foot away. Both were tense, their eyes hard, their jaws tight.

Viper crossed to Ella. "What the fuck happened?"

"I'd put a magical tripwire on my front door," she explained. "If anyone came near it with negative intent, it would go off. Which it did. But whoever set it off had left by the time we got here."

Dice's face firmed. "Shit, Mia, you should have called for me *before* running down here to—"

"Save it," advised Mia, slamming up a hand. "I'm no damsel. I did not feel that my sister and I would be unable to handle whoever had been dumb enough to try to enter an incantor's apartment without invitation."

Viper's gaze sharpened. "They tried to *enter* it?"

"Yup. I thought they'd just come to drop off a note, but there's a shadow on my ward." Ella gestured at it. "They wanted inside."

Viper snarled. "Son of a bitch."

"Indeed." Ella chanted low and soft, releasing a thread of magick that surged up to the ward and pierced its center. The entire ward flickered, glowed, and then settled—the shadow now gone. Sending out a soft wave of magick, she made the four wards once more transparent.

Turning back to Viper, she almost flushed at the covetous look on his face. Huh. *Somebody* liked watching her work magick. If her demon wasn't so pissed, it would have smiled at that.

Door hinges creaked somewhere down the hall, and they each went very still.

Viper caught her wrist as he looked at Dice. "Clubhouse. Main room." He then teleported him and Ella to said room. Milliseconds later, Dice and Mia joined them.

"Wow," breathed Mia. Her gaze bounced around, ricocheting off the reddish brown brick walls, leather couches, pool table, mahogany furnishings, and small bar. It was then Ella remembered that her sister hadn't been here before.

Viper planted his feet as he stared at Ella, still in possession of her hand. "Would only another incantor be able to untangle the wards?"

"Yes," replied Ella. "And they'd have a heck of a time doing it. The process would take literally days, if not longer. But it isn't only incantors who can attempt to damage magickal wards. Anyone with power could make a go of it, they just wouldn't stand a chance of succeeding with mine—unlike incantors."

"The shadow that was on the ward . . . does that mean it was damaged?"

"No. Think of it as a bruise. The ward took a hard hit. It didn't break. No threads of the spells popped. There was just a mark from the impact. I removed it."

"There was no other 'bruises'?"

She shook her head. "Just that one."

"The question is," began Mia, "who was it who left the bruise?"

"I'd say my pen pal gave up on using notes and decided it was time for us to have a showdown."

Or they wanted to take her, Dice telepathically suggested to Viper. *A celestial might do that on behalf of the Uppers to force your hand, knowing you'd return to the upper realm if it would keep her alive.*

Possibly, but . . . *It wouldn't save her life. They'd kill her anyway.*

Mia very theatrically cleared her throat, arching a reprimand-ing brow at him and Dice. "It's rude to exclude us by having private telepathic chats. If you know something, you should share it. This is Ella's safety we're talking about."

"We were just considering whether or not one of our enemies could have come for Ella," Viper prevaricated, choosing his words carefully.

Mia's brow creased. "What, you mean the strix?"

Huh. Apparently Dice had warned her about them.

"I can't see that being the case," Ella said to Viper. "Unless they've seen you and I together—which is highly unlikely—they'd have no reason to come near me. The only time we were ever together in public was the night at the Red Rooms. But since I'd imagine you debauch people often in dark corners of the club, I doubt it would have stood out to any who took notice."

"Well, apart from Neta," Mia chipped in. "Could it have been her who came for you?"

"I don't think I matter enough to the woman for her to risk her life trying to harm me. And it *would* be a risk to her life. If I didn't kill her, someone else would in my defense."

Yeah, *Viper* would do it.

Mia looked at him. "Does Neta care enough for you that she'd try to eliminate Ella?"

"Neta doesn't care for me at all." Viper cut his gaze to Ella. "I had a conversation with her earlier; informed her she's to stay away from you, keep her mouth shut, and that she's barred from the club, the bar, and the pool hall."

Ella blinked. "Wow. Okay. I wasn't expecting that big of a response."

He gave her a pointed look. "Like I told her, I won't tolerate someone trying to come between me and what's mine."

"So you were clear—again—that she has no chance with you?"

Some of the tension in his muscles slipped away when Ella didn't object to being his. "Very clear."

"That could be a reason for her to come at Ella," said Mia. "Are you *sure* Neta doesn't care for you?"

"She doesn't even know me. She turned her attention my way because she badly wants to leave her lair and liked the idea of switching to my club."

"Why does she want to leave?" asked Ella.

"I looked into it earlier," Dice cut in. "Turns out her ex-long-term partner recently took a mate and moved her into their lair."

Realization played over Ella's face. "Ah, so she doesn't wanna see them together. Understandable. If she was a woman scorned, I'd say yeah we should be looking at her for the attempted break-in. But"—her gaze slid to Viper—"as you said, she doesn't know you. You're not important to her. And it isn't as if getting rid of me would solve her problems. It would actually make them worse."

Mia nodded. "Seems safe to conclude that your pen pal made another move."

Ella blew out a breath. "What bothers me most is that, if this asshole is following me around, they saw me come back to my complex. They had no reason to think I'd be at Mia's place. Which means that when they tried to break in, they wanted to physically get *to me*, not just nose around or leave something for me to find."

Rage boiled in Viper's blood. *No one* was going to get near her. Fucking no one.

"Why do you think they left so fast?" asked Dice. "Could they have sensed the tripwire?"

Ella frowned, pensive. "I doubt it. It's more probable that the electric shock deterred them from trying again. They then had no reason to stick around."

Dice blinked. "Anyone who attacked your wards would get an electric shock?"

"Yup."

Viper's entity grinned, liking her ruthless streak. "If you had been inside the apartment but there'd been no tripwire, would you have sensed that someone was taking a shot at the wards?"

"No."

"Then that's what they were expecting. They thought they could dismantle your security measures right beneath your nose." *Bastard.*

Mia puffed out a breath, shaking her head. "Luka's gonna *freak*, you know, El."

She gave a flat smile. "Yeah. Yeah, I do know."

CHAPTER NINETEEN

Arriving at the private area for staff in the Red Rooms, Ella smiled up at Ghost. "Thank you for the ride."

He'd first teleported to Ella's place and then Mia's to collect them. He would have taken them straight to Viper's office, but the president was apparently having a meeting with Dice and Jester there.

Ghost gave a slight bow, his mouth curved. "My pleasure." He pointed to a door nearby. "You can access the main club area through there. I'll let Viper and Dice know you're here," he added, poking his temple as he backed toward the restrooms.

Once he disappeared out of sight, she and her sister began heading for the door he'd indicated.

"It sure is handy having teleporters around," said Mia.

It was also a good way to ensure that not only was it hard for Ella's pen pal to track her movements, but also hard for Kasper and Arman to report her whereabouts to Luka. As predicted, her anchor had gone apeshit on hearing about the attempted break-in at her apartment two and a half weeks ago. From now on, whenever she was inside, one of her guards stood sentry outside the front door.

"Just think," began Mia, nudging her gently, "if you hadn't come here with me that night I badgered you to come, you probably would never have slept with Viper. And then maybe you guys wouldn't have what you have now."

What they had . . Well, it was nothing close to a shallow arrangement anymore. It had been his idea for them to have a little fun here at the club rather than simply go straight to his clubhouse. He did that now. Proposed they go here or there. Sometimes to the movies or restaurants, though she'd use a glamor spell to conceal her identity from others. Other times he'd choose isolated scenic spots, and they might even take a picnic. He never called them 'dates', but that was what they were.

More significantly, he took her out for rides on his bike. She knew it was no little thing that he'd had her on the back of his bike. It showed that he truly considered her his. Not just in a sexual sense, but in a whole other way. And since her own feelings of possessiveness were pretty intense where he was concerned, it was a relief that they both appeared to be on the same page.

Her demon liked him a whole lot; wanted to keep him. Which wasn't necessarily a good thing. Such entities lacked the capacity to feel love, but they did form very strong attachments to people. If that happened, well, the entities wouldn't let them go.

"You should thank me, really," Mia pushed. "I'm basically the reason you two got together."

Brushing a hand down her emerald-green halter neck dress, Ella snorted. "I just knew you'd try to take credit for it." She pushed open the door and stepped out of the staff area.

Her demon frowned at the loudness of the thumping music

and the strong scents of cologne, alcohol, perfume, and musk. It was only the knowledge that Viper was further inside that kept the entity from urging Ella to leave.

She and Mia slowly walked through the club, both bopping their heads to the music. Ella didn't worry that anyone would recognize her, since she'd used a glamor spell to edit her appearance. It had been Viper's idea for her to do that whenever they were out in public together. He didn't want any watchful strix to turn their attention to her. Dice was in the same boat with Mia, and so she too wore glamor tonight.

Of course, for Ella, using glamor had the added bonus of ensuring that her loved ones remained in the dark about her involvement with Viper. But at this point, it seemed unfair of her to keep him a secret. He didn't appear to be upset about it, but it still felt wrong. "I need to pull up my big girl panties and finally tell Mom, Jocelyn, and Luka that I've been seeing Viper."

Mia sighed. "When you do, I'll tell them about Dice. I wasn't going to, since things aren't serious between us. But it'll help take some of the heat off you."

"I wouldn't expect you to—"

"You'd the same for me."

Yes, Ella would. "I had planned to cough it up before now, but then Viper assured me Neta would keep her mouth shut and so I took the out that gave me." Neta really *had* kept quiet.

"What holds me back at this point from making stuff public is that there's still so much I don't know about him," Ella went on. "I'm hopeful that he'll eventually shine a light on things." It particularly bothered her demon—it didn't respect his need for, or right to protect, his privacy. It felt entitled to know his personal business. "I'm also hopeful that I'll get fucked in an alcove again tonight."

Mia laughed. "Dice and I prefer the dance floor. But yeah,

alcoves are fun too. You know, I wouldn't have thought public sex would be your jam."

"That makes two of us. But then, I also wouldn't have thought I'd fuck an angel."

"That makes two of us. We've surprised even ourselves." Her gaze turned inward, suggesting she was having a telepathic conversation. "Ah, Dice said the meeting's over and we can either head to the office or wait for them to join us."

Ella hummed. "I say we both head there."

"I'm with you on that one."

His hip propped against the office wall, Jester said, "We've looked hard. We've set traps. We've checked for any cameras or listening devices. There's nothing to suggest we're being watched."

"I'd like to say that puts me at ease, but it doesn't," said Viper, sinking into his chair.

"Sting could be right that you're being monitored through rumors and business transactions," said Dice, standing on the other side of the desk. "The celestial could be sticking to the shadows."

"Much like the strix," Jester added.

On the one hand, it pleased Viper that the strix were proving elusive. It meant he could focus much of his time, energy, and attention on Ella. But on the other hand, he needed the threat eradicated. Strix were dangerous. Took lives without a qualm. They couldn't be allowed to live.

His annoyance at being unable to locate them was eased by how well things were going with Ella. She and her sister had arrived at the club mere minutes ago, and he was looking forward to having more time with his woman.

He now saw Ella every day without fail. Though she enjoyed alone time, she never made excuses not to see him. Never sent him away if he turned up at her apartment uninvited. Never turned down any suggestions he made for how they might spend time together. She even came up with suggestions of her own.

She shared more with Viper now. Ran a lot by him. Confided in him about things she once would never have mentioned to him. She didn't yet trust him *all* the way, but she was getting there.

Many times he'd come close to telling her of their relationship in her previous life, but he needed to wait until the time was *just right*. He couldn't afford to jack it up. Especially when there was so much he'd need her to accept. It was essential that he treaded carefully.

He brought her to his compound often, wanting her to feel comfortable there. She was at ease around his brothers, having gotten to know them well. She laughed with them, played pool with them, shot the shit with them.

Little items of hers were now scattered around his bedroom. He fucking loved that. Loved having her mark there. Loved that evidence of her feeling so sure she'd return.

"We done here?" asked Dice.

"Meeting's officially over," Viper confirmed.

"I'll let Mia know, then." His eyes took on a faraway look for a brief moment.

"Do she and Ella still use glamor?" asked Jester.

Dice gave a grunt of confirmation.

Jester's gaze sharpened on Viper. "I'm betting it pisses you off that Ella's gotta edit her appearance—you can't be clear to one and all that she's taken."

"It does, yeah," Viper admitted. "But it's more important to me that any strix or celestials who're watching our club don't clock her with me."

"What about when the danger's passed? You think you'll be

able to convince her to drop the glamor? Or is she gonna want to hide that she's seeing you?"

"I don't think she'll wanna keep hiding it. She talks about telling her family. I feel like she's waiting for something. Not sure what."

"You haven't made it clear that you're serious about keeping her. Dealing with the backlash she'd receive from her loved ones won't be worth her bother for a fling, will it?"

Viper gave a moody frown. "What I've got going on with Ella has gone way beyond a fling. She has to feel that."

"She probably does. But she ain't gonna feel positive about it unless you spell it out. I'm surprised you haven't done it yet."

"I need the time to reel her fully in, so that no amount of bitching from Belinsky or her family will make her try to break things off with me," Viper explained. "Those demons are already on edge because of the threat hovering over her. They won't handle this well on top of that."

Jester looked at Dice. "Do you think Mia's anchor will protest to her sleeping with you if she mentions it to him?"

"Yeah, but I don't think it'll solely be because I'm one of the Fallen," replied Dice. "Things went a little sour between them. On the surface, it seems like he's pulled his shit together. She says he's back to normal, though things are awkward. But if you ask me, he's still got his head lodged firmly up his ass. He doesn't make an effort to see much of her. He also doesn't text, call, or even telepath her often to check in."

"Then he's clearly got a problem with her," Jester asserted. "But what?"

"Don't know. If it was Mia who'd put a stop to them sleeping together, I would have said he's bitter about it. But *he* did that, and he's now fucking a woman he works with." Dice rolled his shoulders.

A knock came at the door.

"Come in," Viper invited, expecting Ella and Mia. But when the door creaked open, it wasn't either of their heads that popped inside; it was Prophet's.

"Hey," he greeted with a chin tip. "Any of you seen Merchant?"

They all shook their heads in the negative.

Prophet's lips thinned. "No one seems to know where he is. He's *supposed* to be taking over for me at the bar. Speaking of the bar . . . you and Dice might want to know that your regulars are over there. The brunettes, I mean."

"Regulars?" a female voice echoed, the word brittle, cold, and coated in disgust.

Ella.

Shit.

CHAPTER TWENTY

In front of her, Prophet went stock still. He couldn't possibly be more shocked than Ella.

Betrayal burned her throat and lungs. That fucker. That ass-licking fucker.

Viper had sworn there'd be no other women. She'd believed him. She'd taken him at his word. Hadn't had a single moment of doubt.

My mistake.

Prophet slowly and woodenly turned to face her, releasing the office door as he did so. It steadily swung open, and her gaze slammed on Viper. He was pushing out of his seat, his broad shoulders tense, his face hard.

Ella glared at him, dropping her glamor, barely holding back a snarl. Her heart pounded in her chest, and her jaw hurt from how tightly she clenched it. Her demon longed to punch him in the throat.

Dice took one step toward Mia, and Ella sensed her sister stiffen; heard her low hiss of fury. He halted, his lips thinning,

"Prophet, get gone," Viper ordered, the words coated in frost.

The angel disappeared fast.

Viper's eyes flew back to Ella as his expression softened. "Baby, come inside," he urged, his tone beseeching. "You too, Mia. Jester, give us some privacy, would you?"

"You got it." Jester stalked out.

Ella half-considered pivoting on her heel and marching out of the club. But, no. No, she was going to give this lying son of a bitch a verbal ass-reaming before she did.

Barging into the office, she bared her teeth at him. "You are such a hypocritical fucker. You don't want me sleeping with other guys, but you're fine having other women in your bed."

He lifted his palms, skirting around his desk. "Baby, you've got it all wrong," he swore.

Dice tried taking Mia's arm, but she flinched away with a growled, "*Don't.*"

"It isn't what you think," the VP told her.

As he and Mia began to argue, Ella took an angry step toward Viper and said, "I believed you. I actually believed you when you assured me there'd be no one else. More fucking fool me."

Viper dropped his arms to his sides. "There hasn't been anyone else, Ella."

"Other than for the brunette, you mean?"

His jaw went tight. "She's not someone I fuck."

"So, what, she's all about blowjobs and hand jobs? Because that counts as cheating, in my book."

Viper prowled to her, his face solemn. "I swear to you, I haven't touched another women since you; none have touched me. What Prophet said ... It doesn't mean what you think it does."

Ella guffawed. "What else could her being a regular *possibly* mean?"

He pressed his lips tight together.

She felt her mouth twist into a bitter smile as hot tears stung her eyes. "Right."

He covered the space between them in a blur of movement and caught her face with his hands. "Every word I've said is the truth."

He looked so earnest it was difficult to doubt his words, but how could she not? "Then explain what he meant by 'regular'."

Viper drew in a deep breath and looked beyond her—something he often did when she asked him questions. "Some secrets aren't only mine to share, you get me?" he asked, his eyes returning to hers. "If you react badly, if you tell others, a lot of people could be affected. Even killed."

Ella's skin chilled at the grave note to his voice. He wasn't being dramatic here. This whole 'regular' thing was strongly linked to one of the things he'd so far kept from her. "Those people being your brothers," she guessed.

"They rely on me to keep them safe."

Ella licked her lips, only then becoming aware that her sister and Dice had fallen silent. She looked their way. He was rubbing at his nape while Mia—who'd now also dropped her glamor—stood with her hands on her hips, her chin up in challenge . . . as if daring him to cough up a truth he clearly felt compelled to keep quiet.

"Ella," Viper said, pulling her attention back to him. "I promise you, baby, I have not betrayed you. Never would."

"I want to believe that."

"Then believe it," he implored, his eyes delving so deep into hers it was hard to hold his gaze. "*Trust me.*"

"Why? You don't trust me, or you would just be honest with me here and now about what Prophet meant." She paused. "I guess this answers the question of whether or not you always planned to keep me ignorant. If you're ever willing to share anything with

me, now would have been the time to do it." She pulled her face
free of his hands and whirled, meaning to walk out.

Power rushed through the room. The door slammed shut.
The lock flicked. A growl sounded behind her. Mia sucked in a
breath. Dice cursed low.

Ella furiously spun back to face Viper . . . and froze. His eyes
had changed, becoming all white. A white so pure it faintly
glowed.

What the fuck?

Her skin prickled as the temperature dropped . . . much in the
same way it did when a person's inner demon surfaced. But what
stared back at her was not a demon. Nor was it Viper. *Something*
lived inside him. Something not anything close to holy—a
strange sort of malice oozed from it.

Her demon should have been unnerved. Instead, it was plain
intrigued, the weirdo.

Mia's mind touch hers. *What is happening?* she asked.

I have no clue, Ella replied, swallowing hard.

The entity cocked its head. "You're wary of me," it noted.
"There's no need for fear. I'd never harm you. If it makes you feel
better, I promised Viper I wouldn't."

It was a little worrying that Viper had felt a need to extract
such a vow. "Do you always keep your promises?"

"No." But the entity didn't appear to see why she might not
feel so reassured.

Oookay.

"He's telling you the truth," it went on. "There was no
betrayal."

"Why won't he explain what Prophet meant?"

"He doesn't have your full trust, loyalty, or commitment. He
has no surety that you will hold your silence. In his position,
would you so easily confess a secret that keeps many safe?"

Well, no.

"Maybe you can be trusted to say nothing, but there are ways of extracting information from people. For instance, I could enter your mind, take out anything I wanted—even the memory of this conversation; you'd never know we'd had it."

She went cold all over.

"But I won't," said the entity. "Instead, I propose a geas. You would promise to never repeat what you are told, and you would be bound to silence by his power. It would also mean that no one could take the information from your mind—the geas would keep it hidden from prying psychic eyes."

Ella blinked, having not expected such a suggestion. She'd heard of geasa, of course, but she'd never had reason to use them. Considering that death was often the infraction for violating such oaths, the idea had never appealed to her. "I wouldn't be *bound* to my word. Geasa can be broken."

"Not those put in place by celestial power."

Fair enough.

"We can do something similar with a spell," Mia told the entity. "The magick would bind us to our vow to never repeat whatever we hear."

The entity considered it for a moment but then shook its head. "Another incantor could undo it."

"We overlay our spells with wards so they're not easily untangled."

"But they can be untangled, can't they? I have witnessed many be destroyed or nulled." The entity pinned Ella with a serious look. "You would have to agree to a geas ... or walk out of this club, out of his life, and never know what he might have told you. Never know that he was, in fact, telling you the truth."

Mia telepathed her again, asking, *What do you think?*

I'm not crazy about being under a geas, Ella replied, *but it's not as if I'd reveal what they told us anyway, so it doesn't make much difference.*

You make a very good point. A sigh. *All right, I'll agree to it.*

"A geas it is," said Ella.

Triumph momentarily rippled across the entity's face. "Right decision." It retreated, and Viper's eyes went back to their normal startling blue. Eyes that then intently watched her . . . as though he were searching for signs of revulsion on her part.

He wouldn't find any. Hey, she was leery of his entity, but not repulsed. It would have been hypocritical if she were, given that she had her own inner entity.

An awkward silence fell, but Mia quickly broke it, saying, "Well *that* I hadn't expected." She looked at Dice. "Do all angels have inner entities?"

"Yes," Dice grunted.

"Why do you keep it secret?" Mia asked him. "It's not *that* big of a deal. We demons have our own entities—we wouldn't be spooked."

"But your kind would be surprised," Dice rightly stated. "They think they have the Fallen figured out; that they know all they need to know about us. If they realize they don't, if they realize we kept something like this from them, they'll wonder what else they don't know. We don't want their scrutiny."

Viper drowned out the conversation between his brother and Mia, focusing instead on his woman. She was watching him, her eyes slightly narrowed—not in suspicion, fear, or distrust. It seemed more as though she felt she was seeing him for the first time.

Fuck Prophet for being so damn careless. The angel had telepathically apologized mere moments after fleeing, but Viper wasn't feeling all that forgiving.

Prophet had known that the sisters were in the club. Okay, so he wouldn't have seen through their glamor. But he surely would have sensed that two people were close behind him.

Neither Viper nor Dice had asked to be notified if people they regularly fed from arrived. Still, if Prophet had really felt the need to inform them, he could have done it mind-to-mind. Instead, he'd come to the office—not entered, just stuck his head inside and kept the door partially open—and spoken aloud without a thought to whom could be nearby.

If Viper didn't know any better, he'd think that Prophet had planned for the sisters to overhear.

Either way, Viper could honestly pummel him into the ground and think nothing of it. He telepathically reached out to Dice, saying, *That was careless of Prophet. Careless in a way that makes me a little suspicious.*

Dice's psyche bumped his. *You think he knew they were close enough to overhear him?*

It's possible. He knew the sisters were here; would have guessed it was them on the way to the office—and I find it hard to believe he didn't notice them.

Viper had been mindful of each step he took with Ella. It was a precarious dance that required him to get the timing, moves, and balance just right. And Prophet might have just fucked it all up.

Viper hadn't intended to tell her about his 'diet' yet. His original plan had been to wait until she was firmly attached to him before he told her anything. He'd decided to spoon-feed her the things he needed to reveal as he established his place in her life. Spacing it all out, giving her time to process each reveal before moving onto another, would make it easier for her to digest it all.

She'd begun to care for him. He knew that; felt it. But she didn't yet love him, so he couldn't be sure that his upcoming confession—he really had no choice but to make it or he'd lose her—wouldn't scare her off. He couldn't predict her reaction.

Ella was, by nature, a compassionate and accepting person. The qualities were stamped on her soul. She didn't judge unless it was deserved. And his entity felt confident that she wouldn't hold their diet against them. Viper? He wasn't so confident. Because it was a fuck of a lot to accept—and it was only the tip of the iceberg.

At least she hadn't walked out. Or, as it were, *tried* to. No amount of magick would open the door now that his entity had locked it.

She hadn't tried, though. She wasn't announcing an intention to leave. And she didn't appear to have closed her mind to whatever Viper might say.

He took a slow step toward her, pleased she didn't tense or back away. "You're sure about the geas?"

She gave a decisive nod. "Positive."

It was a good thing for them all, since his entity had been bluffing when it said she could either agree or walk out of his life—it wouldn't let her go. Neither would Viper. Not for anything.

He held out his hand, relieved when she took it without hesitation. "You swear not to repeat what Dice and I tell you?"

"I swear," she replied, her pulse beating fast in her neck.

Viper let a burst of his power blast into her system in a cold, electric wave that made her suck in a breath. The power writhed and glowed beneath the skin of her hand as it bound her to the vow she'd just made. And then it settled, the glow fading.

He released Ella's hand, watching her carefully. She idly rubbed at her palm, staring at him in a sort of awed caution. Not fear, though, thankfully—he couldn't have hacked that.

He arched a questioning brow at Mia, who dipped her chin and stuck out her own hand. He pressed his palm to hers and demanded the same promise of her. Mia gave it easily, and he then used his power to hold her to her word, much as he'd done with Ella.

As he dropped her hand, Mia flinched back with a blink. "Your power is, like, *wow.*"

Viper leaned back against his desk. "Try not to judge me and my brothers too harshly for choosing to fall even knowing what the cost to us would be."

Ella's brow creased. "Cost?"

Slanting his head, he said, "Your entity is a sort of inner darkness, isn't it? Mine was once an inner light. But that changed."

"Changed how?" Ella asked.

"What lives in me, in Dice, in my brothers . . . those entities feel no joy. No contentment. No peace. Their emotional spectrum ranges from dark to darker. The nearest thing they feel to happiness is a shallow sense of satisfaction, which they usually only experience at the expense of someone else's pain or discomfort or humiliation."

Damn, thought Ella. Her demon was an utter psychopath. It felt no remorse, empathy, or love. But it could experience some positive emotions, and not all were shallow.

"One feeling overrules all others for us and our inner entities." He fixed his gaze with hers, demanding her focus. "Thirst."

Ella's scalp tingled as wariness danced in her veins. "Thirst for what?"

He waited a few beats. "Blood."

She stared at him numbly, aware of her sister drawing in a shocked breath.

"The Fallen are cursed—quite literally—to subsist on blood as well as food and water," said Viper, his expression carefully blank. "We go from virtuous beings to decadent creatures. It's why they call it a fall from grace. This is our punishment."

Well, shit. Nothing could have prepared her for this revelation. There'd been no clues, no hints, no rumors. And who would ever think that freaking *angels* would be doomed in such a way, fallen or not?

Her chest panged with sympathy. Maybe she should have recoiled in horror—it would certainly be understandable—but it was impossible when he looked so damn tense, clearly braced for revulsion and rejection.

To have to survive on the life-force of others . . . Ella couldn't imagine what kind of existence that would be. She only knew she'd hate it.

Mia narrowed her eyes. "Do you generally kill those you feed from?"

It was Dice who answered, "Not unless it's during battle."

"I never heard any rumors about how the Fallen might drink blood," Mia said. "Not even a few whispers about it. How are you forcing people to keep it quiet if you're not killing those whose blood you take?"

"They don't remember us taking it," Dice explained. "We can rid them of the memory, and we heal the puncture wounds."

"None of us like our new reality," said Viper. "We were prepared for it. For the cravings, the bloodlust, the unquenchable hunger. But we quickly came to see that there is no real way to prepare yourself for this life. You're a parasite, plain and simple."

Ella's heart ached for him. To consider yourself a parasite, to feel that you'd been reduced to such a creature . . . It would be a mindfuck for sure. He must have had one hell of a good reason to choose to fall.

"We make the best of it," Viper continued. "It's all we can do."

"We also have ironclad rules," Dice added. "We never make the feeding painful. We never drink from the young, the ill, or the weak. And we never take more blood than we need."

"Unless, of course, there's a battle—then all bets are off," Viper tacked on.

As the puzzle pieces knitted together, Ella said, "The brunettes at the bar are people you feed from routinely, aren't they? That's why Prophet called them your regulars."

"Yes," Viper verified. "But let me be clear. I don't fuck the people I feed from, Ella. I take their blood and walk away. That's it."

"Same goes for me," Dice told Mia.

Ella rubbed at her face, considering all they'd told her. She was a little thrown by it. She recalled once catching a glimpse of one of the Black Saints in a shadowy alcove, his mouth on the neck of a woman—she'd thought they were just having a little sexual fumble, hadn't once guessed there was more going on.

Though Viper had talked of how sharing his secrets presented risks to his brothers, she'd half-thought he might be making excuses. But no, it truly *was* risky. There had once been a few blood-drinking breeds of demon. Feeding on life had made them tremendously powerful. Other demonic breeds hadn't liked that, so they'd wiped them out. They would do the same to the Fallen for certain.

"I see why you held this stuff back. If it got out, you'd all be hunted and killed." It wasn't only his brothers at risk, since ... "Any members of the Fallen worldwide would be tracked and executed."

"That's the reason for the geas," said Viper. "It's not that I don't trust you. I just needed the extra bit of insurance. No truth spell or hypnotic energy could force the information out of you—you're literally unable to share it."

"I actually feel better knowing that. I was put under a truth spell once. It was horrible."

His expression went dark. "The fuck? Who did it?"

"It was a long time ago. I was just seventeen. My cousin thought it would be funny to embarrass me by making me blurt out all kinds of private stuff." Secret crushes, her menstrual cycle, the joys of masturbation, what powers she possessed. Hearing herself so casually spill it all, completely helpless to stop it, had been an instance of pure horror. "It's all right, I got my revenge."

"I don't doubt it." He paused, his eyes drifting over her face. "You're taking all of this better than I thought you would."

Her brow furrowed. "Hey, look, it's not exactly happy news. But it's not your fault. Yes, you made the decision to fall, but you didn't *ask* to be cursed. You don't kill who you feed from. You don't take the blood of those who are young or vulnerable. You make the best of a shitty situation. The only people I'm disgusted at are those who created the curse."

Viper felt some of the tension drain from his muscles. She wasn't running. Wasn't judging. Wasn't going to reject him.

His entity cast him an *I told you so* smirk, the smug fucker.

"What happens if you resist drinking blood?" Mia asked Dice, the threads of anger gone from her voice; replaced by compassion.

"We go into bloodlust. That happens, we're isolated until it passes." Dice held his hand out to Mia. "Can we go somewhere to talk? Alone?"

Mia's mouth went tight, but then it relaxed. She placed her hand in his. "Okay." She looked at Ella, her brow flicking up.

Ella gave her a subtle nod, and Viper sensed they were speaking telepathically.

The other couple then left, leaving him and his woman alone.

Viper pushed away from his desk and cautiously approached her, alert for signs that she needed a little space. But she didn't seize up or frown or back away. Her expression was pensive. "What're you thinking?" he asked.

"I'm wondering"—she tilted her head—"if you've fed from me."

"I haven't, no. But I want to." His reply was frank. Unapologetic. Edged with a sexual undertone that he hadn't been able to suppress.

"Why haven't you? You could have made me forget."

"I want you to give me your blood of your own free will. Or not at all."

The line between her brows smoothed away. "But you take blood from others without their permission."

"They don't belong to me. You do." The knots in his gut fell away when she didn't object to that. It meant they hadn't gone a step backwards.

"How often do you have to feed?"

"At least weekly." For his brothers, it was daily. But they weren't archangels.

"Do you make the bites pleasurable?"

"I personally don't, no. We can if we want to, though. Some do. Some don't. Some do it occasionally. Our inner entities generally don't like us to make it pleasurable, being cruel as they are. Though my entity would be different with you. It likes you." Just the mere thought of tasting her blood again made Viper's cock stir.

"You told me a lot tonight, but there's more you're keeping from me—if the rumors about you are true, why you fell from the upper realm, and ... something else. Something bigger. I can feel it."

He placed his hands on her shoulders. "Another time, I'll tell you the rest."

"Why not now?"

"I don't want to pile everything on you at once. My tale is a long story with several moving parts—a lot to take in and process."

Her eyes went slitted. "That's not the only reason you're holding back. Admit it, you're stalling."

Viper slid one hand up to palm the side of her neck. "Be fair, baby," he said, his tone soft. "You're asking me to tell you my deepest, darkest secrets. And you're asking me to do it merely to appease your curiosity. I need the certainty that you're not going anywhere before I lay it all out. You can't give me that yet, can you?"

Her head flicked to the side. "You don't want me to go anywhere?"

"Of course I fucking don't."

She licked her lips, something warm flashing in her gaze. "We suck at keeping things simple, don't we?"

"We do." They had in her previous life as well, their connection too intense; a connection that ran soul-deep. Humming, he delved a proprietary hand into her hair and loosely fisted it. "So I'm thinking I should keep you. It makes sense, since I'd want to rip out the throat of anyone who touched you."

She gave him a wan smile. "Seems we have a bit of a conundrum, then. You're hesitant to tell me until you're confident I'm sticking around, which I get . . . but I can't fully commit to you when there's so much I don't know."

Viper had figured as much, hence why he was intent on reeling her so far in she'd never think of walking away. "For now . . . I say we keep going as we are. Sort of."

"Sort of?"

"Like you said, we suck at keeping things simple. So let's complicate them a little."

"In what way?"

"We stop calling what we have an arrangement or a fling and call it what it really is."

Her mouth quirked. "A relationship."

He nodded, relieved she'd admitted it. "It might not have been in your original plans, but it's what we have. So let's just keep building on it."

Her throat bobbed. "Okay."

Feeling his lips bow up, he lowered his face to hers. "Good." He gave her a quick kiss. "What's with the frown?"

"I'm worried that others might find out your secret. You're sure you can keep it under wraps?"

"My kind have been doing it since they first fell eons ago."

"But with the technology we have today, it isn't so easy to keep secrets. Everyone's a photographer in this day and age, thanks to the cameras on their cell phones."

"Which is why my brothers and I only feed here in the club. It reduces the risk of anyone seeing anything they shouldn't, as does the fog and the darkness. You ever tried to snap a picture in the club? They always come out fuzzy and staticky."

"Hmm, I *haven't* actually attempted it. That you guys are powerful enough to render cameras useless is impressive." She cocked her head. "What about when you feed during battle? That must pose risks."

"Some people found out our secret that way, but none who would tell. They're allies, and they have their own secrets to protect. Secrets we learned and could expose if they crossed us." He stroked her hair. "I'm sorry you found out this way. I didn't want that. It never occurred to me that one of my brothers would let it slip like that, so I thought I had time." Time to rehearse what he'd say, plan where and when he'd tell her.

Her eyes narrowed in suspicion. "Did he let it slip on purpose?"

She was sharp, his woman. "I don't know. It's possible. I'll find out for sure once I talk to him. Right now, I'm only interested in you."

"I'm fine. Really. I mean, it was obviously a shock. But I can deal. I'm not going anywhere. It's not like you drink blood for shits and giggles. That *would* be weird."

"Just weird?" he asked, feeling his lips twitch.

"Okay, weird and gross and the ultimate bad habit. Many other adjectives would also apply. But the truth is you have no choice." She stared at him for long moments, a series of emotions flickering fast behind her eyes. "Do you have to feed tonight?"

He stilled. "I'll have to do it tomorrow at the latest."

She scratched the back of her head, pulling a face.

"What's wrong, baby?"

Her arm flopped to her side. "I don't like the thought of you feeding from other people."

"I told you, I don't fuck them, Ella. I make it quick and clinical."

"I still don't like it."

"I get it. In your shoes, I wouldn't like it either. But it's that or bloodlust."

"Or . . ." She trailed off and rolled her shoulders. "Or you could feed from me."

He stiffened in surprise, his throat burning with thirst at the suggestion alone. His entity smirked once more. "Be careful what offers you throw around, Ella. You need to be damn sure of what you're saying. You offer your blood to me, I'll take it. And if you regret it afterwards, it'll be a punch to the gut for me."

Her tongue slipped out to nervously touch her bottom lip. "You bit me once. Well, it wasn't so much a bite, but you cut my lip when we kissed."

"Not on purpose."

"You scrape your teeth on my neck a lot."

"Teasing myself with what I can't have, hoping that might one day change." He slid his palm from the side of her neck to her nape. "But we're not gonna discuss it any more tonight. You're going to take time to think about it. Really, really think about it. I want you to be sure all the fucking way."

"All right."

"Good." Tugging her closer with the hand gripping her nape, he looped his free arm around her.

"This club . . . you opened it to reel in possible prey."

He couldn't help but smile. "Clever girl. It's better this way. We confine our feeding to the one place. Innocents don't come here. Only those who are drawn to darkness and sin."

"I'm not."

"Sure you are. You're drawn to me, aren't you?"

She inclined her head, her lips curving. "Point well made."

"It is. Now kiss me."

CHAPTER TWENTY-ONE

Slumping into a chair in the clubhouse's meeting room the following day, Prophet glanced from Viper to Dice. There was no nervousness there. No sheepishness. No remorse.

Viper's entity narrowed its eyes. Either the angel didn't grasp the gravity of his behavior last night—which seemed highly unlikely—or he felt he'd done nothing wrong.

At the head of the table, Viper swiveled his chair slightly toward him. "I'm sure you can guess what this is about."

Prophet gave a nod. "I messed up, I know. But I apologized."

"Yeah, you did," said Dice from the chair opposite Prophet, his expression hard. "Our problem is that we're not sure you meant it."

Prophet frowned. "What?"

"Nor are we sure it was an accident on your part," Dice added. "*What?*"

"Our club's ability to live in peace with demons in this realm depends on our secrecy," Viper pointed out. "We're all careful of what we say at all times. We don't accidentally say too much in a public place. *You* don't accidentally do that. You've always been vigilant. Last night, you weren't."

Prophet's mouth thinned. "I didn't know the sisters were there."

Viper shot him an incredulous look. "They were close enough that they overheard you. I find it hard to believe you hadn't sensed their presence on your way to the office."

Prophet's nostrils flared. "This is bull."

His oh-so-innocent routine was bull. "You didn't needed to come to my office. The conversation you wanted to have with us wasn't long-winded or of a serious nature, was it? All you wanted was to ask if we'd seen Merchant and—though we hadn't ever asked to be informed of such a thing—tell us that our regulars were at the bar. You could have done that telepathically. It would have saved you a walk and been less risky."

"I wasn't taking risks, I—"

"No? You didn't enter my office and close the door behind you. You popped your head inside, keeping the door open while you talked. That isn't careless?"

"*I didn't know they were there.*"

Viper leaned forward. "I think you did," he said, his pitch dropping, his voice oozing danger.

"Why would I have wanted them to overhear me?"

"Not them. *Ella.* Maybe you wanted to know once and for all if she would be able to handle our reality. You knew we could edit both her memories and that of Mia afterward. But you had to also know how much I would have *hated* doing that to my woman. You didn't care."

Prophet sighed. "Nothing I say is going to change your mind, is it?" he asked, like a suffering, misunderstood martyr.

"I could always invade yours and get the answers for myself,"

Viper suggested with a shrug. "It's not something I want to do, but it would go a long way to proving your innocence. Unless . . . you're *not* innocent."

Cursing beneath his breath, Prophet shifted in his seat. "Okay, okay, I knew they were close. I thought there was a chance they'd overhear me. I wanted Ella to."

"Why?" Viper bit off, his inner entity seething.

Lines of anxiety set into Prophet's face. "I worry for you. I worry what you'll do if she rejects you when you come clean to her about everything. I know what it'll do to you; what the consequences will be. I felt that if she could accept our diet, there was a good chance she'd accept the rest. It seemed best for you to know that now."

Indignance spiked in Viper's blood. "So, in your view, this was a test."

"I didn't do it for me, though, I did it for you. And look, it worked out in your favor, didn't it?" Prophet spoke as if he'd done Viper a service. "And now there's real hope that Ella can handle the entire picture."

Dice growled low in his throat as his mind bumped Viper's. *He can't honestly think you owe him or some shit.*

He shouldn't think *that, but he does.* "Too many times the Uppers disciplined you for taking it upon yourself to perform reckless acts for 'the greater good'. You never did learn from that, did you?"

Prophet's eyelids flickered, his jaw clenching.

Viper pinned him with a cold stare. "I don't want or need you to 'test' Ella. You have concerns, bring them to me. Do *not* work against me. Do *not* decide you know what's best and act on it."

The angel licked his lips. "Viper—"

"I have been clear since before we fell why I was coming to this realm. Every member of our club knows that I'm here for

Ella. Claiming her as my own is the ultimate goal. You've always been aware of this, correct?"

Prophet's lips tightened. "Correct."

"Then your concerns can't be anything new. Your awareness of the risks must have been there from the start. Am I right on that?"

"Yes." A muttered response.

"And yet, you chose to fall with us anyway. You never made me aware of your concerns or doubts regarding Ella. You decided to take the chance that all would work out well. Is that the case?"

Prophet stiffly inclined his head.

"So what fucking right do you have to suddenly interfere in my plans?" Viper demanded. "You *chose* to take chances when you fell, always knowing the risks. What authority do you have over me that you get to decide what's 'best' for me? That you get to 'test' my woman?"

"I thought I was doing the right thing," he upheld.

Viper's entity snarled at the weak defense. "That's my point. You assumed you knew what was right, and you acted accordingly—arrogantly believing we'd thank you in the end. There was nothing 'right' about it. I can't afford to make mistakes in how I handle bringing Ella into my world. It's a delicate, complex dance. There's no room for wrong moves. What I absolutely do not fucking need is any of my brothers causing missteps."

"I wasn't trying to cause you problems."

"But you *could* have. You also placed Dice in a position where he'd either have to delete Mia's memories or share things with her he hadn't originally intended to share unless he built something serious with her."

"And I cannot tell you how much that pisses me off," Dice gritted out, glaring at Prophet.

"You will not *ever* interfere when it comes to Ella," Viper ordered.

"There will be no more tests. There will be no more doing what you believe is 'best' when it comes to her. Are we clear on that?"

Prophet ground his teeth. "We're clear."

"I hope so," Viper told him. "Because you might be my brother, but she's my woman. She is my priority—always will be. I will eliminate any risk to her. I will obliterate anyone who gets in the way of me making her mine. That includes you. So do yourself a real favor and heed my warning. Because I'm telling you now, there won't be another."

"I want a love potion."

Oh, unreal. Ella blinked at the she-demon beside her. "A love potion?"

The brunette gave a decisive nod. "Yes."

It wasn't unusual for people to come into the store thinking they could purchase such potions. They were the kind of people who watched *way* too much TV and had a dramatized notion of magick and how it worked. They had no real idea of its limitations, costs, or risks.

Turning away from the products on the shelf that she'd been rearranging, Ella gave her a tight smile. "There's no potion that will make someone fall in love with another."

A line formed between the brunette's thin brows. "Of course there is," she said, waving a hand that sported long acrylic nails. "I've heard about them."

"There are potions that can temporarily manipulate a person's body chemistry using magick, much like with a drug. The potions make the brain release oxytocin, the good ole 'love hormone'. Whoever—or whatever—they're looking at while the potion takes effect will become an object of their obsessive devotion. But the potions wear off in a matter of hours."

"Surely you can whip up something stronger than that."

"The magick would never hold. It can't. Because real love is emotion. Emotions can't be manipulated that way."

The woman tossed her head, making her sleek bob dance to the side. "A temporary effect will do, I suppose."

"You're fine with essentially forcing someone to love you? Fine with interfering with their will in such a way?"

"Yes," she answered without missing a beat.

Ella's demon huffed in disdain. It didn't exactly have an issue with forcing anyone to do anything against their will, but it did find the idea of love potions somewhat pathetic. "Even though it won't last, and they'll eventually realize you did something to manipulate their feelings?"

"Why would they realize it?"

"Once the magick wears off, the person who was bespelled can look back through all that happened through clear lenses. They'll be well-aware that their 'feelings' were fake, they'll realize they were caught in a spell, and they'll obviously suspect the person they temporarily 'loved' as being responsible." It wouldn't exactly take detective work.

She lightly scratched her chin with one nail. "He may not suspect me. He's not particularly smart. Where do you keep the potions? I browsed the aisles, but I didn't find one."

Of course she didn't. "We don't stock them, sorry." Ella turned and made a beeline for the counter.

"But you could whip me up one, right?" the woman persisted, trailing after her.

"You want me to help you trick someone to love you? Uh, no."

The brunette practically pouted. "Why not?"

"First of all, it's highly unethical." Ella rounded the counter, moving to stand behind it. "Second of all, I have too much of a healthy respect for magick to ever misuse it." Magick was a force that was *not* to be fucked around with.

The brunette gave her a dirty look. "Fine. I'll get a love potion from someone else."

"Possibly. But you'll run across every problem I just mentioned, *and* also have to deal with magickal karma bitch-slapping you. A misuse of magick always leads to that."

Not seeming at all concerned, the woman swanned out of the store, almost bumping into Kasper outside. He and Arman stood either side of the door, making no attempt to be invisible.

Mia materialized at Ella's side. "What was that about?"

"She wanted a love potion."

Mia rolled her eyes. "You warned her about the consequences?"

"Yup. She doesn't appear to care." Ella cricked her neck, too much tension gathered there.

Mia's face softened as her gaze sharpened on her. "Are you okay?"

"Yeah. Just a headache. It'll pass."

"That's all it is? Often when I glance over, you look sort of . . . introspective. You said earlier that you weren't gonna let what we learned last night run you off, but you've been quiet all day. You're not having second thoughts, are you?"

"No, not at all." Her demon would have put up a fight if Ella had tried to pull away from Viper anyway—it had become a teensy bit attached to him, and it gave not one measly fuck that he drank blood.

"It's not that you're spooked? Because it would be understandable."

"I'm not spooked. Surprised, yes. Pretty bummed on his behalf, yes. And also kind of . . . "

"What?"

Ella cleared her throat. "I'm curious as to what it'd feel like to let a certain someone take a bite out of me."

A slow smile curved Mia's mouth. "I've thought about that

a lot, too. Truth be told"—she leaned in—"I wouldn't mind finding out."

"I told Viper to come to me the next time he needs to feed. But it's important to him that I'm *sure* about it; he doesn't want me to have regrets afterwards."

"And would you?"

"I don't think so." Maybe some would have found the blood-drinking thing a little off-putting. Ella wasn't one of those people. "He said he could make it pleasurable."

"Dice said the same. I didn't volunteer to offer him a vein next time he was thirsty, but I think I will. I know we're not serious, but I still positively loathe the thought of him sinking his teeth into another person's skin—man or woman."

The light click-clack of heels preceded the appearance of their mother. She smiled brightly at them, her hands clasped together. "My lovelies, I have a favor to ask of you."

"No," they both said at once.

Melodie frowned, lowering her arms. "I haven't even told you what it is yet."

"The answer's still no," Ella told her.

"A resounding no," added Mia. "Your favors always center around allowing us to test your new products on us. My hair was like straw for a week when I last tested a shampoo."

"And I got a huge-ass purple rash after trying out one of your soaps," Ella reminded their mother.

"There aren't *always* side effects," said Melodie.

"But there usually are," Ella pointed out, "and I'm not interested in personally finding out *what* they are this time."

Melodie huffed. "*Someone* needs to be a test dummy."

"Neither me nor Ella are gonna be that someone," Mia stated.

Melodie's gaze flitted to the front of the store and narrowed in consideration. "Hmm, maybe *she'll* consent to it."

"Who?" Ella tracked her mother's gaze to see Jocelyn stood outside nattering amiably with *Maxine*. Her inner demon glared at the harpy, rather unpleased to see her.

"Jocelyn is still friends with her?" asked Mia, astonished.

"Not quite," replied Melodie. "Like us, she feels there's a good chance that Maxine befriended her for the wrong reason. But she won't find out for sure if she doesn't give the harpy the opportunity to pump her for information, so she accepted Maxine's invitation to go for lunch." Melodie smiled as both women entered the store. "Maxine, how lovely to see you. I was just wondering how you'd feel about letting me test some new products on you."

The harpy's polite smile faltered. "I'd prefer not to, if it's all the same to you."

"Can't say I blame you," muttered Jocelyn.

"Where did you go for lunch?" asked Melodie.

"The sushi place not far from here," replied Jocelyn. "The food was amazing."

Maxine looked from Ella to Mia, her eyes briefly flashing with something not very pleasant. "Girls."

Not 'Ladies' this time, Ella noted as she telepathically reached out to her sister.

Yeah, that greeting was a condescending slap if ever I've heard one, said Mia. "How's Dionne?"

Maxine's strained smile turned brittle. "She's fine. Well, I'll be off now. I'll touch base with you again next week, Jocelyn."

Once the harpy had flounced out of the store, Ella turned to her aunt. "Well?"

"She asked me less questions than usual, as if being careful not to bump my radar," said Jocelyn. "She also bemoaned how a mysterious someone went to Knox 'falsely' claiming she uses Dionne as a plant. Maxine monitored me *very* carefully when she revealed that little tidbit."

Mia hummed. "So she suspects that it was one or more of us."

"I'd say so. I played clueless and feigned horror on her behalf." Jocelyn's brow furrowed. "I was initially surprised that she asked me to lunch, but I suppose she has to continue on as normal or she'll otherwise look guilty of what Knox accused her of."

"Move, idiot," a female voice hissed, drawing their attention to the couple making their way toward the counter.

Ella felt her lips curve up. She knew Larkin, since *this* harpy was part of Levi and Piper's circle of friends. Larkin's mate, Teague, was someone who most demons in Vegas would recognize on sight. He regularly raced in the Underground hellhorse racing stadium, and he'd never been known to lose. Or to be anything close to sane.

Teague gave his mate a sheepish smile. "I'm sorry, am I bothering you?"

Larkin glared up at him. "*Are* you actually sorry, though?"

He considered it for a moment. "No."

The harpy growled, which made his smile widen.

"Here, let me carry your shower gel," he said, all solicitous.

She held the bottle tighter. "It's shampoo."

"Semantics."

Reaching the counter, Larkin drew in a centering breath, smiled politely at Ella and the others, and plonked the bottle down. "Just this."

"No conditioner, today?" asked Mia.

"Still got some left," replied Larkin. "I shampoo twice, so I run out of that sooner. I don't usually care about brands, but since Piper convinced me to sample your stuff, I won't use anything else."

Having rung up her purchase, Ella bagged it. "I'll have to thank her for being our product-pimp."

Teague courteously took the bag. "I'll carry the soap."

Larkin's eyelid twitched. "It's shampoo."

He made a dismissive sound. "Semantics."

The harpy blinked at him. "I'm starting to think that that word doesn't mean what you think it does."

The couple bickered all the way to the door, though Teague seemed to be riling his mate on purpose. It generally wasn't advisable to piss off a harpy—especially one whose entity had an ugly reputation. But hellhorses weren't exactly the most sensible demonic breed.

"More of those Black Saints are outside again," commented Melodie, staring out of the window.

Following her gaze, Ella noticed a bunch of the Fallen gathered outside the dive bar.

"I'm thinking of starting a petition," Melodie announced.

Mia cocked her head. "To what?"

"Make them stop coming to the bar," their mother replied.

Ella frowned, pointing out, "They own it."

"That doesn't mean they need to be there." With a sniff, Melodie retreated to the workshop.

Wincing, Ella exchanged an awkward look with Mia. If their mother was irritated merely seeing the Black Saints close to the store, she would lose her mind on hearing Ella's news.

"I'll have to tell her about Viper and I at some point," said Ella. "I wasn't sure it'd be necessary. But last night, he made it clear that he hopes this will go the distance."

"Are you hoping for the same?"

"Yes. I feel comfortable with him in a way I never have with anyone else." All her life, Ella had felt like something was missing. It was much the same feeling that you got when you walked into a room and realized that something had been moved or taken. There was an absence that she couldn't explain. Now, with him around, it was gone.

"Do you care for him?"

"Yes, I do. I actually think I'm in serious danger of falling hard for this dude." It would be a first for Ella. She'd done a whole lot of liking. There'd also been plenty of lusting. A time or two, she'd thought she might well grow to feel the big L for someone. But it had just never happened.

"Don't get me wrong, I'm still a little miffed that he hasn't yet told me all there is to know about him," Ella continued. "But I do understand the Black Saints' need for caution. And I don't really have much room to judge someone for keeping things from people anyway, considering I've kept my involvement with him a secret."

"Yeah, we'd be hypocrites to judge them."

"I thought my demon might fight me on agreeing to a relationship with Viper, but it isn't actually opposed to keeping him. Why? Simple and selfish: It's possessive enough of him not to want another woman to have him."

Mia snickered. "Typical."

Ella puffed out a breath. "I guess I better rehearse exactly how I'll break it to our family."

As she later drove them home from work, it was exactly what she did. But no matter what way she approached the matter, no matter what angle she took, she never found a way to voice the news that would make their loved ones take it well.

"I think I'm going to have to accept that there is no way to make them take it well," said Ella, turning onto a single lane. This short-cut to their apartment building didn't see much traffic, instead it was surrounded by grassland. "I'll just have to bite the bullet and tell them anyway."

"I think Mom and Jocelyn will eventually come round, once they see that Viper makes you happy. Luka? He might hold it against Viper until the end of time."

"I wish I could say you're wrong, but—"

Something landed on her car and rolled off it.

Ella slammed her foot on the brakes, bringing the car to a screeching halt.

Ghost. It was Ghost who'd hit the car. He was now pushing himself up off the ground . . . and glaring at the two strix looming over him. One strix lashed him with a whip of—*whoa*—black fire while the other blasted him with flaming orbs.

And then . . . everything happened superfast.

Several members of the Black Saints appeared, *sans* Viper.

Ella's guards rushed out of their car behind hers and began charging forward.

More strix came sprinting across the field on her right, as if they'd been waiting there.

The rest of the Black Saints materialized, Viper included, and shed their jackets in a wickedly fast movement.

All hell then officially broke loose.

CHAPTER TWENTY-TWO

Ella fumbled for the door handle, ready to jump out and join the battle, when she noticed something that made her freeze. "What the . . . ?" The strix were volleying balls of hellfire at the Black Saints—that was normal enough—but the angels were retaliating with ultraviolet orbs of who-knew-the-fuck-what.

Mia leaned forward. "What *is* that stuff they're conjuring? It's not holy fire, and it's not hellfire."

"Maybe it's some combination of both."

Something *blasted* out of Viper. A shimmering, ultraviolet wave that rippled through the air.

And sliced its targets in two.

Ella flinched back, her demon as impressed as it was leery. "Well. Fuck."

More of those waves were tossed around, killing multiple demons at a time.

Hearing a vicious muffled curse, she looked to her left to see Razor baring his teeth at a strix. He whipped out his arm, telekinetically throwing it at another demon that had been fast approaching, sending them both flying to the ground. Yet another flip of the same arm sent a third strix soaring right over Ella's car and into the grassland beyond it. All three strix were on their feet again within moments, only to be taken out by a series of ultraviolet thingies.

Her heart jumped when a cluster of strix surrounded Kasper and Arman.

And killed the guards in seconds.

She hissed in anger, clenching her hand on the steering wheel. "Jesus Christ. We have to—" She started in surprise as a strix approached the front of the car, sniffing. Its red eyes zipped from her to Mia, a combination of intrigue and bloodthirst there. The demon coiled its body, preparing itself to lunge.

Ella grimly smiled. "That's it, motherfucker, come on."

It pounced on the bonnet but then shrieked as electric magick shot through its feet and surged through its body. Its eyes rolling back, it violently convulsed as it toppled backwards and fell to the ground. A puff of ashes ballooned up, telling her that it was dead.

Viper's psyche bumped hers, and his voice floated into her mind: *I'd be wasting my breath telling you to stay in the car, so instead I'm going to tell you to watch your back. They like to pounce from behind.*

As a thought came to mind, Ella turned to her sister. "I have an idea."

Hyped up on adrenaline, rage, and protectiveness, Viper grunted in satisfaction as yet two more strix burst into ashes. Typically, he wouldn't rush a battle. But Ella was stuck in the middle of this one. She could take care of herself just fine, yes, but there were many strix here. So Viper kept hurling one archangelic blast after another, cleaving in half several demons at a time.

He didn't have to worry that any humans would arrive and see things they shouldn't. He'd instantly thrown a forcefield over the area to conceal them—a forcefield that for anyone outside it would give the illusion of 'roadworks ahead' traffic signs.

Surrounded by the scent and sight of blood and death, Viper's entity was high on sadistic glee. It was particularly enjoying watching these strix die, because they'd *dared* go near Ella. She hadn't been their target, but it didn't matter.

A roasting hot orb connected with Viper's head, burning his ear, making him hiss out a pained curse. He whirled to find his new attacker and—*there*. It was in the process of hurling another orb at him. He squatted low, evading it, and then lobbed several orbs of unholy fire at the demon. Only once it was ashes did he briefly check on his brothers, noting that none had allowed their inner fire to cover them in flames, careful what they permitted the sisters to see.

He glanced at Ella's car.

And his gut dropped.

She and her sister were both fucking hanging out of the sunroof, back to back, as strix charged the car. Their palms crackling with vibrantly colored magick, their lips barely moved as they chanted low and fast; ramming the aforementioned strix with magickal strikes.

Normally, Viper would have sat back and enjoyed watching Ella wield her magick. Right then, his focus was on the battle.

A focus that shifted to his left as more demons rushed him.

Viper grunted as an orb of hellfire smacked his already charred skin, popping blisters and making his skin sizzle. More came, and he batted them away with orbs of his own before slicing the bastard in half with another lethal blast.

He wanted to teleport to his woman's side, but the strix were mainly coming at *him*. It was best that he wasn't stood near her right now.

Crackling balls of flame arrowed through the air toward Viper—one, two, three. He sidestepped two, but the third clipped his shoulder. Even as he killed its source, a heavy weight crashed down on his back and teeth bit his injured shoulder *hard*. The force felt like needles driving into his flesh and scraping bone.

Viper looked at Jester. "I am so done with these bastards."

As yet another strix fell victim to her magick, Ella allowed herself to quickly check on Viper. She glanced his way ... just in time to watch a strix unlatch its teeth from his skin and slip to the ground, agony painting its face. Huh. That was weird. She had to—

A hellfire orb slammed into her shoulder like a flaming rock, sending a brief sensation of numbness down her arm.

Ow. Focusing on her attacker, she chanted as she emitted twisting streams of magick that rammed into its heart hard enough to make it stop. Like that, the demon was dead.

But then another took its place, launching orbs at her *and* the car. The latter move was a mistake, because those orbs bounced off her vehicle's transparent protective shield and took down the strix who'd conjured them. Ha.

An alarming cry of pain came from Mia.

Ella tensed. "Are you—"

"I'm okay, just wasn't expecting how hot that black fire is," said Mia. "Their numbers are massively down, I'm thinking this will be over soon."

Fingers crossed.

Always chanting, always tossing out magick, she and Mia

snapped necks, broke legs, ruptured organs, and sent ashes scattering everywhere.

They didn't always attack strix that came their way ... because the strix didn't persistently come at the sisters, too focused on the Black Saints. As such, Ella and Mia were also able to cover the angels' backs. Not that the guys *needed* help. They actually appeared to be enjoying themselves.

If they weren't grunting and cursing, they were laughing like loons. The strix were more animalistic, hissing and shrieking and making guttural cat-like sounds.

"I don't know where the smell of acid is coming from, but it's making my nose tingle." Ella wasn't crazy about the scents of sulphur and brimstone either.

"I think it's coming from whatever the Black Saints are conjuring."

Noticing that three strix were hightailing it across the field, Ella narrowed her eyes. Apparently, some had decided they were fighting a lost cause. Good decision. That didn't mean she'd let them leave alive.

But before she had the chance to cut their run short, they bounced off something she couldn't see. A containment forcefield, maybe? She wasn't sure. Whatever it was, the strix battered at it with fists.

Chanting, Ella slammed them with heavy gusts of magick that punched their backs hard enough to knock them down. Before they could fully rise, she hurled a loop of magick that curled around each of their necks and contracted tightly, cutting off their air supply.

Another tried running. She did the same to it.

Another made the same attempt, and it met the same fate.

A strix sped toward her car with an enraged hiss, its eyes boring into hers. She launched a blast of magick square in its face, causing its head to wrench back. Before she could act again, an ultraviolet blast sliced through it.

She whipped her gaze to her far left. Viper was looking at her, his breaths coming a little heavy ... and she saw that the battle was over. No strix remained, no others were attempting to flee. All the fallen angels appeared fine and were slipping their jackets back on.

"You okay, Mia?"

A relieved sigh. "Yeah. Just wondering something, though."

"What?"

"Well, the strix somehow sent Ghost tumbling over your car and onto the road, didn't they? How did they manage to see him when they call him Ghost for a reason."

Considering he'd once claimed to Ella that people only saw him if he *wanted* them to see him ... "I really have no idea."

Ghost tipped his chin toward a stretch of grassland. "They were waiting out there to swarm me, V. My cloak dropped for just a few seconds, and then they were on me. For them to wait here, they know my routine. They've been watching me—probably all of us."

Just as Viper had suspected. "There are two things I don't get. *How* they could know your routine when your presence is cloaked, and how the hell they could make that cloak drop."

Ghost shrugged. "Beats me. I'd like to know the answers as well."

Viper crossed to Ella's car just as she and her sister hopped out of it. Pulling his woman close, he searched her from head to toe. "Were you bitten?"

"No, the strix never got that close to me. I'm okay, just a few minor wounds."

"I'll never consider any injury you suffer 'minor'." Viper pressed his palm to hers and then pushed healing energy into her.

Her eyes widened. "Oh. You kept that nifty ability quiet." She looked at Mia, who was receiving the same aid from Dice.

Satisfied she was fully healed, Viper caught Ella by her nape. "I know it's not who you are, but I can still wish you'd stayed in the damn car."

"Technically, I did."

He felt his nostrils flare. "Not with every possible entry and exit closed."

"As you said, that's not who I am."

"It should be totaled," said Rivet, eyeing the vehicle.

Ella shrugged. "A little magickal protection goes a long way."

"Was it my imagination, or did your car actually zap a strix?" asked Blackjack.

"I'd set the trap for my note-writer, but the strix suffered for it." Her attention drifted to the two dead bodyguards, and her eyes dulled. "They were killed so fast I didn't have a chance to do anything to stop it."

Picking up on the guilt lacing her voice, Viper gave her a pointed look. "The strix are to blame, not you."

"My words, your mouth," Mia said to him before then turning to Ghost. "I'm guessing the strix barreled into you out of nowhere, since you went hurtling through the air."

He stiffly inclined his head. "They did."

"I never see you," said Ella. "I catch glimpses of your brothers in the distance sometimes, but never you. How did *they*?"

"I can cloak my presence, which is why I can stick close to you without being seen," Ghost replied. "For just a few seconds, the cloak dropped."

Ella frowned. "But . . . how could they have made it drop when they couldn't see you?"

"They must have guessed I was here when they saw your car. They somehow know I watch over you and that you use this route. They were prepared for an ambush." Ghost absently rubbed at dried blood on his jaw. "Don't know how they lowered my cloak, though."

"Maybe they didn't," said Dice. "Maybe a celestial is working with them. They hate hell-born demons, yeah, but the Uppers are desperate to take Viper down. They could have decided to make an exception."

Ella's gaze flew to Viper, a pinch of fear there. "They want you *dead*? Why?"

Hearing the worry in her voice, he felt his heart squeeze. "Baby, they're not going to get their wish. Soon enough, they'll come to terms with that and back off." Maybe. "In the meantime, they'll send other celestials on what are basically suicide missions."

"If a celestial *was* here just now, surely they wouldn't have hidden and watched the battle," said Mia. "They would have struck while you were preoccupied with the strix."

Viper shook his head. "I threw up a forcefield. It hid the battle from view, and it would have stopped anyone outside it from landing any hits of their own."

Ella poked him. "You didn't answer my question."

"You didn't stay in the car. *Fully*."

"We talked about that already." Ella looked at Ghost. "Speaking of the car, how are you managing to keep up with it if you're not driving? Do you have wings or something?"

Ghost's lips curved a little. "Or something."

Viper thought Ella might push for an answer, but she sighed, her gaze again drifting to the dead guards.

Sadness once more seeped into her expression. "Shame they couldn't hide their presence like you can, Ghost. I really liked those guys. Luka's gonna freak when I tell him what happened." Ella looked up at Viper. "This would have been a good time to tell him about you and me. I'd like to just get it over with. But . . . "

"But he's going to be furious enough on learning you were attacked by strix, and you don't want him to be in a murderous frame of mind when you tell him about us," Viper understood.

"Instead of admitting that Ghost is your guard, just say you got caught in the backlash of strix blindsiding him as he walked innocently across the street," Jester advised her. "A wrong place wrong time thing."

Ella pulled a face, not wanting to keep more things from Luka than she already was. But seriously, given how her anchor operated, what else could she do?

Sometimes, as Viper had recently shown, the truth was just best kept quiet. It would be better for her to present the Black Saints as her saviors rather than revealing that they'd been the targets. Luka would otherwise blame them for her being in the sight of the strix.

"If there's anything you lot don't want him to see, now is the time to hide it," Ella warned the Black Saints as she pulled out her phone. She brought up Luka's contact entry and pressed 'Call'.

He answered after a few rings, "Yes?"

"Hey, hope you're okay." Ella scratched the back of her head. "Be warned, you're not gonna like what I say next. Mia and I got caught up in a strix problem, and your guards sadly died in their attempt to save us. But the Black Saints showed up, so we're fine."

There was a long pause, then, "*What?*"

She winced at the growl. "Really, we're good."

"Where are you?" It was a snarly demand.

She rattled off the location, and then the line went dead. Sighing, she pocketed her phone. "He's likely gonna have someone teleport him here." Hence why she was backing away from Viper. "You might want to lower the forcefield so he'll see us."

"Already done," Viper told her.

Proving her prediction correct, Luka materialized nearby no more than thirty seconds later. He headed right for her with his guards and a third demon—no doubt the teleporter—at his back. His expression black, his mouth a thin slash, he studied her appearance. "You're all right?" he asked, his voice gruff with anger.

"We're fine, I promise," Ella assured him.

Mia leaned into her. "I really don't think he's asking about me," she said, as ever amused by how he considered everyone other than those closest to him to be somebody else's problem.

Luka's gaze swept over the Black Saints, eventually settling on their president. "Viper."

Viper inclined his head and greeted, "Belinsky."

"I'm sorry about Kasper and Arman," said Ella, feeling seriously shitty about them getting caught in the middle of all this fuckery. "I liked them. They were good guys."

Her anchor gave her a hard look. "Don't take the weight of their deaths on your shoulders. It is not your fault." He planted his feet. "Now, I have questions. Starting with how exactly does one get caught up in a strix issue?"

"A Black Saint was crossing the road in front of us when, bam, down he went as some strix barreled into him. Your soldiers jumped out to help, got attacked for their trouble, and then the rest of the club appeared. Mia and I stayed in the car while a short but sweet battle ensued that the Black Saints did indeed win." Aside from the first sentence, it was pretty much the truth, she'd just omitted a few details.

Luka's eyes flew to Viper. "I suppose you're going to call in a favor for protecting my anchor."

He shook his head. "The girls got caught up in our shit. They owe us nothing."

The legion narrowed his eyes slightly, a glint of suspicion there. But then his attention resettled on Ella. "Come. I will take you home."

"No need," Ella assured him. "I have my car, it didn't sustain any damage."

"I don't care. I want to be sure you're home safe before I leave you. Mikhail can drive the car back to your building."

Viper's psyche stroked Ella's as he said, *Let him take you back to your apartment so he can feel sure you're all right. I'll come pick you up as soon as he's gone.*

Knowing that Luka wouldn't budge on this anyway, she agreed, *Okay. I'll text you when I'm ready.* She then smiled wanly at Luka. "Fine. You can take me home."

Stepping out of Viper's en suite bathroom wearing only a fluffy towel, Ella sighed at him. "You're *still* brooding?"

"I'm not brooding," he denied, sitting on the bed. "I'm concerned."

"There's no need to be. I'm fine."

Which wasn't the point. "You should never have been caught up in my shit." He scrubbed a hand over his jaw. "They somehow know he's tailing you, which means they're also aware that you're important to the club. They would have killed you today in the hope that it would piss us off."

"But they didn't."

Viper wanted to gather her close, squirrel her away, and hide her somewhere where no one would ever find her. That she was powerful in her own right and didn't need such protection didn't quash those instincts.

It had been hard for him to let Belinsky take her away earlier.

So fucking hard. What Viper had most wanted was to take her to his compound and not let her out of his sight. But he'd known that the legion wouldn't leave that spot without her, and the quickest way for Viper to get her alone had been to let Luka feel assured that she was safe.

Viper rose to his feet. "I don't suppose you'll let me put you someplace safe until all this is over, will you?"

She bristled. "Uh, no. No, I won't."

"Strix are dangerous, Ella."

"I know. Gosh, if only I could use magick or something."

His entity snickered at that. "I'd be the last person to imply that you can't handle yourself—I've seen you in action, and I know you're strong. I just . . . I don't want to lose you."

Her face softened. "I'm not the main target here."

"But you're *a* target purely because you're of interest to the club."

"True, but you have guards on me. Be satisfied with that. I get that you're still wound tight after what happened earlier, but I'm fine. See for yourself." She dropped her towel.

Predictably, his body stirred. "You think you can distract me with sex?"

Humor lit her gaze. "That is my hope. But my intention was to seduce you in any case."

"You don't need to put effort into seducing me, Ella. I'm easy when it comes to you."

"That works both ways." She crossed to him. "Now instead of fretting over what could have happened, can we celebrate that it didn't?" She tilted her head. "Or shall I cover up?"

"Stay as you are." Because there was no way for him not to fold like a cheap pack of cards when she was naked in front of him.

Viper edged closer and inhaled deeply, savoring the feel of her scent slamming into his senses and making his cock harden.

He stared down at her hauntingly beautiful face. Fuck, she made him ache. Covet. Crave.

Her eyes lowered as she doodled a circle in the hollow of his throat. "You, um, you said yesterday that you need to feed tonight at the latest. I thought about it. Hard." Her gaze flew back to his. "I want you to take my blood."

He stilled, greed and excitement bursting to life inside him. His entity grinned, fucking ecstatic. "Be sure, Ella. If I drink from you, it'll get intense."

Her brow dented. "Intense how?"

"With others, I keep it clinical. Feed and then walk away. You're not just prey to me, you're mine. There'll be nothing impersonal about what happens. I won't only take your blood, I'll take you *while* I feed."

She swallowed hard, her eyes heating in a way that made his gut twist.

"Which means it won't be a gentle feed. It won't hurt—you'll love it, Ill make sure of that. But it'll be intense, like I said."

She hummed in thought. "Well, go big or go home, Viper."

"*Be sure.*"

"I'm positive. And why you think that 'intense' will ever be a turn-off for me, I don't know. Honestly, it's like you're new here."

His lips twitched. "Fine. But don't say you weren't warned."

Tired of him drawing this whole thing out, Ella fisted his tee and tugged on it hard. "I won't, I promise. Now do me already."

In hindsight, she shouldn't have gotten all demanding. Whenever she tried to rush him, he only made her wait longer. So it was no surprise that he lowered his face to hers inch by slow inch.

Finally, their mouths touched. It was a mere brush of lips. Featherlight. Barely-there. And yet, her nerve-endings sprang to attention.

He sipped from her mouth once, twice. Then he took it. Took it with a hungry, bruising, unrestrained kiss that made every part of her ache.

Releasing his tee, she slid her hands up to grip his shoulders. The kiss went on and on, interspersed with nips and scrapes of his teeth. All she felt in that moment—the heat, the connection, the chemical bliss—strangely calmed her mind. Her body, on the other hand? Oh, it was a hot mess as sexual sparks arced between them.

She leaned into him, seeking more. He kissed her harder. Deeper. Hungrier. Dragged her right under his spell, like always.

Viper pulled his lips free, his pupils blown, his face cold. "I'm gonna fuck every other man from your mind," he said, his voice thick with a need that made her skin pebble. A finger tapped her temple. "I'll be the only one up here. And you'll never get me out."

Ella felt a little shiver take her. And then his mouth was back on hers, his tongue was sliding against her own, his hands were in her hair . . . and up in flames she went.

She impatiently yanked and pulled at his clothes, shedding them piece by piece, scattering them all over the bedroom floor.

Hands snatched her hips and lifted her, plopping her down on his dresser. His mouth dipped to her neck, licking and nipping and suckling. Covetous hands stroked over her skin, a hint of reverence in his touch as well as the distinct stamp of ownership.

She palmed his head, letting tufts of his hair sift through her fingers as she closed her eyes. Ella officially lost herself in the moment, in the sensations, in the excitement winding through her. At this point, her core *hurt* with need and—

He raised his head, slamming a carnal gaze on hers. And shoved a finger inside her. Her gasp got lost beneath the growl that rumbled out of him.

"So slick and ready," he roughly whispered.

"Exactly, so can we cut the foreplay short?"

"It's like you read my mind."

Ordinarily, Viper would have spent more time gorging and savoring. But right now, knowing he was about to feed from her, he was too wound up to hold out. His cock was harder than it had ever been.

He withdrew his finger, snapped his hands around her thighs, and hauled her closer. "I want to take you bare, Ella," he said, the edge of a growl in his voice as he lodged the head of his dick inside her. "You still good with that?"

They'd discussed it only yesterday, agreeing it was time to scrap the condoms. She was on birth control, and both their kinds were immune to STDs.

She nodded, curling her legs tight around his hips. "Yes."

Thank fuck. Urged on by his entity, he rammed his hips forward, driving his cock deep. Her inner walls gripped him tight, making his teeth grind.

"Mine, Ella. You're mine and only mine." Digging his fingertips into her thighs, he fucked her hard.

She slapped her hands down on the dresser and elevated her hips slightly, allowing him to slam even deeper. "And you're mine."

Those words gripped his balls and squeezed. "Only ever yours."

It was true. No one had ever owned him until her. None had ever marked him.

So long he'd wandered the Earth at the bidding of his superiors, never really being *seen*. People had interacted with him, yes, but they'd forgotten him afterwards—he'd used his power to ensure it. It hadn't worked on her. Even her soul itself had retained those memories.

Until they'd been scrubbed away—he'd 'watched' it happen when raiding one of the Seven's memories.

Recalling that, recalling how she'd been taken from him, he couldn't help but up his pace. He fiercely powered into her, drinking in the gasp that crawled up her throat.

Speaking of her throat . . .

Viper dipped his head and scraped his teeth over her pulse there. She tilted her neck in offering. "You're gonna have to ask for it, Ella," he said, a note of challenge in his words. "I need to know you're still with me."

"I'm with you. Take what you need."

He growled. "I've fucking ached for this."

There was a flash of pain as he sank his teeth deep, but then a liquid heat fired through Ella's body and dialed up her need. As if someone had injected her with a goddamn aphrodisiac. *Oh, hell.*

Viper groaned, grabbing a fistful of her curls. He tugged hard on her hair as he drank, every *pull* of his mouth making her core clench.

She arched into him, her breathing going to shit, her mind blissfully empty of everything but *how fucking good* it felt.

Tension swirled in her belly, moved through her muscles, and tightened her inner walls. Then that tension broke.

Ella shattered with a silent scream, her eyes going blind. His dick plundered, thickened, pulsed, *rammed so deep.* And then he stilled, shuddering and jolting with every blast of his release.

Viper dislodged his teeth from her neck as the strength seemed to drain from them both. Fuck, he hadn't felt so sated in a long time. It wasn't simply that he'd taken her blood as he possessed her body, it was that she'd *allowed* it. Welcomed it. Showed that element of trust, moving them a step closer to where they needed to be before he could claim her.

He blew over the bite mark to heal it and then raised his head. "You okay?"

She double-blinked, her lips kicking up. "We are *definitely* doing that again."

He smiled.

CHAPTER TWENTY-THREE

After she and Mia parted ways in the lobby of their complex the following Saturday after work, Ella nabbed her mail from the lockable box there. With one of her new guards at her back, she then made her way to her apartment. As always, he remained outside her front door when she entered—an order from Luka.

Breezing through the living area, she yawned and cricked her neck. It might be good for her to have a nap before texting Viper. At the very least, she'd need to knock back some painkillers first. She had a wicked headache, and the herbal tea she'd drank at the store had done nothing to relieve it.

In the kitchen, she scanned the bundle of envelopes in her hands. Bills. Shit-mail. And . . . whatever was in the plain brown envelope at the bottom of the pile.

Curious, she dumped the rest of her mail on the counter, along with her purse, and then tore open the envelope. As she fished out a small piece of paper that had been folded over, her belly did a fast flip. *Motherfucker.*

Her demon stirred, uncoiling like a snake as its mood instantly darkened. Ella tossed aside the ripped envelope and opened up the slip. One word. Only one word was printed on it: *Everleigh*.

Her brows snapped together. Who the fuck was Everleigh? Seriously, what was *with* this asshole?

Like with the other notes, there was a gleam of compulsive power in the ink. But the message itself . . . she didn't know what to make of it.

Was Everleigh a person? A song? A mere attempt to baffle Ella?

The only thing she knew for certain was that she wanted to pummel its author's face with a baton.

Ella tore into the note to disengage the snare and then slapped it on the counter. She hadn't expected any to be posted to her address. In fact, as time had gone by and no more had come, she'd thought maybe the writer had given up on using this tactic. But oh no, apparently not.

She dug her cell phone out of her purse and texted Viper: *I got another note*, not bothering to add where he could find her. He'd know that already, since Ghost would have told him she'd arrived home safely.

She probably should have begun the text with a 'hi', but she wasn't really in the mood for pleasantries. She was in the mood to cut off a certain note-sender's balls.

Movement in her peripheral vision snagged her attention. She turned to see Viper stood in her living room, his face like thunder. Clearly not in tune with her mood, her hormones got a little excited.

His jaw hard, he stalked into the kitchen, his eyes glittering blue gems of anger. "Gotta tell you, baby, I'm getting real sick of this bastard."

"You're not alone in that," she mumbled.

"Ghost said your car was clean."

"It was. This particular note was posted to my address."

Viper clenched his teeth, furious. "He clearly didn't think he had any other way of getting it to you." He palmed the back of her head. "Where is it?"

She swiped the slightly ripped slip of paper from the counter and handed it to him. "He only typed a single word this time. A name."

Viper dipped his gaze to the note . . . and felt every muscle in his body go rigid. He stopped breathing as shock stole the air from his lungs. His entity went equally still, just as taken aback.

"What is it?" asked Ella. "You know an Everleigh?"

Viper clamped his lips shut. He could only stare at her, having no fucking clue what to say.

Her brows knit, lines of unease creasing her face. "What? Who is she?" Ella fixed him with a wary stare that made his chest pang. "Is she an ex or something? Another of your regulars?"

Fuck, he did *not* want to explain that now. He wasn't ready yet.

He could slip in a few lies to divert her line of questioning . . . but then later, when he finally divulged the entire truth, she'd be pissed at him for bullshitting her.

"Viper, *who is Everleigh?*"

He crumpled up the note. "She's connected to the things I haven't yet told you," he fudged.

Ella narrowed her eyes. "You're not gonna ask me to let you explain in your own sweet time, are you? Because that's not happening. I need to know what this means. I need to know how whoever wrote this note could know anything about the stuff you've yet to share with me."

They could only know if they knew who she was to Viper. Which meant a celestial was behind the notes. A celestial who'd figured out that Viper *had* tracked down his woman.

A long, rough sigh eased out of him. "I told you once that

my tale has a lot of moving parts. This is one of them. There's no way for me to explain this without also telling you the rest and . . . and you're right, I can't expect you to wait for an explanation." In her shoes, he wouldn't have agreed to wait either. "But before we get to that, I need to show you something."

She blinked. "Okay."

He took her hand and teleported them to his bedroom at the clubhouse. "The third drawer of my dresser." He jerked his chin toward it, letting a hint of a dare sound in his voice as he said, "Open it."

Curiosity trampled all over her features, overlaying the lines of impatience. Once he released her hand, she crossed to the dresser and did as he asked.

"The denim vest on top of the pile," he said. "Take it out."

"Why?"

"It's yours. I had it made for you."

Her brow creasing, she pulled it out of the drawer.

"Turn it around."

She did so . . . and her breath caught as she stared at the embroidered clothing patch on the back. A patch that read: *Property of Viper.*

He watched her throat bob with emotion. His woman knew enough about bikers to know what it meant; to know that this vest was his way of publicly and officially claiming her. "It's been in that drawer for weeks."

She cleared her throat with a deliberate cough. "Weeks?"

"I was waiting for the right moment to give it to you. That moment being the one where, on hearing all I've so far kept from you, you assured me you could deal. I don't know if we've reached that point. I'd hoped we'd have more time." He sighed. "I'll spill everything. But first, you have to promise me something."

Her eyelids lowered slightly. "What?"

"Promise you'll stay with me until I've explained everything. Promise you'll hear me all the way out."

Her brow pinched, as if she had no idea why he'd ever assume she wouldn't do him that courtesy. "I'll hear you all the way out. You have my word." She carefully—and, to his surprise, hesitantly—returned the vest to his drawer.

His entity noted the hesitance. Was pleased by it. But it didn't grin smugly. Not when it knew that what Viper next told her could jack everything up.

Blowing out a breath, she walked to him. "There has to be another geas in place, right? It's fine, I get it." She offered him her hand. "I'd rather know that the information can't be forced out of me."

He gripped her hand. "Do you swear never to repeat what I tell you here and now?"

"I swear it." Ella gasped as his power—cold and prickly and *old*—flooded her system and crackled through her veins. With that deed done, he let go of her hand.

"Now come on, out with it," she prodded. "What's so terrible you worry I can't handle it?"

Viper lowered himself into the armchair. He stretched out his long legs, crossing them at the ankles, and splayed his hands on the armrests. He lazily let his head loll back to hit the headrest as he weakly indicated the bed, inviting her to sit.

So nonchalant. So casual.

A *ruse*. She wasn't fooled. Nor was her demon. His discomfort was evident in his unnatural stillness, the minute tightening of his jaw, the too-lazy blinks, and how deliberately slow and even his breathing was.

"I'm about to bring you fully into my world now, Ella. It's not a pretty place. You're going to hear things you don't like. Things that may upset you. Scare you. Confuse you. Piss you off." He paused. "Remember your promise."

Ella sat on the bed. "I'll hear you all the way out." Growing more uneasy with each second, she watched his chest expand as he drew in a breath. He stared back at her, seeming braced for . . . something.

"The rumor about me is true. I am an archangel. But I doubt that comes as much of a surprise to you."

It didn't.

"Archangels aren't creations of God."

She felt her brows knit. "Really?"

"We are the handiwork of Chaos, the Creator. God was his first creation, and we were told to serve him. So we do."

That she hadn't expected to hear. "Are angels creations of Chaos?"

"No, they were fashioned by God. They're essentially his own version of archangels."

Interesting. "Is the rumor that you're one of the Seven also true?"

He gave a slow nod.

That didn't particularly surprise her either. "Which one of the Seven are you?"

"I went by many titles." The words were casual, but tension crept up his arms and into his shoulders. "The Destroyer. The Chief of Tempters. The Archangel of Darkness and Death."

Realization dawned on her fast, making her eyes widen slightly. "Samael." A whisper.

"Samael," he confirmed.

Well, damn. A lot was said about him. That he was the most beautiful of the archangels. That he walked among humans. That he wasn't evil but had a backward moral code.

"For the most part, the Uppers are protective of humans."

"For the most part?" she echoed.

"They like to tempt the inborn darkness inside humans, and they used me exclusively to do it. I've tricked, tempted, seduced, punished, and destroyed. I've sparked wars, taken souls, and engineered the falls of 'the wicked', as the Uppers refer to them. You've no doubt heard the tales of my deeds."

She had. "You did all this at their bidding?"

Viper nodded. "Which, of course, doesn't excuse my part in it." He swiped his tongue over his teeth. "Killing became too easy. It stopped marking me. You get desensitized to the darkness after a while."

Ella dragged in a breath, her mind working through all he'd revealed. She couldn't lie—to realize he was Samael was mildly disturbing. She'd heard of his many 'exploits'. It was really no wonder he'd been endowed with so many grim titles.

Her demon wasn't quite so disturbed. It actually liked the idea that he knew darkness just as well as it did. Well, what *didn't* the entity so far like about Viper?

"I really should have guessed you were Samael. The clue is in your chosen name." Vipers were venomous, weren't they? And Samael went by another title: The Venom of God. "Did you choose to fall because you were tired of doing what they asked of you?"

The stiffness in his shoulders bled up to his neck, making the cords stand out. "It was part of the reason. I was . . . tired. Weary. A little lost. I didn't like how my responsibilities had increasingly ate at my inner entity. But it wasn't until a certain person came into my life that I felt truly motivated to fall. I meant to do it a long time ago, but I was betrayed by the rest of the Seven. Convinced they were saving me from myself, they took from me the certain person I mentioned before. Hid that person. Swore I'd never find them."

Memories of their first conversation at the Red Rooms came rushing back to her. "They're what brought you to Vegas?"

"Yes. It took me a long time, but I found them. Her." A triumphant glint danced in his gaze. "When I did, I left the upper realm. It was the only way I could keep this one thing I needed. I wasn't going to lose her again." He leaned forward in his seat and rested his arms on his thighs. "The first time you and I met, I knew you by another name."

"The first time we . . . I'm sorry, what?"

"It wasn't in this life. It was in your previous one."

She sucked in a sharp breath.

"Your name then was Everleigh," he added, answering her unspoken question. "We fell hard. Fast. You were prepared to accept me, curse and all, if I left heaven to be with you. But things didn't go as we planned."

Her lips parted as she gaped at him. "Wait . . . you're saying . . . "

"I'm saying we were together in another life. You just don't remember."

Ella's thought processes stuttered, her mind struggling to keep up. She knew souls were often reborn. But his claim that they'd encountered each other in her past life seemed so surreal. And yet, it made sense.

She'd always felt that he reminded her of someone—he'd been familiar to her from the start. The first time they'd locked gazes, she'd felt sure she'd looked into his eyes before. More, he'd never really felt like a stranger. She was comfortable with him in a way she generally wouldn't be with people she didn't know well.

And hadn't she always felt that something was missing? Hadn't there always been a sense of absence that had only disappeared when he came into her life?

Her breath snagged when she suddenly once more found herself recalling the wraith's words ... *He will come for you.*

It had meant Viper. Samael. The freaking Archangel of Darkness and Death.

No wonder the wraith had laughed its tits off.

Licking her lips, she gave her head a little shake. "Why ... why didn't you say anything sooner?" Where was the point in seeking her out only to keep her ignorant?

His head tipped to the side. "If I'd told you this right off the bat, how would you have reacted?"

Mostly with disbelief. And ... "I probably would have thought it was a lie. That you were fucking with me for your own entertainment."

"Because you didn't know me. I needed that to change. Needed for you to feel safe and comfortable with me."

"I've felt that way around you for weeks now. Yet, you said nothing."

"Because, like I told you before, it's all tangled up in everything else I haven't yet shared with you."

"Okay. Tell me more."

"Before you, no one I came upon here on Earth ever remembered me after that first meeting. You did. I don't know how, but you did. And you drew me in without trying."

People *forgot* him? Jesus.

"You became an obsession for me. To the point where there was no letting you go. You were the only thing I'd ever claimed as mine." He pushed out of his chair and then walked toward her. "When you learned of the curse, you didn't turn me away. But there's more to it in my case. I hadn't yet told you that—, you were taken from me before I had the chance." The pain of that spiderwebbed through his expression. "Taken by people who were intent on me not paying the price for falling."

She looked up at him as he halted before her. "What price?"

"I'm not merely doomed to drink blood, Ella. That's not even the worst part." He wrapped his fingers around her wrist, tugged her to her feet, and then teleported her to the yard. He dropped her hand and flicked his own, saying, "Look around, Ella. What do you see?"

She scanned their surroundings a little uncertainly.

"Flowers? Fresh grass? Animals? Any signs of nature thriving? No. And you won't see those things. Because of me."

She frowned. "What?"

"Have you ever been at the pool hall, the club, or the dive bar when I was there and *not* seen a fight break out? Of course you haven't. And again, it was because of me."

She gave another shake of her head. "I don't understand."

"The strix I've battled who bit me . . . they all died. Know why? My blood is acidic."

Her gut squeezed. "Acidic?"

He stepped closer, towering over her. "My presence stunts growth, kills animals, invites sin, incites violence, makes even friends turn on each other. That's what it means to be the incarnation of a deadly sin. That's what becomes of one of the Seven archangels if they fall."

CHAPTER TWENTY-FOUR

Ella could only gape at him, her brain hiccuping and spluttering as it strived to process his words. Not once in the times she'd chewed over what he could be hiding had she *ever* considered this. Why would she have? She'd had no idea that such a fate could befall anyone, let alone a fallen member of the Seven.

Originally, she'd wondered if he was being a little dramatic in his insistence that his secrets were so dark. Oh, how wrong she'd been to doubt him.

He was the incarnation of a deadly sin. *A deadly sin.* Her demon, as stunned as Ella, couldn't quite wrap its head around it.

His gaze vacant and unblinking, he watched her very carefully, seemingly intent on soaking in her every reaction. His body was so rigid he could have passed for a statue.

What was she supposed to say? Or do? Her mind gave her no answer. It was still busy struggling to work through his revelation, and so all she could do was stand there gawking at him.

No wonder he'd hesitated to tell her. His presence fouled and corrupted everything and everyone around him. What did that knowledge even do to a person? What kind of mind fuckery would it cause? And how did it even come about?

She licked her lips. "How . . . how can falling cause that?"

His empty gaze drifted over her face. "Each of the Seven archangels is one of the seven virtues," he said, his voice slow and flat. "The fall, though, it warps us. Once upon a time, I embodied patience. Now, I embody wrath. I infect people with it without even trying."

"And this is a punishment for falling?"

"It was intended to be more of a deterrent. It's certainly effective since, to my knowledge, no member of the Seven fell before me." He paused. "The strix came after my club because what I am *draws* any kind of evil like a magnet. We don't need to hunt the hell-born. They seek us out."

Oh, Jesus. While that would make his self-appointed job easier, it would also mean that danger constantly chased him and his brothers. And to know that evil would *literally* be drawn to you, would come for you, follow you . . . Who wouldn't hate that?

She rubbed at her chest. "But you have some kind of control over how you affect people, right? I mean, I never feel wrathful around you."

"It doesn't appear to work on the people I care about, such as you and my brothers. Everyone else? I can attempt to lessen the impact, but it doesn't work for long."

Which totally explained why he never spent much time around outsiders—even Mia. "Why did your brothers fall with you?"

"It was a show of loyalty. I led their branch of the holy host. I'd trained them, watched out for them, fought at their side, saved their asses more times than they could count. They didn't want to answer to a new archangel, and they didn't feel they could trust the rest of the Seven after what they did to me."

She looked toward the clubhouse. "They're not normal angels, are they?" She'd sensed that much.

"My inner circle—Dice, Jester, Razor, Omen, Darko, and Ghost . . . People call them 'the Burning Ones'."

She froze. "Seraphim." *Well, shit.*

"Seraphim, the most powerful and dangerous of the angels. The rest of my brothers are dominions. Slightly less powerful but still dangerous."

She swiped a hand down her face. The shocks kept piling up. His club . . . It was far more deadly than she ever could have imagined. If the demon world as a whole understood that, she was quite sure the club would be massacred. Her own entity was a little unnerved by all this, to be truthful. And not much daunted it in general.

"No wonder you guard all your secrets so tightly," she said. "I'm surprised you made alliances with demons. Surely it would be safer to keep to yourselves."

"It would have. But I needed to gain a foothold in your world. I needed access to the Underground so I could watch over you there and be certain you were safe. And I knew I had a better chance of situating myself in your life if you thought some of your kind trusted me."

"Cunning."

Viper didn't take offence, seeing mirth bloom in her gaze. Well, demons didn't generally have an issue with 'cunning'. They were incredibly devious themselves and respected such a quality in others. "Yes, but necessary."

She carved a hand through her hair, looking the epitome of dazed. "Anymore bombshells you need to drop?"

"None." He took her wrist and teleported her back to his

bedroom. "Well, maybe one. Though it isn't bad or huge." Viper peeled up his tee and gestured at the ink above his heart. "You asked me what these writings say."

Her gaze dipped to the strange symbols.

"It's two words: *Only her.*" He let his t-shirt drop. "*You,* Ella. No one else found their way under my skin. Just you."

She scratched at her scalp, clearly overwhelmed. "That's . . . I don't know what to say."

He didn't need her to say anything. All he wanted was for her to not walk out. She'd promised to stay until he'd relayed everything. He'd made it clear there was nothing else to tell her, so this was the point where she could declare her intention to leave. But she hadn't. More, there were thousands of queries in her eyes.

Queries were good. They might mean she'd hang around longer. He'd been deliberately vague about certain aspects of his story, hoping it would spark her to linger—even if only to ask for elaborations.

As she'd said, cunning.

"You say you settled in Vegas for me," she began, "but you've been here a while. You didn't approach me or anything."

"I couldn't. I knew the Uppers would send slayers after me. They did. The entire time I spent fending them off, I established my club here in Vegas. And I watched you from afar."

"Hence why you where there when I interfered in the mugging," she realized.

"Yes. I couldn't explain that before now but, if you think back, I didn't lie to you when I spoke of why I was close by. I simply kept some details to myself."

She flicked up a *That makes it okay, does it?* brow but then sniffed. "The pool hall, the dive bar . . . you bought those because I frequented them, didn't you?"

"And your apartment complex."

Her eyes widened. "Oh, my God. You're the new mystery owner who came along and fixed the place up."

"I wanted to better its conditions and improve its security, so it fucking galled me when the bastard writing you notes still managed to get inside." Viper could have warded it against teleportation, but it would have prevented any demonic residents with such an ability from gaining entrance that way. "In buying the place, I pretty much fucked up."

Her brows dipped. "Fucked up?"

"As the Everleigh-note has proven, only someone who knows exactly who you are to me could be sending the notes. That means someone from the upper realm has been watching me. Someone who figured out by my business transactions that I had a vested interest in you."

"They would have realized that I was the unifying element," she reasoned, her expression thoughtful. "I live in the complex. The pool hall was my long-time haunt. The dive bar was next to my store. Although . . . all of that also applies to Mia."

"Yes, but anyone watching me while I was near you would have noticed I paid attention to *you*. They would have guessed who you are to me—it was a given that I would seek you out after I fell, if not before." He held his breath, braced for her to yell at him; blame him for the shit she'd recently had to deal with. But she didn't.

"I never considered that the notes were connected to you. I received the first one before you and I even spoke." She folded her arms. "Who exactly would do this? One of the Seven? You said they betrayed you, though you didn't really go into detail."

"Back when you were Everleigh, they came for us, taking us by surprise. They put us both to sleep, took us to separate locations, and killed you knowing your soul would be reborn. They took measures to ensure I wouldn't find you."

They'd tried lying to him, tried convincing him that the Uppers were responsible for her disappearance. He hadn't bought it. Gabriel had been too twitchy and nervous, and Michael hadn't been able to look Viper in the eye. So he'd delved into Raphael's mind and seen all; seen how he, Uriel, and Azrael had led the 'mob'; watched as Raphael wiped Viper's imprint and memories from her soul.

"Believe it or not, they thought they were doing the right thing by us." His entity snorted, finding them ridiculous.

Her head jerked back. "How is killing me the right thing?"

"It isn't. But in their mind, it would free us both from each other. They felt you were better off without me, and vice versa; felt that parting us was the only way to stop me from falling." They hadn't cared that she was the only thing that brought him peace; had disregarded what she meant to him, more concerned about what he'd become on falling.

"I don't believe any of them are responsible for the notes," he went on. "Their motive for separating us was to prevent me from falling. It's too late for that now, so it'd be senseless for them to go near us. Besides, I put them through some serious pain when I realized what they'd done. They won't want to risk that happening again. And they're not the vengeful type, unlike me."

Her eyes went slitted. "You said they hid me. How? I mean, I'm right here."

"I'd imprinted myself on your soul. Marked it—and yes, you were aware of it. You agreed to it. They removed that mark before killing you, because it would have otherwise enabled me to track your soul. They should have known better than to think it would be enough to keep me from searching for you."

He took a slow step toward her and offered, "I can show you what they did."

Her brows met. "You were there?"

"No. But I psychically punched my way into Raphael's mind afterward and snatched the memory of what happened right out of his brain. Want to see?"

"Yes, I want to see."

"I'll have to touch you," he warned.

She rolled her eyes. "I'm not scared of you."

Relief pounded through him. His entity relaxed slightly, though it was still on edge. They weren't out of the woods yet.

Viper closed the space between them. "There's more I could show you."

"Like, what?"

"Glimpses of times we met in your past life. Some of those memories were soaked into your soul. When we met again, those memories would have begun to surface." His lips thinning, he added, "But Raphael had wiped them away."

"Will it hurt to show me?"

"I would never do anything that would cause you pain."

"Will it hurt *you*? You'd be invading the mind of a demon—it takes a toll on celestials."

"There'd be some discomfort, but it wouldn't drain me because it would take only seconds. It will be like uploading a file to a computer."

She planted her feet and rolled her shoulders. "Okay. Show me. I want to see what happened. I want back what they took from me."

He placed the heels of his hands against her temples. "Close your eyes."

Ella pulled in a preparatory breath, bracing herself for the psychic impact, not entirely sure what to expect.

And then it happened.

Images flickered through her mind, fast and vibrant. Memories played out there in fast-forward but dug in deep, planting themselves in her own mind.

She saw all of their personal journey. The talks they'd had, the kisses they'd shared, the attention he'd lavished on her body, the way he'd kept coming back to her, the love that had crept up on him little by little until finally it had filled every space inside him.

And then she saw *them*. The rest of the Seven. They'd stared at her so dispassionately as they pinned her to a wall and took what they'd had no right to take. Not only her life, but her memories of Viper. The motherfuckers.

As she watched it all play out, she frowned. The replays plucked at elusive recollections, bringing images and sensations and emotions to the forefront of her mind.

Buried as she was in the past, it was hard to snap back to the present. It was his scent that led the way; that gave her something to focus on.

Leather, allspice, and bay rum with an earthy undertone.

Soft pulses of his breath fanned her face, and she could almost *feel* him watching her with that hawk-eyed gaze. She lifted her eyelids . . . and met startling-blue eyes that, steely as a bird's, honed right in on hers. Longing clutched at her throat, her emotions toward him so much more intense now that she'd seen flashes of their history.

A history that had been *stolen* from her.

"Those rat bastards. They had me pinned to a wall." The latter words rang with the anger she was struggling to suppress.

His nostrils flared. "I know. They paid for it."

Cold fingertips raced up her spine at the menacing note lacing his voice. "Good."

Given he'd fallen for her at a time when her soul had hosted a different body, she might have worried that he looked at her and saw only Everleigh—a person he'd lost. But as he'd shown her their past, she realized it wasn't like that. She would have otherwise sensed it in his memories, in the emotions attached to them.

He looked at her and saw only the woman he'd claimed as his.

And strange as it might sound, that time didn't feel like a 'past life'. It felt more like her years as Ella were a continuation of her years as Everleigh ... but with some differences. Just the same, his time as Viper would be a continuation of his life as Samael ... but with a few variations.

Their names, prior circumstances, and new realities didn't matter. Not to her, not to him. Their connection went beyond that shit; ran too deep for any of it to make a single difference.

"You know, I don't think they did a thorough job of making me forget you. I'd look at you and think, 'Hmm, he reminds me of someone.' Your eyes seemed familiar somehow. I dismissed it, not for a second thinking we'd met before. And those memories you showed me ... they *pulled* at little scenes that I have vague recollections of. I think I might have been dreaming about you."

Which would explain why Mia's talisman hadn't worked. They hadn't *really* been dreams, she'd been seeing flashbacks of her time with Viper.

His brow creased. "I did wonder if maybe I seemed familiar to you. If your soul did manage to retain some memories, being around me would have triggered them to surface. They would have come to you as you slept. You didn't remember them on waking?"

"Only brief flashes here and there. Nothing I could ever piece together." She cocked her head. "Could that be why it felt like my dreams were taking a toll on me?"

He nodded. "Your brain would have been sifting through and trying to soak up the memories. It would have been tough on your psyche."

Then that totally explained it. Although . . . she didn't think she'd dreamed of—well, had flashbacks of—him in weeks. Yet, she still felt weighed down by fatigue.

She puffed out a breath. "You're nuts coming back for me and choosing to live a cursed life when—"

"The life I led was dark and dull and left me feeling dead. Until you." He palmed her jaw and swept a thumb over the side of her face. "I talked about you to the rest of the Seven, trusting them to keep it secret from the Uppers. That was my mistake. One you paid for. Never again," he swore. "I don't know who's sending the notes, but I won't let them hurt you."

"Do you think whoever did it put a compulsion in the ink that would force me to stay away from you or something?"

"Maybe."

"You'd think they would have given up sending me snares, considering the other three notes failed to work."

"I don't think they thought the most recent one would work either. I think their intention was to make you ask questions and leave me no choice but to tell you everything."

She frowned. "How would they know you already hadn't told me?"

"They won't believe in a million years that you'd accept a man who's the embodiment of a deadly sin. I'm not even certain you will." An intensity gathered behind his eyes. "But I won't let you go. I came to this world knowing I would stain it. I don't then have the right to claim something good from it. But I'll do it anyway. I need you." He slid his hand from her cheek to her hair. "Never needed a single person in my life except you."

The raw honesty in his voice was the good kind of punch to

the chest. Much as he'd done some verbal ducking and diving and weaving since they first met, he was clearly set on being truthful here and now, even if it meant exposing his emotions. The guy seemed too damn self-assured to feel vulnerable doing so.

"You have no idea how close I've come to permanently binding you to me so you'd never escape me," he said. "I'm selfish enough to do it; to ignore what that would mean for you."

Her pulse skipped a beat. "Then why haven't you?"

"Same reason I wouldn't take your blood without your consent. I *need* for you to want it. Want me. I get that the thought of irrevocably belonging to me might not be so thrilling. Still, I can't let you go, Ella. You have to know I won't."

She licked her lips. "You're throwing around words like 'binding' and 'irrevocably'."

"Because when I claim you, I will *own* you. Every inch of your body, every part of your soul, every thought that passes through your head—it'll all be mine. You'll be shackled to me just as surely as you're shackled to your psi-mate. My claim will be *that* irreversible."

Ella's skin pebbled at the intensity with which he spoke. "I didn't know angels could lay those kind of claims."

He smoothed a hand down her hair. "I didn't fully claim you last time because it's a binding of souls; I wasn't sure if my falling would somehow stain yours if we were that tightly connected, so I chose to wait."

But then the rest of the Seven had taken her.

"I'm not pushing you to consent to it here and now, I'm just making it clear that it *will* happen. Not only because I want that, but because it's the only way I can ensure that no one can take you from me again." He lowered his face toward hers. "Fact is I love the fuck out of you, baby. There'll never be a time when I don't."

He'd spoken so matter-of-factly, no awkwardness, no shame, no hesitation to give her such honesty. He needed to stop with these verbal feel-good punches. They were affecting even her demon at this point, and not a lot touched it emotionally.

"You're not there yet. I know that. But you'll get there. Unless you let what I've become poison what you feel."

Maybe it should have poisoned all she felt. It wasn't as if he hadn't told her some *major* shit. But it would seem that not even such revelations could change how she felt about him. And even if it *had* been too hard to accept, how could she ever have held it against him that he'd fallen when he'd done it for her?

"What I said at the Red Rooms still applies: That you're cursed isn't your fault. Yes, you knew what the consequences would be; you knew how it would impact everything and everyone around you. But you're not responsible for the curse itself, or for becoming the personification of a deadly sin."

"But you're scared," he sensed, his lips bowing down.

"Not of you. I'm scared *for* you. If my kind find out what exactly you are . . . "

"There's no reason they ever would."

She anxiously rubbed at her nape. "What if the Uppers let it leak?"

"They wouldn't. Not even to ensure my death. They use this realm in various ways, such as dumping angels here and forcing them to earn their halo. If demons learned what could become of a fallen archangel, they'd come for me. But what else would they do?"

"Kill the rest of the Fallen, as well as any non-Fallen angels, in case there's other stuff they don't know about your kind."

He nodded. "Demons outnumber celestials here in this realm, so we'd be wiped out fast and hard unless those in the upper realm sent backup, and I'm not sure they would. They know there'd be no real winners if a war broke out between the light and the dark. But if they let us be slaughtered, demons would then essentially own this realm. There'd be no angelic presence here. The Uppers will never want that."

Viper badly wanted to haul her close, kiss her, hold tight to her. But his baby was so overwhelmed and off-balance that he knew she needed personal space right now.

She'd handled things far better than he ever could have hoped. She was still here, no distrust or misgivings in her expression. She wasn't looking at him any differently than she had before. But yes, she was definitely overwhelmed. "I've given you a whole lot to think about, haven't I?"

"My synapses feel fried." She eyed him curiously. "You could have just taken the memory of the note from my head, couldn't you? You could have delayed having to tell me all this—I would never have known any different."

"I couldn't do something like that to you. It would make me no better than the last fuckers who meddled with your memories." He could be a cruel bastard. He'd own that. But he'd never direct such cruelty at her.

Even his entity, sadistic shit though it was, would never wish to betray or hurt her. And despite that it was an incredibly selfish being, it wasn't urging Viper to disregard her current emotional state and push her to give them all they wanted from her. It was prepared to give her some time and breathing room if it was what she needed.

As such, it didn't cast him annoyed looks when he took a step back. She, however, narrowed her eyes at his retreat.

"Why are you backing away?" she demanded.

He shrugged. "Figured you might want some space to process."

"Well, you figured wrong. And you were wrong about something else, too." She flushed, turning all awkward and fidgety. "I didn't realize it until now, if I'm honest." She shifted from foot to foot, avoiding his gaze. "You're not the only one who's riddled with soppy emotions."

Viper felt his mouth curve, warmth blooming in his chest and spreading through his system. "Is that your way of telling me you love me?"

She cleared her throat. "Kinda."

He hooked an arm around her neck and drew her closer. "You always did struggle to say it," he said, his lips moving against her forehead. "As if it would somehow jinx everything."

"Yeah, I saw that in the memories you showed me," she mumbled.

He kissed her temple. "As I said before, I won't push you to let me claim you here and now. I don't want your mind whirling when I do it. I don't want your thoughts preoccupied with other things. I want you with me one-hundred percent, completely certain it's what you want. But don't make me wait too long, Ella."

"Or?" she asked.

The word was a tease. Pure playfulness. Still, his entity rose up and took over, saying, "Or I'll take the matter into my own hands. You're mine as well as his. Neither of us are going to let you go."

Her eyes bled to black as her demon came to the fore. "If she wants to leave, she will leave," it told the entity, haughty.

"But she doesn't," it stated, "and neither do you."

Her demon gave a prim little sniff and then subsided.

Ella blinked as her eyes returned to normal. "They don't seem to get along all that well."

"It's their version of foreplay."

She twisted her mouth. "That claiming thing you mentioned—"

"We're not gonna talk about it anymore today. I just piled a fuck of a lot on you. Some of it was heavy shit. I want to give you time to let everything fully settle up here," he added, gently tapping her temple. "From the beginning, I've pushed and pushed to get what I want from you. I don't want to push when it comes to something as serious as binding you to me. It's not as if I'm asking for a little thing here. I want you to be sure you're ready for it."

Ella narrowed her eyes, her gut stirring. "It's not just that, is it? As you said, you've pushed from the start. It's been you who made every advance; you who nudged us into a relationship. You need for me to do my own pushing."

His brow creased as he weaved his fingers through her hair. "You'll never need to push me to claim you, baby—I'm all for that. I came to this realm for that reason. But yeah, I'd like to feel that we're reaching for each other; not that it's me leading this dance." He framed her face with his hands. "We'll put a pin in all that for now. Come for a ride with me."

Her lips tipped up. "Okay."

He pressed his forehead to hers. "Will you wear it?"

"The vest, you mean? Hell, yeah, I'll wear it."

He grinned.

CHAPTER TWENTY-FIVE

Walking into the clubhouse's main sitting area the following morning, Viper frowned on seeing every one of his brothers there. "How come you're all gathered here?"

"We're waiting to hear if we're right in guessing that Ella now knows everything," replied Dice from the sofa. "Blackjack said he saw you teleport her to the yard last night; said you were gesturing for her to look around and that the conversation looked intense."

Viper planted his feet. "She now knows everything."

"How'd she take it?" asked Darko, leaning against the pool table.

"Far better than I thought she would." Viper was equal parts proud and relieved. "Don't get me wrong, she was shocked to hear what I'd become. Probably a little unsettled, though she didn't admit to it. But she rolled with it. Rolled with all I told her about our history and situation. Doesn't hold the curse against me. Most importantly, she still accepts my claim on her."

"I figured that," began Ghost, who was sitting on Dice's left, "since I noticed you two leave the compound last night on your bike and she was wearing the vest you had made for her."

From his stool near the bar, Razor slammed a glare on Ghost. "You didn't tell us that."

"What goes on between a man and a woman is their business," said Ghost.

Pushing away from the wall, Omen shot him a hard look. "You know we've been standing around asking each other how we think Ella might've reacted to all he told her. You could have put our minds at rest."

Ghost lifted his shoulders. "It was more entertaining watching you all sweat over it."

Razor clenched his jaw. "There are times I tell myself, 'You know, he's not really *that* much of a prick; I'm hard on him.' Then you do shit that reminds me you are, in fact, a total prick."

Ghost put a hand to his chest, as if hurt. "*I'm* not the one slandering my brother's good name."

"It ain't slander when it's true."

"It ain't true, so it's slander."

Viper lifted a hand, palm out. "Stop."

Razor moodily grunted. Ghost only smiled.

Sprawled on an armchair, Jester looked up at Viper. "How come you never gave us a heads-up that you meant to finally unload it all on Ella?"

"Because it wasn't planned. I only told her because I didn't really have much choice." Viper paused. "She received another note. It said, 'Everleigh'. Which means they're definitely being sent to her by someone from the upper realm. My business decisions virtually led them straight to her. It's the only thing that makes sense."

It pissed Viper off something fierce that he hadn't considered someone would do that. He should have been more careful for her sake. "She naturally wanted to know who the note referred to; she'd sensed from my reaction that I knew."

Dice twisted his mouth. "They'd obviously guessed that you hadn't told her everything; they were placing you in a position where you had to."

"Yes," Viper agreed. "They'll want her dead. Not merely to punish me, but to make a point to any current or future member of the Seven: If you fall to be with your own personal Ella, such a move will only lead to that person's death."

Razor grunted in agreement. "Is there any way to lure this bastard out into the open?"

Hustle sat up straight on the other armchair. "We could ask Ella—"

"We are *not* using my woman as bait," Viper snapped. His entity wanted to slap the angel for even suggesting it.

"It wouldn't work anyway," Omen remarked. "They'd know that Viper would never leave her unprotected; they'd guess it was a trap."

"I don't think we'll need to lure them out," said Dice. "Their last note basically announced their presence. They're probably bored and want to go back home. It won't be long before they step out of the shadows. We'll be ready when they do."

"Interesting choice of breakfast."

Looking up from the clubhouse's kitchen table, Ella cast her sister an unapologetic smile. "You want some. You know you do."

Mia snorted at the bowl of ice-cream and then made her way to the coffee machine.

It wasn't uncommon for them to see each other at the Black Saints' compound, since both spent many nights here. On those occasions, they had breakfast together before heading off to work. Today, however, they'd get to laze around due to it being Sunday.

Shifting a little on the stool, Ella scooped up yet more ice-cream and all but shoved it into her mouth. "I had a massive talk with Viper last night."

Mia's brows lifted in interest. "Really?" she asked as the coffee machine came to life.

There was still a sense of surrealness to all he'd told and showed Ella. She'd barely fully absorbed it. It hurt to think of how they'd once had their chance at happiness stolen from them. But now, thanks to him, they had a second chance. That he'd searched for her, fallen from the upper realm for her, so shrewdly infiltrated her life in his determination to keep her ... it made her love him all the more.

"Well, don't leave me hanging. Elaborate."

"He told me everything. And I mean, everything. His story ... well, it's a doozy. But I'm under a geas, so I can't share it." Ella gifted her with an apologetic look.

"Dice once hinted at it being kind of dark; he was worried you'd reject Viper because of it." She took a moment to scrutinize Ella's face. "As you look happy, I'm going to assume that you're not here against your will."

"Huh?"

"Well, I don't for one moment think that Viper would let you leave him, so it struck me that if you *had* rejected him he could very well have trapped you here."

Honestly, Ella wouldn't put it past him to do such a thing. "I didn't reject him. I'm here of my own free will. I ... "

"Love him, I know. 'Bout time you realized it."

What the fuck? "You knew?"

"Of course I knew."

"Why didn't you tell me?"

"You needed to work it out for yourself."

"Heifer," Ella playfully tossed out before shoving the last of her ice-cream into her mouth. "You're always so stingy with information."

"Right back atcha. You learned *lots* that you're not sharing."

Ella dropped her spoon into her empty bowl. "I can share something else."

Mia's eyes lit up. "Ooh, what?"

"Unfortunately, it's not happy news. I got another note. I can't say what it said, because you'll only ask what it meant and I won't be able to explain. But, for reasons I can't go into, we're thinking it was written by a celestial. One who seeks to punish Viper for falling and thinks they can do it through me."

Mia's brow furrowed. "But ... the notes were coming before you got involved with him. Unless you two were sleeping together for longer than I thought but you didn't tell me?"

"No, it's not that. Let's just say they were able to detect his interest in me." Ella scratched at her nape. "I don't know if I should tell Luka about the note. I mean, he'll have all kinds of questions. Some of which I won't be able to answer, which will lead him to ask *more* questions. Learning I'm in a relationship with the president of the Black Saints is going to make him mad. Hearing that Viper put me under two geasa will only enhance that fury."

Mia nodded, pouring coffee into her cup. "He'll hate that there are secrets he isn't privy to. Rationally, he'll know that that's how it goes with couples. But you're his anchor, so he'll ignore rationality. Especially when he won't want you to be with Viper. And if Luka hears that a celestial is on your ass, he's gonna be pissed at Viper. He'll hold him responsible for the danger that you're in."

"And by telling Luka it's a celestial, I'll be dragging him into a situation that I don't want him to get tangled up in."

"It might be best to not tell him about the note. You might not like the idea of hiding stuff from him, but there'll be plenty of stuff that he doesn't tell you regarding his own business—mostly for your protection. This is no different."

Ella lifted her brows. "That's true."

"My advice? Keep him ignorant. It's for his own sake as well as all those whose secrets you need to protect. You'll have to keep Mom and Jocelyn ignorant, too." Mia exhaled heavily. "You have practice at that sort of thing, at least. But you did *try* to tell them about your love life this week. Twice, actually."

The first time, she'd gently raised the subject of the Black Saints . . . only for both Melodie and Jocelyn to talk about how they really needed to get started on petitioning to have the fallen angels removed from the Underground.

In response, Ella had thrown in a comment about how well the club had integrated itself into demonic society; claimed that they could only have made important allies like Knox and Maddox if said allies felt certain that the club meant no harm whatsoever to the demons existing in this realm. Melodie and Jocelyn had strongly disagreed, tossing out stories of the deaths of past incantors who were wronged by the Fallen.

The second time Ella had tried broaching the subject, Melodie had scowled and said, "*Don't make me think about them, I'm too annoyed that Knox refused to forbid them entrance to the Underground.*" Ella hadn't even known until right then that her mother had actually made such a direct appeal to him.

Ella rose from her stool. "I've given up on the idea of *gently* breaking it to them. The fact is they're not going to take it well no matter what approach I take." She crossed to the sink and plonked her bowl and spoon into it.

Mia's brow furrowed as she stared at the bowl. "What made you settle on having ice-cream for breakfast? You on the rag or something?"

"No, but it helped me ignore the weird taste on my tongue."
Ella grimaced. "It's been there since I woke up. I was going to
scoff on a banana instead, but the smell of it turned my stomach." She wrinkled her nose at Mia's mug. "Same goes for your
coffee, actually."

Mia poked her tongue into the inside of her cheek. "Hmm."

"What does 'hmm' mean?"

Mia set her cup on the counter and then curled her fingers
around Ella's upper arm. "Sweetie, why don't you come sit down?"

Allowing her sister to usher her back onto her stool, Ella
frowned at the odd expression she wore. "What is it?"

Mia clasped her hands and hesitated, seeming intent on
choosing her words carefully. "Having ice-cream for breakfast
isn't exactly normal for you, is it? You have headaches that
come and go. Also not normal. Certain smells are bothering
you. Again, unusual. Now you also have a funny taste on your
tongue. *Definitely* abnormal. And maybe it's nothing, but ..."
Mia trailed off and bit her bottom lip. "When was the last time
you had your monthly code red situation?"

Ella went very still, startled by the question. "I'm not pregnant," she breathed.

"When was it?" Mia gently persisted.

"Well, it was ..." Ella frowned, struggling to recall the last
time she'd had her period. Her belly began to churn. "Shortly
after I slept with Viper at the Red Rooms the first time." She
scrubbed a hand down her face, feeling the blood drain from it.
Her demon wasn't one to panic. Ever. But its unease was amping
up with every second.

Mia gave her a gentle smile. "I think you should let me check
you over, just in case."

Ella's pulse started to kick up. "I can't be pregnant."

"It's possible that I'm wrong. Let's be sure, though."

Swallowing, Ella rubbed her palms over her thighs. "Okay."

Her sister gave a satisfied nod. "Just relax. Stay nice and still for me." She rested a splayed hand on Ella's stomach and closed her eyes.

Her nerves winding tight with anxiety, Ella worried her lower lip. She fought the urge to tap her foot restlessly, impatience battering at her. Finally, her sister's eyelids lifted. "Well?" Ella all but croaked.

Clasping her hands again, Mia smiled. "Congratulations, sis. You're going to be a mom."

Oh, fuck.

Ella's ability to think coherently promptly went right out the window. She sat there in stunned silence, her mind whirling; her thoughts jumbled; her hearing tinny.

Mia kept talking, but Ella didn't take in a single word. Couldn't. She was stuck trying to absorb what she'd just heard.

Ella barely registered her sister disappearing from her side. What could have been minutes or hours later, a warm cup was pushed into Ella's hand.

"Drink this," her sister coaxed. "It's just herbal tea. Safe for pregnant women, I promise."

Pregnant.

Maybe it was the sensation of warmth from the mug that snapped Ella out of her panic. Maybe the word 'pregnant' hit hard enough to make the entire situation sink in. Whatever the case, she felt her brain begin to slow its roll.

Her demon's shock swiftly became buried beneath the avalanche of parental protectiveness that had rained down on it. The wellbeing of the child now its sole concern, its sense of hypervigilance shot into the stratosphere.

"Do you know what you want to do?" The careful question from Mia was empty of judgement.

There was a lot that Ella didn't know, but she felt certain of one thing. Setting down the cup, she said, "I want to keep the baby."

Mia cast her a supportive smile. "I'll be terribly surprised if Viper doesn't feel the same."

Her child wouldn't be the first half-celestial-half-demon to be born. Some of the Fallen had bred with demons when they first fell eons ago—the eventual result being the creation of the breed of demons known simply as descendants.

It was believed that some archangels had also fallen back then; that they, too, had reproduced with demons. In fact, some thought that Raini's mate Maddox had archangelic blood. But Viper was the incarnation of a deadly goddamn sin, which made this situation a little different.

Ella wouldn't care if her child was half rhino—she'd love it no matter what. But she feared for it. The demon world wasn't even kind to descendants; considered them mutts. They weren't going to welcome her baby.

Mia gently squeezed her shoulder. "You need to tell Viper."

"Tell me what?" he asked, striding inside.

Ella jumped, almost knocking over the cup of tea; her palm flying to her belly in an unconscious protective movement.

Viper's brows drew together. "What's wrong?"

"Nothing's wrong," her sister quickly assured him. "Ella just has some news."

He frowned. Squinted. His gaze dropped to the hand on her stomach. Then his blue eyes widened, his broad shoulders turned stiff, and his facial muscles went slack.

Viper's gaze slammed back on Ella's, disbelieving. "You're pregnant."

"Yeah," she rasped. "Yeah, I'm pregnant."

*

Holy shit. Viper could only stare at her, stock still. His gaze again dropping to her stomach, he felt a fierce surge of possession rise up inside him. His woman was pregnant with his baby. He swallowed hard, his throat growing tight; emotions burning brightly in his chest.

And, inappropriate though it might be, he had the visceral urge to take her to the floor and bury himself inside her—which his equally pleased entity was all for.

What they *weren't* pleased about was the fear in her expression.

Protectiveness dancing around his system, Viper walked straight to her and caught her face in his hands. "You're going to be fine," he firmly stated, refusing to consider any other possibility. "Both of you will be."

"I love how you think that the force of your will alone is all that's necessary to ensure that," she said, mirth playing over her face and chasing away some of the fear.

Mia smiled at them both. "This is so awesome!"

"Also slightly terrifying."

Viper moved a little closer, hugging Ella to him. "When did you find out?"

"Just now. Mia suspected it, so she did a little magickal scan to check." She looked at her sister. "Thank God you did."

"How far along do you think you are?"

"No idea," said Ella, shaking her head. "I've been feeling iffy for weeks, but part of that was because my sleeps weren't restful. The . . . dreams I talked about *seemed* to have stopped, but I still felt tired. This could have been why, I don't know. The symptoms of demonic pregnancy don't always start straight away. I had my last period over a month ago."

They'd always used condoms until recently, but she was on the pill. So either the pill hadn't been effective, or they'd come across a faulty condom at some point.

Viper palmed her stomach as he touched his mind to that of the child inside her, being sure to include her in the psychic 'loop' he opened: *Hey there, little one.*

The young, underdeveloped mind stirred. It ever so gently bumped his, contentment traveling along the 'channel'.

She gasped, her eyes going wide. "Was that the baby?"

"Yes."

"I-I never felt anything like that before."

"The baby won't be able to reach out on its own yet; only to respond to you when you open a telepathic door. As soon as your mind withdraws, that door closes. The baby's too young to open it alone."

"Wait, so you heard it?" asked Mia.

He shook his head. "It didn't speak, just responded with emotion. It feels content." He looked back at Ella. "Going by its psychic development, I'd say you're at least three weeks along."

Her mouth dropped. "Wow. Demonic pregnancies generally last thirty weeks."

"Celestial pregnancies go on for roughly twenty-six weeks. There's no saying how long exactly yours will last."

Seeing pure male satisfaction glittering in his gaze, Ella said, "I don't need to ask if you're happy about the pregnancy."

"I'm fucking overjoyed." A line briefly appeared between his brows. "Though I worry for you. It's not easy for non-celestials to carry archangelic babies."

Ella glanced at her sister, expecting her to react in *some* way to hearing Viper's confirmation that he was in fact an archangel. The woman didn't bat an eyelid, so she'd apparently decided for herself that the rumor was true.

"An ultrasound scan might help give you an idea," said Mia.

Ella grimaced. "I'm not keen on making this public yet."

"There are doctors who'll be discreet and won't ask questions.

I know of one. I can contact him and arrange a scan for you, if you want," Mia offered.

Viper gave a curt nod. "Do that."

Ella frowned. "But what if this doctor isn't keen on being so discreet when they see *you*? They'll assume you're the father and then know that the baby must be half celestial."

"We can conceal his face using a glamor spell," Mia suggested.

Ella blinked. "That's a good idea."

Her sister shrugged. "You would have thought of it yourself if you weren't flapping."

Ella squeezed her eyes shut. "God, everyone is gonna lose their mind when they find out."

Viper took her hand and gave it a supportive squeeze. "We'll tell your family and anchor together that you're pregnant and that the baby's mine."

"But they might say mean stuff to you."

He felt his brow pinch. "You think I'm going to let you have that conversation alone when I know how hard it's gonna be for you?" She wouldn't ever again have to do anything alone. He'd be right there, as would his brothers if she needed them. "I want you to consider moving into the compound."

"That's a good idea," Mia chipped in. "It's got better security measures than our complex. Not to mention it's inhabited by a bunch of people who would die to protect you and the baby if need be."

Viper could have kissed the woman. He could have. She'd said exactly what he'd been thinking, and it was clear that Ella was now ruminating on it.

She cleared her throat. "Well, yes, but . . . "

"Hey, I know it's a lot of change all at once," said Viper. "If you'd rather I moved into your building with you, I can do that."

Mia lifted a hand. "My personal recommendation would be

the compound. Or some kind of walled-off estate where you can have crazy security measures."

"Is that really necessary?" asked Ella.

Just then, the air temperature dipped as Viper's entity surfaced. It lowered its glowing-white gaze to her flat stomach and rested its hand there. "Not a lot of things come as a shock to me, but this did. You should not worry so much about the reactions of your relatives and anchor." Its expression turned grave. "It is not them who are a danger to the child."

Her gut tightened. "Danger?"

"The people in the upper realm won't like that Viper has a child. If they find out, they'll try to kill it before its even born."

Ella's breath hitched, and her demon froze. "You're serious?"

"Oh, yes. Viper wouldn't want you to know that. He wouldn't want to scare you. But you need to understand the threat-level if you're to properly protect the little one here. Also, I find that fear is a good motivator—you should let it motivate you to relocate here, where you and the baby will be safest." It nipped her lower lip. "Take care of it and yourself. We'll talk again soon." It retreated, and Viper's eyes went back to their normal startling blue.

She swallowed. "Was it telling the truth? Will some in the upper realm truly think of harming the baby?"

His lips flattened. "Yes, but it won't happen." A firm, hard statement that allowed for no doubts. "There's no reason they should learn of your pregnancy. At least not for a while, providing we're careful. They'll be reluctant to act if and when they do, since you're a demon. It could risk starting a war."

Oh, Ella would set fire to the fucking Earth if anyone or anything tried to harm her child. There'd be a war for certain.

He gave her a hard look of reassurance. "I won't let anything happen to you or the baby, Ella. No one will touch either of you."

No, they wouldn't. She'd never allow it. "Will it need to drink blood?"

He hesitated. "Possibly. I can't know for sure. The baby will tell you if so. Once it can reach out on its own, of course."

She felt her brow pinch. "Tell me?" she echoed.

"Likely using telepathic images. Archangelic babies are highly advanced both intellectually and psychically. Our child might only be half archangel, but that won't make much of a difference. Even now it'll have a very good understanding of the things happening around it."

She stared at him dumbly, her brain stuck on 'highly advanced'.

"The baby will see we're not living together, for instance. It's doubtful that they'll like it."

Her brow hiked up. "Oh, so I should move in here because the baby won't otherwise like it?" Not that she was going to argue about relocating.

Viper brushed his nose against hers. "Like I said, I'm willing to move to your building. But I would hope you'd prefer to be surrounded by the kind of protection you might turn out to need if things go to shit. Especially when we have strix hanging around. They can't get in here. Not ever. Your complex? I don't know about that."

Ella sighed. "I'm not going to fight moving in here. It's not like I'm supremely attached to my apartment anyway. And with the danger the Uppers represent, I'll take whatever precautions necessary."

Relief flashed in his eyes. "Good. The baby will be pleased by that."

She snorted. "Like it's really affected either way right now."

"It is, as I explained before, highly adva—"

"I don't want to hear that part again, it's freaking me out."

A thought occurred to her, and she leaned forward. "Can the baby wield power?"

"Yes, though not a lot. Give it a month or two, and you'll probably see some *real* displays of power. That's generally how it goes with archangelic babies."

She felt her jaw drop. "You're serious?" The words came out on a choked whisper.

"Very."

Oh, fuck. "What sort of things will they be able to do?"

Viper pursed his lips. "I'm not sure. They're half archangel half incantor. That's one hell of a mix. Their demonic nature could put a spin on their archangelic abilities, and vice versa. On the other hand, their gifts might be either more celestial or more demonic."

She blinked rapidly. "I don't know what to say."

He gave her hand a reassuring squeeze. "Don't stress over it. There's no need to. The baby will be fine. They'll have better control over their abilities than a demon baby. That's good, right?"

"Good," she echoed numbly.

His lips twitched. "I know it's early days so you might be reluctant to share it with more people but, given how we'll want to step up security measures, I'd like to tell the whole club about the baby."

His woman absently dipped her chin. "I'm good with that."

He telepathically reached out on his club's channel, saying, *Club meeting, be here asap.* "When do you want to pass on our news to your mother, aunt, and anchor?"

Another sigh. "Soon. But not until after the scan." *What will you being an incarnation of a deadly sin mean for the baby?* she asked telepathically, worrying her lower lip.

Maybe something, maybe nothing. There's no history of this happening before, so I've no idea what to expect. But we'll handle what comes together. He tugged gently on her hand, urging her to stand. "Come on. Let's go share our news."

Not long after, they were in the meeting room, her sat on his lap while the others settled themselves on the chairs gathering around the table. "I'll get straight down to it. Ella's pregnant."

"She's what?" spluttered Hustle, shocked.

His face going slack, Dice straightened in his chair. "No way." He exchanged glances with the others, who were all equally stunned. "This is . . . I mean, it's good, but *whoa.*"

"Whoa works," mumbled Ella, still a little dazed.

Ghost smiled, rubbing his hands. "Well, congratulations."

The rest of the club passed on the same sentiment.

Viper nodded his thanks. "We don't know how long the pregnancy will go on for—the lengths differ for archangels and demons. We think Ella's roughly three weeks along, so that gives us something like four or five months before the baby is here."

Raising his hand, Darko bit his lip. "I hate to be the voice of doom and gloom—"

"No, you don't," argued Jester. "You love that shit."

"—but you know what the Uppers will do if they find out, right?"

"We've always been prepared for them to 'visit'," Viper reminded Darko. "We'll be ready if and when they do. They will not touch Ella or our child."

"No, they damn well won't," agreed Razor. "Every person in our club will fight to keep them safe. If the Uppers do come here, they won't know what hit 'em."

CHAPTER TWENTY-SIX

Sitting in the clinic's waiting area the following day, Viper idly scanned the room. It was fairly basic with its white walls, generic framed pictures, rows of padded seats, informational posters, and wall-mounted TV.

It was apparently typical of the doctor to hold private ultrasound scans during out-of-clinic hours. Which explained why the receptionist desk was unattended.

The only people there were him, Ella, Dice, and Mia. The VP would guard the door while the rest of them went inside for the scan. Mia had nagged at Ella to allow her to attend the ultrasound, and she'd eventually caved.

Ella had worked a glamor spell on him and Dice, altering their appearance to conceal their identities. They didn't want word of the pregnancy to get out before they were ready to share it.

She turned to him, worrying her lower lip. "I just telepathically reached out to the baby. They're nervous. Why would they be? Is something wrong?"

"They're nervous because you're nervous. They'll respond to your emotional state."

Her face fell. "Now I feel bad."

"Don't." To distract her, Viper splayed his hand on Ella's thigh as he asked, "Where and how do you want to break the news of the pregnancy to your family and Luka?" They'd decided to do it tomorrow, but they hadn't gone into specifics yet.

Grimacing, she replied, "At my apartment would be best. We want to keep the pregnancy on the downlow, so a public place is out,—the risk of them using their indoor voices is minimal. And we can't exactly take them to the clubhouse. I suppose I could invite them for dinner and just blurt it all out there and then; tell them all at once."

Sitting on her other side, an eavesdropping Mia said, "That'll work. I don't think you should tell them ahead of time that Viper will be there, though. They'll arrive all worked up. That won't help."

Dice looked at Ella. "Do you think your family or anchor will want you to get rid of the baby?" he asked, a deceptive casualness in his voice.

"No," she replied without missing a beat. "But they'll be pissed that I kept my relationship with Viper from them."

"They'll be equally pissed at me," Viper pointed out, "so at least we can shoulder their reactions together."

Ella pressed her lips together. "Don't take this the wrong way, but say as little as possible to them."

He felt his mouth kick up. "Just smile and look pretty?"

"The more you remind them that you're there, the more annoyed they'll feel."

"I'll let you do the majority of the talking. But if they step out of line, I will speak up. They don't get to yell or give you a hard time." Viper draped his arm over the back of her chair. "I doubt they tell you every little thing that happens in their lives. Just keep that fresh in your mind."

Ella placed a hand on her belly. "I worry they'll say stuff that'll upset the baby."

Viper covered her hand with his own. "It won't hurt them. I don't think."

Her head twitched to the side. "You don't think?"

"Well, if it feels threatened or worries you're unsafe, it might at least try to intervene."

She went still, unease flickering over her face. "Define 'intervene'."

"I can't. I don't know exactly what tricks the baby's got in their psychic hat yet." Viper was intrigued to find out. "They're less likely to act if I'm with you because they'll feel more secure. They'll trust that I'll keep you both safe."

A door to their left opened, and a middle-aged blonde in a white lab coat stepped out of the room. At that, they all stood.

She aimed a professional smile at their group. "Mia, I didn't realize you'd be here. I'm guessing this is your sister, Ella. Hello, there." Her gaze moved from Viper to Dice. "And you two men are?"

"Remember I said there'd be questions we may not answer?" Mia asked the doctor as they all approached her. "This is one of them."

"Fair enough. Let's get the scan underway."

Viper gently urged Ella into the room. Mia followed, but Dice remained outside to stand guard on the other side of the door.

The room they entered was a clinical white with only three chairs, a small table, a narrow bed, and a bunch of medical equipment.

The doctor offered her hand to Ella, who quickly shook it.

"I'm Dr. Greene. Mia tells me that you're roughly three weeks into your pregnancy."

"That's right," Ella told her with a nod. "I drank plenty of water in advance, my bladder is as full as it can get."

"Excellent. It'll make the ultrasound image clearer." Greene turned on the ultrasound machine and pressed some buttons. "If you could just lay down here for me and raise your t-shirt, that would be great."

Ella lay on the bed and inched up her tee. She grimaced when the doctor squirted gel on her stomach.

"What's wrong?" Viper asked, his brows snapping together.

"It's cold," she groused, taking his hand. A hand she squeezed tight when Greene placed a handheld probe over her lower abdomen. "I'd better not pee."

Stifling a smile, Viper dropped a kiss on her head. A frantic beat sounded. Fast as butterfly wings. And then a somewhat cloudy image popped up on the screen.

Sidling up to him, Mia spoke to the doctor. "I thought you said having a full bladder would make the image clear."

"Generally, it would," Greene told her, not looking away from the screen as she moved the probe along Ella's belly. "But there seems to be an extra layer around the fetus. Almost a womb within a womb." She glanced at Ella, curiosity lighting her eyes.

"No questions," Mia reminded the doctor.

She nodded. "Right."

Anxiety battering at her, Ella telepathically reached out to Viper and asked, *Why would I have two wombs?*

His mind softly stroked hers. *You don't. All celestial babies grow with their own protective film; it's normal. Our baby may be half demon, but it seems they still have the added layer.*

And this is a good thing? It's basically extra protection for them?

Yes. Viper gave her hand a light squeeze. *Stop worrying, all's good.*

Blowing out a steadying breath, she concentrated firmly on the monitor. She could make out the baby's outline. Could see the little head and body. The vision made her swallow hard, her mouth automatically curving.

"I can't tell you the gender, but I can tell you the fetus is more physically developed than I would have expected." Greene spared Ella a swift glance. "I think you may be further along in the pregnancy than you thought. At least by another three weeks."

Or Ella was simply destined to have a shorter pregnancy, much like celestials. But she couldn't say that.

Viper swiped his thumb over the back of her hand. "Does everything look good?" he asked Greene.

"It's hard to say for absolutely certain—the image is just so murky because of the added layer no one wants to explain to me," Greene replied, moving the probe this way and that.

Ella gasped as the baby kicked at it.

Greene blinked. "Oh, the fetus doesn't like that, does it?"

Ella felt its consciousness flutter against hers, and she had the impression of cold and discomfort.

The image on the screen froze as the machine faltered, stuttering and rattling. And Ella just *knew* the little menace in her womb was responsible.

As Greene removed the probe and began pressing buttons on the machine, Ella exchanged a look with her sister, who looked close to laughing. Yeah, her demon thought it was hilarious too.

Ella lightly touched the baby's mind. *You're fine, the machine can't hurt you, I promise.*

Eventually, the ominous noises stopped.

She peered up at Viper to find his eyes smiling, a hint of pride there.

Greene let out a long breath. "I think we'd better print out the image on the screen in case the machine stops working altogether." She jabbed a button. There was a short whir as it printed out a small black and white picture. The doctor handed it to Ella with a smile. "Unfortunately, it's not the clearest image."

It was *perfect*. Would have been perfect no matter what, because it was her baby. She looked up at Viper again, finding him staring down at the picture, his lips curled; his eyes twin gems of wonder and contentment.

His gaze breezed over to hers, and his mouth canted up a little more. *They look kind of like a peanut, but I'm all there for it.*

She snorted, gratefully accepting the paper towel Greene handed to her, listening as the doctor reeled off all the various symptoms she could expect to experience. One made her blink. "Wait, power-hiccups?" she repeated, wiping the gel from her abdomen.

"You may not have the same level of control over your demonic abilities, or it may be that you instead struggle to access them," Greene explained. "You may not experience the issue, but I thought it best to warn you." Having switched off the ultrasound machine, she stood. "Avoid alcohol, caffeine, and raw fish. We'll have regular scans so we can keep an eye on things. Mia gave you my number; call me any time if necessary."

Ella righted her tee and slipped off the bed. "Thank you." She shook the doctor's hand once more and then walked out of the room with the others. Smiling down at the picture she held, she swallowed. "Psychically, the baby doesn't feel so small. It has a strong presence, if you know what I mean. But it's *so tiny*." She showed the picture to Dice, who smiled down at it.

Viper curled an arm around her shoulders. "I can see you're

panicking at just how physically vulnerable the baby is right now, but no one will harm them, Ella."

Maybe not *physically*, she thought, but the reactions of her family might emotionally hurt the baby.

Ella wanted her loved ones to be as excited by the pregnancy as she was. She wanted them to welcome the baby. More, she wanted them *not* to plot Viper's death.

If the baby was really as advanced as Viper claimed, it wouldn't be at all oblivious to their reactions. It would know if they were unhappy. It'd be hurt. She *loathed* the thought of that.

God knew how her demon would react to her family's disapproval about the pregnancy. It didn't love them—had no capacity to feel the emotion. But it valued them; it had formed a strong attachment to each of them. Still, it would want to butcher them alive if it perceived them as any kind of threat to the baby.

Ella didn't for one second believe they'd harm the baby or in any way press her to abort it. No, they'd be disapproving. Worried. Wary of what it might be able to do. But they'd love it. Her demon would know that *deep down*. The problem? She couldn't rely on the entity to be entirely rational when it was so on edge with hyped-up overprotectiveness.

It wouldn't kill Luka, of course—to kill its anchor would be to harm itself. But it would certainly put him through a shitload of pain.

Outside the clinic, they walked to a nearby alley and—once sure no one was watching them—teleported back to the compound. Viper led the way into the main area . . . just in time for them to watch Razor hurl a coaster at Ghost like it was a damn boomerang.

"Stop being an ass," Razor growled at him.

Ghost shrugged. "I don't know how." Noticing that Ella and

the others had returned, he grinned. "Quick question: what about the name Clark for the baby if it's a boy?"

Jester sighed. "Stop suggesting names of superheroes. Why are you so obsessed with them?"

"Not obsessed," Ghost objected. "I just identify with them, you know?"

Jester stared at him steadily. "No, I don't know. There's no reason why you should."

Ella only rolled her eyes at the spectacle. Her sister and Dice headed over to the little bar while she allowed Viper to lead her out of the room and into the hallway that led to the kitchen. It didn't do much to muffle the noise coming from the main area. The place could never be described as quiet, but she didn't mind that. And she liked that her child would be surrounded by people—all of whom she just knew would be glad to shower it with whatever attention they could.

Again, she looked down at the picture in her hand, smoothing a crinkle out of the corner, marveling at the sight of her baby. She was honestly a little terrified to be a parent, but it was a good sort of fear. The kind that was edged with excitement.

She looked at Viper, only then realizing ... "You never talk about your own parents."

He spared her a quick glance. "I never knew them well. I'm a fourth son. We're given to the holy host when we're young."

Her lips parting, she halted in a horrified shock. "Oh, my God. *How* young?"

He stopped walking. "Six. We're put through all sorts of education and training to prepare us for the life of a soldier. Parents know this is going to happen, have no way to stop it, and so tend to hold back from you in the hope it will make the separation better for all concerned."

He said it all so dispassionately. As if it was nothing. But then, maybe a person would have to convince themselves it was nothing in order to emotionally survive it. "This is a rule in the upper realm?"

"Exemptions are made for some—mostly those with status— but not many."

"That's just so unbelievably cruel."

Viper looped an arm tight around her. "Don't feel sad for me, baby. It's cold, I know, but I never knew any different growing up. It's such a common thing that it's accepted as normal. That said, I'd never intended to have children for that very reason." His gaze lowered to her belly. "But this is different. I'm not up there anymore. No child we have would be taken from us that way."

Unless the Uppers tried to kill the baby, which Ella was resolved would *never* happen.

Viper pressed a kiss to her forehead. "Don't let this spoil your mood. I'd take you on a ride to cheer you up, but it ain't safe while you're pregnant."

She knew that, but still she pouted. "I'll miss it."

"After the baby's born, we'll go out for a ride—you and me. My brothers will watch over Peanut for us."

"Or Mia can do it." It was more of a statement than a suggestion.

His brows lifted. "You don't think my brothers would make trusted babysitters?"

Ghost barreled out of the door clad in a damn superhero suit and started dashing down the hall with his arms out straight at his sides, mimicking a bird in flight.

Ella cleared her throat. "To be honest, no, I don't."

"So Ghost wouldn't make a good sitter," Viper ceded. "But the others would."

Just then, Razor came striding down the hallway with a blade in each hand—both of which were covered in crackling ultraviolet flames. "You're dead, Ghost, I fucking *swear* it!"

Her nose wrinkled. "Hmm, you sure about that?" she asked Viper.

He sighed, shaking his head. "Fuck these assholes."

She chuckled.

CHAPTER TWENTY-SEVEN

Hearing a knock at her front door the following day, Ella blew out a trembly breath and twisted her fingers. She knew it would be Luka, since she'd just buzzed him into the building.

"Want me to get it?" asked Jester, moving slightly as it to lift the elbow he'd rested on the fire mantel. Both he and Dice were here to guard their president while Ella broke the news about the pregnancy, concerned that Luka and his own guards might attack Viper.

Not an unnecessary concern, unfortunately.

"No. No, I'll do it." Her belly rolling with nerves, she glanced at Viper over her shoulder. He looked casual as anything, his arms loosely folded, his hip propped against the kitchen doorjamb. Behind him, Mia poured drinks while Dice leaned against the counter.

"You've got this, Ella," Viper assured her.

Another knock, this one harder.

Muttering beneath her breath, she padded over to the front

door and pulled it open. Luka stood on the other side of it, his guards close behind him. Ella smiled. "Hey. Glad you could make it," she said, backing up for them to enter.

They stalked inside . . . and then went completely still. Luka's gaze darted from Jester to Viper.

As she half-turned so that she no longer had her back to Viper, the archangel inclined his head at her anchor and smoothly greeted, "Belinsky."

Luka's brow furrowed. "The fuck are you doing here?"

She snorted. "Charming."

Luka refocused on her. "Why would you have invited *these* three to a family dinner?"

"I'll explain that once Melodie and Jocelyn get here. It's a long story, and there's no point in me starting to tell it to you only to have to restart it once they arrive."

Luka pressed his lips together and stared at Viper, his gaze now speculative. "You know . . . it once occurred to me that you hang on the periphery of Ella's life. I didn't think much of it at the time. Now I'm wondering if maybe I should have."

Viper stared at him steadily, one corner of his mouth *ever* so slightly bowing up.

Ella inwardly sighed, having no faith that the upcoming conversation would go well. There was no way to reveal the overall picture—minus certain details, of course—that would result in merely smiles and a round of congratulations.

Luka turned to her, folding his arms. "What's this about?"

She straightened. "I told you, I'll explain everything when my mom and Jocelyn get here."

"Or you could do it now."

She didn't, but he carried on pestering her to spill *something* right up until the intercom buzzed again.

As expected, it turned out to be her mother and aunt. Ella

admitted them into the building and soon after opened the apartment door wide for them. They breezed inside, their smiles easy. Smiles that froze when they spotted the Black Saints.

Melodie turned to Ella. "Something's wrong, isn't it?" she guessed, her smile flitting away. "What's happened?"

"And why are *they* here?" asked Jocelyn, so much contempt lacing the word 'they'.

Closing the door, Ella inwardly sighed. "Let's all go sit down." She turned and headed straight to the kitchen. Viper backed up, allowing her to pass.

At the table, Mia briefly looked up, clearly a bag of nerves. "Hi, everyone." Her greeting was just a little *too* bright. Each and every guest narrowed their eyes on Dice, who still leaned against the counter. "Dinner will be ready soon."

"I hope you're going to in the meantime explain what's happening, because I can't wait until after we're finished eating," declared Melodie.

Ella gave a slow nod and settled at the head of the table. "Everyone please sit."

Luka took the chair directly across from her, Melodie claimed the seat on Mia's right, and Jocelyn sat beside Melodie. Viper stood behind Ella's chair while Jester stood beside Dice. Luka's guards planted themselves at his back, their uneasy gazes flitting from celestial to celestial.

"Well?" Melodie prodded, anxious.

Ella calmly rested her hands on the table and linked her fingers. "It would help if you could all stay quiet until I've finished talking, because there's a lot to unpack."

"We'll say nothing," agreed Melodie with a nod.

Ella subtly heaved in a long breath. "First of all, I'm pregnant."

"*What?*" her mother burst out. "You are joking!"

"Oh my God, who's the father?" demanded Jocelyn. Her eyes

drifted to Viper, and her body went still. "Please don't tell me it's *him*."

Ella clamped her lips together.

A growl rumbled out of Luka. "You have got to be fucking kidding me."

And then the ranting began.

The comments were mostly disparaging remarks about the Fallen and an insistence that celestials and demons shouldn't mix. Each one rang with outrage and something close to horror.

Sighing, Ella briefly exchanged a tired look with Mia. It had been too much to hope for that the others would give her a chance to explain, wasn't it? Especially when Viper's very presence would make them react more negatively, what with him unintentionally spreading wrath around—he only had so much control over it. Hence why he'd earlier said that if it looked as if things would get out of hand, he'd leave the room.

Ella raised a palm to silent the shouts. "I'd appreciate it if you could stop bashing celestials, since the child in my womb is not only part celestial but advanced enough to understand everything you say."

A stunned silence descended.

Jocelyn shook her head, confused. "You don't have a bump, how pregnant are you?"

"I'm not sure exactly." Ella scratched at her arm. "Roughly three weeks. The prenatal scan wasn't very clear."

"You've already had a scan?" asked Melodie, sounding hurt that she'd only heard about it now.

Ella nodded. "I had it yesterday. I wanted to be sure all looked good before I passed on the news."

"Was it a one-night stand?" asked Luka, his voice toneless, his expression vacant.

"No. Viper and I are together."

A muscle in her anchor's jaw flexed, and she saw a snake-like shape writhe beneath the skin of his throat. "How long has it been going on?"

If you counted the first time they'd had sex, which she did . . . "About a month."

Mia raised a hand. "Also, I just want to throw out that Dice and I are knee-deep in a fling."

Their mother's eyes fell shut, and Jocelyn's jaw dropped.

"This is just unbelievable," muttered Melodie, lifting her eyelids. "I honestly think I might be sick."

Mia rolled her eyes. "Stop being dramatic and *listen*. Ella is sitting here telling you that she's in a happy, solid relationship. Isn't that what you want for her?"

"Not if her partner is a fallen angel I don't, no."

Luka fixed Ella with a hard stare. "I suspected you were seeing someone, because you were smiling all the fucking time. You swore I was wrong; told me you were happy being single. You lied."

Ella scratched at her temple. "You were asking too many questions. I wanted to shut the line of conversation down fast so, yes, I told a little white lie."

"It doesn't matter if it's little or white, it's still a lie," reprimanded Melodie. "You lied to all of us by saying nothing of this until now."

Annoyance surged through both Ella and her demon. "And you're all entitled to know my private business, are you? Is that what we're doing now, sharing our innermost secrets with each other? Sweet. You go first, Mom."

Melodie briefly looked away. "This isn't the time for smartass-ness."

"That isn't a word," said Mia.

Melodie shrugged. "Who cares? You should have told us."

"Why?" Viper challenged. "You haven't told your daughters how you usually spend your Friday evenings. The harbinger's name is Clarence, right?"

Ella blinked. Wait, what?

Watching her mother's cheeks warm, Mia spoke, "You're seeing someone?"

Viper's attention shot to Jocelyn. "Or we could talk about how much time and money you spend at the hellhound racing stadium."

Melodie gaped at her sister. "You promised you'd given up gambling."

Jocelyn looked down at her lap, her jaw going tight.

As Viper's gaze settled on Luka, the legion stiffened and warned, "Careful."

Viper shrugged. "I'll watch my words if you'll watch yours."

Jocelyn notched up her chin as she glared at him. "Are you an archangel? An ex-member of the Seven?"

Ella bristled. "Why is it you think you have the right to demand answers from him?"

"They're pertinent questions," Jocelyn insisted, a sass to her.

"You're just looking for reasons to imply he's not good for me."

"I don't need to find reasons, they're already there. Or have you forgotten that our relatives suffered dearly at the hands of his kind?"

"But not at *his* hands. Viper had nothing to do with it."

Jocelyn gave a dismissive shake of her head. "It doesn't matter. They can't be trusted. They betrayed even their own kind by jumping ship and turning their back on their realm."

She gritted her teeth. "Recall that the baby understands what you say."

Sensing his woman was getting worked up, Viper placed a

calming hand on her shoulder. "I shouldn't have to point this out," he said to the others, "but it ain't good for a pregnant woman to be stressed, so maybe you can dial shit down." It was a pressing suggestion.

Melodie pulled in a breath and made a visible effort to dig for calm. "What happens when he's decided he wants to head on back to the upper realm, Ella? Where does that leave you?"

"Not a chance would I ever go back there," Viper told her. "I wouldn't leave Ella and our baby for anything."

Ella carefully placed the ultrasound picture on the table. "It's a little fuzzy, but . . ."

Melodie carefully lifted it, her face softening as she greedily soaked in the image there. She reluctantly passed it to Jocelyn, whose gaze warmed as she stared down at it. Jocelyn held it up for Belinsky to see, and the legion took a long look at it.

Exhaling heavily, Melodie reclaimed the image and then gently set it on the table. She rubbed at her neck. "I'm happy about the baby, sweetheart. Children are always a blessing. And I want to be happy for you. I just . . ."

"We'd prefer that you weren't going to shack up with one of the Fallen," Jocelyn finished.

"I would never have guessed," Ella deadpanned. "So you'd rather I was a single parent?"

"Yes. No. Ugh." Melodie shook her head hard as if to clear it.

"I would," claimed Jocelyn. "Setting aside that he's a fallen angel, he's also a biker. They're all the same. Misogynistic. Irresponsible. Reckless. They only care about their 'brothers' and being 'free.'"

Mia frowned. "Oh, and you would know this how? Do you hang with bikers? Have you ever spoken to one until now? Or are you just babbling clichés?"

"You can feel however you want to feel about me being a

celestial and a biker," said Viper, his voice deadly calm. "What you won't do is make me turn away from Ella. I'm here to stay. You might as well accept it." Viper personally doubted that would happen here and now, though.

Catching Viper's eye, Luka unfolded from his chair and plucked at one cuff. "You and I should chat," he said, tipping his chin toward the living room. "In private."

Ella stilled. "Luka—"

"It's fine, baby," Viper assured her, having already anticipated that the legion would want to talk with him alone. "Stay here."

Ella pinned her anchor with a look. "If you hurt him . . ."

"I won't, but I *am* going to make my feelings clear." Luka indicated for his guards to remain in position and then strode out of the kitchen.

Stay here, Viper telepathically ordered his brothers. He followed the legion into the living room, finding him stood in its center—feet planted, arms folded, expression alive with fury.

Luka snarled. "The only reason I haven't ripped your throat out is that—much as it pisses me off—I can see that Ella cares about you. Why she does, I don't know. She can do a fuck of a lot better than you. She *deserves* a lot better than you."

"I'm not gonna argue that," said Viper.

"But you're gonna be a selfish fucking bastard and stick around."

"You'd rather I walked away and left her to raise our baby alone?"

"There wouldn't be a baby if you'd protected her. But you didn't. You scrapped the condom and didn't care about the consequences, just as you don't care that you being in her life endangers her."

Annoyance tap-danced all over Viper's skin. "You're making assumptions, and they're bullshit."

"What's bullshit is you having the fucking nerve to stand here and act like I'm not entitled to disapprove of your presence in her life," Luka clipped, getting up in his face.

Viper felt his jaw tighten. "Having *you* in her life puts Ella at risk to some degree. *You* didn't walk away from her. That make you selfish as well?"

Luka pressed his lips tight together. "There's a difference. *I* protect her. *You* don't. The strix ... it was no coincidence that she happened to be around when they attacked your brother. She got caught up in that because she's with you."

"And they died for trying to harm her, so I *did* protect her."

"But you didn't have the balls to tell me the truth when I turned up at that scene. You kept silent while she blew smoke up my ass."

"Because she didn't feel comfortable telling you about our relationship—and that, Belinsky, is on you."

"Me?"

"You're her anchor. Someone she should be able to trust to always have her back, no matter her choices. But she didn't trust that you would in this case. And she was right not to, wasn't she? *She's* the injured party here, not you. Not her mother. Not her aunt. *Ella*."

Luka snapped his mouth shut, something wriggling beneath the skin along his jawline.

Viper inwardly sighed. He didn't want to be at odds with his woman's anchor—it'd be something that would hurt her. And truth be told, Luka wasn't a bad guy. Just exceedingly overprotective. And nobody could claim that the legion's concerns weren't valid.

Still, Viper wasn't going anywhere; he needed the guy to see that. "You're not gonna believe this, because you're too busy clinging to your anger. Fact is, though, that Ella means a fuck of a lot to me. More than you can know. I love her."

Luka's expression didn't alter. "You're right, I don't believe it."

Just then, Ella entered the room; the others trailed behind her.

"Everything's fine, baby," Viper assured her, not liking the worry on her face. Addressing her anchor, mother, and aunt, he said, "To be blunt, I don't give the first fuck how anyone here feels about me other than Ella. But I do care that this is a time when she needs the support of the people around her. No one other than Mia and my club are giving it to her right now. That should bother all three of you."

Silence fell as the trio exchanged unhappy looks.

Ella's mind bumped Viper's. *They're not going to back down, are they?*

Not right now, no. Though his presence likely wasn't helping, his absence wouldn't improve the situation either. They were too worked up.

Ella sighed. "Maybe you should go," she told them.

Melodie's eyes widened. "What? You're kicking us out?"

"We're just going round and round in circles, and I refuse to keep defending my choices as if any of you have a right to make them for me," Ella clipped. "I'm also not going to tolerate you spouting more mean and petty remarks. So unless you're going to quit with that, yes, I think you should leave."

For a few moments, nobody moved.

"Congratulations on your pregnancy, Ella," Luka said stiffly, though the words weren't empty. "I can't claim to approve of your choice of father for the baby. I want you safe. *He* is not safe. On the contrary, he's a highly dangerous being."

"Never to Ella," Viper firmly asserted.

Belinsky responded with a blank look. Without another word to anyone, he left with his guards.

Melodie smoothed a hand down her top. "We'll leave, Ella, but not because we're unhappy about the baby. I want to be clear on that. We'll go because to stay would only be to disrespect your wishes and make the situation worse. I don't want that."

Looking troubled, Melodie and Jocelyn then absconded.

Viper stroked Ella's hair. "Well . . . did it all go worse or better than you expected?"

"Neither. It was as ugly as I'd thought it would be. What did Luka say to you?"

"Just that he thinks you can do better—I don't disagree there—and he feels you'd be safer if I wasn't around. I can't really disagree with that either, but I'm going nowhere. I made that clear to him, and I was also clear about how much you mean to me. Give him time; he'll back down. They all will."

Ella squinted slightly, an accusing light in her eyes that was tempered by a warm amusement. "You went digging into their business."

He shrugged. "I suspected they'd yell at you, and I wanted to be able to shut that shit down fast."

"I'm sorry they all acted like dicks to you."

He lightly splayed his hand around the front of her neck, the weight of his palm barely there, the pads of his fingers featherlight. Yet, his possessiveness came through loud and clear. "I get it. Luka . . . he's just overprotective. Your mother and aunt were bound to react badly. Their ancestors—"

"Weren't killed by you, so no one should be trying to hold you accountable for it," Ella finished, sliding her hands up his chest. "My hope is that they'll come round soon, but it's more likely that they'll drag their heels in silent protest."

"I'm sorry about that for your sake, but I won't give a flying fuck if they don't accept me. All that matters to me is that they don't talk you into leaving my side."

"They could try. Probably will. But it won't work."

"Promise?" he asked, searching her gaze.

"Promise."

Viper's lips curved. "That's my girl."

Yes, yes, she was.

CHAPTER TWENTY-EIGHT

Setting down the role of packing tape, Ella cricked her neck. "I'm never moving again. I just wanna throw that out there."

"You said that last time you moved," Mia reminded her, putting together another box.

"Yeah, well, I seriously mean it this time round." Over the past five days, Ella had gradually relocated her belongings to the compound. There wasn't much left to go.

Viper and his brothers had done all the heavy lifting, treating her like she was made of spun glass. But since she wasn't a fan of hauling stuff around, she hadn't complained. In fact, she and Mia had had fun observing all those male muscles bunching and rippling.

"It puts a slight downer on things that I don't have the blessing of *all* the people I love before taking this big step," said Ella. "Stupid, right?"

"Not stupid. They *will* pull their acts together eventually. Even Luka."

Ella sure hoped so. He wasn't being a *total* ass. He'd taken to texting her twice a day to check in and see how she was doing. He also called her regularly, his overprotective nature on hyperdrive due to her pregnancy. But he refused to acknowledge that Viper was her child's father.

She'd asked Luka how he'd like it if *she* acted this way toward *his* partner. He'd merely stared at her, his expression one of total incomprehension. In hindsight, she shouldn't have tried appealing to his sense of empathy—it was too detached.

She didn't want there to be a rift between her and Luka, but that could potentially happen. Because how could she *ever* pick his side—despite being his anchor—if he made any kind of move against Viper?

Neither male would go down easy in a fight. Blood would be spilled, and both were the type to keep battling until someone was dead.

Viper wouldn't end Luka's life—that would risk ending hers. But Luka might not pay him that same courtesy. And if her anchor somehow succeeded in killing him, Viper's brothers would seek revenge by executing Luka and his entire lair.

She didn't want *any* of them fighting. Didn't want to see any of them dead—not Viper, not Luka, not the Black Saints.

She also didn't want her mother or aunt to put some kind of hex on these particular celestials, but it could very well happen. Melodie and Jocelyn were visibly pleased by the pregnancy. They just annoyingly acted as though the child was an immaculate conception.

Whenever Ella mentioned Viper, they would either lapse into silence or quickly change the subject. It was ridiculous, but at least they were welcoming toward the baby.

"Do you regret telling Mom, Jocelyn, and Luka about you and Viper so soon?" asked Mia.

"No. It wouldn't have mattered when they found out, they were always going to react badly. And why should I have to hide something that brings me happiness?"

"I almost didn't tell Joe about Dice when he asked if I was seeing anyone yesterday. But I'm done keeping it secret to pander to other people's feelings. Still, I didn't expect Joe to flip. Even more shocking was his admittance that he'd ended the fling because he'd thought I'd protest."

Yeah, it transpired that—rather than simply *ask* Mia if, like him, she'd come to want more—Joe had decided to test her by putting a stop to the fling to see how she'd react. While it seemed nuts, it did explain why he'd recently acted like a jilted lover.

"At least he acknowledged that he should have manned up and handled things differently," Mia continued. "I feel bad, because it must have stung him to realize I didn't care for him the way he did me. I hate that I hurt him."

"Him being upset didn't entitle him to turn into a complete jerkoff. It wasn't as if you'd done anything to make him believe that you two were building a relationship."

Mia nodded her agreement. "I'd had boundaries firmly in place. We hadn't gone on dates or done any romantic stuff."

"I wish I'd been there to see Dice give him a dressing down." Apparently, the seraphim had gone almost nose to nose with Joe, who—struggling to stand his ground in the face of all that badassery—had gone from mouthy and snarly to silent and unsure.

Ella went on, "Dice was right that Joe expects a lot when it comes to you. He expects you to want what he wants, feel how he feels, chase after him when he pulls away, and put up with his shit. He *always* expected to be the center of everything for you."

Mia sighed. "I know. He always pressured me to cancel plans I had with others. He never had anything nice to say about any guy I got involved with. That Dice is one of the Fallen just gives

Joe an excuse to piss and moan. I really hope he doesn't take too long to fix things."

Ella went to speak, but then Viper teleported into the room. She felt her mouth curve. "Hey. Didn't think you were coming until later."

His lips canted up. "I managed to shuffle some things around so I could come sooner." He inclined his head at Mia and then crossed to Ella, staring down at her with a possessive gleam in his eyes. "How are you and Peanut doing?" he asked, dropping his gaze to her belly as he gave it a light rub, practically brimming with masculine contentment, like all was right in his world.

"We're okay." A smile warmed her chest as she heard Viper's voice float into her mind as he babbled sweet greetings at their baby, whose mind stirred and fluttered against theirs. Something that never failed to fill her with wonder. "I'm almost done packing the last of my stuff."

He frowned. "I told you to wait until I got back; I said I'd help."

"I didn't need help with packing clothes—they're not exactly heavy. Still, Mia gave me a hand."

"I'll reach out to my brothers. They'll help with carting more of your stuff to the compound." His eyes skipped from hers to Mia. "You both look a little down."

"We were just talking about how our anchors are acting lately," said Ella with a sigh. "It tends to shit on our mood. I know *you're* not bothered that Luka pretends you don't exist, but *I* care. Especially when his behavior emboldens my mother and aunt, making them feel it's okay to do the same. I've decided that I'm going to give them a few weeks to get over their crap. If they haven't done it by then, I will have a serious talk with them."

It wouldn't come to that, because Viper had already discussed with his club what would happen if this continued. He wouldn't wait as long as three weeks to make his move. Not with how much it was getting to Ella. She didn't need the stress, and she shouldn't have to be saddled with it.

Ella sighed. "Right, call your brothers so we can teleport all my stuff out of here. I want to go home."

Home. He fucking loved that she called his compound that. "All right. It's pizza night apparently, you good with pizza?"

Her brow creased. "You guys have pizza night?"

"Not until an hour ago—Darko decided it's gonna be a new tradition."

She snorted. "I'm good with pizza. After we've scoffed some down, we can go to bed and you can fuck me stupid."

"If I must."

"You must."

Ella really did love when Viper put that tongue of his to work.

She lay flat on her bed, fisting the sheets, as his velvet-soft tongue flicked and lapped and pumped. She occasionally felt the edge of his teeth—a scrape here, a nip there.

He'd been at it for … she wasn't sure, she'd lost track of time. She only knew that her orgasm was already on her. She just needed his tongue to stop with these maddeningly shallow pulses.

Ella tugged hard on his hair in demand, knowing he liked it.

A low, deep growl fanned her slick flesh. Viper then tilted her hips and sank his tongue deeper. *Oh, thank the good Lord.*

His tongue pumped, pumped, pumped just as his hand pushed down on her navel. Oh Jesus, it put the best kind of pressure on her G-spot. *Game over.*

She came, her back bowing, her thoughts splintering.

Viper slinked up her body and lowered his weight onto her, his muscles bunched with barely restrained need. A hand palmed her ass and lifted it as he nudged the broad head of his cock inside her. "You ready to be fucked?"

Ella licked her lips. "I'm ready to be claimed."

He went completely rigid, tension crawling into his frame; his gaze piercing hers, searching and studying.

He wasn't going to find any doubts there. All he'd see was excitement and certainty. Those same emotions coursed through her demon. The idea of performing the binding—whatever it entailed—appealed to them both.

She understood why he'd asked her to wait. Understood he'd wanted to be certain she was fully committed to him in mind, body, and soul before he bound them together. But if he asked that they wait longer she was gonna throat punch him. *After* he'd fucked her, of course. She wasn't going to do herself out of another fabulous orgasm.

"You're sure, Ella?"

"I'm sure."

"I'll claim everything that you are," he warned. "You'll never get any of it back."

"I won't ever want it back. It's all already yours anyway."

Viper pulled in a breath as relief, triumph, and male contentment rooted themselves deep in his belly. "Mine." With a low growl, he closed his mouth over hers and slammed his cock deep.

He swallowed her sharp cry as he rode her hard, urged on by his smug-as-fuck entity. Viper had originally intended to take her slow and easy. But his restraint was a distant memory. All he could think about was taking, possessing, gorging, *claiming*.

So long he'd yearned for this. He'd almost had it once, only to lose her before he could lay his claim. Now it would finally happen.

His entity pushed to the surface and stared down at her. "We own all of you now. You'll only ever belong to us."

Ella swore in surprise as the entity began to ferociously fuck in and out of her. She tightened her legs around its waist, digging her fingers into the hard muscle of its back. Every thrust was savage, relentless, entitled.

Pure white eyes became a striking blue as Viper resurfaced. "Open for me."

She felt him, then; felt his mind stroking against hers insistently. "It'll hurt you to be in my mind."

"It'll hurt a lot less if you drop your shields. Open for me, Ella."

Even as her belly fluttered with nerves, she lowered her psychic shields. He poured into her mind, fast as water gushing along river rapids; filling every space, marking every corner, leaving pieces of himself.

Then . . . it was as if her very being *lifted*. Floated toward him, like it had been called. She recalled that he could do that; could call souls, take them.

Their souls touched. No, *joined* with a warm click. And, God, now she felt every bit of pleasure he was feeling.

That pleasure soared through her, amplifying her own.

Then his teeth sank deep, a flash of pain spiced her spiraling pleasure, and *boom* she fractured.

By the time she came down from her high, he was slowly and idly gliding his softening cock in and out of her as he blew over her bite, healing the puncture marks.

Ella blinked at him. "Wow. That was intense."

His lips curved. "And now you're irrevocably mine. Good luck with that."

She chuckled, sweeping a hand up his back.

Withdrawing his cock, Viper nuzzled her temple. "Love you, baby."

Her lips trembled. "And I love you."

Fuck, his heart hurt in the best way. She always *showed* what she felt for him; never hid it from her voice, expressions, or body language. Saying it aloud simply never came easy to her, so it meant that much more when she gave him the words.

Right then, the cell on her nightstand began to ring but she ignored it, her gaze turned inward as she let his hair sift through her fingers. "Even though you're gone from my mind, I can still feel your 'touch' there. Your psychic fingerprints, for lack of a better term."

"I had to be inside both your mind and body in order to reach your soul," he explained, rolling them both onto their sides facing each other. "Our souls are now connected." Satisfaction dripped from every word. He could not be more fucking content right now. It genuinely wasn't possible.

"What does that mean for us?"

"Many things. Our hearts now beat in sync. You'll age as I age. We'll forever be connected—nothing could pry our souls apart." Viper paused, suspecting she might not like what he said next. "And neither of us can exist without the other."

She stiffened against him. "So if I died—"

"That won't happen."

"But if I did, despite how powerful you are, you'd die along with me?"

He dipped his chin.

She gaped at him in horror. "Why would you do that? Why would you make yourself vulnerable this way?"

"You'd be my one vulnerability either way, Ella. I've lived a very long life, but I never *felt* alive until you. Before, I followed and served and did extremely dark deeds. My entity was the only light I had, but then it lost its light when I fell. *You're* that for me. Without you, I'd be the living dead. I'd do terrible things once more. It's better that you'd take me with you."

Ella felt her throat thicken. He'd spoken so matter-of-factly, no hesitance in being so bluntly honest. And his words, oh, they hit her hard. "I . . . I don't know what to say to that."

One of his fingers traced the shell of her ear. "Just say you love me again."

"Later. I'm too busy being mad that you'd essentially tie your lifespan to mine." She loved that he'd claimed her; loved that they officially belonged to each other. But she didn't like what it meant for him. Her demon didn't particularly understand her problem, but it wasn't in the habit of putting other people first, so . . .

"Not sure if you've considered this but, being half archangel, our baby is not going to have an average lifespan. Now, neither will you."

"*You* won't either if I die before you," she pointed out.

His gaze turned severe. "Nothing is going to happen to you. I'd never allow it."

She was about to remind him that he couldn't control everything, but then her cell began to chime again. "I think it might be Luka. I can feel his psyche buzzing against mine." He didn't feel whatsoever happy.

"He might have felt my mind briefly fill yours," mused Viper.

She nabbed her still-ringing phone from the nightstand. "Yeah, it's him." She answered, "Hello."

"What just happened?" Luka demanded.

She bit down on her lower lip. "Uh, I got claimed by Viper."

"What does that mean?"

"That we're permanently bound together."

Several Russian curses streamed down her ear. "This shit just keeps getting better and better," he groused.

Pretending to misunderstand, she smiled and said, "Agreed."

His response was a low growl. Then the line went dead.

Ella jerked away from her phone, frowning. "He just hung up on me."

Viper nuzzled her neck. "What else would you expect? He hasn't gotten used to me being in your life yet. He will, though."

"He'd better," she muttered, tossing her phone back on the nightstand. "But I'm not holding my breath." Her eyes bled to black as her demon shoved its way to the surface and took over. "I do not want to talk about him anymore," it told Viper.

"Okay. What do you want to do?"

"Claim you right back." The demon slapped its hand on his chest, the flesh beneath its palm began to burn ... and he realized it was branding him.

His cock came to life once more, and the demon had barely finished leaving its mark before he'd slammed his dick home again.

CHAPTER TWENTY-NINE

"He's here."

At Jester's words, Viper looked up from his cell phone. "And early, it would seem." It shouldn't surprise him.

"I wasn't so sure if Belinsky would accept your invitation."

Viper pushed off the sofa. "I knew he'd come if for no other reason than he wouldn't want to miss out on being able to throw shit in my face. He could do that any time, yeah, but not without seeking me out—something Ella would have been furious at him for. This way, he can make out like I'm to blame for whatever argument might ensue."

It had been two weeks since Ella had made her anchor and family aware of their relationship. Things hadn't gotten better. They still refused to acknowledge that he was part of her life.

She hadn't said as much, but he knew his woman; knew it was getting to her more and more. He genuinely couldn't care less if they did or didn't accept him, but he did care that it upset her.

There'd be no reasoning with Melodie or Jocelyn—they

were blinded by prejudice. Belinsky, however? His irrationality stemmed from a *good* source: overprotectiveness. Viper could work with that.

Thanks to his old profession, he'd done his fair share of manipulating people. He was confident that he could talk Belinsky into backing down if he handled things right. As for Melodie . . . she was as stubborn as her daughters, so Viper figured the quickest way to make her crumble would be to convince someone else to do it first. She'd very likely follow Belinsky's lead, and Jocelyn would no doubt then fold as well.

As plans went, it had potential. But if he didn't pull off the first step, he'd have to regroup.

Viper slid Jester a swift look as they walked toward the exit. "If Ella wakes, try to keep her inside." She'd been dead to the world when Viper exited the bedroom earlier. He'd been replying to some business-related emails while waiting for her to rouse. "I want to talk to Belinsky alone."

Jester's brow pinched. "I thought you asked him to come at noon, knowing she'd be in work then."

"I did. Arriving early is his way of trying to take control and communicate that he isn't at my beck and call."

Pushing open the main door, Viper watched as Belinsky and his two personal bodyguards slipped out of a black town car. All three scanned the area before focusing on Viper.

His entity sneered at Belinsky. It didn't like him, or that the legion had a claim to Ella. Honestly, neither did Viper. Much as he preferred that she was bound to her psi-mate, he didn't like that another male had a psychic link to her.

Belinsky stalked to him, his expression hard. "Viper," he greeted with a grunt, his tone not in the least bit welcoming.

Viper inclined his head. "Belinsky."

"Is Ella here?"

"She is. That you'd show up at a time you knew she'd be here, well, that kind of pisses me off. Because you *know* it'd hit her hard to see us at each other's throats." Viper stepped up to the edge of Belinsky's private space, ignoring how the legion's guards stiffened. "You and me had a problem before. You just made that problem bigger."

Belinsky inched closer to him. "Oh, we have a lot of fucking problems."

"No one's asking you to like me. I really couldn't give a fuck either way—already made that clear. But how you're acting is hurting Ella, and I'm nothing close to okay with that."

"You're exaggerating," accused Belinsky. "She's annoyed. She's not hurting."

Viper bristled at the male's flippancy. "Wrong. You're her anchor, someone very important to her; someone who's supposed to be a central figure in her world—one who's supportive and protective. But you apparently find it more important to give me the ice-cold shoulder than be there for her during her pregnancy."

The legion's brows lowered. "That's not how it is."

"No?" Viper challenged. "Here you are, on the outside of a really special part of her life. You're missing out, which means *she's* missing out. The latter isn't acceptable to me, and it shouldn't be acceptable to you."

Belinsky's neck turned so stiff the cords stood out. "I call and text her daily. I see her as often as I did before."

Her mother and aunt saw her constantly as well, but they were on the outside looking in just the same. "But she doesn't feel she can share with you as openly as she did before."

"Of course she can," the legion upheld, clearly outraged that Viper would insinuate differently.

"How is that? She can't talk to you about every aspect of her everyday life anymore, because I'm so much a part of it—you don't want to hear about anything relating to me. She doesn't feel she can confide all her fears about the pregnancy to you because she's leery of saying anything that will make you be more of a dick to me."

"What fears?" demanded Belinsky.

"Typical anxieties that come with being pregnant. But just because they're typical doesn't make them any less serious." Anxieties ate at Viper from time to time, too. The pregnancy was going well, there'd been no hiccups or complications. Still, he worried that might at some point change.

The fact was they were dealing with the unknown. She was an incantor carrying the baby of a fallen archangel who embodied a deadly sin. It wasn't heard of before now. They had nothing to compare their experience to.

"She doesn't need to be scared, she will be fine," Belinsky decreed. "I can understand if she is concerned about birthing a child who is part celestial—we don't know what exactly that will mean for her—but she'll have the best care."

"She plans to have a homebirth."

The legion's eyelids flickered.

"Ah, you didn't know that?"

"She should be in a medical facility."

"She'll be surrounded by fallen fucking angels—all of whom can heal her if any complications should arise. If anything comes up that we can't handle, I will of course take her wherever she needs to go." Viper could teleport her anywhere in a second flat.

"She needs healthcare professionals—"

"She's set on a homebirth. Her mind won't change on that." Viper edged closer to him. "Think what that'll mean for you. You won't come visit her here at the compound, you refuse to see it as her home. So you won't be anywhere near her when she goes into labor. You won't be one of the first to see the baby when it's born. You'll hear about the birth via a text or phone call. That gonna be good enough for you?"

Clenching his jaw, Belinsky briefly looked away.

"You're fucking yourself over. Is flipping me the finger really worth that? Right now, because you refuse to visit her at her home, you only see her at times she can come to you. You don't think she'll come to you less and less over time, hurt that you won't support her?" Viper raised his shoulders. "Why not just accept that what's done is done?"

"She can do better than you."

"No one's disputing that. But it makes no difference. I claimed her. I wear her demon's brand. She has my baby inside her. Nothing you or anyone else does will change any of that, so where's the fucking point in keeping up with this shit?"

Belinsky tipped his head to the side, eyeing him speculatively. "I wouldn't have taken you for someone who'd urge another man to be more involved in their woman's life."

"The truth? I don't much like that she's linked to someone else, or that you're so close to her. When you've got a woman of your own, you'll understand. You'll also understand why I'm standing here now pushing you to set aside your own personal opinions about me."

The legion squinted. "You actually do care about her."

"Took you long enough to figure that out."

"Here's my issue. If you're an archangel—and I'm betting you are—there'll be beings who won't like that you've fallen, especially if you were once one of the Seven. And they *really* won't like learning you have a child. I don't want her or the child she's carrying being targeted by celestials."

"Those in the upper realm will be somewhat displeased,"

Viper fudged. "But they won't touch Ella or our baby—I'd never allow it."

"She got caught up in your strix problem."

"And those who harmed her no longer exist," Viper stated. "You treat me like I'm the enemy. Truth is, we're both on the same side. We both want the best for Ella. We both want her to be happy and safe. We've got a better chance of ensuring that happens if we're united."

"United?"

"I'm not talking an alliance. I've made plenty of those; don't need more. I'm saying that a divide between us—the two main men in her life—is a weakness in her security. I don't like that. And I'm betting you don't either."

Belinsky glared at him, put-out. "Do you have to fucking make sense?"

"Yes. Because she's hurting. I'm not okay with that. Make it stop."

The squeak of hinges came from behind Viper. He half-turned to see Ella in the doorway, her expression wary.

Beside her, Jester shot him a sheepish look. *Tried keeping her inside. She threatened to zap me with magick.*

Viper felt his mouth curve slightly. "Hey, baby. Don't worry, no shit's about to go down; all is good." He looked at her anchor. "Ain't that right?"

The legion only grunted, but it was a sound of resignation.

She cautiously approached, glancing from him to Viper. "What brings you here, Luka?"

"Viper and I were just—"

"Bonding," Viper finished.

The legion slammed a hard stare on him. "There was no bonding. There will never be bonding." He looked back at her. "I stand by what I said before: he's done nothing to deserve you, but"—he gritted his teeth, drawing in a long breath—"I won't kill him."

"Or torture him," Ella prodded. When he didn't answer, she pushed, *"Or torture him."*

Belinsky looked close to rolling his eyes. "Or torture him." His gaze fell on Viper. "Unless you hurt her."

Viper could have pointed out that the legion wouldn't stand much of a chance against him, but that would only lead to an argument. "Got it."

"Then there'll be civility." The words seemed torn out of the legion. He flicked up a brow at Ella. "Good enough?"

Her lips tipped up. "Good enough." Her mind bumped Viper's as she telepathically spoke, *How did you manage to convince him to back down?*

Viper draped an arm over her shoulders. *Who says I had anything to do with it?*

He's too stubborn to do it of his own accord.

I just pointed out that he's hurting you and missing out on a lot.

They invited the legion inside, but he turned down the offer as he needed to attend a meeting. After rounding up the conversation, he gave her a hug, nodded curtly at Viper, and then disappeared with his bodyguards.

Looking up at her archangel, Ella tilted her head. "You invited him here, didn't you?" It touched her that someone so proud would make the first move.

He shrugged. "It was time he and I talked, so I made it happen."

As they walked toward the main door, she heard laughs filtering out of the open windows. "Thank you for being the bigger person in this scenario." She pressed a grateful kiss to his cheek.

He looped an arm tight around her waist. "My hope is that your mother and aunt will each now decide to dismount their high horse. I figured that if I could get Belinsky to dismount his own first, the others would follow suit."

"I'm hoping you're right. Peanut does not need the stress of all this. And I know they've got to be affected by how tightly wound I am." Ella paused as he pushed open the main door and they walked into the clubhouse. "Honestly, I don't feel like spending time around Mom or Jocelyn today."

"Then stay home," Viper urged, guiding her into the main area. "Mia can handle things without you, right?"

She pursed her lips, her mood improving at just the thought of it. "I suppose so. She's handled it without me in the past." Ella stopped talking as a bang drew her attention to the corner table.

Rivet had knocked over his chair, his face morphed into a glower that was fixed on Hustle. "How did you do it?"

"Do what?" asked Hustle, shuffling cards.

"We both know you just cheated. *How?*"

Hustle sank into his chair, relaxed. "Oh, so because you lost, you think I conned you?"

"I think you conned me because you conned me."

On the sofa, Jester sighed at Rivet. "Why would you play against someone you know will swindle you?"

"He promised he'd play fair," said Rivet, righting his chair.

"And it didn't occur to you that he was likely lying his ass off?"

Rounding the bar, Sting frowned at Jester. "Why do you constantly accuse people of lying?"

"People lie—it's a fact of life," Jester sagely asserted.

"They don't do it *all* the time," said Sting. "Stop being so paranoid."

"I ain't paranoid."

Hustle pointed at Jester. "That right there was pure bullshit."

Jester shrugged. "As I said, people lie."

Ella exchanged an amused look with Viper as they strode out

of the room. She liked his brothers; liked how welcoming they'd been and that there was a real sense of family there.

The only angel who was ever a little awkward around Ella was Prophet, but Viper had explained how this particular Black Saint worried what exactly her archangel would do and become if he lost her.

"How much persuading will I need to do to convince you to spend the day with me?" Viper asked her, pulling her from her musings.

She hummed. "Not a lot." None at all, in fact. Her demon very much liked the idea—it tended to become annoyed and bored when they were apart. It had become extremely attached to him, hence why it had so far branded him three times.

A demon's inner entity often left such marks on lovers if they felt possessive enough. The tattoo-like brands were always personal. So he sported an 'E' on his ass, a handprint on his hip, and a burst of magick motes zigzagging around his chest and trailing up his spine.

Such brands faded as the entity's interest in that person faded. Viper's marks would never disappear, though. It was cute just how smug he was at being claimed by her demon that way.

"Does this mean I need to take you back to bed to convince you, or will a bowl of ice-cream for breakfast be enough?"

She snickered. "Either will work just fine. You have anything in mind you want to do today?"

"How about we go out somewhere?"

"Like . . . for fun?"

"Yeah." Viper's entity frowned, not liking the idea. It would prefer to keep her here at all times, where she was out of the reach of any danger that might come her way. It generally didn't worry about anything, but the life of Ella and their baby? Totally different situation.

The entity also had its concerns about the birth, unsure how it would go. Viper was confident—or, more to the point, told himself he had every reason to feel confident—that the birth would go fine. Still, the further she got into her pregnancy, the more often anxiety crept up on him. Partly because this was something out of his control.

He was a man who liked control; who was used to having it. This wasn't something he could ensure went exactly how he wanted it to go.

Ella drifted her fingertips over his face. "You hate the idea of going out," she softly accused.

"I don't hate it. I can't lie, I feel better when you're here, where you're safest. But we shouldn't stop living our lives just because a celestial is hanging around."

"I don't want you going stir crazy from worry that someone's gonna jump out of the shadows to grab me."

Viper pulled her closer. "We'll take several of my brothers with us. And if there's any sign of danger, we'll teleport home in a second's notice."

Her mouth curled. "Okay. I'm up for it. I'd like to not use glamor, though. There's no reason for us to hide who we are to each other anymore. The strix knows. A celestial spy knows. My family and anchor knows. We could make this our first public appearance as a couple."

He hummed, considering it. "Yeah, it's time. And I like the idea that everyone will now know you belong to me."

She snorted. "Of course you do. Now, where do you want to go?"

"You choose. I want to take you somewhere you can relax and wind down and forget about all the shit that's happening around us."

Her smile widened. "I know just the place."

*

"*Yeah, go! Go! Go! It won! Boom!*" Conscious of her mate's eyes on her, Ella tore her attention away from the hellhorse racing track. "What?"

He stared at her, his brow furrowed. "You really find this relaxing?"

"You don't?"

"No."

And if the looks on the faces of Jester, Dice, Darko, and Ghost were anything to go by, they didn't find it relaxing either.

Sad head-shakes came from the group of six hellhorses who'd joined them. Like Teague, they didn't belong to a lair and were instead part of his unofficial clan. She'd learned that there was an alliance between said clan and the Black Saints. She got the sense that these guys knew who Viper was, though they were likely unaware of what he'd become on falling.

He gave her a confused look. "What's relaxing about watching hellhorses face a series of sadistic hurdles that can burn, bruise, and slice the competitors—as well as cause them to topple into nightmarish pits filled with shit like spikes, snakes, and boiling oil?"

Ella grazed her teeth over her lower lip. "It's not obvious?"

Cleaning his glasses, the lean, brown-eyed clan member decked out in golfing gear turned to her. "It's the celestial blood in him. He'll never get it. He'll never understand the rush." Leo slipped his glasses back on. "You should pity him."

"Or kill him," Slade chipped in, idly scratching at his blond scruff. "I'd personally prefer death over such a poor quality of life. You'd be doing him a solid."

Viper narrowed his eyes as he swept them over the group. "Doesn't Teague have a VIP box for your clan to use?"

"We prefer being in the stands," Gideon explained, batting away his wavy shoulder-length red hair before taking a swig of his beer—the guy very rarely didn't have a drink in his hand, from what Ella had observed. "The atmosphere here is better."

"And we can sic people on each other when we feel like it," Leo added.

"How?" asked Darko, curious.

"Observe." Leo tossed a coin at someone on a lower tier. That same someone swung around with a scowl, seemed to decide that the person behind him was responsible, and dived at him. Honestly, demons were way too easy to provoke.

"I reckon the taller one will win," said Leo.

Archer pulled a doubtful face. "My money's on the ginger."

No one could call hellhorses normal. Or stable. Or anything close to safe. And yet, they didn't send her inner alarms going wild.

Due to her pregnancy, her protective instincts went electric whenever she was out in public, as did those of her demon. But hellhorses were just way too funny to make her nervous.

Right then, Archer pulled a mushroom out of his little paper bag and offered it to her.

She felt her nose wrinkle. "Uh, I'm good, thanks."

Stood at his back, Saxon cuffed Archer over the head, knocking his short dark ponytail aside. "Stop handing them out to people like they're chips."

Archer didn't even flinch at the hit, despite that his well-built clan member had put some strength behind it. "Why? Sharing is caring."

"You don't warn anyone that they're psychedelics, that's why," Saxon complained before taking a bite of his hotdog. "I had to watch Khloë chase an imaginary pixie around our goddamn camp the other night."

Indignancy flared in Archer's blue eyes. "First of all, Teague warned her that these are magic mushrooms—she ate two anyway. Second of all, your negative opinion of them is unwarranted. They're of the Earth."

"So is poison hemlock. Would you eat that?"

"If I was hungry enough."

Tucker blew out a breath and lifted a dark-skinned hand. "I think I speak for all of us when I say—"

"Don't," said Saxon, tossing him a quelling look. "Don't speak for us. We're good."

Tucker raised his shoulders. "So no one else is thinking that Archer will be the first of us to die?"

Leo twisted his mouth. "I *wasn't* thinking it. But I am now."

"Nah, Gideon will drink himself to death *way* before I pop my clogs." Ignoring Gideon's eye roll, Archer looked at Ella. "I tried to get him off the drink. But some people ... they just don't care what they put in their bodies, you know?"

Watching him plop another mushroom in his mouth, Ella nodded sagely. "I know."

Tucker leaned toward her, blanketing her with the scent of marijuana. "The word you're looking for is 'oblivious'."

"Watch where you're leaning," Saxon groused, glaring at him. "You almost made me drop my hotdog."

Tucker gave him a superior look. "It'd be better if you had, Baldy, since you still haven't washed your bloodstained hands." He shuddered.

Saxon sighed. "Back to that again, are we, little man?"

Tucker bristled. "I'm not short."

"Okay," Saxon agreed.

Slade looked at Viper. "I'm still not happy I got kicked out of your club."

Viper spared him a sideways glance. "You weren't kicked out. You weren't even inside the club. You were stood outside doing your best to get a rise out of Sting."

Slade flapped a hand. "Semantics."

Ella cocked her head. "So, like Teague, you don't know what that word means?"

"No, they don't," Tucker confirmed for him.

"Why were you bothering Sting?" Jester asked Slade.

"I heard he's a good fighter, so I challenged him weeks ago to a brawl in the Underground fight pit," replied Slade. "I bet him two hundred dollars I'd kick his ass. He waved away the challenge; said it'd be like taking candy from a baby. Who gives candy to babies?"

"Archer probably would," Saxon muttered. "And mushrooms."

A fond, nostalgic smile curved Gideon's mouth. "You know, my mom used to put brandy in my bottle to make me sleep."

Leo stared at Gideon for several seconds. "That explains so much."

Yeah, it kind of did. She spared Leo a quick look when he adjusted his golfing glove. "So, you heading off to play golf after this?"

Leo seemed both surprised and confused by the question. "No. Why'd you ask?"

"Well, because you're dressed for it."

He swept the ungloved hand down his body. "This is my normal, everyday attire."

"Why?"

Tucker snickered. "Because he's a goddamn weirdo."

Leo threw him a snarky look over his shoulder. "Fuck off, Frodo."

His mouth tightening, Tucker leaned toward him. "I'm not short."

No, he was just smaller than the others. But he was as wacked as they were—that was for sure. He just seemed to consider himself the only normal member of the clan.

After watching several races—and winning a nice clump of cash—Ella and Viper began making their way out of the Underground, hand in hand. It garnered them plenty of looks, all of which she ignored. His brothers remained close, on high alert.

"Thank you for tonight," she told him. "I didn't realize how much I needed some time to just chill."

Viper sighed. "And I still don't get how all that made you feel chill."

"Oh, my sweet summer child."

He gave his head a quick shake. "Forget it."

CHAPTER THIRTY

Cursing aloud as the blanket in her hand burst into flames, Ella dropped it on the nursery floor in surprise. "I am sick and tired of this shit."

Beside her, Mia quickly dowsed the fire with a flick of her hand, her expression sympathetic. "Dr. Greene warned you that your abilities might—"

"I know, I know. But she said the power-hiccups happen in the third stage of pregnancy. I'm not even fully out of stage *one* yet."

"Only by typical demonic pregnancy standards. I think the gestation period for you is going to be more that of a celestial."

As did Viper. It was kind of unnerving. As was the fact that, according to him, the baby was psychically developing at a faster rate than expected. That would mean Peanut was *physically* developing at much the same speed. Hence her bump.

"If that is the case, you're firmly in stage two," Mia added. "You should be pleased by that. It means you'll get to meet your little ball of wonder sooner than you thought."

"But I can't do something as simple as place a protective spell on one of the baby's blankets without damaging something," Ella sulked.

It had gotten to the point where people held their breath whenever she tried using her abilities. Sometimes she'd manage to conjure only a spurt of magick rather than emit a long stream of it. Other times, it would be vice versa.

Plucking the scorched blanket from the hardwood floor, she grimaced. "It's completely ruined." Her voice cracked.

Mia took the blanket from her, tossed it out of the open door, and put a hand on her shoulder. "Hey, it's all right. I'll bet Peanut's not upset about it."

Ella touched the baby's mind, and she had the impression of laughter. She huffed. "At least someone finds it funny." It no longer felt strange that the baby was so advanced. She'd gotten used to it.

Each time she and Viper touched Peanut's mind, they found only contentment. Providing, of course, it wasn't tired, sleepy, or annoyed by something happening outside the womb. Like when strangers boldly tried touching her belly—it really didn't like that.

Mia rubbed her back. "Peanut's got more blankets where that one came from. And after the birth, you can put protective spells on them all. Though the baby's safe enough here. You put wards all over the room."

Of course she had. It wasn't that she didn't trust his brothers, it was that you could never be too careful.

Mia had added her own magick to the wards, strengthening them. As had both Melodie and Jocelyn when they visited two days ago.

Viper's plan to make them back down had worked. Her mother had Ella called the morning after Luka's visit to the compound a week ago, apologized for her behavior, promised to make it all right, and then suggested they try the family dinner thing again.

During the meal, Melodie had been perfectly polite toward Viper. Jocelyn had been equally polite, though a little tense. Luka had thankfully stuck to his word and kept things civil. Though Luka's civility held a standoffish edge, there was a little mirth there. Ella got the feeling he got a kick out of the 'friction' between himself and Viper; like it would be part of their dynamic.

Despite that the dinner had gone without incident, Ella was taken aback when her mother and aunt asked to stop by the compound a few days later. They'd wanted to see where Ella lived.

While they were here, Viper had introduced them to his brothers. The visit had gone better than expected. Probably because it was plain to see that these particular fallen angels weren't as cold and scary as they seemed.

Okay, they could certainly be scary. And they were more dangerous than people assumed. But they could joke, laugh, shoot the shit, and come across as somewhat normal. Neither Melodie nor Jocelyn had been able to keep smiles off their faces.

What *really* won them over was how obvious it was that the entire club were not only supremely protective of Ella but were helping take care of preparations for the baby—including with decorating the nursery.

Ella let her gaze scan the room. It had been painted a lemony yellow and furnished with a crib, rocking chair, dresser, and wardrobe. Toys practically spilled out of baskets. Clothes had been washed and placed in drawers. A baby monitor stood on the dresser near the crib. Other items such as feeding essentials, diapers, hooded towels, and a bathtub were neatly positioned here and there.

As something hanging on the wardrobe door caught her eye, Ella frowned. "Who bought that?" It was a sleepsuit with a devil on one shoulder and an angel on the other. Apt.

Looking at it, Mia gave a wan smile. "Not sure. Probably Ghost."

"No, he bought the tiny superhero suit." Ella thought it was super cute how the Black Saints were as bad at buying baby stuff on impulse as she was.

Things *appeared* in the nursery all the time. Some were necessities, others were cute stuff like plushies and toys. Darko had even had a little biker jacket made for the baby.

"On the subject of Ghost," began Mia, "want to tell me why you shoved him off the sofa and zapped his ass with magick?"

Ella scowled. "He went whining to you about it?"

"No, Omen told me; thought it was hilarious. What did Ghost do?"

"We were sitting together in the main area. I'd fallen asleep. I woke up to find him reading to the baby."

"And that's bad?"

"He was reading *The Exorcist*."

Mia clamped her lips shut, clearly fighting a smile.

"He even did the demonic voice," Ella griped. "The baby thought it was funny. I didn't. And neither should you."

"I don't."

"Your eyes are laughing."

"How can eyes laugh?"

"I don't know, but yours are cracking up."

Mia held up two placatory hands. "Ghost would never read a book like that to the baby, he had to have been messing with you. He probably hadn't read a single word from the book until he saw you start to wake."

"Didn't look like it to me." With an indignant huff, Ella rested her hand on her slightly swollen belly.

"You're not gonna be able to hide that bump with baggy clothes for much longer," remarked Mia.

"I know." Ella sighed. "That's when I'll have to be *real* careful. Stuff travels fast through the demonic grapevine, so the news of my pregnancy will spread like wildfire. And considering I'm often seen with Viper, people will be quick to assume he's the father. Not all will like it."

Ella was already well-protected—she was never alone outside the compound, and she now drove the brand new and much safer vehicle that Viper had bought for her. But the Black Saints would likely step up the security around her even further when her pregnancy became common knowledge.

Some demons would be unbothered by the baby being half celestial. Others? There would be those who were merely concerned or wary. However, there'd be demons who would be downright rude and unfriendly to Ella, as if she'd betrayed her race by procreating with 'the enemy'.

A part of Ella chafed at being so coddled, but she accepted the overprotective security measures for the sake of her child—and also because they made her demon less tense. Having been claimed by Viper also seemed to have settled something in her demon.

A phone beeped, making Mia dip her hand down the pocket of her jeans. Fishing out her cell, she frowned. "It's Joe."

Ella felt her brows knit. "Why would he text you when he can just telepath you?"

Mia exhaled heavily. "He finds telepathy intimate, so he'll avoid talking to people mind-to-mind when he's unhappy with them."

Hello, man child. "What does he want?"

Mia angled the phone so Ella could the read text: *Can we talk?* Ella wasn't exactly in a 'let's forgive Joe' frame of mind.

However, there was the little problem that a lot of physical distance between anchors could cause them issues psychically. So Ella wasn't going to urge Mia to ignore Joe's request. Besides, it wasn't her decision to make.

As such, Ella softly asked, "What are you going to do?"

Mia rubbed at her throat. "What I *want* to do is tell him to wait awhile before we talk again. None of the recent conversations we've had have really helped our situation. But I want it resolved once and for all. Before all this, we never had a single problem. I would never have imagined we'd be where we are now.

"The person he's been lately . . . it's not *him*. It's a hurt, defensive, guarded version of him. We can all get twisted up inside when we're in pain. I don't like knowing he has to feel very alone right now. You'd be the same if it was Luka."

Yes, Ella would. And so she knew . . . "You're going to respond to the text."

"Yes. I have to know if he *finally* means for us to move forward." Mia typed out a response and then showed it to Ella. It read: *Depends what you want to talk about. Lately, it's never been anything good.* "Do you think that was a little mean?"

"No," Ella assured her. "I think you needed to make it clear that you acknowledging his message doesn't mean he isn't still firmly in the dog house."

Another beep came. Mia angled the phone so Ella could easily read the text as well. It simply said: *I deserved that.*

Mia snorted and typed: *Yeah, dude, you did.*

I don't want to fight, we've done enough of that. I can't claim my head is on straight yet—it'd be a lie. I need time. But I want us to at least be on good terms. I hate that we're in a situation where I hesitated to telepath you because I wasn't sure you'd welcome it.

Ella hummed. "He's saying all the right things."

"Yeah, but he does that. And each time I think, hey, maybe he's really done being an ass, he proves me wrong."

Another message came through: *I'm outside the Black Saints' compound right now. You don't have to let me in if you don't want to, but can you at least come outside and talk to me through the fence? I want to be able to apologize to your face.*

Ella stilled. "Wait, he's here?"

You don't have to come alone, he added. *You can bring someone with you if you want.*

Mia shook her head. "I really wouldn't have expected this. He must genuinely mean to apologize. Though that doesn't mean we won't end up bickering again. Would you come with me? I just think he's less likely to start an argument if there's someone else around."

"Of course." Ella would prefer it that way.

Mia texted him again: *I'll be right out.*

Together, they left the nursery and made their way toward the exit. Just as they neared it, a bunch of the Black Saints filed inside. All frowned on realizing that Ella seemed about to go outside.

"Where are you two ladies heading?" asked Merchant.

"My anchor's outside. He wants to talk." Mia raised a reassuring hand. "I'm not going to invite him in here, so relax."

"I don't much like the idea of you speaking to him out there either," commented Blackjack, his brow creased. "He's a dick."

"I'm going to hear him out. Ella will be with me. And we'll stay within the gates."

She and Mia walked out of the building, their arms linked. Some of the Black Saints followed them outside but lingered near the bikes—making no attempt to hide that they would be keeping an eye on things.

Joe stood beyond the chain link fence several feet away from the gates. His stance was casual, but his face was lined with tension.

They moved to stand opposite him, keeping the fence between them.

He paid no attention to Ella, his eyes focused on her sister. "Hey, Mia," he said, an odd hitch in his voice.

Something's wrong, Mia told her telepathically.

Ella didn't let her expression change. *What do you mean?*

I don't know, I can't explain it. There's just something off *with him psychically. Like when you hear a song and there's an off-note that jars.*

Her belly roiling, Ella was just about to suggest—okay, insist—they return inside. But she froze as his hands splayed against the fence, his fingers poking through the diamond-shaped gaps.

Fingers with black tips, like they'd been charred.

Mia gasped. "Oh my God, what happened?" She instinctively reached out and touched his hand.

Like that, Ella felt a *wrench* on her body as she and Mia were swiftly teleported out of the compound.

A field. They now stood on an open, wide-ass field. A tall, blond, winged male who carried an aura of power faced them—*archangel*, Ella thought. On his left was a slender grim-looking male who didn't seem entirely sure he wanted to be there. On the archangel's right stood none other than goddamn Maxine.

Son of a bitch.

More, as if the situation wasn't bad enough, they were surrounded by dozens upon dozens of strix.

Fuck.

The archangel looked at Joe. "Sleep."

Like that, the demon toppled to the ground at the sisters' feet, out cold.

Oh, hell.

In a matter of milliseconds, three things happened.

Ella's demon went AWOL.

The archangel took a step forward.

A ring of ultraviolet flames formed around her, Mia, and Joe. Flames that grew and curved and swam . . . before then forming a glowing-ultraviolet shield.

Mia slid her a sideways look. *That wasn't me.*

It wasn't me either. It was Peanut. And that wasn't scary at all.

Through the shield, Ella watched the archangel curiously cock his head.

"That I did not expect," he said.

That made two of them. *Call out to Dice, Mia. Do it fast. We need to get away from here right the fuck now.*

Grabbing his ringing cell phone from his office desk, Viper looked at the screen. *Teague.* He felt his brow dent. It wasn't often he heard from the hellhorse.

Leaning back in his leather chair, he was just about to answer the call when Darko materialized in front of him. his expression hard.

"Don't go postal, okay," urged Darko, "but you should know that, uh . . . Ella and Mia disappeared."

Everything in Viper and his entity went rigid. "What do you mean they disappeared?"

"They were there and then they were gone. *Poof.* Mia's anchor teleported them away from the compound."

Rage and dread clawing at him and his entity, Viper shot out of his seat as he tried touching Ella's mind. Nothing but dead air. "I can't reach Ella telepathically, so she isn't close by." *Fuck, fuck, fuck.*

Terror took him over. Terror for her, for their child. Terror that he'd lose them both.

Dice. He should contact Dice and have him reach out to Mia.

Viper would have done exactly that if the seraphim hadn't right then appeared beside Darko.

"I just heard from Mia," Dice clipped, his eyes hard. "Fucking Joe took her and Ella. Only it seems like he was forced to do it by an archangel. A blond archangel with dove-gray wings."

Realization smacked Viper right in the face. "Ophaniel," he snarled, his entity bashing at his insides, demanding they track and kill the archangel. "Either he lied that he hadn't taken up the Uppers on their offer, or he's since then changed his mind." Viper took a quick step toward Dice, urgency gripping his gut. "Where are they?"

"They don't know. Mia said there are no landmarks, nothing that stands out. Just grass and trees and dark fucking clouds. Oh, and strix. They're fucking *surrounded* by strix. Ophaniel is working with them somehow."

It had to have been him who'd lowered Ghost's cloak and possibly even targeted Ella. "Then his plan must be to allow the strix to do his dirty work." Viper gripped his still-ringing phone tight.

"He's having trouble with that right now, because your kid decided to pop up a protective shield."

The startling news made both Viper and his entity go still. "A shield?"

"Yeah, one constructed of ultraviolet flames." Dice shook his head, stunned.

"The shield is a good thing, but only to an extent."

"What do you mean?" asked Darko.

"I mean Ophaniel will know there's no way Ella could pop up a shield of unholy flames . . . unless she was pregnant."

Darko's jaw dropped. "Oh, shit."

Right then, Viper's phone finally stopped ringing.

Moments later, Dice's began chiming.

The VP checked his cell phone screen. "It's Teague." He dismissively canceled the call. "I say we head to the spot of land I was at earlier. The strix aren't there, but maybe there's something I missed, something—" He stopped talking as Viper's phone again rang.

Cursing, Viper jabbed his thumb on the screen. "Teague, I'll call you back—I got some shit going down."

"Well, I figured that," said the hellhorse, "since your woman and her sister have been taken."

Viper stiffened, and his entity narrowed its eyes. "How would you know?"

"I'm looking at them right now. Me and my clan have been scouting for strix. We found them. They're circling the sisters and some guy who's now unconscious. Looks like there's two celestials in the mix as well. Also a she-demon who Larkin says is from her lair."

"Where are they?" Viper bit out, his heart pounding.

"Don't come in hot. There's a lot of the fuckers, and we need to move carefully or they'll scatter."

"*Where*, Teague?"

CHAPTER THIRTY-ONE

The strix curiously crept closer to the shield, though not *too* close. They were fairly salivating, like they hadn't fed in weeks. But Ella knew it wasn't blood they thirsted for here and now. It was vengeance. They would kill her in lieu of Viper.

There had to be at least fifty of them. It was the first time she'd seen any female strix. Plenty were here, and they all looked as fierce and battle-ready as the males.

Damn, this was bad. Very, very bad. Especially since her sister hadn't been able to give Dice even a general idea of their location.

Their scenery was a vast spread of pastureland that featured straggly trees, fence posts, barbed wire, and wildflowers.

The archangel had no doubt deliberately chosen a location that had no landmarks, since it was well-known that demons could telepath. He wouldn't want either she or Mia calling out for aid.

Ella's entity was in a blind fury, eager to magickly fuck up their enemies' shit. But she didn't dare release any magick, since it might ricochet off the walls of the shield and rebound back on her.

Admittedly scared for her child, Ella touched Peanut's mind with her own. *It's okay, we'll get out of this.*

Its young psyche fluttered against her own, humming with a fear-tinged determination. Her heart broke. She could do nothing to get the baby to safety. There was just too many enemies and nowhere to run.

While the protective shield was invaluable right now, she worried what the strain of keeping it in place might do to her child. Psychically advanced or not, they were still a baby.

"What are you even doing here?" clipped Mia, and Ella quickly realized that her sister was addressing Maxine.

The harpy's mouth curved into a somewhat sadistic grin. "I like to see those I help bring down finally meet their end."

Those she'd helped bring down?

"I do hope you're not counting on a rescue—no one will find you."

Something about the *way* Maxine said that, about the glint of cunning in her gaze, made Ella's scalp tingle in suspicion. She again reached out to Mia. *Do you think our surroundings could be an illusion?*

I had the same thought, funnily enough, replied Mia. *Something just feels wrong about this picture.*

It did. There were none of the sounds you'd expect to hear in such a place—no birds crying overhead, no shushing of breeze-rustled grass, no insects buzzing. Only the creaking of something metal, the flapping of cloth, and the rustling of leaves. Instead of the scents of manure, flowers, and earth, she could smell garbage, mildew, and rust.

A tall, long-haired female strix moved through the lines of demons, haughty as any royal. This had to be the queen of the colony. Two muscular strix—one male, one female—followed the queen, their posture protective. *Guards*, Ella thought.

The queen smirked at the archangel. "Your plan worked."

"Of course it worked." There was no pompous arrogance in the statement, only an unshakable confidence in himself.

The queen's red eyes slid to Ella, and her smirk deepened. "My brethren and I are going to have a lot of fun with you." She clicked her fingers at her male guard.

Ella's heart jumped as the strix obligingly moved toward the shield.

The archangel lifted a cautioning hand. "Wait." Not a command, more like an advisory statement.

The queen bristled, her red eyes glaring at him. "We want her," she said, pointing at Ella.

"You'll have to wait until the shield lowers," he calmly told her. "Relax. The child will not be able to hold it for long."

Ella's stomach dropped. Oh, fuck, he knew she was pregnant.

The queen's brows met. "Child?"

"Yes, she carries Viper's offspring," he revealed.

The queen's eyes lit up in devious delight, the lines of hunger in her expression deepening.

"As soon as the shield winks out, you can attack."

"Why can't we just do it now?"

The archangel flapped a hand. "See for yourself."

The queen nodded curtly at her male guard. He rushed forward, collided into the shield—and disintegrated into ashes just like that.

Ella felt her mouth drop open. *Oh. My. God.*

Mia gasped, her hand gripping Ella's arm tight. "Go, Peanut," she whispered, awe in her tone.

That same awe coursed through Ella's inner demon, along with a healthy dose of parental pride.

"It's constructed of unholy fire," the archangel explained to the queen. "It will cause death on impact. But you can keep at it if you wish—your choice." He gave an uncaring shrug.

Who *was* this guy? One of the Seven, maybe?

It was weird that he was so chill. There was no anger, no sense of urgency, no distaste as he looked upon either Ella or her sister. He honestly seemed largely unaffected by their presence. And yet, he'd played a part in them being brought here and he clearly wanted them dead.

The slim guy at his side took a nervous step back from the shield, as did the traitorous bitch Maxine and the majority of the strix. Only the queen and archangel remained in position, appearing unfazed.

"How long before the shield drops?" the queen asked the archangel, her tone huffy.

"Not long. Then you can slaughter them all."

Anxiety punched Ella's chest, and she pulled in a breath. It hurt, as if her windpipe had narrowed. The shield *would* drop—that was a fact. There were far too many strix to hold at bay, not to mention two celestials *and* Maxine to combat. There was a very real possibility that she, her child, Mia, and Joe would die today.

And if Ella died, Viper would too due to their souls being bound. *Fuck.*

Tamping down the panic that tried to rise, Ella cocked her head at the archangel. "Who are you?"

He regarded her for a moment. "Name's Ophaniel."

Never heard of him, Ella telepathically told her sister. *You?*

No, never.

A groaning sound came from Joe, but he didn't wake.

"What's wrong with his hands?" Mia asked the archangel, gesturing at her psi-mate.

"I burned them with holy fire," Ophaniel answered matter-of-factly.

A low hiss came from Mia. "You tortured him?"

"Of course not. I simply *suggested* he put his fingers into one of these." Ophaniel conjured a golden, fiery orb. "I'd hoped the burns would shock you enough that you'd reach out to him—it was the only way he'd be able to teleport you here. It is pure luck that your arm was looped through that of your sister." Looking at Ella, he let the orb disintegrate. "I had thought I would need to get to you by insisting on a trade—you for your sister."

"You said he burned himself at your suggestion," Mia remembered, flicking a concerned look at her anchor. "So, what, you controlled his actions somehow?"

"Not quite," Ophaniel responded. "I suppose there's no harm in explaining, since you won't live to share the information. I steered his will, though it took some time to get a real grasp on it. With humans and angels, I can easily slip into their minds, put them asleep, and use their bodies without their knowledge. I can also plant thoughts, suggestions, or ideas in their heads. The latter doesn't work as well with demons. It's also impossible to use them as puppets."

Thank God. Because he could have otherwise wreaked all sorts of havoc. "If you're so good at slipping into celestial minds, why didn't you attempt to control any of the other Black Saints?"

"They're unfortunately too powerful," he replied, a note of faint resentment in his voice. "A dominion proved helpful, though—something he's unaware of. 'Prophet' he calls himself these days. He is all tangled up in regret, bitterness, self-loathing, and fear. A mind is easier to invade if a person is vulnerable, but—what with him being so powerful—I could only pick up his surface thoughts. Still, it made him a good involuntary source of information."

Right then, Mia's mind stroked hers. *Dice just telepathed me, he sees us.*

It took everything in Ella not to smile. *He found us?*

Teague's clan did. The Black Saints are all here, but they can't get close. Archangelic wards have been placed around to keep people away—it seems Ophaniel isn't taking any chances.

Oh, fuck. *Can they unravel the wards?*

Viper can, but Dice says it won't be a quick process.

Panic again beat at Ella, and she almost cursed aloud. At least they *could* be unraveled. That was something.

She tried mentally reaching out to Viper. Nothing. He wasn't close enough for her to psychically touch, then.

"Are you the newest member of the Seven?" Mia asked Ophaniel.

"No, just one of many slayers." His wings rustled slightly. "My superiors offer me the jobs that no one else wants to do. And they want Samael dead."

Maxine's head whipped to face Ophaniel, her lips parting in shock. Ah, she hadn't known who Viper was. The other celestial displayed no such surprise.

Ophaniel looked at Ella. "My superiors also want *you* dead. Samael cannot be rewarded for falling by being allowed to live happily ever after with you." He studied her expression. "You did not react on hearing his true name, so you must have already known it."

Ella said nothing. She *couldn't* really confirm it, due to the geas. "You wrote the notes I received."

"Freddie wrote them," said Ophaniel, gesturing at his celestial companion. "I embedded power in the ink."

Ella's brow knitted. "What were you trying to compel me to do?"

"The first two were intended to make you suicide. The latter two would have caused you to kill Samael."

Her demon snapped its teeth. It wanted to tear out the insides of each person outside of the shield, but more particularly this archangel. "You *had* to have eventually realized I wasn't going to fall for a snare, so why keep trying?"

"The fourth note was more of an attempt to force Samael into confessing all. I knew from Prophet's surface thoughts that Samael was keeping you partially in the dark. I thought if you knew the truth about him, you might just do the smart thing and kill him." He exhaled heavily in annoyance, as if he'd expected better of her.

"You were also the one who tried breaking into my apartment."

"Guilty," he admitted, though he didn't sound at all regretful. "I would have taken you, had it been possible. You're too heavily guarded for me to get near you. Joe is the only teleporter in your circle, but you would not have allowed him to take you anywhere."

"You said you can't use demons as puppets, but it clearly worked with him," said Mia.

"No, he merely eventually succumbed to the suggestions I planted," Ophaniel told her. "I was only successful because he is currently vulnerable—haunted by jealousy, pain, and bitterness. I had to wait until he was so eaten up by those emotions that his defenses were down before I could really influence his will. He probably wouldn't have been half so problematic for you recently if I hadn't been working on him daily. His subconscious fought me hard, not wanting any harm to come to you."

The shield flickered like a faulty light bulb.

Ella's heart slammed in her chest, and her demon spat a curse.

Ophaniel's lips tipped up, though the smile didn't reach his eyes. "The child's psychic strength is faltering, I see."

She telepathed her sister again. *Ask Dice if Viper is close to unraveling the other wards yet.*

Just did, said Mia. *He says they need a few more minutes.*

Ella wasn't sure they *had* a few more minutes.

Ophaniel's gaze bounced from her to Mia. "Your eyes keep going out of focus, so I would imagine you're having telepathic chats with each other. Or is it with your men?" His mouth curved. "Samael must be going wild right now, unable to get to his mate and child. Such a shame."

Ella couldn't fight a frown. That smile . . . it wasn't triumphant or cruel. In fact, it was more like nostalgic. As if thinking of Viper brought him pleasant memories. The "Such a shame" part even sounded genuine. "You know him well?"

"Well enough."

"Setting up his mate and unborn child to die doesn't bother you?"

A shrug. "It's nothing personal. I'm simply doing my job. You understand."

"No, no, I don't. I don't understand how *anyone* would want to harm a child."

Ophaniel's sapphire-blue gaze sharpened on Ella. "You are not stupid. You know why my superiors would be disturbed by the life in your womb and want it destroyed. They can hardly permit a half-demon half-fallen archangel to walk the Earth."

If the Uppers knew of the baby from Ophaniel, then he'd been aware of her pregnancy *before* now. But how? Suspicion pricking at her, she looked at Maxine, who only smiled. "How did you find out?"

"It was more of a guess really," replied the harpy.

"Maxine is well-known among celestials," said Ophaniel. "Always a wondrous source of information for the right price."

Unreal. Ella had assumed that Maxine used what information she scrounged up to blackmail or manipulate other demons. She hadn't for a moment suspected that the woman would be passing it on to celestials. "Why? Why would you betray your own?"

"Why not?" Maxine challenged with a casual shrug.

Ella blinked at her. *Why? Not?*

"Oh, you were expecting some tragic, traumatic backstory?" Maxine gave a gentle shake of her head. "No, dear. Call it a . . . family business. Generations of us have been such sources. It is how we initially attained wealth."

Son of a bitch. "Dionne wants nothing to do with the 'family business,' does she?"

The woman's eyes hardened. "She will change her mind."

Ella refocused on Ophaniel. "You asked her to befriend my aunt and wring her dry of any helpful information."

He conceded that with an incline of his head. "Your aunt wasn't very forthcoming, unfortunately."

"And so Maxine planted her daughter at our store," Mia surmised.

Maxine sighed. "She didn't learn much either. But when I recently noticed your aunt and mother buying baby clothes and took into account Ella's recent habit of wearing loose tops, I had an inkling that she was pregnant."

"A surface scan of Prophet's mind confirmed the suspicion," Ophaniel added. "And so I passed on the news to those in the upper realm. Just be grateful they don't instead wish to take and raise the child to use for their own purposes. They would . . . not be kind."

Ella had the feeling he spoke from experience. Maybe, like Viper, he'd been forced into a life he didn't want. It would explain his complete lack of enthusiasm here.

"You may judge me for my actions," he began, "but know that Samael has done far worse deeds, even going as far as . . . "

His words faded as Mia's voice again poured into her mind: *Two wards are unraveled, there's just two more to go.*

Ella felt her pulse spike. *Good, because I don't think this shield will stay up for much longer. And those strix want to rip me apart and get to the baby.*

"You know," began Ophaniel, his voice tipping up in volume, "it's rude to have telepathic conversations when someone is speaking to you." He gave a mocking *tut, tut.*

Ella lifted her chin. "Can't say I was interested in listening to you try to excuse your own behavior by comparing your acts to those of Viper. He might have done some dark shit in his time, but he never harmed children."

She slid her gaze to Freddie, who still appeared remarkably uncomfortable. He wasn't an archangel, but she got the sense that he was some form of celestial. "It doesn't bother you that you'll have contributed to the death of a child?"

His throat bobbed, and he plucked at his tie. "It is not a child, it is an abomination." Harsh words. But there was a shake to his voice, as if he was repeating an opinion that he didn't entirely agree with.

"Freddie is eager to earn his halo and return to his family in the upper realm," said Ophaniel. "When my superiors hear that he aided me, they will grant him what he wants."

Ella frowned. "Good deeds earn halos. He'll have innocent blood on his hands."

Ophaniel gave her a look that could only be described as one of gentle condescension. "None of you are innocent."

"Neither are celestials."

His lips twitched. "Quite so. Holy blood doesn't ensure goodness." His gaze zipped from her to Mia. "But you both *have* killed, have you not?"

"My baby hasn't."

"But it will." Ophaniel sighed. "In this realm, it is rare for your kind to go without taking lives due to the brutality of the demon world. The fetus may be half archangel, but it'll still be firmly in that world. And it may very well carry Samael's curse—perhaps even share his inability to avoid drawing evil like a magnet." He gestured at the strix. "Case in point."

"How did you manage to gain *their* cooperation?"

Ophaniel shrugged. "I simply promised I would help them kill Samael. They're very eager to make him pay for the deaths of their brethren."

Again, the shield flickered—this time for several seconds, making Ella fear it would wink out altogether. But it didn't.

"Not long to go now," said Ophaniel.

Snickers ran through the crowd of strix, their eagerness to charge almost tangible.

"I would much rather not hang around for this part," he said. "It will bring me no real pleasure to see two women—demons or not—savaged by strix. But my superiors will be angry if they're not able to watch the replay of your deaths via my memories."

His superiors needed to have their necks snapped. "If I'm going to die, I'd like to know one thing first."

He tipped his head to the side, a brow hiking up in question.

"Why didn't you act sooner? Why use notes and subtle moves? Why try hijacking the wills of others? You're an archangel. It shouldn't have been all that hard for you to kill me."

"That's several questions, but I don't mind answering. Truthfully, I would have much preferred if my assignment had been a straightforward execution. But I'm under strict orders to ensure that your deaths do not taste of celestial interference—people would, after all, immediately suspect we'd targeted you to punish Samael for falling. That meant being very careful how I proceeded. We can't have a war breaking out, can we?

"When you die at the hands of the Black Saints' enemies, people will blame them as well as the strix. Joe will share some of the blame as well. But I'm quite sure he'll die here and now, so he'll be spared any punishments from your lair." A smile lit his eyes as the shield began to ripple, its brightness fading. "Ah, here we go."

Fuck.

The shield dropped. Ophaniel grinned. The queen let out a bloodthirsty roar, sparking her brethren to do the same. The strix all moved to charge ... only to freeze as the pastureland around them disappeared, revealing their true whereabouts.

Seeing the rows of rusted, vandalized mobile homes and trailers, Ella realized they were on the grounds of an abandoned trailer park. Some trailers had been tipped over and lay sprawled on the leafy gravel roads.

Overgrown grass and weeds were all that was left of the lawns. Damaged portable canopies and smashed garden furniture lay haphazardly here and there. There was debris everywhere—bike wheels, satellite dishes, crates, and car parts.

Before the strix had a chance to recover from their surprise, the Black Saints appeared within the circle that the hell-born demons had formed around Ella and Mia.

Oh, thank all that's holy and unholy. Her demon grinned, equal parts relieved and delighted.

The strix hissed, shifting uneasily as they found themselves facing the fallen angels, who were all stood with their backs to Ella, Mia, and Joe.

Only one Black Saint stood within the circle. And he was glaring right at Ophaniel, his eyes hard as granite.

Viper.

CHAPTER THIRTY-TWO

Protective fury whirling in his veins, Viper glared at the archangel who stood a few feet away. He wanted to rush to Ella, hold her, soothe her, check every inch of her. But he didn't dare turn his back on his foe—this celestial was an accomplished slayer.

Ophaniel cast him a faint smile. "Samael, good to see you again." He sounded so genuine that Viper could almost believe it.

His entity crept close to the surface, wanting to tear apart this male it had once called a friend. "Given the circumstances, I really can't say 'likewise'."

"Perfectly understandable." Again, so genuine.

Viper touched his mind to Ella's and asked, *You all right?*

I'm fine, she assured him. *So is Peanut. Ophaniel didn't harm us, he planned on feeding us to the strix.*

Viper knew that. He'd heard much of what the archangel said as he fought to unravel the closest wards.

He wasn't sure who Ophaniel's demonic sidekick was, but he

recognized the angel as being the same one Ophaniel had used as a puppet the last time he'd played messenger.

A snake-like hiss came from the crowd of strix. Viper saw her, then. A tall, pale-skinned brunette. *The queen*.

His entity's attention locked on her, hate roiling in its gut for this creature that intended to feed on its mate and child; who had come at his club again and again; who had killed many humans like they were nothing.

Viper let his lips curve into a taunting smile, wanting her attention on him, not Ella. "Finally crawled out of your hole to face me yourself?"

She flashed him her fangs, her expression feral. "You're not supposed to be here."

"None of us should be here." Viper darted his gaze from her to Ophaniel. "You both should have left well enough alone."

The archangel gave a slight shrug. "It's really nothing personal on my part."

Viper felt his jaw clench. "You took my woman and unborn child. You set them up to die. You would have *watched* them die. That makes it seriously fucking personal."

"Yes, I suppose it does. But even you have to have reservations about this child. Already it makes displays of power and conjures unholy fire. It should not be born. It will embody too much darkness."

"You don't care about that. You don't care about anything that's happening right here and now. You're as numb as I once was."

Ophaniel wouldn't even be fazed by the thought of dying. He might even look forward to it. Viper had been the same way once. It was Ella who'd saved him.

The archangel was quiet for a long moment. "I find I'm not so numb that I would wish to have a literal hand in killing you, so I will allow the strix to finish you off."

Vines shot out of the ground and nabbed Ophaniel's feet before he could teleport away. His body swayed slightly as his eyes widened and landed on Ella.

Viper looked to see that his mate had her palms planted firmly on the grass, chanting low, her gaze hard on the archangel.

She shot Ophaniel a little smirk. "You thought you were going somewhere?"

Viper's entity grinned, approving.

The angelic sidekick glanced around, as if seeking a savior. The she-demon went as if to run. Then both also found their ankles bound by vines.

Ella's smirk kicked up a notch. "You should have left when you had the chance. Not that it would have mattered. I'd have hunted you both down."

Maxine snarled. "You think you'll get out of this alive? Look around you. You're severely outnumbered."

"Yes, I've noticed."

More thick, prickly vines right then sprouted out of the ground, twig-like ropes coiled around them. They formed a circle between the strix and the Black Saints—twisting, linking, looping, growing higher and higher.

Then they fell outwards, landing hard on the strix, squashing many and trapping others. The demons struggled and hissed, attacking the vines.

Viper returned his attention to the slayer. "You might be reluctant to kill me, Ophaniel, but I'm not feeling the same reluctance toward you."

Ophaniel's face tightened. "Don't make me call out to them, Samael. They would not settle for merely relocating her soul this time, and we both know what they would do to that of your child. This way, your loved ones will at least be reborn elsewhere and live other lives. Be content with that."

"You know I won't." Viper frowned. "I could almost think you came here to die, because I don't see how you thought you'd live through this."

Ophaniel's eyes flickered. Yes, he hoped to die here. He could have taken his own life, but he'd prefer to suffer an 'honorable' death by losing his life in battle.

Viper's entity snorted, now not particularly wanting to end the archangel—it wasn't feeling inclined to oblige him in *anything*.

"Release me," Ophaniel ordered.

"You don't truly want that," said Viper. "And even if you did, the answer would be no."

The slayer sighed. "You're right. It would bother me none to die here today. But you and your child must die also—neither of you can be allowed to exist."

Mere moments later, six figures appeared behind Ophaniel and his sidekicks. Viper gritted his teeth at the sight of those he'd once thought of as family. Ella must have recognized them from the replay he'd showed her of the death that her soul had once suffered at the archangels' hands, because she spat an ugly curse.

Ophaniel angled his face slightly toward the newcomers. "Just to bring you up to speed ... the redhead in the blue sweater is the infamous Everleigh, and she is pregnant with his child."

Viper skimmed his gaze along Michael, Azrael, Raphael, Uriel, Raguel, and Gabriel. "Leave. You will die here if you don't."

Gabriel twisted his lips. "We were thinking more along the lines of doing this." He struck out with an archangelic blast that cleaved Ophaniel and his sidekicks in half.

Huh. His entity's brows hiked up in surprise.

The queen let out a battle cry, and the strix who'd managed to escape the tangle of vines then charged.

The six archangels swiftly fell into place among the Black Saints, braced to fight. Hooves thundered along the ground as seven hellhorses galloped out from between the trailers, their legs moving with such speed they were a blur. Among them were five black-furred, crimson-eyed bloodhounds and five oversized ravens.

Viper rushed to his mate and teleported her, Mia, and Joe out of the circle and to the clubhouse. Unsurprisingly, indignation flared in the sisters' gazes.

"No," objected Ella. "I wanted to fight with—"

"Think," he bid, cupping her neck. "You've got our baby in your belly, he or she needs protecting—including from themselves, and we can't trust they won't try to help us fight and then drain themselves psychically. Also, I won't be able to keep my thoughts straight if you're surrounded by danger, not to mention anywhere near the archangels who once took you from me."

"They seem to be on our side."

"Doesn't mean they're on *your* side. Doesn't mean they think our baby should live." He put his hand on her slightly swollen belly. "Keeping them safe is the biggest job, and I'm leaving that to you. The best way you can do it is by staying here." He looked up at Mia, who stood over her anchor. "I'm trusting you to watch over her."

The sisters exchanged a look, their shoulders slumping.

"Honestly, I don't want to leave her or Joe anyway," Mia admitted.

Ella sighed. "You'll have to come back for me once it's over. The enchanted vines won't disappear until I get rid of them."

He gave her a hard kiss. "I'll be back for you."

"Be careful."

"Always am, baby." Viper teleported back to the trailer park just in time to watch the hellhorses charge right into the gathering of strix, mowing them down and trampling on the bodies. Some roared out hellfire, others puffed out noxious smoke that misted the air.

Tossing around unholy orbs, Dice shot him a sideways glance. *The girls safe?*

Yes, Viper replied.

Though the colony's attention was now divided, two came right at Viper without delay. He flicked his hand, sending out an archangelic blast of unholy fire that chopped them in half.

A female strix sprung high, its eyes on Viper. And got plucked out of the sky by a vine that contracted around it like a boa constrictor.

He scanned the colony, searching for the queen. A tight cluster of strix caught his attention. They were surrounding her, he realized.

He wasn't fooled. The queen was a fighter. She wouldn't truly hide behind her brethren. She knew Viper wanted her dead, and she hoped to lure him away from those who had his back. His entity was insulted that she thought him so easily fooled.

He'd wait her out. She'd come at him sooner or later. She wouldn't be able to help herself.

Do you think we can trust the Six? Dice asked as Viper telekinetically tore a post sporting a flapping country flag from a mobile home.

Viper telekinetically swept the pole outwards, knocking down several strix in one swoop. *I don't know.* His entity didn't trust them for a second.

The archangels—currently alternating between volleying golden orbs of holy fire around and striking out with archangelic blasts—had joined their fight, yes. But just because they were slaughtering hell-born demons didn't mean they wouldn't later turn on the fallen angels around them.

Viper pitched an ultraviolet orb at an approaching strix, catching it full-on in the face. A pained cry crawled out of the demon as it staggered backwards, digging the heels of its palms into its eyes. A vine shot out and wacked it aside—sending it crashing into a hellhorse. The steed whirled on the strix and bit off its head.

Okay.

The smells of sulphur and brimstone proceeded the cracking of a whip. The black fire slapped his chest, searingly hot and corrosive. The pain was surreal.

Little black chips rained down on the offending strix, melting its flesh and killing it. *Hell-ice.*

Viper didn't need to look up to know that Teague's mate would be hovering in the air above. Larkin could shoot hell-ice, and she liked to attack while in flight.

More strix came at him, and Viper let his focus center on the battle. Fury, adrenaline, a thirst for vengeance, the addictive release from violence—it all coursed through him, drove him, fueled him. Power hummed in the air from a combination of hellfire, magick, unholy fire, and archangelic power.

Around him, his brothers fought like savages. The archangels battled just as mercilessly, as did Larkin. Hellhorses kept on galloping back and forth, ruthlessly knocking into strix like battering rams; stomping over the fallen bodies; exhaling streams of hellfire. The hounds barked and pounced and tore into flesh. Ravens flew down to attack faces, pecking and clawing.

The colony outnumbered them, but Viper didn't believe that would last long. Not with the assault that the strix faced. But they either didn't feel the same way or weren't letting it impact them, because they fought like trojans. There was relentless biting, clawing, pouncing, hellfire-throwing, and whip-lashing.

The more the battle raged, the more insane the noise level became. The snapping of whips, the spitting of flames, the barking of hounds, the stomping of hooves, the crackles of magick, the squawks of ravens, the whooshes of zooming orbs—the combination was near deafening.

Hearing a pained neigh, he looked to see a hellhorse sprawled on the ground on its side, three strix crawling all over it. Viper lobbed one with ultraviolet orbs while Larkin swooped down and snatched away another. The steed then surged up, the movement so abrupt it flicked the last strix off like a fly. Before the strix could rise, Viper telekinetically lifted a trailer and plonked it on top of the offending creature, squashing it.

On and on they all fought, both sides primal and determined. Ashes wafted on the breeze that whispered over his skin and tousled his hair.

At one point, Viper took a moment to quickly let his gaze zip around. The strix's numbers had dropped notably, to his entity's supreme satisfaction, but they were still fighting hard. They wouldn't retreat unless their queen ordered such a move.

His brothers were covered in burns and rake marks, but they were alive and on their feet—most were also smiling. The hellhorses were still hard at work, burning and biting and barreling into strix. The hounds and ravens attacked just as viciously.

The archangels had broken away from the Black Saints. They were now soaring around, having joined Larkin and the carrion birds in attacking from above.

Meanwhile, the enchanted vines continued to writhe along the ground, popping up to wrap around strix, flick them away, or drag them off.

An owl dived down toward his face, its talons extended. Viper reacted fast, telekinetically batting it aside. It screeched but managed to keep to the air. Then it was coming at him from another angle . . . and got snatched out of the air by a hellhorse's teeth . . . at which point another steed appeared, and they began playing tug war with it.

We should invite the clan to our battles from now on, Ghost telepathed along their club's channel, a laugh lacing the words. *They're seriously entertaining.*

A loud familiar curse caught Viper's attention. He snapped his head to the side, noticing that Omen had been shoved onto the garbage pile and had two strix feeding from him while a third tried yanking off his head.

Viper teleported over there, grabbed one strix by the hair, and yanked it away from his brother. It whirled on him fast, dragging its nails down his face, slicing through skin. Viper retaliated with a telekinetic punch to the solar plexus that made it stagger backwards, trip over a vine, and tumble onto its back.

And then a passing hellhorse crushed its skull with one hoof, leaving it mere ashes.

By that point, Omen had managed to overpower the other two strix with the aid of a bloodhound and was now locked in battle with a different—

A body clamped around Viper from behind, nails digging into his chest. He sharply pitched his upper body forward, flipping the demon off. It landed hard on its back with an *oof*.

Viper fisted its hair, dragged its body upwards, and sank his teeth into the crook of its neck. Blood flowed into his mouth and, ignoring its charred taste, he drank it down in greedy gulps—deliberately making it painful, ensuring he had enough to heal his wounds.

Done, he snapped the demon's neck.

Ashes fluttered down.

A female roar of fury rang out.

And Viper smiled.

CHAPTER THIRTY-THREE

Tracking the roar, Viper looked to see the queen shrugging through the strix circling her. Apparently, she'd finally conceded to herself that he wouldn't take the bait.

A bloodthirsty glee curving its mouth, his entity snaked closer to the surface, not wanting to miss a single detail of the pain she was about to endure.

Pinning Viper with a baleful glare, she contracted her fingers like claws. "This ends now." She bent her legs slightly and leaped toward him.

His eyes on her rapidly descending body, he pelted her with a hail of ultraviolet orbs that knocked her balance and fucked up her trajectory, sending her sailing slightly to the left.

She landed awkwardly and rolled once, tumbling into a bed of overgrown grass.

He could have taken her out with a mere archangelic blast, could have ended it right there. But no—he was gonna make this bitch suffer.

Viper waited for her to get to her feet and then launched several orbs of unholy fire her way. Two she dodged. The third caught her hip while the fourth smacked the side of her face, burning it badly.

She hissed her rage, squeezing one eye shut. "Bastard." She sprinted at him, fingers contracted again.

He telekinetically punched her blistering cheek, making her head whip to the side and her pace falter.

Those red eyes once more lasering in on him, she conjured a ball of flames. A ball that winked out of sight as her shoulder flinched, clipped by a golden orb of holy fire that brought with it the scent of clean rain. The smell swept through the air, cleansing it of other scents such as acid, blood, and Sulphur.

More golden orbs sailed her way, all coming from up above. Dodging most, she leaped onto a small shed and then launched herself at Viper.

He moved back, but didn't manage to get fully out of her reach. Nails caught his shoulder, carving deep grooves, as she swiped out her arm. His entity snarled at her triumphant laugh.

Viper went to hurl an orb but—*too slow*. She shifted into mist before he had the chance.

The clump of mist darted backwards, evading—

A biting cold wind gusted down and sent the mist whooshing and twisting and rolling. A wind he knew had come from a hard flap of Larkin's wings.

The queen shifted again as she landed hard on the ash-laden gravel road, grimacing as the stuff stuck to her. To add insult to injury, a vine wacked her right over the head, making his entity snicker.

"You're not looking too good over there," he taunted.

Her eyes boring into him, she bolted upright, and lashed out with a whip of black fire that looped around his calf. Before he knew it, he'd been yanked off his feet and was skidding along the ground toward her. *Fuck*.

Viper slammed the badly burned side of her face with an ultraviolet orb, coming to an abrupt halt as the whip disintegrated and she cried out in pained fury.

She scampered behind a pile of debris, taking cover. A garden gnome came flying at his head. Then a flower pot. Then a tire.

Three hellfire orbs dropped down on the queen's head. *Larkin again*.

While the queen screeched up at the harpy, distracted, he telekinetically scooped the strix up and threw her aside, sending her colliding into a mobile home.

Again and again he telekinetically picked her up and tossed her around. First into a power pole, then a mailbox, then the garbage pile, then an old tarp-covered truck. On and on it went, until she was panting and bleeding and swaying.

Just as she weakly climbed her way off a clump of tires, he telekinetically hefted up a ladder and tossed it like a frisbee. It smacked into her hard, sending her crashing backwards into one of her brethren.

With an angry roar that held a tinge of humiliation, she again struggled to her feet . . . at which point he telekinetically scooped her up, shoved her up high and then dropped her down so hard on a trailer roof she went right through it.

He heard coughs. Curses. An enraged hiss. Then a swirl of molecules zoomed through the broken roof and rushed at Viper, reshaping themselves fast. The queen snarled and lunged at him. He reared back to avoid a swipe of razor-sharp nails and slipped on loose gravel.

She took advantage, pouncing on him. He hit the ground hard, her atop him. He snapped his hand around her wrist when she went to dig her long nails right into his throat.

She bared her teeth. "I will kill—"

Viper wacked her temple with a telekinetic punch, dazing her, just before a vine snagged her by the neck and dragged her away from him.

He fluidly rose to his feet, watching as the long, thick vine curled around her like an anaconda, pinning her limbs to her sides. It bashed her against the gravel road again and again and again.

Working alongside Ella's magick, he hit the queen's head with one orb of unholy fire after another, until her face was a mass of blisters, burns, black patches, and broken teeth.

A defeated rage blotting her gaze, the queen curled back her split upper lip as she glared at him, her breathing labored, her eyes bloodshot.

Viper gave her a reprimanding look. "You would have been better off not challenging my club."

She flashed him one chipped fang. "You would have hunted us anyway."

"True. But your death wouldn't have been half so painful if you hadn't turned your attention to my mate." He picked up a piece of an old metal antenna and used it to slice his palm.

She frowned. "What are you doing?"

Viper looked at Dice, who waited on his left. "Pry her jaw open."

The VP obliged, ignoring her efforts to avoid his hands.

Viper smiled at her. "Enjoy." He hung his injured palm above her mouth and let a few drops of his blood hit her tongue. Then he and Dice stood back and watched as her eyes widened, her mouth fell open in a silent scream, and she died in a sheer and delightful agony that made his entity feel all warm and fuzzy.

Uriel's psyche bumped his. *So it's true,* he telepathically said to Viper. *When one of the Seven falls, they become a deadly sin and their blood turns acidic.*

Viper looked over to see that all six archangels stood off to the side. *Yeah, it's true.*

And yet, you have no regrets?

Not one. "If you've come here for her—"

"We have not," Raphael assured him. "I still wish you had made a different choice, but I understand why you did not."

Raguel nodded. "We shouldn't have interfered."

"She is really pregnant?" asked Gabriel, tilting his head to the side.

Viper tensed. "Yes."

Azrael's lips thinned. "You know the Uppers will never allow the child to live."

"It's half demon," Viper pointed out. "So unless they want a war on their hands, they'll have to just let it go. The demon world will already be tremendously pissed when they hear that celestials targeted their own. If the Uppers want to make that worse, they can go ahead and do so. But then whether or not my child lives will be the least of their worries."

The six archangels exchanged looks.

"If I were them, I'd pull all Earth-bound angels back to the upper realm. You wouldn't want them getting hurt in lieu of the celestials who can't be reached so easily."

Jester sidled up to Viper, his gaze on the archangels. "Why did you fight at our side?"

Michael sighed. "We owed Samael. And whether he still considers us family or not, we still consider him family." He looked at Viper. "We will leave now. I would advise you to keep a close watch on the woman you claimed. You make a good point that the Uppers will hesitate in going after a child who is half demon, but the key word is 'hesitate'."

"Perhaps they will leave it be, but likely not forever," said Raphael. "It could be years from now, even decades, but I would imagine they *will* eventually come for it."

"They'll die if they do—as will anyone else who thinks to harm my child."

"I believe you," said Michael. "Take care, Samael."

Viper gave a curt nod. "Same to all of you." His entity only stared at them blankly, still considering them the worst kind of traitors—their roundabout apologies meant nothing to it.

After they'd teleported away, he scanned his surroundings. His brothers had gathered around. They looked a little fatigued, but mostly amped up. The vines still writhed around in search of strix—reminding him that he'd need to bring Ella here in a moment.

The hellhorses had shifted back to their normal form and were pulling on jeans, their hounds at their sides; their ravens lazily circling their heads. Among the clan stood Larkin, who—no, scratch that. It wasn't Larkin behind the wheel. Her eyes were pure black, signaling that her inner demon had taken over.

That black gaze roamed over Viper's face, blank. "I like the shape of your skull."

Whipping up an arm, Teague crossed to the demon. "Uh, no, just no."

It gave him innocent eyes. "I did not say I would *take* his head—"

"You were considering it," Teague accused.

"But behold his bone structure, it is—"

"I said no."

Tucker smiled at her demon. "Let's not forget that Viper's unlikely to let you behead him."

The entity slid him a haughty look. "Quiet, small man."

At that, Saxon bust a gut laughing.

Flushing, Tucker burst out, "I'm not short."

Snuggling against Viper's naked front as they lay on their sides on the bed, Ella listened as he relayed the entire battle to her. He'd given her a bullet point version while they were at the trailer park when she destroyed the magickal vines, and he'd expanded a little while they showered afterward. But she wanted more deets. Her demon listened eagerly, hungry for every detail.

Relief had left her weak in the knees when he earlier teleported back to the clubhouse, alive and well. She'd had every confidence in his ability to protect and defend, but still she'd feared that something would go wrong; that he wouldn't return; that more Uppers might arrive or that the six archangels might turn on him.

Both she and her demon had hated not having his back during battle. But they *had* understood why he'd wished for Ella to remain at the clubhouse. And, honestly, it was for the best that she had. Neither her pride nor her craving for vengeance were anywhere *near* as important as ensuring the safety of her child. Even her demon conceded that.

Joe hadn't woken until after Mia took him home. Remembering all he'd done, finally understanding how he'd been manipulated by Ophaniel, the guy was devastated and had apologized profusely. Which hopefully meant he was done being a jerk.

As Viper right then fell silent, Ella blew out a breath. "I have to admit, it delights both me and my demon to hear that the queen suffered like that. It's just a shame that the deaths of Ophaniel, Maxine, and Freddie were so quick. They deserved worse."

He wove his fingers through her hair. "Agreed."

"Knox is going to be pissed when he learns about Maxine's

family business. Every relative she has who's part of it will meet a *real* sticky end. As for the rest of them, they'll never be fully trusted by their lair regardless."

"Your aunt will probably feel guilty for allowing Maxine to befriend her. Be prepared for that." He paused, drawing his teeth over his bottom lip. "A part of me feels responsible for what the rest of the Seven did to you in your past life; feels that I shouldn't have trusted them to not come for you."

Ella felt her brow furrow. "It wasn't your fault."

"I know that. I'm just saying that emotions aren't always rational."

No, they weren't. And neither were her family, which was why . . . "I don't look forward to telling my mom, Jocelyn, and Luka about the battle. But I can't really hide it, since Joe knows."

Thankfully, having been unconscious, Joe hadn't actually heard any of what Ophaniel revealed. Viper would have otherwise stolen the memories from Joe's head.

"They'll be upset, but they'll be mostly relieved that you're safe and well," Viper assured her, dragging his fingers down her spine. "Their anger will be mainly directed at the Uppers, not so much me and my brothers. To wish that you hadn't gotten involved with me would be to wish away Peanut's existence— they'll never do that."

"Speaking of Peanut . . . I was not expecting the shield."

A slight shrug. "Archangels can create shields and containment forcefields."

"Even in the womb?"

"Oh, yeah. My mother once told me a story of how I didn't like people touching her swollen belly all the time, so I put a containment field around us that lasted quite a few hours."

Whoa. "Peanut's power display won't have caused it any harm, will it?"

"No," he instantly swore. "Peanut will sleep awhile but be fine."

She let out a relieved breath. "We'll soon have to tell everyone about the pregnancy. More celestials could come." Her demon's eyes narrowed at the thought.

"Or they'll listen to the point I made to the archangels earlier and leave Peanut alone to avoid a war."

"One can but hope." She idly doodled patterns along his collarbone. "I know the archangels helped you, but do you think their words were genuine?"

"Yes. I think they came to realize that, since I'd fallen anyway, their actions toward you were pointless. All they'd done was delay my fall, and in the process they'd betrayed me. They don't feel good about it."

"So you don't think they'd come for the baby? Even if the Uppers requested it of them?"

"If the Uppers had trusted that any of the six would harm me or mine, they would have sent them after us. They didn't."

True enough. "I noticed that Ophaniel and the six archangels have wings. Did you ever have any?"

"Who says I don't anymore?"

She blinked. "Well, I would think they were visible, and I don't see any."

"An archangel's wings can be 'tucked away', as we call it."

"So you can still call on them?"

He smoothed his hand up her back. "Yes."

"Can I see them?"

He twisted his mouth and then teleported to the side of the bed, his back to her.

Propping herself up on one elbow, Ella watched as a set of glowing-white wings *appeared* out of nowhere. He fanned them out and, *damn*, he had one hell of a wingspan. "Oh, wow. Do you ever fly?"

Tucking them away again, he teleported back to the bed and was once more lying on his side next to her. "Can't."

"You can't?"

"It's part of the curse. You get to keep your wings, but they won't work."

Grimacing, she leaned into him, resting a hand on his chest. "That sucks. I hate that curse so much."

He trailed a fingertip down the side of her face. "I'd rather have you than a pair of damn wings."

Maybe, but it didn't alter the fact that . . . "You gave up a lot for me."

"I was drowning, Ella. Drowning in darkness. You pulled me out of it. There's nothing I wouldn't have given up to be with you."

Oh, there he went hitting her in the feels again. "I love you."

His face went all soft and warm. "I love you, too, baby. More than you'll ever know."

CHAPTER THIRTY-FOUR

Five months later

"The answer is still no," Viper told the scruffily dressed fallen angel in front of him. "*Go home.*"

Lou—or Lucifer, as some called him—planted his hands on the compound gate. "Oh, come on. I thought we were friends."

"Why?"

"We used to hang out once upon a time, remember? Back before we both fell?"

Viper hadn't spent time with him *willingly*. Plus . . . "That was a long time ago."

"Neither time nor space can impact the strength of true friendship."

"We never *had* a friendship." They'd been work associates, no more. "You were asocial then, and you're still asocial now."

Lou frowned. "Hey, I have lots of buds."

"Your only real 'bud' is a six-year-old kid." Knox Thorne's son, Asher, to be more accurate.

"Age is just a number. Now come on, let me see her."

Viper sighed, and his entity rolled its eyes. Three times a week since his daughter was born a month ago, Lou had turned up at the compound asking to see her. But Viper wasn't really keen on having the devil anywhere near his baby girl.

Not that Lou was the pure-evil, all-powerful figure that humans imagined him to be. In fact, he was a mercurial, finicky, emotionally immature individual who—though on the psycho-pathic scale for sure—was more interested in getting high and annoying people than causing actual destruction.

"You don't think I'm going to kidnap her and deliver her to the big G or something, do you?" asked Lou, incredulous. "Because that'd be dumb of you. And I never took you for dumb. Callous, vindictive, cynical, and devious, yes, but not stupid."

"You sure have flattery down."

"You want flattery? Let me in, you big sexy thing, you."

"Jesus, Lou—"

"Don't bring *him* into it."

"—just go home."

Lou pouted. "It's not fair that everyone gets to see her but me."

"Actually, barely anyone has seen her." Neither he nor Ella had taken the baby off the compound yet, not even using teleportation. You could say they were a little paranoid for her safety, as were their inner entities, but it wasn't without reason. They were only allowing Ella's family and Luka access to the baby *for now*.

No celestials had come for the child, nor had any demons. But if they were going to, then now—while she was at her most vulnerable stage—would be the time to do it.

Ella's kind hadn't exactly welcomed the idea of another

half-demon half-celestial, but they'd been more bothered by how the Uppers had targeted Ella, Mia, and Joe. So bothered, in fact, that they'd gone after Earth-bound angels in retaliation, just as Viper had predicted they would. All Earth-bounds had since then been called back to the upper realm for their own safety, which they were probably thrilled about, since most weren't fans of Earth.

"This is the thanks I get for being courteous enough not to barrel right past all your security measures," Lou huffed. "You know I could. But I pressed the buzzer, all polite and shit. That should earn me greenie points."

"Brownie points."

"Them, too."

Door hinges behind Viper creaked, and then . . . "You're here *again*?" asked Jester, his tone far from welcoming.

Viper peered over his shoulder to see Ella, Jester, and Darko filing out of the clubhouse.

"Hey, little bro," Lou called out to Jester, grinning. "Still not a smiler, huh? That's all right, I'm not taking the lack of warmth personally."

"You should," said Jester.

As the trio walked toward Viper, Ella looked from Jester to Lou, her eyes wide. "Wait, you two are brothers?"

"*Half*-brothers," Jester clarified. "And I resent the familial connection."

Lou's brow pinched. "Ah, don't be like that. Holding grudges isn't healthy."

Ella frowned at the devil. "What did you do to him?"

"Nothing," replied Lou. "He'll never forgive me for falling from the upper realm and leaving him alone."

Jester's brows snapped together. "I never gave a fuck that you fell. Life was easier without you. We actually had a party."

Darko smiled at the memory. "That was a good night."

"Then what's with the grudge?" Ella asked.

"No grudge," Jester told her. "He just pisses me off."

"Who doesn't? Oh, right. No one." Lou turned to Viper. "Now, back to why I'm here . . . Just let me see the baby this once. Five minutes. Then I'll go."

Viper cocked his head. "Why do you wanna see her so badly?"

"I'm curious," Lou explained.

"Again, I gotta ask why?"

"She's a singular being. Who *wouldn't* be curious?"

Ella psychically reached for Viper, letting her mind bump his as she said, *Maybe we should grant him his wish this once. If we don't, he'll only teleport straight into the clubhouse one day. Mayhem would then ensue.* For some reason, no security measures appeared to keep Lou out. *Or do you think he'll hurt her?*

He wouldn't hurt her, he loves *the idea of her,* Viper replied. *He'd be more likely to protect her with his life purely because her mere existence pisses off the people he most hates.*

Ella had figured as much. *Then I say we grant him his five minutes.* "If we do let you in, will you stop coming here every day?"

"Absolutely," Lou told her, nodding slowly.

"He's lying," said Jester.

Lou put a hand to his heart. "My word is my bond, bro."

"And now he's lying again."

Ella looked at Jester. "You know, now that I know you're brothers, I see why you're always so sure people are feeding you bullshit. You grew up with a compulsive liar."

Lou flinched back, offended. "Who says I'm a compulsive liar?"

Ella hummed. "Larkin. Piper. Levi. Harper. Jolene—"

"Jolene?" Lou grimaced. "She blurts out more porkies than anyone else. I tell you, I'm uncomfortable with how much time she spends around Asher. She's not a good influence on children."

Ella lifted a brow. "And you are?"

"Totally. I played a big part in raising my little bro, you know. And look what a fabulous job I did. He's cold. Ruthless. Asocial. Intolerant. Hates everyone and everything."

"I can see why you'd be proud," she deadpanned, but her sarcasm appeared to go right over Lou's head, because he looked immensely chuffed. Her inner demon shook its head, incredulous.

Are we letting him inside or what? she asked Viper.

He heaved a sigh. *Fine.*

"Five minutes," she told Lou. "Then you leave, and you don't return."

The devil grinned in delight and then teleported to her side. "I always did like you, Ellen."

"It's Ella."

"I'm just using my pet name for you."

"Right." She led him into the clubhouse, unsurprised at the unwelcoming looks he received from the Black Saints they came across. Entering the nursery, she shot Mia a quick smile. "We have a visitor. He's not staying long."

Mia straightened in the armchair at the sight of Lou, her psyche touching Ella's. *You sure about this?*

It seems the best way to get rid of him, and I don't read him as a danger to the baby. Ella and Viper moved to stand at one side of the crib while Lou and Jester stood at the other. The rest of the Black Saints stayed close, protective.

Lou smiled at the cooing baby girl in the crib who was kicking her little legs and munching on her fist. She had Ella's facial shape, but she was *all* Viper—dark hair, gem-like blue eyes, demanding nature.

Her cooing stopped as she stared up at Lou through assessing eyes that were far too *aware* and sharp for her age.

"Oh, she's just like a tiny doll," said Lou. "What's her name? Tell me it's something cool like Cruella."

"Her name is Lilibeth," Ella told him.

His brow creased. "Why?"

"We gave her three options. That's the one she chose." She'd sent Ella a psychic nudge of approval on hearing the name 'Lilibeth'.

Lou's eyes rounded. "Really? How fascinating. Can I hold her?"

Viper's brows slid together. "No."

"Oh, don't be a grump," Lou complained. "I'm not gonna hurt her."

"Answer's still no," Viper told him. "She wouldn't let you anyway."

"Why not?"

"You're a stranger."

Lou recoiled, as if hurt. "I'm practically family."

"In what reality?"

"Can I at least *try* to pick her up? I'm curious as to what she'll do."

Viper sighed. "Go for it."

Looking all gleeful, Lou reached into the crib ... and got wacked by an ultraviolet wave that sent him skidding backwards.

Ella's demon snickered, as proud as it was comforted by Lilibeth's ability to fend people off in such a way.

As for Lou ... well, he laughed. "Oh, that is *fantastic*. I adore this kid."

He would.

Lou walked back to the crib and grinned down at her. "Such a merciless little sweetheart, aren't you, Lilibeth? Yes, you are." He flinched as a telepathic slap hit his cheek.

Ella wrinkled her nose. "She doesn't like it when people do all that baby babble. Finds it condescending." As would any advanced infant, she supposed.

Lou joined his hands, his eyes bright with sheer delight. "*Please* let me adopt her. I will do literally anything—"

"No," both Ella and Viper stated.

Lou dropped his arms to his sides, his face falling. "You're such selfish people."

"And your time is up," said Viper.

"Can I bring Asher with me next time I visit?"

Viper's jaw went tight. "There won't be a next time."

"I told you he was bullshitting," Jester piped up.

Lou smiled at his brother. "You've missed me. I see it now." At Jester's growl, he raised his hands. "Fine, I'll go. I don't believe in outstaying my welcome." He waved at Lilibeth. "You take care, Missy. Uncle Lou will be back to see you soon." Then he was gone.

Ella weakly shrugged. "At least he'll stop coming several times a week."

"Don't be so sure he will," mumbled Jester as he and his brothers trickled out of the nursery.

"As you're back, I'm gonna go pee," declared Mia, pushing out of the chair before then leaving.

Viper scooped up Lilibeth and cradled her against his chest, his palm supporting the back of her head. "You had fun kicking that idiot's ass, didn't you, baby girl?"

Ella felt her mouth flattened. "I thought we agreed that we wouldn't curse around her."

Viper gave Ella a look of amused affection. "Baby."

Yeah, okay, it probably *was* unrealistic to think that a club of bikers could avoid swearing altogether, but they could at least give it a shot.

"Now that there's only us three"—Viper's gaze dropped to her chest—"you gonna finally show me what's under that bandage?"

"You act like I've been hiding it from you for weeks." Ella sent out a gentle wave of magick to close the door and flick the lock. "Raini only finished, like, twenty minutes ago."

She whipped off her tee and, wincing as the tape tugged on her skin, peeled off the bandage on the swell of her breast. A tattoo of a little heart-shaped bottle filled with crimson liquid sat on a diagonal angle, a tag attached to it that read: *Drink Me*.

She'd had Raini do it because, as the mate of a descendant, the succubae already knew about the curse that befell fallen celestials. Any other tattooist might have asked uncomfortable questions.

"It's fucking amazing," he breathed.

It was. "I can hide it with glamor if I ever need to, though I don't think anyone would see the ink and think, *Ooh, Viper drinks blood*. I'm not interested in risking it, though."

"You said you were getting a magick-related tattoo."

"So I lied because I wanted to surprise you," Ella said with a *go sue me* shrug. "You marked yourself for me. No way was I not gonna do the same for you."

"And I fucking love that you have." He pressed a quick kiss to her mouth. "I'm also gonna take you up on that *Drink Me* invitation as soon as we're alone."

Ella smiled. "I'll look forward to it."

"So will I."

Lilibeth let out what could only be described as a *give me attention* shriek.

Ella chuckled. "Feeling left out, huh?" She carefully took the baby from Viper and nuzzled her soft hair, loving the smell of her. "She's perfect."

"She is." Viper curled his arms around them both. "Just like her mom."

"Ooh, smooth."

"I don't suppose there's a joint on the floor anywhere here, is there?" asked Lou from somewhere behind Viper, who went stiff as a board. "I think it might have fallen out of my pocket when Lilibeth whammed me."

"Go," Viper bit off without even looking his way.

"But I can't find my—"

"It isn't here, go."

"So rude." Lou must have gone up on his tippy toes, because his head appeared in Ella's line of sight as he waved at the baby again. "Bye, bye, Lilibeth. I'll see you very—ow, kid, that hurt." Rubbing at his cheek, he disappeared once more.

Lilibeth's small mouth hitched up, and she let out a high-pitched coo of what might have been amusement.

Viper gave her a look of approval. "Yeah, we don't like him, do we? So if he comes back, feel free to slap him as many times as you want."

Ella blinked. "You're actually encouraging our daughter to attack the devil?"

"Do you *want* her to be like Asher and call him 'Uncle Lou'?"

"Not for a second."

"Then we keep up the hostility."

Ella snorted. "Fine. But I'm not so sure he'll be bothered that much. He seemed to find her antics supremely entertaining." She smiled at Lilibeth and then kissed her downy cheek. "We all do. How could we not?" Ella looked back at Viper, finding him staring down at her wearing the most intense but warmest expression. "You okay?"

His lips tipped up. "Never been better, baby. Never been fucking better."

ACKNOWLEDGEMENTS

Thanks to my family—you're all godsends, you really are. I have no clue what I'd do without you.

Thank you so much to the amazing people at Piatkus, particularly Anna Boatman. I always boast that I have THE BEST publishing team, and it's no word of a lie.

Last but never least, I want to say a huge thanks to every reader who takes a chance on this book. I hope you enjoyed Ella and Viper's story! Love you all!

Want more of the
Dark in You series?

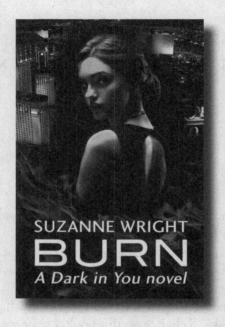

Go back to the beginning
and meet Harper and Knox.

Available now at

No one really knows what they are.
Only that they're the first civilization.
Aeons, they call themselves.

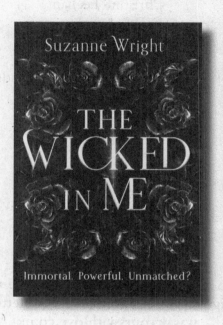

They're immortal. Powerful. Secretive.

Available now at

Do you love fiction with a supernatural twist?

Want the chance to hear news about your favourite authors (and the chance to win free books)?

Christine Feehan
J.R. Ward
Sherrilyn Kenyon
Charlaine Harris
Jayne Ann Krentz and Jayne Castle
P.C. Cast
Maria Lewis
Darynda Jones
Hayley Edwards
Kristen Callihan
Keri Arthur
Amanda Bouchet
Jacquelyn Frank
Larissa Ione

Then visit the *With Love* website and sign up to our romance newsletter:
www.yourswithlove.co.uk

And follow us on Facebook for book giveaways, exclusive romance news and more:
www.facebook.com/yourswithlovex

PIATKUS